THE BOY WHO SAW IN COLOURS

LAUREN ROBINSON

LAUREN ROBINSON

Paperback: ISBN 978-1-83853-354-0

Hardback: ISBN 978-1-83853-355-7

Author website http://laurenrobinsonauthor.co.uk

Cover design, editing and typesetting by Henry Hyde https://henryhyde.co.uk

For the friends who gave me the stories.

PROLOGUE

I CAN STILL REMEMBER HOW THE COLOURS USED TO MAKE me smile.

My fingers are crumbling; my breath is whispering. I'm not afraid of death, but I didn't want him in the room when it happened. He was the last one, leaving the fluorescent light glowing just the way I like it.

People are rather punctilious about death, and it's avoided at all costs in conversation. It's a last choice topic, not embraced in a meaningful way. People cover their eyes on the way down to save themselves from the terror.

I've always wondered why.

There are many reasons, really, but here are two.

One: it's scary as hell.

Two: it's the exact opposite of what so many people obsess over – youth, productivity, vitality, results.

But regardless, you can't run from it, escape it, or cower in the corner. It will find you and drag you out if it has to. It's not afraid of you.

And if death is inevitable, you should try to die well. Die right.

I'm not sure if I did. Was my life lived in full? Did I take up enough space without taking up too much? Righting all of my wrongs and adding a little wrong to my rights? I don't think there is a way to know for sure. There is no handbook for these things. Almost everything has rules except for the most critical details.

How to die. How to live.

Excuse me for barging in like this. I'm sorry if I did too much damage to the door. Please, trust me. If you don't know how, trust anyway.

But of course, an introduction. A name to a face. A voice.

A beginning.

Where are my manners?

My name is Josef Schneider. That's Josef like Yosef. You're with me, *ja*?

That wasn't always my last name, and I didn't learn the forgotten name for many, many years after it was stolen from me. Ripped from my identity and in its place, a new name was sown.

Where did it go?

Masked, coated men took it away.

But we will get to the specifics soon enough. Until then, I will tell you this. I am, of course, a person. Or a shadow of what used to be a person. A memory that's still alive in the hearts of some. Over the years, your perception was shaped to result in you abusing me with defamation, calling me "evil", saying, "he deserved it."

"Rot in hell, you Nazi pig." That one is my personal favourite because I was never a member of the NSDAP. I was seventeen when World War Two ended. One had to be twenty to vote.

Yet, at times, I would agree with you. Maybe I did deserve it. Perhaps it was a way to atone for my sins.

You can decide for yourself, however pointless that may be. You don't know what it was like. We are the only ones who can say anything about it.

The survivors with the scars.

The people who were actually there.

But I suppose you have to blame someone.

That's what humans do, isn't it?

Find someone to blame.

And you can't blame just one person. So, blame a whole generation? What about the ones with their lives on the line? The lives of their families? The children? Do we blame them, too?

Anyway, I think such black and white thinking is dangerous.

Everything needs a bit of colour.

But that's enough of that. Like I said before, you can decide for yourself.

Which brings me to me, a colour. Do you want to know?

Well, I'll tell you who I am.

Or who I was.

I was the boy who saw in colours.

A boy who had paint on his hands and a dried smile.

But now, all I will ever feel is an everlasting numbness of all senses. Everything is black, with what seems like no chance of even a glimpse of light.

Just dust and me – floating in the air.

All I will ever hear is my own breathing and the sound of the smell of my footsteps echoing in the world.

Forever.

Some background.

I loved to paint. Although, just saying that I loved to paint would be an injustice. It spoke to me from within. It expressed my deepest core, translating my messages when words weren't enough. If you will, painting for me was worth more than a million syllables.

Ever since I was a little boy, I was always curious about art because I couldn't find its rules. It wasn't until I was six years old that I realised art had no rules. It was a field without a convention, and that's what made it so exciting to me.

I always thought of the world in a much different way than most tend to.

I see in colours.

I see people in colours.

I see memories in colours.

I see you as a colour, too.

I know that the number four is mustard yellow. Mother always insisted that numbers couldn't have colours; or months, or letters, or people, but I thought that was nonsense.

First the colours, then everything else.

That's how I see.

Odd perhaps, but that's the way it is.

I see myself as red. I like red. People said it suited me.

I do, however, try to enjoy every colour I see – the whole rainbow: a million flavours and scents, none of them quite the same taste and sound as the last. If you put a colour to your ear, maybe you can hear it. Listen.

The number six is the colour of the night. A hug smells sticky, like chocolate, and listening to music tickles the back of my neck – everything blending into one sensation.

Who wouldn't want to experience the world in full sounds and colours? I've learned to fear the silence because that's where the bad memories live. The colours keep me company.

Why do I require the company of colours?

The guilt.

The survivors.

The ones that didn't make it.

The remaining scraps of humans left over.

I drowned the sheets of grief until it rendered me useless. There are people I still cannot bear to look at, but over time visions came slowly creeping into my senses, and I could feel their frightened souls and beat-up hearts floating in the colours. Sometimes, they'd smile at me, nod and pat me on the back. That hurt even more.

Which brings me to the story I am telling you tonight, or today, or whatever time and colour.

It's just a small story, really.

- About two brothers,
- A doomed friendship,
- Some colours, and;
- Quite a lot of swearing.

The story I'm about to disclose cannot be found in any history book. They say that history is told through the eyes of the survivors, but no one groups us with those reported survivors, and even fewer people tell stories about us.

Until now.

I was born and raised in coffee-stained Germany. This Germany was ageless and waited up for me at night. It had no beginning and no end. I belonged there, and in my heart, I will always belong there. Whether or not the Germany of my childhood was saved or lost in the end, you will have to decide for yourself. This is a true story. I was there, and I remember.

Innocence. Love. Childhood.

I think about them now and then; think about the old days when I was a child. If only now. I would feel free, unrestricted, like paper in the sky. Jumping over fires and wishing that the world would never end.

Floating. Flying.

The colours. I've collected them, you know. I placed them in a book, and I gave it a name.

THE COLOUR THESAURUS

I love to collect colours. They help me find my voice when words just won't do. I will let you look at it, and you can fill your own stories with them if you like.

First off was ghost white – the brightest white you could imagine. Blinding, almost. And I know what you're thinking, white isn't a colour. It's just some nonsense – a light. Well, I'm here to tell you that it most definitely *is* a colour. It's not just a colour. It's every colour you could ever think of smashed together and blended to create a beautiful, new colour – a base for everything.

We were travelling to God knows where. A desperate journey.

We would have made it, too, if it wasn't for the cold fingers and smell of agony.

I knelt next to my grandmother's side; her lips were a corroded brown colour, peeling away like cracked paint in desperate need of redoing. Her hands were slippery and cold, like ice cream. And her dark eyes stared blankly at the ceiling.

She lay on the floor.

My thoughts scurried, as did my breathing.

Why Oma?

Why now?

Why?

HOW IT HAPPENED

She was begging. "Please," but she would never finish her sentence.

Then quieter. "Please."

Then she stopped begging.

She began to relax, started to struggle for breath, moaned, and exhaled.

She mumbled a bit. We couldn't understand it.

My grandfather took her hand, and her eyes flew open. She lifted her head and her gaze locked on his. He was startled and began to cry. He told her he loved her. She said she was sorry. And she began to fade.

There was a shiver, a slight twitch, and she was gone.

She just decided not to exhale anymore.

To my right, my little brother's arms were folded. His face was blank and decorated with frozen tears. He shook her arm, but she was gone.

At twelve years of age, I became intimate with death. I witnessed the extraordinary transformation from body to ghost of this particular life lived. She became something else, something immaterial, like memory, love, and presence.

My heart, at this point, was slippery. And loud, so loud. It tasted metallic. The whole world could hear it.

Grandfather knelt, holding his wife's limp, lifeless body in his swollen arms.

Our mother and father were asleep. They were holding hands. Soon, they would wake up with the same distraught look in their eyes as our grandfather, and Mother could only utter two small words.

"Oh, Jesus."

For me, the next thing was a staggered, onslaught of thoughts and massive movements. If you can't imagine it, think battling for breath and suspended sorrow. We were hanging in that room.

We wrapped her body in a sheet. The unsavoury thought of throwing Grandmother overboard was enough to make us get off the boat when it docked. There was nothing else to do but to go home and pretend as though nothing had happened. Death interrupted our plans.

Next, is grey.

It was, if you like, the darkest moment before the dawn.

The second time I saw a dead body, I was barely sixteen years old. There was a crack in the air as loud as thunder, but without the raw power of a storm. I recall a blank-faced man lying on the ground in his stiffness. It took me a few hours to realise that he was dead. His last words stuck to his lips like paper.

There was a man, staring, whose face was a white slate of nothing. My mind doesn't want to recall anything from that day. However, sometimes, I must. I force myself to believe that it happened at all.

A man with kind eyes took off his coat and covered the body with an enormous amount of sadness in each movement. He started pulling at my jacket. "Don't be afraid." The last thing I remember was a van and screaming. I forget the rest, but I know it was painful.

The last moment, the moment I remember most vividly, was red.

Red is a theme in my life.

I looked up. The sky was not like the sky. It felt more like the sun had swallowed it whole. It was apocalyptic, catastrophic. In some places, it was crumbling ash, and there were veins in the redness. Earlier, my friends had been playing there, on the street that looked like an oil painting. I can still hear their colourful echoes, their feet tapping on the road with aqua breaths, their voices laughing. They seemed to be spoiling in the sun, but they didn't care. They embraced it.

Then came the Americans, the Germans, and the bombs.

All together.

I heard a man shout some words, and then a second explosion.

Within minutes, there was a sudden outburst of shrapnel and words; anger sprinkled in for good measure. A river of blood streamed down the streets until it led to the bodies that would be frozen there forever – stuck on the pavement like glue. There was a man whose chest was cut open – he screamed that he had no more legs. Next to him, a shaking man. I could feel him grabbing at my coat. The damn air felt sick. He spoke to me, but I ran. I could feel no cold, but I was shaking.

People at the scene were chasing away photographers, not wanting their agony to be material for the world. They were trapped in a moment of awful sorrow, and they didn't want it to be a spectacle shared by strangers. The journalists were looking for someone to blame, and we were right there – Hitler was not.

"Was this what the Nazis wanted?"

"Was this what Hitler promised?"

"Do you think this is a punishment?"

"Is that the reason for all of this?"

Of course not.

Don't be stupid.

It probably had more to do with the bombs that were thrown down by the tiny humans hiding in the clouds.

Dust filled the air, my lungs, and my eyes. God, that awful dust stung. It made me cry soapy howls of despair and rage.

I felt it all.

I was kneeling in a pool of rubble.

The wall saved my life.

Apart from anything else, all I wanted to do was go home.

To paint, to draw, to see my little brother. Just one last time. I was dying for it – the safety of it – the home of it, but I couldn't move. Also, home didn't exist anymore. It was now part of the mangled landscape. If the end of the world were a place, I was sure it looked like that.

My eyes bled from all the colours.

The trouble was, who could ever come and save me? Who would crouch down? Take me in their arms? Tell me everything will be okay?

No one.

That didn't happen.

No one crouched. No one spoke.

That wasn't allowed.

Would you have?

Be honest.

Instead, I picked up my battered soul from the rubble and continued on the path that was no longer there.

I tripped.

I fell.

I got back up.

Now, when I look at the memories in my hands, I see a long line of colours, but it's those three alone that resonates with me the most. Over the years, the colours have become a jigsaw puzzle. Sometimes the black fits just right, then the white and the red. Other times, they are jumbled so wholly that the colours are unrecognisable. Once in a while, I see them so clearly, I am back in the skin of the scared, little boy.

Yes, even now, I am reminded of it, and I have kept this story stored away to retell it over the years. I do this as an attempt – an immense leap of an effort – to prove to you that my life was worth it.

The hardest for me was the beginning. Everything has an opening, and everything needs one, but it's difficult to pick a moment that is the beginning. Once it begins, it's simple. You just have to keep going.

The only thing I know for sure was that it began with my grandmother, death, and some snow.

Yes, let's start with that.

Here it is.

My story.

What was it like to hear colours, see scents, and taste sounds?

Come with me. I'll show you.

If you want to.

1

THE DAY THE WORLD ENDED

*DARK CHESTNUT*DEEP SPACE SPARKLE*DEEP MOSS GREEN*

It was December 13, 1939.

I was twelve.

The fun that was World War Two had just begun.

My grandmother died.

Empathy whispered to me that she was dying months ago. I asked many questions I got no answers to, so I let them build and build until it would eventually come out in rage.

Things were getting mad. We boarded a boat to an imaginary land, but Grandmother didn't reach our destination, as you know. Mother and Father went mad, answering questions we didn't ask and trying to take us to destinations that didn't exist.

"She's not in any pain now," Mother explained. Father's eyes were narrow with grief. He bit his lip, and his forehead wrinkled like he was trying not to spill the world's secrets.

I had no idea where I was that day. We were on the train for hours and hours. It was past the city, past the countryside, and the landscape blended into one. It was all white, and for me, that forest was nameless. It was there that my Grandmother, Hedya, was buried. The witnesses: a Rabbi, Mother, Father,

Grandfather, Tomas, two shovel-men, and me. We were all stapled together, family strangers, and the trees.

The shovel-men were there for the money, but they still complained.

Everyone wore white shawls of snow. The snow found refuge in my boots. Trees wore thick blankets of ice, and there was more snow to come, judging by the sky.

I painted the scene in my mind, later with my paintbrush. Grandmother taught me how to paint when I was a little boy. Before I ever painted, I learned to draw. If you can draw, you can paint, but it's hard to go the other way.

The first thing I painted was a colour wheel with secondary and tertiary colours. The second was a single pansy blossom. It was terrible, but it hung over my grandmother's fireplace anyway.

Everyone was struggling to hold something back: sadness, of course, but mostly anger. Tears flowed steadily and silently down immobile faces. We felt bruised inside.

Numbness. Emptiness.

Meh.

Although she was gone, my soul was unwilling to acknowledge the finality of death. We were never to look upon her face again, or feel her embrace, see the warmth in her eyes, or be surrounded by her love. Words from the Rabbi and speeches brought a fresh onslaught of tears. Well-spoken words, a tribute to my grandmother's life and loves. A picture painted by me, her young apprentice, was thrown carefully into the dug-up hole in the ground. I had recreated the pansy blossom. The quality improved, but only slightly.

My grandfather watched as the dusty pink roses lowered. *"Auf Wiedersehen, meine Geliebte."* His pain still smelt fresh. "Goodbye, my love."

"Why are we leaving her here?" I asked, staring at the snow.

The question wasn't directed at anyone in particular, but it was Mother who chose to dodge it entirely. "I don't see why we can't take her home."

"Yes, darling."

I tried again. "Why aren't we burying Oma in a graveyard?"

The reason was probably due to the vandalism – the painted swastikas. The graffiti was tattooed, too, on the faces of my family. I could see it in their eyes.

Mother looked at Father briefly. She answered by patting my back. In hindsight, I realise the sticky situation she was in. How would you explain to a child what an adult couldn't even comprehend?

Even though it was a very sad day, Mother still looked very beautiful. I kept trying to think of a way to tell her, but every way I thought of was weird and wrong, so I just kept it to myself. I kept a lot to myself.

Father had a white, waxy face with dark whiskers. He didn't shave in weeks. No money.

"We must be quiet, Josef," Mother finally said. "Show the Rabbi respect." His hat was funny. I stared at that for the remainder of the service and wondered what his head looked like underneath.

As much as he tried to hold it in, Father's pain came out from his throat, one syllable after another, without a sign of stopping. Like he had hit the wall and tried to scream, but his voice was melted by the sound of the silent wood.

"I'm sorry, Papa," I held his hand.

Why do we always say sorry to the grievers?

The muffled sobs wracked against his chest. His world turned into a blur, and so did all the colours. The sounds. The tastes. The smells. Everything was gone. The last painful emotion slammed against him before he lost the feeling of feeling and finally just stood, breathing it all in.

His hand was squeezed, and I soon started daydreaming about a man they called the Führer. He kept me company on the radio as I painted, and his words lingered in my memory. That was before Mother or Father would shut it off and play their music.

In the dream, I was attending a ceremony at which he spoke. I was listening contentedly to the torrent of words spilling from his mouth. His sentences glowed in the dark. My face glowed listening to them. In a quieter moment, he crouched and pinched my cheek. "So you're an artist, little one?" Just as I was about to respond, I was shaken from the dream by the shovels hacking into the snow. Their words, too, hacked at my skin.

Digging to my brother's right, the older one was warming his hands and cursing the snow.

"That snow's a cunt." He let his partner do all the work.

"If we didn't owe you, we wouldn't be here, Ben. It's freezing." I could see his icy breath, Father nodding in submission.

"Should have told Mama to die on a warmer day, Papa."

My grandfather only had to stare to hush him. "Ben, you know your mother had a flair for the dramatics." His laugh was strange.

There were no more words from the shovels.

A few minutes later, we left. Mother was thanking the Rabbi for the ceremony. I kept looking back.

I watched as my little brother stayed.

His name was Tomas Schneider. Again, that wasn't always his last name.

He was two years younger than I was – ten.

He was standing there, frost-bitten hands in his coat pockets, and looking so tiny amongst all the snow. Blue eyes sparkled like storm clouds right before lightning hit. Clouds of grey and blue threatened floods and fury while his pupils dilated in misery, eyelashes catching the snow.

In shock, his tiny hands reached to us. "Come back."

He wept nice and hard, welly boots in the snow. "We can't leave her here…"

Within seconds, the snow had carved itself into his skin, his knees were purple and his nose was red.

Somewhere in all the snow, I could see his broken heart in two pieces. Each half was glowing and beating, under all the white. He realised Mother had come back for him only when he felt the boniness of her hand on his shoulder.

A warm scream filled his throat, and my mother and brother sat frozen in the snow for a few seconds. She was rocking him gently. When it finished, they stood, embraced, and breathed.

A final, forlorn farewell was let go of, and we all turned around and left the wood, looking back several times to a place we would never return.

We hurried back to the train platform and boarded the next train to Berlin. We boarded just before four. The crowd was very crowd-like, trudging through whoever was in their way, all huddled together with frightened faces. I had to be careful not to be trampled. Mother and Father made us walk in front.

The sky was still white, but no snow had fallen just yet. In places, it was becoming dusty pink with the setting in of the evening.

We played with dominoes on the train floor. Not an easy task. Footsteps struggled to avoid walking into us. We wondered if we would stay awake long enough to see who could spot the most rabbits from the train window. It became a game Tomas and I liked to play when we would go on trips. However, not long after boarding, we succumbed to the heavy fatigue in our eyes, as much as we tried to fight it. We were asleep within the hour.

When I awoke, the carriage was quiet and dark – everyone had fallen asleep, and I could hear only the train, the rumble of the tracks, the funeral of the horn, the hiss of the brakes, the clanking of the couplings, the clickety-click of the wheels.

I could see people walking past the train carriage like a piece of the night. Like someone had carefully cut around them and peeled them away, leaving only their blackness behind.

Before I had fallen asleep, Tomas was winning the rabbit spotting game – three, whereas I only spotted one. It was brown, with white spots on its ears. I think. I tried drawing it, but I was asleep before I finished drawing the basic outline. My head was resting on Father's shoulder, and my legs were on my grandfather's sleeping lap. I was sure he carried the memory of Grandmother heavy on his lips. His eyelids were like raisins.

Tomas and Mother were asleep opposite us. She was holding onto him for dear life.

Father received a book from a neighbour in Berlin a few months before his mother's death, but he could never seem to get past the first few pages without putting it down. He placed his hands on his face to disguise the thoughts – a trench-coat and sunglasses, but his words would be tattooed on his hands.

"Such a miserable book," Father's hands said. "Who does he think he is?" He never said such things in the company of others.

Another unsuccessful attempt was made on the way home.

Book: 2

Father: 0

The pages were filled with numbers, equations, and various doodles. Father was an accountant, not an artist, so they weren't outstanding. It would be rather challenging to read a book with blocks of numbers hiding the words.

Lodged in between the pages, something was sticking out from the top, something pencil-sized. I recognised it after a few seconds. A paintbrush. It was glowing under the words and numbers. I couldn't take my eyes off it.

I reached down to loosen it from the book, and as I was making some progress, Father's eyes shot open. Most people wake up drowsy; some people wake up energised. He woke up dead.

He held a smile for as long as he could. "You're a curious boy, aren't you, Josef?"

"What's th—?"

A finger to the lips. "Shhh. Let's go get some fresh air," he said, as he stood and made his way down the carriage.

I had nothing better to do.

On the train, there were people of every stature, but among them, the suffering were the most easily recognised.

Children without mothers.

Wives without husbands.

People completely alone.

And sniffing – there was so much sniffing.

Everyone was leaving their old lives behind, thinking that by the end of the train ride, everything would be different – everything would be better. Some fled wearing nothing but their summer clothes and sat freezing in the German winter snow. Orphaned children relied on siblings and kind strangers to get them to relative safety. You can run away and pretend all you like, but at the end of the journey, you will be left with only yourself, your thoughts, and your problems to keep you company. And what if you have to return to the place that broke you? Then what?

When we finally made it to the back and opened the door, there was a fresh blanket of snow decorating the small platform. I was reluctant to walk out because I didn't want to destroy its beauty, but Father walked out anyway, his shoes creating patterns in the snow like a beautiful painting.

We stood in silence.

I watched as the snow fell gently to the ground and perched

on Father's shoulder. He tried to light a cigarette with great difficulty. All that human-made wind created by the train. It was his
first smoke in three weeks. The older shovel-man gave it to him.

"You want to know what was in my book?" Finally, the light
took to the end.

I looked at his tallness, smiled, and nodded.

"Here." He shrunk in front, his knees carving the snow. The
smoke blew me a grey kiss. He stunk, but we all did.

"Your Oma gave it to me, but I know she would have
wanted you to have it."

He held it out. "You're the only artist left in the family."

The paintbrush had chipped wood and cracked paint. The
bristles were hard and sticking out. Even it looked sad that
Grandmother, its proud owner for so many years, was gone.

Everyone has to leave something behind when they die. A
child, a book, or a painting, or a house; a wall built, a pair of
shoes made, a garden planted.

Or a paintbrush.

Something your hand has touched in some way, so your soul
has somewhere to go. And when people look at that house, or
wall, or garden, or pair of shoes, or paintbrush, you're there.

I truly believed that her soul was attached to the paintbrush,
and as long as I had it with me, she would always be there too.
Somehow.

I held it firmly, examining the coloured stains of blue and
green and purple.

"*Danke*, Papa."

Father painted a smile on his face.

"Thank you, Papa."

On the back of the brush, there was a small, painted blue F.

"What's that?"

Father examined it himself, eyes squinted.

"*Freiheit.*"

He inhaled the smoke. It further lit up his brown eyes until he blew it out.

"Freedom."

A barrier of silence stood beside us. I broke it.

"Can I have a smoke?"

Father was surprised.

"Absolutely not. You're twelve."

I smiled into the wind.

A SPECTACULARLY TRAGIC MOMENT.

Just after eleven that same night, my grandfather walked up an empty city street in Berlin with a suitcase full of food, warm clothes, and papers. German air was in his lungs.

His last words: "It has to be this way."

The houses on the street were like milk cartons and squashed together. Some bruised and battered, with smashed windows and painted defamation.

"All Jews' deser've shot dead," was sloppily painted on a bus stop.

Under it, people corrected the culprit.

The stars were on fire and at peace simultaneously. When grandfather made it halfway, he looked back at our house. He could not see my tiny figure in the bedroom window, but I could see him. I waved, but he did not wave back.

I could still feel his mouth on my forehead.

"Take care of Mama and Papa." I could hear his breath whispering through heavy sleep. Mother was sobbing in the hallway.

Father's questions.

"Why do you have to go?" Then to a whisper. "Things might die down later. It couldn't get that bad. It's too absu—"

Mother's voice interrupted. "They won't be able to make

sense of it all." A pause. "I don't know what we're going to tell them."

More words were exchanged.

There was a silence for about ten minutes, and then nothing but the creaking of the floorboards.

"Opa?" I got up. "Opa?"

But he was gone.

And he did not come back.

When I finally made it downstairs to the kitchen, Father was leaning over the table. His face was swollen with shame and anger. Mother had her elbows planted and covered her face. They didn't even realise I was there.

"Mama? Papa?"

No answer.

They stayed like that for a good thirty seconds – or forever.

The harsh kitchen light was so unkind.

I squinted.

Somewhere near Munich, a suited German was sitting in a cold office, with yellow-stained walls, licking an envelope. The contents inside would seal our fate forever. But we were not taken. Not yet.

A few days later, the men with the uniforms would come, and sometime later, the masked monsters.

Nothing would ever be the same again.

See, on the outside, we looked like a perfectly normal family, seemingly completely intact. Mother would laugh at Father's jokes, and Father would never lay a hand on Mother. We would eat dinner together, and there was absolutely no bad blood between any two members of the family.

However, desirable this may be, this picture-perfect deception of a close-knit family can be deceiving on many levels. Underneath the smiles and poses, hurt can be found. Mother only laughed at Father's jokes when we had guests, and I knew

Father had laid his frustrated hands on mother on several occasions.

Once, they found her throat.

But it wasn't always that way.

The rise of hatred made everyone shout and scream at each other, and it made Mother and Father hate each other, too.

See, my mother, Lissette, a German woman from a respected family, was married to Ben, the accountant and, more perturbingly, a Jew.

Given what we know about the thirties, their union was a tragedy in the making. It was a shameful secret.

But let me share with you a story. A short story.

Mother and Father talked about it over the years, and I've heard various accounts from characters whose names I do not remember.

Forgive me if I get some of the facts wrong or mixed up. It's a story of my mother and father's beginnings. A little background information is always essential, after all. Don't you agree?

2

THE GERMAN WHO LOVED THE JEW

*GOLD FUSION*GRULLO*GRAPE*

LET'S LOOK AT SOME NUMBERS. IN 1933, WHEN THE NAZIS assumed power, there were about 35,000 mixed marriages in Germany.

In 1939, there were 20,000.

The reason for this was not purely due to divorce, but because of death and migration.

Mother and Father were two of the Germans who broke the rules.

I will not tell you the specifics of my parents' story, because, like all great love stories, it lived and died with them, just as it should have. It began with a handshake and ended with a kiss.

Mother's parents are what Herr Hitler would be pleased to call Aryan Germans. Father's were German Jews. There was a difference, apparently. There was no doubt that Mother loved Father, yet family ties are so strong. With the memory of a happy childhood in the Fatherland, she often found herself trying to see things from the Nazis' point of view and had excuses for the things that they did – to the dismay of their liberal-minded friends and the hurt confusion of Father.

Tomas and I often felt like we were pulled in every direction during our childhood. The situation became even more sticky when Mother's Father, my Grandfather, got her a job in the factory that Hitler opened to lower unemployment rates of women in Germany.

The factory lingered with middle-class women who pledged their allegiance to the Führer and sang his praises for making work more accessible. A snowball of a woman with greasy, red hair commented that she would marry him. Believe it or not, about half of Hitler's followers were women. Most thought he was handsome, and an excellent public speaker, but the other half voted due to the promise of employment. The thing about promises, however, is that you should only believe them when they come from a power-hungry madman like Hitler if they are in writing and signed with golden ink.

Mother and Father were a fervent love match, made more fervent by the fact that they had waited in secret for two years until Father earned enough money in his profession to support a family. Mother's factory job didn't pay very much, but it was enough to get by.

He had known other girls, and as Mother was twenty five before she was married, she had the attention of other men as well. Other German men, who would have made life a lot easier for her. But she liked the challenge and ran towards it with a smile. Mother's beauty wasn't that of magazines. To me, she was like a piece of art, and art wasn't always supposed to be beautiful but meant to make you feel something.

Consequently, their marriage was not the hasty, impassioned leap of two people soaring on the wings of first love. The love between them was as calm as the night, deep as the sea; in the light of it, they both knew that they would never look upon another. Even as a child, I could see it. I could smell it. They determined that no obstacle would prevent them from their union, and there were plenty once both their families learned of their children's intentions.

"Child," implored my grandmother, who deep in her heart had always hoped that Mother's superior intelligence, careful upbringing and attractiveness would land her a "good Aryan man," well up in the social levels. "Think about what this means for yourself, Lis. You will be barred from certain circles just because you have Ben's last name."

"That makes not a whit of difference to me," Mother stubbornly maintained. "I love Ben. I'd marry him if he were a blackie."

"But, child, remember the racial and religious differences between you." She sniffed the air. "Your children will be teased."

Father's parents attended an Orthodox synagogue, and although he looked with affection on the parental habits of his childhood, he eschewed them for himself and his family. He went to the synagogue, once a year, to please his mother, but our parents raised us wavering between agnosticism and downright atheism.

"Mama," Mother said quietly, "Remember that the greatest man who ever walked the earth was a Jew – Jesus."

That held her for a minute. "Yes," she murmured, "It is a great paradox."

For Europe, the day was bright. The harsh sun shone through the stained glass window and hit my grandmother directly in her eyes. She had to wipe at them occasionally.

"And another great Jew," Mother added quickly. "Spinoza, for instance, and Einstein."

Grandmother looked at Mother a little sadly. She wasn't convinced, but she was, for now, out of arguments.

"A nice day we have, Lissette." Grandmother often tried changing the subject when things got a bit too heated. For her, stubbornness was not worth losing her only child over.

What Father's parents said to him, I can only imagine, as he never spoke of it. At least not the truth.

"Ben," his mother most likely said, "it grieves my old heart that you have to marry a *shiksa* rather than one of our own. We have a need, as never before, to stick to our own people and traditions."

But loving her son above the rest of her children, she might have embraced his head in her wrinkling hands. "Above everything else, I want you to be happy." Or she could have used those same hands to slap him hard across the cheek.

When Tomas and I were born, things got better between the families. Mother's family were glad to see that I had inherited Mother's quick blonde-red hair and that Tomas had inherited her cheeky, blue eyes.

The Jewish and German women met, embraced, and promptly forgot their differences in purely feminine discussions of painting baby rooms and clothes. They could have maintained a negative attitude and still have preserved the family peace. Even, gradually, as they learned to know my father better and saw how fine he was, and how good he was to their only child and grandchildren, there came shy words of affection and admiration.

I remember when I was about five, Father's mother was teaching me how to hold a paintbrush properly. She gifted me a small, blue book, intended for young children, but I read it daily and well into my pre-teens. The book was the colour of the sky and felt like my hands over a warm fireplace. I heard my other grandmother comment proudly as she sipped on expensive tea.

"He's a fine little boy with a great future." Sip. "But I'm glad Tomas and Josef are not all Jew in their makeup. They don't look Jewish, and their ways are not Jewish. In fact, you wouldn't think they were Jews at all."

Mother piped in right around there and breathed hot tea

into her lungs. "The children are neither Jew nor Christian. They are just Josef and Tomas." Her father chuckled to himself. "A stubborn girl we raised," and he would smile in her direction. My grandmother's nose turned up so much that I thought it was going to touch her eyebrows.

In later years, Mother and Father would form their small band of merry men and have their late night, secret meetings at our house. Lots of whispering was involved. At certain times, when my parents thought I was asleep, I would listen to the soft words from the stairs.

The secret conversation.

Man 1: "They must be able to tell how bad things are. This is ridiculous."

Father: "Of course they do. They're just too blind to see it. There must be something we can do. Start a secret club or something."

Man 2: "I must say, Ben. We're off to a bad start."

Father (mumbling): "We're safe behind these walls. No one is listening."

Someone was always listening in World War Two Germany.

Man 1: "Aren't you two scared? For your families?"

Father: "Of course. But we must keep going for them. I love my country, but I hate politics. We have to fight for what we love."

For man 1, the love of his country would lead him to the gallows. Hung up like the washing on a lamppost, for conversing with a Jew and being a member of a secret club. He hung there for days with his mouth open, and children would throw pebbles into it.

The man would not discuss where the club originated, but other peoples' lips weren't so tight, especially when the punishment was death. I couldn't really blame them.

We watched the hangman. I said nothing, but Tomas had some words. "What did he do, Mama?"

"Something, darling."

After hurrying us inside, we stared at our half-eaten breakfast, and none of us said a word.

3

BAD DECISIONS

*BUFF*BURNT UMBER*

STRANGE THINGS OCCURRED AFTER THE WHITE DAY IN THE woods. Tomas and I couldn't go to school anymore, because according to Mother, "What they're filling children's heads with is rubbish."

It was a month after Grandmother passed away, and we heard not a whisper from our grandfather.

Surprisingly, we found Mother in our room, pulling our belongings out of our wardrobe and piling it into one big box. Some of our parents' belongings were in there, too.

Other things, like toys and radios, were thrown into a larger box at the other end of our room and labelled "For sale". As you might imagine, I was shocked to see that my paints, crayons, sketchpads, and even the blue book Grandmother had given to me, were in that pile too.

Our toys had been disappearing for months.

We finally had answers as to why.

I picked up the book and held it to my chest. Mother looked at me like she might cry before dusting herself off and rising from her knees.

"What are you doing, Mama?" I asked.

Things were too unclear for us to be upset.

Father always told us to be polite to our mother, to treat her with respect, and not to imitate the way he sometimes spoke to her.

She shook her rolled-up jumper and pointed to the doorway behind us.

"Downstairs, boys. Downstairs."

She was a very tall woman with sand-coloured hair that was slovenly piled on top of her head in great curls, each one as stiff as day-old pasta. She wore a greenish-blue gown made of soft, satiny fabric that was long and loose, always smelling of soft cotton, regardless of the time of day. Her beauty was less clean than most other mothers. Less polished and reminiscent of an old, worn book. Damaged, but beautiful.

Tomas chimed in now. "Mama, what's going on?"

Delicate, blond hair fell onto his brow; his skin was so pale that it almost rendered him stark against the bright walls.

"Boys, please, wait for me downstairs, and I'll explain everything, okay?" Mother tried an unexpected smile. She was already walking.

We ran past her on the staircase. I stood for a moment without saying anything and just examined Mother's bare face. Her eyes were a lot more black around the rims than they usually were, just like mine when I got in trouble and ended up crying. I wondered if she had ever stopped crying since the previous night.

For the first time, Mother had no words. She knelt like a leg-rest by our chairs.

"Now, you two have no reason to worry." She clapped. "Everything is going to be alright." She rubbed her hands and the words. "If anything, it could turn out to be fun."

I swallowed.

"What is?" Tomas paused for a moment, gathering his ten-year-old thoughts. "Are we being sent away?" His body slumped on the chair, and his chin was tucked into his neck.

"*Nein*, darling... not really..." Mother said, looking for a moment like she might actually smile, but then thinking better of it.

"You, Josef, Papa, and myself – all four of us actually."

Another trip to an imaginary place.

My eyebrows sank.

"Where are we going this time?" Tomas said, slightly raising his voice.

She played with her dress, not looking him in the eye. She thought some more. "To the moon, Tomas!"

He laughed.

Mother wouldn't tell Tomas where we were going because he was too young, and he'd accept anything as an answer anyway, so I had to do the thing that big brothers do and ask for him. I thought for a moment, and then with great care, I delivered the words.

"But where exactly are we going? Why can't we stay here?"

She thought about this carefully before answering, and she put her hand on her face as if she had a horrible headache. The position grown-ups usually take when they are conjuring up a lie.

"Papa's job," she replied. "You boys know how important that is, don't you?"

I didn't know. Not really. All I could say for certain about Father's job was it was something most people didn't need at the time. At least, that's what he said.

"It's a very important job," said Mother, hesitating for a moment. "A very important job that requires someone very important to do it. You boys understand that now, don't you?"

We looked at each other and nodded.

She went on to explain that the man Father worked for wanted him to go to Vienna. "*Versteht?* Understand?"

"And we all have to go with you?" I asked.

"Of course you do, Josef. You wouldn't want me to be all by myself, now, would you? I would miss you an awful lot," she added, in mock sadness.

I smiled.

Tomas' eyes strayed away many times during the conversation as if he was trying to find answers in the walls, on the bookshelves, in the cupboards.

"Who do you think you would miss most – Josef or I?" Tomas asked.

"Josef or *me*, Tomas," she corrected him.

Tomas hated nothing more than when adults corrected him about stupid things, especially when what he meant was quite clear.

"I would miss you both equally as much, you silly boy," she finally answered.

She said she was a great believer in not playing favourites, even though I knew that Tomas was her favourite. He didn't ask as many questions as I did, and Father didn't have to give him as many 'talking tos' about painting all day and being rebellious.

She continued for a good ten minutes before she stopped to deliver a difficult, but very necessary lecture.

"But boys," Mother said, now lowering her tone and standing up to deliver the speech. I knew it was important. She made us stand.

We stood with our backs to the wall, and her shadow loomed over us.

"You two have a very important role to play, too, okay?"

Tomas and I exchanged glances again.

"What is it?" I asked.

"We mustn't tell anyone that we are going away, okay? This has to be our little secret."

"Why?"

Mother sighed. Her sigh was of a sort of deflating; it was as if the tension had lifted yet left her with a melancholy instead of relief.

"Different people are fighting to be in charge. People that shouldn't be. We don't want to upset anyone."

Above Mother, the words were being painted and perching on her shoulder. Soft cotton did cartwheels near her head.

"... But what about our house?" I asked. I sat back down, and Tomas mimicked me.

She looked around, as though she might never see the room again. It was a beautiful house with two floors, with a small basement where Mother would cook, and Mother and Father would go to swear at each other. We owned a lot of beautiful furniture when I was a child, but it was sold, mostly to buy food and other household things that I didn't understand the importance of.

"We'll have to leave it for now. Maybe we'll come back someday when things die down."

"Maybe?" I questioned. "What do you me—"

"And what about Oma and Opa?" added Tomas.

"*Ja*, what about them?" I agreed.

She stiffened slightly, like an animal just before it attacks his prey.

"They will be alright, boys. But that's enough questions for now. Go upstairs and help pack. Quick quick."

My brother left the room. Tomas knew the importance of obeying orders.

When my figure remained, Mother knew there would be more questions.

"How far away is it?" I asked.

"Du verarscht mich doch!" Mother slapped the table with a laugh, although it was a strange kind of laugh because she didn't look happy at all and turned away from me like she didn't want me to see her face. "You're a pain in the ass!"

"What about my book?" I blubbered, a thing I knew I wasn't supposed to do, but hoped I'd be forgiven on this occasion. "Oma got it for me as a gift."

"We will get you a new one when we settle in, darling, and no blubbing."

"But I don't want a new one," I said, my voice coming dangerously close to shouting, which was not allowed in our house, especially to Mother. "That one was from Oma…and…"

"But Papa's jo—"

"I don't care about the fucking job! Or the house!"

I was shouting now. So loud, in fact, that I was sure people on the other side of the city would have heard me. "I don't want you to sell my things." More short breaths. "You didn't even ask."

"Josef, that's enough!" Mother said, now snapping at me and standing up to show me that she was serious.

"Honestly, you just don't know what your Papa and I are risking for this family." She added. "We are moving to keep our family safe… and together."

Safe and together.

If only I knew the importance of that phrase back then.

"And to move, we need money, and to get money, we have to sell things that are precious to us." At that moment, I noticed that Mother wasn't wearing her wedding ring. "Now, that's enough! Give me the book and go upstairs with your brother."

Mother's eyes flashed indignantly, much like lightning on a pitch-black night. The unmoving gaze was accompanied by deliberate, slow breathing like she was fighting something back and losing.

She kneeled before me, managing to soothe me enough to calm me down. My voice lowered. "What is happening, Mama?"

Hysteria, Josef.

Crouching down and grabbing hold of my shoulders. "Josef, listen to me." Stern business. Mother began feeding me sentences. She made certain that I was focused.

"Things are going to get crazy, and you will see a lot of scary things. But look for the helpers. There are always going to be people who will help."

"But..."

"We've talked about interrupting, Josef. We don't want to make a big fuss. Maybe someday we will come back and live as... as a family again. Maybe not. *Ich weiss nicht.* I don't know."

There was that word was again – "maybe".

Maybe.

Maybe.

The meaning of "maybe" in the grown-up dictionary: never.

Like the time I wanted to get a new bicycle, because I had fallen off my old one and broken a pedal off, and Father said maybe he would buy me another, but I never did get that bicycle. In my mind, I tried to make the definition of maybe turn into definitely, to keep me sane – to keep me holding onto some hope that we would return home soon.

Tears welled.

"Are we leaving because of the men in uniforms?" It was a dangerous question and one that I should have asked that day. Maybe then Mother would have seen me as a child capable of understanding grown-up emotions. Perhaps then she would have shared her calm instead of joining in on my chaos. "*Ja*, Mama. I understand."

I wanted to tell Mother that day how hard it was for me to leave and how hard it was for me to tell her how hard it was for me to leave. I was scared. Maybe if I said, "I'm scared," things would have been different, and Mother would have known who I was. But I couldn't. I buried things too deep inside me for too long, and now I couldn't find the words, and Mother didn't understand the language of the colours swarming around in my mind.

I left with a hole punctured in my back. Not one big enough to see with the naked eye, but big enough for things to come leaking out of it.

I kicked my chair, about which Mother made no fuss. If it were a normal day, I would have been given a talking-to, but this was no typical day. I knew that nothing I could have said would have made a difference. After all, grown-ups make the rules, and children just have to follow them. I knew that pleading was useless because no matter how much I begged, she would never understand what painting meant to me. It would be like trying to explain to her what colour the number two smells like. Lemon colour, for those of you who care.

Tomas had been standing at the other side of the door, listening carefully.

"*Geht's dir gut?* You good?" Tomas asked, when I exited the room.

"*Ja*," I said back, trying to fight back the disappointment I was hiding behind my eyes.

We made our way upstairs slowly, holding onto the banister with one hand. I wondered if the new place would have a delicate banister to slide down as this one did. Sliding down the banister was a pastime. We liked to race.

I looked around for a moment and remembered all the happy times we shared in our house. The place where the Christmas tree stood in December, and how every year we took turns to be lifted to the top of the tree, with branches that touched the clouds, and perch the angel on top. The porch where we took off our muddy shoes when we went splashing through the puddles in the winter months.

The hall where my paintings hung. The sports awards on the floating shelves. We were good at long-distance sports, and we often got the attention of many notable people, like the men in funny hats.

Father's books sighed on their shelves.

The picture of the Führer hung gloriously on the wall above the stairs. When we got it, it caused quite the stir, but everyone soon got over it.

It wasn't much, but it was our home. It was ours.

Sometimes having to say goodbye to a house you grew up in is just as hard as saying goodbye to a person you knew your whole life.

I heard Father entering the office. There was mumbling for many sentences.

"Why would you sell his book? It would only be worth a few Pfennigs." Inaudible. "You know what he's like."

Until Mother spoke loudly to Father.

"We need all the Pfennigs we can get, Ben. He must learn to sacrifice for family…"

Which caused Father to speak louder than Mother could, and that put an end to their conversation.

"He's twelve! The children didn't start this! Why punish them?"

Then the door of the lounge closed and I couldn't hear any more. I buried my head into the banister of the staircase.

Tomas was close to crying.

He looked at me. I wanted nothing more than to pull him into the cardigan that grandma had knitted, but I didn't. Instead, I placed a hand on his shoulder, and I whispered, "Everything is going to be fine."

But the truth is, I didn't want everything to fine. Fine is

boring. Fine may as well be awful. I was afraid of fine. I was afraid that every time life let me down, I would keep telling everyone that I was fine and fine would be my reality forever. I would live secret emotions, them peaking over walls from time to time, reminding me that I am still alive.

"I'll race you." Tomas stood up, wiping the streaks on his face and propping himself up on the banister. "Stop being sad like a wussy."

My face managed a smile and ran to the top of the banister.

"I bet I can beat you down."

"Only if you can catch me!"

4

QUESTIONS AND MELTING ICE-CREAM

*QUEEN PINK*QUINACRIDONE MAGENTA*

SOME OF THE TRUTH HAD ALREADY REVEALED ITSELF. IT came exactly one week before Christmas, and stress was stacked high on Mother and Father's backs. They tried to hide from us, and perhaps they had successfully lied to Tomas, but I knew that things just haven't metamorphosed for no apparent reason.

The reason for my curiosity came that day, just a few days after my grandmother was buried. Father still wore the grief of losing his mother like a fresh coat of white paint. Lines on his face gave away the pain that he tried to conceal.

We were walking along the rough, cobbled streets that made my feet ache.

It was a Tuesday. The colour was indigo blue.

We were going to buy sweets as a reward for our co-operation. Or simply so Father could get away from Mother for a few minutes, Mother told Father that he shouldn't go, but he was persistent. She was unravelling. And fast, snapping at us for simple things like saying "hello" to father's friends or sticking our tongues out at sad-looking boys in the marketplace, where our aunt worked.

We walked carefully beside Father, him holding Tomas' hand tightly like he was afraid that the wind might carry him away.

It was a miracle I went at all. I was painting a new picture of the rabbit I had spotted on the train. I tried to use the old paint-brush, but the bristles were too hard, and trying to soften them with water wouldn't do, so I decided to go.

The buildings were tight together and loomed over us, like a forest of stone. When I looked up, the roofs were so close that I could only make out a sliver of the blue sky that was mirrored by the tiny stream of light – the alleyway, where the shop was, twisted and turned back on itself. Whether I'd look in front or behind, I saw nothing but stone – and people.

Then came the staring.

Every lethal stare felt painful and piercing as if their glare was tearing me apart with a blinding, teal light.

I couldn't breathe. It felt like the air was choking me. A terri-fied, but composed look from over Tomas' shoulder confirmed that he could feel it too. Father kept walking, keeping his eyes focused on the stacked-together buildings.

I looked at my hands to make sure that I was still human. The peoples' eyes stared with such hatred that the colours were force-fed – every cold stare after another.

Staring at father, this time with more momentum. He couldn't hear my fear. The man that stared back was not my father at all. He had that same dead look in his eyes that he did on the train.

He looked pale. Defeated.

My mind once again drifted to the colours – for comfort.

Tomas' coat.

Blue.

Like a midwinter night an hour before pitch dark. That colour you see as velvet no matter what texture it is. Yet, even under my chilled fingertips, the fabric was far from soft.

Father wore a sandy-coloured duffel coat with sable toggles and straps. On his neck, he wore a pendant with the star of David. He had only just started wearing it.

People were coming from everywhere.

I had never been claustrophobic before, but in that powerful swell of humanity, I felt the panic rise in my chest. When Father and Tomas moved, I had to move with them, quickly, and if my feet failed to keep up, I risked being trampled.

People were gaunt and serious. There was hardly a single utterance, save for a few frightened yelps from other children. There was nothing for it, but to move with the crowd. I could smell them too, the people, I mean, an unholy agglomeration of perfumes, body odour, and over-applied cologne. A siren came from behind the buildings, startling the seething mass.

When we arrived, I could spot two figures. They looked like two miniature army men. But when I squeezed my eyes together really tightly, those toys turned into people. As you might expect, they were Nazis in uniforms. One was short. The other very tall. I realised that I knew these men. They were friends of our mother and had been in our home on several occasions.

"Look, Papa – Niklas and Hans!" Tomas' eyes widened.

My breathing calmed. When we would meet the soldiers in the company of Mother, we would all beam at each other. We slapped each other's backs and shook hands, chatted over glasses of pale tea. Sometimes they would offer us chocolate, which was very exciting because we rarely got any.

It was odd, though, because I'd never seen those men standing there before, and we had made many trips to the shop over my twelve years.

I don't like odd things. They never seem to mean anything good.

"Ben," Niklas called. His voice was indignant. The small

man always spoke first, even though he wasn't in charge. "We don't want any trouble here." He pointed to a sign on the door, "*Juden Werden Heir Nicht Bedient* – No Jews served here."

I was startled by the harshness of his voice. I knew that whatever would come next wouldn't be good. The way he stood, the way he stared at us, even his breath smelt like trouble.

"I'm not here for trouble." Father's eyes were shivering, and he wore his shame on his shirt like a tie. "I am here to get my son's sweets." His arm stretched out to the tall man. "Come on. You know me. I'm Lissette's husband."

The tall man, Hans, sighed. His sigh was intense, but not subdued. It was frustrated but not yet sad. "You know the rules, Ben."

Father remained. "I've come here many times without any problems," he finally spoke.

He looked as if his brain had shut down. He was clammy, and there was the glisten of cold sweat.

He pulled us behind him. "Please. I promised my boys."

"Can't you read?"

"It's illegal to serve a Jew in this establishment."

"I'm sorry… I'm no…" Father tried to form a sentence.

"I'm an accountant. I pay my taxes. I'm entitled to everything inside that shop."

"An accountant?" The small, fat guard laughed.

"*Ja.* I'm a graduate of the University of Milan. You know this."

The duo shared a patronising look and laughed in my father's face. Then the smaller man spoke. "An educated Jew? That's as rare as hen's teeth."

Then it happened.

Quickly.

The small man's hand travelled towards me before another hand hastily elbowed it away.

"Don't touch my son."

The hand that held firmly onto me and my brother let go.

An arm was swatted.

I watched Father as he was forced to kneel.

"I have a gift for you," Hans said.

"Josef… Tomas. Look at the snow, darlings. Look …" Father said.

Tomas diverted his eyes to the snow strewn along the road.

Father realised, however, that I was determined to keep my eyes on him, and perhaps it was something that I should have seen.

Tomas stood with me in the cold, winter air. We did not speak.

"*Schweinehund!*" A swing of a fist. "You filthy pig!"

He was cracked hard across his face, catching his ear, collapsing him to the ground. On his back, he was hit again. Each time, he would try to get up and look for us.

He should have stayed down.

I looked. I swallowed hard as Father was beaten.

Tomas screamed.

Civilians came to witness the humiliation. Among them were humans who hung their heads in shame. Some tried to pry our gaze away. Some watched, glowing German pride. We got lost in the crowd.

I wished for someone, anyone, to step in and stop it. Catch my father in his arms and stop the madness.

But no one did.

Father was hit with the soldier's fist six times before he collapsed to the ground, and this time, he did not get up. His face was burning five lines of fire. His knees were aching on the pavement.

The Star of David necklace kindled under his shirt, and father made several attempts to put it out. But it was no use.

Father coughed.

I felt sick.

When it finally did end, I managed to fight my way through the crowd to help Father up. I entered from the back. There were many voices, words, and sunlight. Tomas leaned forward. The skinnier of the men reached down and ran his gloved fingers through my brother's hair.

"Such beautiful children too. Shame." His eyes were genuinely filled with sorrow.

I dragged father towards the back of the block of shops – for fresh air.

Tomas followed in disarray.

No one came to our aid.

A few younger men called Father a 'Kike' from the crowd.

He didn't do as I expected. He didn't tell the soldiers that there had been some mistake. He didn't scream or yell at them. He didn't even try to make a joke to comfort us.

Nothing.

He collapsed down the side of the wall.

"Papa, are you all right?" I asked him.

He couldn't answer.

All he could do was pull Tomas and me towards him, wrapping his arms around us tightly. He was decorated with hopeless fear, clutching his Star of David pendant.

All three of us just sat on the ground, unable to say what needed to be said. Tomas' eyes were wet. I clung to myself.

We were kneeling in the shadow. In an hour, it would all dissolve into the blackness of the coming night. Breath collapsed. It slipped down over Father's throat. He managed to speak. "I'm sorry, boys." He said it to my forehead.

More slabs of breath.

"We'll get sweets another time, okay? We'll have Mama take you."

Then there was an image, fast and hot.

A large glob of bright orange.

Niklas stood over us with a hollow smile.

Father dragged himself behind us, holding the men's gift in his hands. Blood soaked his coat.

The same, sorrow-eyed man that had beaten Father approached us, two ice creams in hand. We stood before him, expecting another handful of derision, but we watched as he bent down, and he offered them to us. We took them.

Tomas thanked him. I didn't.

The man left.

Father watched.

I didn't even eat the ice cream. I simply held it until it started to melt and watched it run down my arm.

Later that night, when we went to bed, we debated the events of the evening.

"Why were Mama's friends so horrible to Papa?"

"Don't know. Maybe they're unfulfilled."

I laughed.

We often heard grown-ups talking to our mother and father about this topic, when they thought we weren't listening.

In the end, we fell asleep. We talked our way to unconsciousness.

I could feel the ice-cream running down my arm, and I counted blue stars in my head.

5

SECRET SUITCASES

*SAPPHIRE*STRICKEN BLUE*STARRY-SHOULDER
BLONDE

THEN CAME JANUARY 1, 1940 – WHEN IT ALL WENT WRONG.
The night that destroyed my family forever.

Mother left a forbidden letter, and we took the secret suitcases. We hid them under the sink until it came time to go. I would never know the contents of the letter, and Father would never learn about its existence. When Mother wrote the words, her pen was heavy. She had to keep putting it down. Then in a final guilt-stricken motion, she slid the envelope under the dresser for someone to find.

I suppose she thought it would take longer for it to be discovered, and by then, we'd be in Vienna. I wish I knew how lonely she was at that moment. But alas, not a day after we left, there would be two German visitors. They knew we had gone the moment they walked in, and it was not long until someone spoke.

You don't realise till you're packing everything up forever just how many memories you have made in a place. But by then, it's too late. The memories are gone, and we are left with a feeling of nostalgia in our bones. You can live your life exactly the way you wanted, and you would still have that regret, at the end, when you're packing it all away.

A man I didn't know stood at the doorway of our house, and we were rushed out. I recognised his voice from the secret conversation. Man two, obviously.

"It feels cruel. To give you hope like this. Just cruel."

"It's all we have."

The man passed an envelope to Father. That envelope was our escape, and our only hope of us all staying together.

The contents: four train tickets to Vienna, departing in two days from a village in the countryside.

We would wait there until it was time.

It was a risk, but a risk my parents were willing to take.

The man then gave Father every last Pfennig he had to make the trip, shook his hand and he was gone.

His last words: "Be careful."

You couldn't always get what you wanted in Nazi Germany, but if you had enough money, there was always a way.

We walked around the corner of the cobbled street towards the car. I'd never been in one before. Sadness was tied around my neck like a rope and getting tighter, but still, I was determined to fight back the tears that were trying to elbow their way out. Then, after the last footstep and glance at my childhood home, we were gone. I thought about the footprints that would remain inside the house forever and the missed memories of the past. I will miss the twelve-year-old boy that left. He was ripped out of me like a sheet of paper and discarded like trash.

I was like a phoenix on that street, and I knew that soon I would have to burn to become anew.

Goodbye Josef.

On the ride in, there wasn't much room for conversation. Everyone's silence fought against each other. Blue squares were trapped in my eyes, unable to float and dance around like usual.

It hurt. I don't remember much, except for Mother crying and me drawing. The light was scarce, but the moonlight glow was enough to see the page at least. Art was the only way I could run away and still stay at home. Occasionally, I would sneak a ticket out of Father's coat pocket, and stare at the golden lettering on the front. It wasn't really gold, but it's how it looked to me.

When we first arrived at our in-between home, my mouth hung with lips slightly parted, and my eyes were as wide as they could stretch. Everything was the exact opposite of our old house, and I was glad that we were only staying there for two days. The house in the city stood on a quiet street, and alongside it was a handful of other homes that were fun to look at because they looked exactly like ours, but not entirely.

This house stood alone. A single-level, stone cottage, with a large chimney, which poked out of one side of the roof. The wooden-framed sash windows were propped open with sticks. And the brickwork, perhaps once a jaunty yellow, looked dirty with what looked like a hundred years of grime. A small rose garden was planted in front, and although it had once been carefully planned and loved, it was riddled with weeds.

There were two small rooms, one with a tiny, wooden table and woollen mattress. It was hard. A small shed at the back served as a chicken coop, but unfortunately, there were no chickens there anymore. A neat pile of chopped wood was stacked against the house.

"I think it was a bad idea coming here," I said, a few hours later, when Tomas and I were helping Father clean the cottage a little. Mother said we shouldn't unpack.

She was "taking care of some business", and we weren't to disturb her.

"It'll just be for a few days, Josef," father replied, as he was unpacking his toothbrush and some cologne. "Then we all go to Vienna."

"Papa, I think it might better to go home," Tomas said.

Father smiled and breathed the new air. "We don't have the luxury of thinking, son."

I understood to some extent, what the phrase and Father's smile meant.

I was at the age where the puzzle was starting to fit together, only I couldn't find all the correct pieces.

Ever since the incident with the men and the shop, he always kept his head down and never looked up from the floor. I would try not to stare too long.

Something was growing inside of me. Something so big that when it worked its way up to the outside world, it would either make me shout and scream that the whole thing was unfair, or just make me burst into tears instead. I was determined not to reveal it in front of Father because, even though he tried to hide it from us, I knew that he, too, was upset about coming here. I could see it in his eyes.

I explored the house with Tomas, hoping that we might find a small door or cubby hole where a decent amount of playing could be done, but there wasn't one. Just two doors facing and waving at each other.

"This isn't right," I said under my breath. We only had a few belongings each; some clothes, vanity items, and a few toys for Tomas. I had outgrown toys a few years ago, but I still liked to play the odd game of toy soldiers with my brother.

"Papa said it's only for a few days," Tomas said.

Tomas was always a great believer in focusing on his blessings, not on his misfortunes. Even in a place like this, where I was sure that no one could ever be happy again. He was the kind of boy who made the stars want to climb out of the sky and perch on his shoulder.

I threw myself on the mattress and sank into it.

6

MONSTERS AND THE MIDNIGHT MARATHON

MURKY-DISASTER

OVER THE COURSE OF THE NEXT DAY – AND LET'S STEAL A phrase from Father here – "life continued like everything had happened."

Father spent most of his time playing with us, which was quite grand. Mother, contrarily, kept very quiet during the day and had quite a lot more of her afternoon naps. Some of which weren't even in the afternoon, but before lunch. She became a hermit-like human, only ever coming out of her comfort for survival basics. She lived in the walls.

Tomas peeked through the door, only to find Father prying her traumatically from the mattress. She cried as if the idea of getting out of bed physically hurt her.

When she did manage to unstick herself, she came outside to where we were playing and, for a minute, she watched us. I found her eyes, and she looked as though she would smile, but it dissolved into her sunken face just as quickly. I was running to her, but brick by brick, her walls came tumbling. As she ran from us, her tears turned the rainy day into a whirlwind of greys and yellows. Being the inquisitive little boys we were, we followed.

She fell to the floor, on her knees.

The greys and yellows followed her.

"What have I done?"

She sobbed.

"What have I done?"

There were things she wanted to tell us but couldn't because it would hurt us. So, she kept them inside and let them hurt her. Let them eat at her skin.

She didn't mention the forbidden letter. Not even to Father. I thought it best not to bring it up.

The sobs punched her, ripping through her muscles, bones and guts. She pressed her forehead against her bony hands and let her heart tear in and out of her chest.

She was hollow.

Then Tomas was there, patting her head and rubbing her back. He reached into her hollowness.

As much as I wanted to look away, my body refused to let me. Even as my lips trembled and my shoulders heaved with emotion, I was unwilling to back down. I joined the two on the floor, but I was reluctant.

"Apparently, when the Gestapo comes into your home and asks to take your children away, you're supposed to say yes."

Silence.

"What are you talking about, Mama?"

No answer.

The night the monsters came for us, the sky was nothing at all. It was like a child began to draw on it with a pencil and then erased it all in a way that smudged and spread the grey.

Father burst into the room where we were all settling down for the evening. We were asleep at either end of the mattress.

"They're here. Lissette. They're here."

His face looked like he was being injected with darkness.

The monsters weren't the kind with three heads and tentacles coming out of their hands. They had faces like mine; they wore clean, crisp suits and uniforms, carried guns, and wore medals on their jackets. The kind of monster that you wouldn't be able to spot until it was too late. Until you were being dragged under the bed by your foot.

As was always the case, I kept my grandmother's paintbrush close.

Mother and Father fought and argued about what they were going to do next. The situation was unappetising, to say the least. In the end, it was decided that we would flee from the back door in the hopes that we'd make it to the next town and find refuge there. Through the woods. That was the safest option.

First bad decision.

We were going to run.

A few small steps to freedom.

I don't have to tell you we didn't make it.

The dusky, grey peaks gave the bottom of the sky a jagged edge, and the clouds above soothed it with charcoal swirls. The rain streaked, invisible until it hit the sodden ground.

I had one eye open, one still in a dream. A full dream would have been better, of course, but there was no time for such luxuries.

We had to go.

We had to go quickly.

Mother tried to wake me up. I could see her floating figure above me in the darkness. "*Komm schon, Liebling. Komm schon.*" Her voice sounded like a butterfly's wings. But I would not wake up. "Come on, darling. Come on."

No time.

They were coming.

She lifted me sideways.

Second bad decision.

Her feet dragged out of the house and limped through the snow. Father was in front, Tomas in his arms. His breath was heavy that night if I remember it correctly.

I held the paintbrush's hand.

Mother struggled, almost dropping me on several occasions.

We were at the starting line.

The marathon had begun.

The pistol was fired.

Mother hobbled and stopped.

I was getting heavy.

I had no idea where we were running.

All I could feel was the cold biting at my skin. I stared at the house in the distance, faded from sleep. I could smell Mother's perfume on the side of her neck.

In the far distance, black figures with guns were forming. There must have been about four of them – only Tomas saw them at first. He was starting to regain consciousness, and from the bottom of his throat, he formed a cold, two-syllable note. "Monsters!" He pointed at the darkness, colours in his breath.

Mother and Father had to pick up their pace now. Their legs were sinking deeper into the snow. The faster they ran, the slower they became. The heavier we became.

The world was getting heavy now, too, due to all that snow.

Mother tried to be careful and wrapped her arms tightly around me. She did not see the object buried in the snow. How could she have?

She tripped.

She buckled.

She dropped me.

For a moment, it must have felt like she was hanging suspended, free of everything, or perhaps losing control. Then gravity took over, and she came plunging towards the snow. Instinctively, she pulled my arms and legs towards her chest, but I fell out of her grasp.

In my unconsciousness, I knew I was falling. I could feel the sensation of cold and darkness everywhere. I was so scared I could have screamed. Only when I opened my mouth, nothing happened.

She saw my feet, legs, and body slap the snow. A scream forced its way out of her mouth, jolting me awake and alerting the monsters. I could hear their echoes, or perhaps that was from Father, who was now running back for us. He left Tomas in the snow. My heart was heavy. She picked me up again, slung me over her shoulder and carried on.

"Oh, I'm sorry, darling. I'm sorry." She kept a calm, steady voice, despite the tears.

The monsters arrived about ten seconds later.

Quickly.

A gunshot.

A scream. "Papa!"

One of the black-masked monsters ordered Mother to give me to them.

Mother howled. She wouldn't let go of me. She couldn't.

I wouldn't let go of her.

I could feel the leather hands grabbing at my waist.

The goodbye was chaotic. It was soaking, with my face buried into the worn, woollen shallows of Mother's dressing gown: my body collapsed in the snow. I clung to her legs. There was kicking. I was dejected, swollen with realisations of my fate. There was more dragging.

A veil was over my skin, grey and cold.

I fell asleep in a dream, and I woke up in a nightmare.

I watched the petals and the twigs swaying on the trees. There was a creeping sorrow. It sat like rain on my skin, enough to chill what was once warm – the grief had all condensed right above my head into a cloud big enough to block the watery white-silver glow of the moon.

Papa tried to elbow through, but he was held back.

Monsters shouting. "Run!"

Tomas called out for Mother. The monster's arms held him as he winced.

I was silent.

All I could hear was a haunting ringing in my ears. I tried to block out the emotions that blocked my vision, but they escaped.

I don't remember how we got there, but we were thrown into the back of a small van. There was a boy there too, and he looked at us like he wasn't expecting our company either.

Driving away, I desperately searched for my escape. Looking out of the back window, I caught sight of Mother falling to her knees. She was reaching awfully for the van, and when it drove too far away and she couldn't anymore, she hammered her fists into the pavement. For a moment, her squeals ceased and words came out, but they were too far away. I couldn't hear. I liked to imagine what she said.

My imaginary recollection of Mother's words: "Don't forget who you are."

I'm sorry, Mama.

I forgot.

I'm sorry.

It's sad to lose a mother at a young age, but it's tragic when a child is taken from a mother.

It's harassed my memory, and sometimes I thought that it would have been better if I never looked out at all. But then the regret would have been not looking.

Life is funny.

You look, you lose.

You don't look, you lose.

The monsters didn't just steal us that night. They stole our mother and father's lives, too. Without us, they were not Mama and Papa; they were just Ben and Lissette.

Tomas wore a face of misery. I looked at him, so he didn't feel so alone. He didn't understand what had happened to us, nor did I.

But we knew it was awful.

An explosion of words poured out of my brother's mouth at intervals. He choked on them. "Open the door! Open it now! OPEN!" He was hysterical.

"Will you shut up?" Monster One said.

"It's all right. It's all right. Calm down," Monster Two said.

But he did not calm down.

I inched closer to my little brother and calmed him softly. We cried into each other's shoulders.

The other boy sat in the corner of the van; he could've been a much skinnier reflection of Tomas, with hair darker than mine. His lips almost moved, but his eyes darted back to the frayed laces of his boots.

He had a quiet cry.

We fought ourselves to the point of exhaustion, and we fell asleep, rocked ever so gently by the van drifting through the night.

I thought back to the darkness, to our old home in the city.

It all began to make sense. Dots connected. But it wasn't until later I thought of a noteworthy point.

We were runners. Star athletes. If they just let us run, then maybe we could have made it.

7

DARKNESS AND MATCH-STICK SOLDIERS

*DUTCH WHITE*DUST STORM*DUKE BLUE

YES, DARKNESS.

A shadow version of Tomas sat before me, light outlining his silhouette, colours dancing in the margins. I had been in the process of drawing a new concept for a painting, the grey of the pencil further illuminating all that white still left. It was one of my simpler sketches; Tomas and Mother sitting together, reading by the fireplace. I didn't usually draw people, but I did like moments. I liked how they tasted.

Darkness, Tomas, and four voices downstairs.

Another one of our mother and father's secret meetings I suspected.

I wondered how they managed to keep it a secret with all that shouting.

Somewhere, in all the darkness, we sat playing with our makeshift match-stick soldiers. It was all we had since our toys were gone. Mother and Father thought we were asleep long ago, and surely they would have scolded us for playing with fire, yet there we were. We were engaging in a childhood pastime on the floor.

Tomas emptied the contents of the matchbox onto the carpet. Some were burned out.

We could just make out the voices: a deeper voice, a softer voice, Father's voice, and Mother's voice.

Their voices kneaded methodically at the door as we played with our pretend men.

Blankets were set up to look like rolling hills, rolled up socks were used as obstacles, and broken pencils were used as guns. But soon, the centre of our attention was focused solely on the matches and the lighting of them. All children did this at least once in childhood. Why are we so obsessed with destruction and fire? Perhaps I was just a strange child.

I was setting it up carefully, making sure to get it just right. More beautiful. The destruction would have been much more satisfying that way. We would light each match, one by one. Watch as it fuelled the next. Smile a kindling smile, and throw it into the candle to hide the evidence.

The smell would be harder to disguise, but we hadn't planned that far ahead.

"Can we light them now?" Tomas asked.

"*Nein*," I said. "Not yet."

"Please." He said after a slight pause.

"*Nein*, Tomas. I'm not done yet." I smiled. "Soon."

A battle would take place.

I struck the match.

The voices were attacking each other now. One heaping itself upon the other to be heard. A fight of colours. I imagined them colliding like dust clouds.

"Nein," Mother's voice said. It was repeated. "Nein." Then more. "Tomas and Josef aren't fit for a place like that."

Mother would not back down. "They would hate it there."

The colour of darkness flashed in my eyes, and I had no choice but to listen to the argument from the softer voice.

"Those boys are top of their class. They are already interested in them."

Who are they?

Tomas struck another match. The sweet smell of carbon and fire lit up the room and my brother's face. The fire danced behind the glass of the candle holder as our match-stick soldiers burned.

They were silenced once more by Mother's voice, but now it gained momentum. "Not my boys."

I listened.

Father's voice entered. It sounded almost gratifying. Not to Mother, but the men. "Lis, perhaps they are right…" I could feel his heart stop in mine. It hurt.

The air was still, and the flame from the candle barely even flickered. It was steady and bright enough to relieve the darkness in our room, but it was not enough to read by. I picked up Grandmother's paintbrush. Nothing but black on the paper.

The items around the candle cast shadows that radiated out as hands, like that of an old analogue clock. The wick blackened, and the wax slowly turned to liquid, running down the side and onto the glass plate the candle sat on. Tomas made brief eye contact when he saw the change in my face that night.

I continued. I struck another match and relit the candle.

"I've heard what happens there." That was the unmistakable voice of Father. It was shaking now.

Where is there?

I was curious now.

I sat and listened as best I could.

The stars outside were brilliant and set fire to the roses on our carpet.

"Josef, light another," Tomas said.

"It would be a privilege for them. Turn them into fine young, Aryan men," one of the deeper voices answered.

"Josef?!"

"I know it's a good school. But the nature of the... I just can't." Mother argued. "No."

"Josef, the matches are going out again."

I waved at Tomas, dismissing him.

"Lissette, I know that. I know. They are your little boys... Of course, you don't want to give them up."

I was now fixated on the voices downstairs.

"You're running out of options, I'm afraid. Lissette, Ben – use your minds. Your father will organise everything."

The voice stopped and lowered to a whisper. "To object to their names being put forward for an elite school is tantamount to treason against the Reich and the Führer." The deeper voice piped up again.

As far as the voice was concerned, we didn't belong to Mother and Father.

"They don't belong to the fucking Reich. They belong to me!"

No, Mother. That's naïve.

We belonged to the Führer. To Germany. To the Reich.

"Josef, the light is going out."

"What?"

"The matches are going out."

The arid voices, low and matter-of-fact, had an answer for everything.

"Our school is the finest ever established..."

All was silent.

"Lissette, they will come for Ben. They will take Josef, too. I don't know." The voice tried to sound unconcerned. "It might not be tomorrow, next week or even next year, but they will... Lissette, please..."

He added later, for further impact: "Look at your house! What you gave up already."

"I can see!"

I could listen no longer.

As I got up from the floor, the candle burned out – too much movement. Darkness flowed in.

Tomas struck another match and reignited the candle. The dance behind the glass resumed. We continued playing for a good twenty minutes before we heard the voices leave, and as they did, I gathered the courage to walk downstairs into the dust cloud of colours.

"Where're you going?" Tomas shouted from his crossed-legged position on the floor.

"Ssssh. Nowhere. I'll be back soon. Stay here."

When I approached the large oak door, it opened with Father's beaten figure standing there – frozen.

Mother sat crying, forearms flat on the table. Her palms were facing upwards.

Father raised his head. It was heavy.

"Josef, what are you doing down here?" Father asked, wiping his eyes. "Go back to bed."

"Sorry, Papa. I couldn't sleep. Who were those—?"

I paused when I noticed his eyes trailing off and staring at nothing on the door behind me. "Are they going to take us away?"

Father's expression was sharp and definite, freshly cut. "No."

It gave me more questions than answers.

A wooden hand wiped at the splinters of his beard, and he made several attempts to speak.

"Papa?"

But when I began walking farther into the room, it was not Father who I walked towards.

I walked to the table and took hold of Mother's upturned hand. She squeezed mine hard. There was some level of discomfort, but I did not let go.

"What's wrong, Mama?"

"Go back to bed, Josef." Her voice was firm and sounded like confused love.

And angry, but I didn't know why. I thought she was angry at me.

"I'm sorry, Mama."

"Take him back to bed, Ben." She said, throwing the light blue words across the kitchen table.

Mother and Father would not disclose how the conversation ended that night. If only I had kept listening, just for another few minutes...

"It'll be alright, Josef," Father said. He tucked my curiosity back into bed with a pat; a gentle kiss on the forehead. He commented on the smell. "Why does it smell like damn burning in here?"

He opened the window and invited the air inside.

"It will be alright, Josef." He said it again.

I was just a child, but I could tell that it would most likely not be alright. That didn't make my father a liar; it made him my father.

Maybe, if I'd intervened. If I had burst downstairs, into the kitchen and said, "I'm here. Take me," it might have changed everything.

Three possibilities:

- We could have stayed at home.
- The monsters would still have taken us, and Mother and Father would have still protested.
- But maybe, just maybe, they would have lived.

The cruelty of fate, however, did not allow me to enter at the opportune moment. I stopped. I walked away. I continued playing with Tomas.

I killed my parents.

8

THE CASTLE ON THE CLOUDS

*CAMEO PINK*CAL POLY GREEN*CARIBBEAN GREEN

THE MASKED MONSTERS SPOKE OF A PLACE CALLED INLAND.
That's where they were taking us.

Munich was the breeding ground of Nazis, so it was only
fitting that one of Hitler's elite schools was built there. In
Munich's heart.

"You'll go to school. Inland is a place where the bravest, and
strongest boys go to become soldiers for the Führer." A reply
delivered to Tomas when he asked where we were going. It felt
scripted. Wooden. It was shaped by fear.

I didn't want to be a soldier, but in Inland, there were no ifs
or buts. Children didn't get to say, "But I don't want to…"

There was none of that.

Nevertheless, from then on, Inland is where we would call
home. Or a place of residence at least.

Rustic cabins dotted the grassy hills as trees stood up like
spikes, zigzagging the border of brick roads and unpolished
homes. Rivers streamed through deep valleys. The buildings
looked as though they were falling on top of each other,
squashed together by a giant's thumb.

It was raining – the usual soundtrack of Germany.

The school was government-funded, and unless you were personally selected to attend due to skill or social class, big money was paid to get in. And so, most of the children of Germany's higher echelons attended.

It was run by Herr Erich Dohman, simply known as 'Dohman'. Children in Inland saw very little of him, and only when they got in some serious trouble. No one ever wanted to see him at all. As far as dispositions go, his wasn't the most convivial. With that said, Inland was one of the most elite schools in Germany and had a good track record with graduating students. Most went on to become respectable German citizens, fighting for the Fatherland. At a minimum, the children got the papers needed to attend university.

Apparently, Dohman had straightened a few boys out.

With a fist.

We held onto the futile hope that we'd somehow get lost, or they'd change their minds and take us home to our parents. Or something like that. My thoughts were not gardened by logic, but I suppose in times like that, logic is just a five-letter word. Absurd and completely meaningless.

"*Schaut doch aus dem Fenster!* Look out the window!" The monster in a pretty, powdery blue dress said as she pointed her finger at the fogged-up window. "It's your new home." She said the words with such optimistic excitement.

I traced a circle on the glass and looked out through the rain-curtained window. I was shivering, bundled up in my useless woollen pyjamas. Tomas clung to me. Or I clung to him. Or maybe both. Yes, I think it was both. It created some degree of warmth, but it wasn't enough. I held Tomas' hand to stop him from biting his nails. He did that when he was very nervous. There must have been some degree of anger in Tomas that day, too. For when I looked again, he was biting his lip –

something he only did when he was conjuring up thoughts of anger.

I couldn't feel emotion. Yet.

Frozen blood was dried across my knuckles. I laid in a few punches during the scuffle before.

The dark-haired boy was frozen in the corner. At times, I thought the boy was dead, but he was just sleeping.

It was a long road to the school. I thought we were travelling to the sky. Murky snow was spread out for us like a carpet. Clouds gathered to watch the arrival of Inland's newest inhabitants.

The building was something medieval. If it wasn't for the destructive air raid of 1945, people would have come from all over the world to marvel at its beauty.

It looked as though it sat on the clouds and was held by the sky. Despite my fear, it was hard not to find its beauty inspiring, even if it was just a little bit. Our stomachs rose and fell due to the bumpiness on the road.

I held the paintbrush in front of me. We had conversations in my head. Why are we going to this place? Are they going to kill us? Feed us to a bear? All were viable in the mind of a twelve-year-old.

I ran my fingers through the soft bristles. We held hands. The thought occurred to me that they might take it away from me, so I hid it in my sock. The monsters didn't even attempt it, however. After all, what threat could a tiny paintbrush possibly be?

Quite a big threat, actually.

That paintbrush gave one boy, stuck in his German circum-stance, hope. And hope is a very scary thing sometimes, espe-cially when it's all you have.

When it came time for me to tell my story with the paint, I started to wonder when my gift became more than just a gift, and when painting went from just meaning something to meaning everything. Was it when I was first introduced to Grandmother's paintbrush by my father in the snow? Was it when the man with yellow-stained fingers gifted me the sketch pad? Or the day I gifted my first painting? The answer itself has always been unclear. Maybe you can decide for yourself.

Anyhow, I'm getting ahead of myself now.

I do apologise. I will do that a lot. The excitement gets the better of me.

Before we get to all that, I think we first have to tour the beginnings of our time in Inland.

There's a lot more story to tell first. Don't you agree?

One of the monsters stayed with us in the car, while another disappeared inside. He didn't speak much. Must've been there to force us inside if we protested. However, later, when the real fun began, he merely just sat there and watched. A rather useless addition if you ask me, but I don't think anyone was asking me.

Several minutes passed, and eventually, the monster returned with the unnaturally tall Herr Dohman. Following closely behind him was a younger man, who couldn't have been any more than twenty four years old: Oskar Frederick. He carried the perfect balance between danger and charm, with a cigarette clenched between his two, yellowing front teeth. He always rolled his own. It was cheaper.

The tall man walked straight, like he had an invisible string holding him up, walking with his hands in his pocket. I heard the wrappers and coins struggling as he lumbered on, boulder-like towards the van. There was a chocolate smell to the air.

"*Kommt schon. Kommt heir.*" Dohman tried luring us out, but we wouldn't move. We were afraid to take a breath of the Inland air. "Come on. Come here."

The dark-haired boy departed first. Starvation got the best of him, and when Dohman had an offer of sweets on the table, how could the boy refuse? The snow stuck to his hair like white paint onto a black canvas. He had sores on his lips. Everything about him was undernourished, and it looked like smiling was painful.

After perhaps five minutes, Tomas was enticed by a green lollipop. He was never the type of boy to waste time fighting. Better to go quickly and quietly. No furore. Also, the green ones were his favourite.

I wouldn't move, and I would not speak.

"*Was ist dann verkehrt mit diesem Kind?*" Dohman's hands said to the monster in the dress. "What's wrong with this child?"

He squatted unnaturally outside the open door, looking as though he was going to snap in half. His face wrinkled like a maze as he chewed on a hard sweet – swept, silver hair blowing in the faultless, German wind. I looked away.

"He isn't slow, is he?" He, again, addressed the monster, who assured him that I was indeed not 'slow'. We can't have that in Inland.

The second door was flung open. A trail of light invited me out, but still, I wouldn't budge. Dohman muttered something inaudible to the monster beside him. It wasn't that I wasn't listening to him, just that my eyes were now fixated on the young man behind him. He was pointing his finger to the side of his head and circling it around, miming the words "he's crazy".

I managed a smile. His warm colours were inviting me out, almost like a beacon, but still, I wouldn't move.

It took an hour to coax me out.

Oskar did it.

The conversation.

"*Hallo*, Josef."

He hunkered below my fear-coloured feet. "That's your name, isn't it?"

Nothing. Not even the sound of a nod.

Oskar rolled a cigarette. Eye contact would have been favourable, but was unessential. Small shavings of tobacco blew away with the wind, and the young man's reaction made me laugh above tight, withholding lips.

This was nicer, Josef.

Oskar had his vantage point, and he entered.

"Don't you laugh at me."

Some smoking later: "Will you come out and let me have a look at you?"

He had me charmed just the right amount, so I left the comfort of the van and walked towards Oskar's words.

When I looked at him, the sun blurred his face. Stars appeared. "Oh, yes. You're alright." He dusted off my pyjamas. "You can't tell right now, but I know that you are very brave."

He did it all quietly. A point that was the most noteworthy to me.

I had watery bite marks of snow on my hands. Oskar held me by my coat-hanger arms and gently tugged to keep me moving. Sometimes he would speak to me.

"*Du wirst in Ordnung sein.* You'll be alright."

The next hurdle was the front door.

I would not enter when I saw the shadow people inside.

Frozen tears trudged from my eyes. A group of children gathered as children did and were telling jokes at my expense. I was struck by the abundance of blue-eyed and blond-haired strangers. Their laughs were the kind that could only come from children – so cruel and cold.

Then came Oskar's announcement: "Get on with it, dick-heads. Don't you have someplace to be?" And they retreated whence they came.

"Oh, come on, Josef." Oskar was getting somewhat impatient. "It's not that bad." The words spoken were both stern and gentle. If you find that hard to believe, that such a combination is possible, imagine being hugged so tightly, to the point it hurts, and immediately being punched in the face.

That's what it was like. That's what he was like.

Eventually, he must have got tired of waiting, and he ended up dragging me tenderly inside. His hand had a tight grasp on mine and my other hand was clutching at the fabric of my shirt.

I eyed Dohman inside, from the small opening of the half-closed door, speaking with Tomas and the other boy. Despite being so afraid, a smile still came as naturally to Tomas as breathing.

Our eyes kept meeting and darting off to the various distractions in the room. Pictures of boys in uniforms, banners, trophies, and like in all German buildings at the time, the Führer with his gaze.

Colours and circles reunited and ran in front of my eyes, zigzagging and mingling with whatever sunlight was present from the window. I pressed my fingers against my head – too many colours.

I had a strange feeling in the pit of my stomach.

When we arrived in Inland, we had some inkling that it was for our own good. It didn't bring us much comfort, though. If Mother and Father loved us so much, why would they send us to such a place?

Why?

Why?

Why?

Why?

I listed off a hundred, a thousand, possibilities in my head. Bullet point form:

- They lost their jobs and thought sending us here would be best.

- Maybe they wanted us out of the way for a while so they could get some important business done.
- The fault could have been placed on Mother and her afternoon naps.
- Or maybe, as Tomas suggested, they sent us here to give us an education money can't buy. They would visit soon, he assured me.

But that wasn't to say I accepted any of them as legitimate reasons for our abandonment. Nothing changed the fact that we were small, cold, and frightened little humans. Also, they made Tomas cry, and in my eyes, that was unforgivable.

9

BOY: UNKNOWN

HEAVEN

On a boring hallway chair in a place called Inland, there sat a child with legs dangling in the air, clearing the floor by several inches. But his legs weren't swinging in a carefree way. Each swing was more like a kick, sharp and pointed. There was anger in that kick.

I was mesmerised by the navy and white stripes on his pyjamas, far too big for his body, and all lopsided around his shoulders. It looked like he was drowning in them. His eyes were hard open as he stared at the scary looking clown on the wall – a doctor's waiting room. Inland had its own.

Oskar was rolling more cigarettes on his lap, one leg over the other. He searched in his pockets for the make shift *Zigarettenfilter* and matches that always seemed to be misplaced.

I grabbed Tomas' hand to steady mine. He smiled in an inappropriate and deadly way, but not smugly. He smiled to hide his fear. More like a reflex action.

Tomas could be best described as a smile.

He smiled then.

He will smile now.

And simply because he believed that life was too short not to. You can cry, but don't waste time on such nonsense.

Oh, how I wished I was like my brother back then. I know I was thinking it as I desperately tried to fake my best smile.

The silence of the waiting room made my blood as cold as the air that crept through the open window. The leaves outside were stubborn, refusing to be moved by any wind, and hung limply until they fell of their own accord. There was no whispering noise or rustling. It was all as if nature conspired to keep us in the dark, not daring to whisper the reassurance we craved. Oskar sat with a face like a polished stone.

A doctor would come.

There would be an examination.

The boy from the van would also take part.

He was fragile. His arms were like twigs, and he wore a potato-sack shirt. I thought that if he were to spin too fast, his limbs might snap off. It was hard to get his attention under the mop of dark hair that dominated his narrow face. I was sure that there were eyes in there somewhere. He held himself tightly, and his clothes looked at least a size too small for him, only exaggerating his skinniness.

He looked like a boy lost in a crowd. I wanted to know his name, but Mother told us we shouldn't speak to strangers, so I sat beside the words and stared.

When our time came, Oskar escorted us down a long, narrowing hallway. Nearing the end, we met a slender nurse. Her hair was grey and her eyes were bulging; the staring kind that always seemed to be jumping out of their sockets – caused in some degree, perhaps, by the black-rimmed glasses she wore around her neck. Father referred to them as the 'virgin glasses'. If you wore them, you wouldn't be planning on having sex for the next hundred years.

She took us into the examining room.

"Stand here. The doctor will be with you soon," she instructed us. Her voice was significant and direct.

My hands were clammy.

The doctor was much the same. Most adults in Inland were all the same. He walked in with a face like a brick. His movements were all sharp and with purpose. Examining our clothed bodies for a few seconds, he looked up, and a careless smile flashed across his face. "You boys are fortunate to be chosen to attend Inland."

Luck had nothing to do with it. It had more to do with a cruel twist of fate. Twisted words. Twisted people. Twisted colours. Everything in Inland was twisted.

The doctor looked at me with a sharp nod. "You have dangerous golden eyes, boy." He would not stop sneezing and sniffing, and he did not wear gloves.

Golden eyes were not desirable in Germany at the time.

Nothing different was.

"Where did you get eyes like that?" I didn't answer. Luckily for me, golden hair was in trend. My hair lit up the colour of acorns when it hit the sun that shone through the blackened window. "The rest of you is... pure Aryan," the doctor said.

ARYAN

The word Aryan gave me some degree of confusion. For although Hitler and the Nazi party certainly popularised it, it was not Hitler who created it. The idea wasn't a new one. It was taught throughout history, long before the night of the broken glass.

Yes, welcome to a history lesson by Josef.

The earliest known Aryans came from prehistoric Iran and later emigrated to India. So, no, the first Aryans did not have blond hair and blue eyes.

I will give you a moment to audibly gasp and recover from the shock. It's big news.

Now, if you've fully recovered, we will get back to the story.

The doctor lifted my face with his thumb. Left. Right. Left. Right. The thickness of my lips were measured.

He smiled at Tomas for so long; after a few moments, what remained were only teeth. Brown ones. "You're a gift to the Führer –– beautiful blond hair and blue eyes."

The nurse was beginning to secure her black-framed glasses, to get a better look. She folded her arms across her pigeon chest, nodding intently.

Tomas stood in submission. It didn't seem fair to me that he was a gift to the Führer, but I had dangerous eyes. The only thing I knew for certain about my eyes was that I got them from my father. Now, I added "dangerous" to the list.

Lastly, it was the boy's turn. The doctor made him turn his head from left to right and back again in the same fashion. He was taller than both of us and looked at least two years older. The doctor didn't say a word to him, but his expression said enough. I could feel it.

He weighed and measured us as the nurse wrote it all down in a brown notebook. Even our teeth and nose shape were taken into consideration. I didn't know there would be a test.

That was the easy part.

It was nothing compared to the humiliation that was to come.

"Remove your clothing." The doctor's voice spun on a chair.

All three of us looked at each other. The window was open. Perhaps it wasn't too late to run. All were reluctant to get undressed first, searching in each other's eyes for the mutual sympathy we craved.

The doctor decided on me.

"Josef, zieh deine Sachen aus," the doctor said. "Josef, clothes off."

I forced myself to bring down my trousers with rattling hands. The sneezing doctor pressed at me to keep me moving. Tomas shuffled in like he was going to help, but thought against it.

I stood in just my underwear and one sock. The other must-have got lost in the snow. During the examination, I couldn't help but think of that small, solitary sock, alone in the snow forever. Indeed, a scene from a painting.

"And the underpants."

"What?" My hearing worked fine.

With much discomfort, they similarly came down, and it was with an amplitude of humiliation that I stood in just my skinniness, with my self-respect around my ankles.

The tall nurse started hurrying Tomas and the dark-haired boy now, too. Their faces were wooden. I was afraid to look down but felt my eyes drifting anyway. My eyes also worked fine.

I hadn't noticed before, but in that tiny room, standing so vulnerably by my brother's side, I realised that he was at least half an inch taller than me. I suppose I hadn't looked up at him until that point. He held his head higher. His back was straighter, and he stood so proudly that one was ashamed to do otherwise after him.

I stood like hands were pressing down on my shoulders, as if my very thoughts weighed me down.

The room was cold.

We stood, shivering.

Three naked boys were examined.

"Move your hands now," the doctor instructed.

Tomas did as he was told immediately, with a nervous grin. I refused to move my hands.

"Why?" I asked. I breathed it rather than spoke it, so neither the doctor nor the nurse heard me.

"I said, arms out!" He sneezed into his hand.

They had to make sure we had both balls in there.

I pried my hands away from my penis and held my arms.

"It'll only be for a second," the nurse promised. "You're going to be part of the Führer's new master race. That's exciting, isn't it?"

Master race?

I didn't feel like I was part of any master race, and if such a master race did exist, that doctor would be the first to go, with all his sneezing and rudeness.

Luckily, though, I didn't speak.

The doctor cupped our genitals.

"Breathe in."

He gave us instructions we were to follow promptly.

"And out."

Our examination came to an end with our photos being taken for our new identity cards and birth certificates, the nurse doubling as a photographer. The camera's mechanical whirring and clicking startled me.

"Noch einen. Noch einen." I blinked, so the photo was retaken."One more. One more," the nurse said.

I thought about the family photos we had taken yearly.

How Mother dressed and washed us pristinely. Nothing was out of place, despite us playing in the summer puddles a few hours before. Father made us laugh for the photo. He never liked the fake, polished smile that usually came with photographs – preferring for us to smile naturally. So, every time he gazed upon the photo, he would be reminded of happiness. Pure, unconditional bliss that only young children can master. We try to censor our joy a lot more as we get older, covering our mouths like we reject the idea altogether.

"Twinkle, twinkle little *cow.* What? *Cow?*" Try as I might, I was unable to suppress the laughter.

"Tomas, did you change the words again?" Father sang so exuberantly.

I can still remember the sound of my little brother's laughter, the way the words and the bright, vivid, yellowish colours bounced off his teeth. It created the colour of music. I'm reminded of that day often.

That was our father, and we loved him.

My eyes fogged up. I wiped a small opening, just enough to see out.

"*Lächle. Lächle,*" the nurse instructed. "Smile. Smile."

My face smiled, but my eyes couldn't.

Stripped of half our dignity, we were allowed to put clothes on again, which we did in record-breaking time, might I add. We were given hand-me-down clothes. My shirt had a large hole at the bottom of it, so I tucked it into my trousers.

As we left, we could hear the discussion taking place in our honour. From the side, I listened to the cotton colours, but when I turned, they were gone.

"I'm thinking the first and second one. The third one isn't fit."

The nurse hesitated before mumbling in agreement. "… They… happy with the first and second."

I frantically tried to remember who was first and who was second, but my mind failed me.

"What numbers were we, Tomas? Do you remember?"

"I think I was second, so…" He shrugged.

Was I first? Second? Third? Was Tomas first? Was he third? Please don't let him be third.

"We'll be alright," he finally answered, putting his hand on my shoulder. Panic rose.

But the doctor knew who was first and second. The nurse knew. The monsters did. You know. Even I did, to some extent.

Soon after, Oskar came back out and took Tomas and me into one room, and the boy was led into another.

I never saw him again.

And I didn't even know his name.

10

THE FORGOTTEN NAME

FRENCH ROSE

WE WERE NO LONGER TO CALL OURSELVES JOSEF AND Tomas ____, which you already know I have no memory of. The new name was beaten into our heads, forced on us like an unwanted kiss from an aunt at a Christmas party.

"Tomas Schneider," Dohman pointed to my little brother. "And you – Josef Schneider." Our previous names were not German enough. The way he held his lanky frame and gestured with his hands screamed comedy. The man seemed to sink into his forties like an old armchair.

In a somewhat ironic turn of events, the name Schneider was also of Jewish decent.

"That's not our names," Tomas argued. "Our names are Tomas and Josef____" You don't want to be the kid who argued with Dohman.

"Shut up," Dohman said, cutting his sentence in half.

"Those were poor excuses for names." He was polishing his glasses with spit, stamping authority.

Tomas nodded. His face was cracked. After a few minutes,

he gathered up the courage to speak again. "Herr Dohman, where's Mama and Papa?"

Dohman put his glasses back on. He thought about the answer until he decided on a simple one.

"Gone." Blue, lantern eyes stared at his desk. "And there will be no speaking of your Mama and Papa either, *ja*?"

"Why not?" Perfect unison.

I sank further into the chair, hoping that it would swallow me whole. Playing with the buttons on my shirt, peeling them off by their tiny threads, gave me some comfort. The urge to speak out or punch him was growing on me, like weeds. I could feel Tomas' gaze.

"Don't interrupt me," Dohman said sternly. It seems that all adults don't like it very much when children talk over them.

"Mama and Papa are dead. From now on…"

"What? Mama and Papa aren't dead. We saw them… just a few hours…" Tomas' words were swift, and he came to a moment of realisation.

The gun.

He also heard it.

He wept some more. "Josef…"

"What did I just say about interrupting?" Dohman looked down at his desk, like he would be able to fashion a suitable response from the papers littered on it. "They were hung for their crimes against the Reich."

Crimes? For wanting to keep their children? For marrying each other? For swearing?

Eyes down.

"You two are better here than with those traitors." The wall now seemed to have answers in its shadows for Dohman eyeballed it. Germans at the time could never escape the shadows. Aware of who had fathered us, Dohman had conflicting thoughts that day. He plucked the shades of grey in his mind like harp strings. The colours coloured his behaviour, but it was messy and didn't keep inside the lines. His face spoke, even when his lips didn't move. "If Jewish people are inferior, then how could these children have Jewish blood and still appear to look Aryan?"

To reconcile this dilemma, Dohman propagated the idea that we were descendants of pure German blood, and we had more of our mother's traits, despite that being untrue. The guilt convinced him that the Nazis were not stealing children, but reclaiming what was always theirs.

"It was our duty to remove you from such an environment, so you could grow the proper way," Dohman spoke to his desk.

"No. No. No." Tomas repeated.

"I'm sorry. W-what do you mean?" My eyes diverted between Tomas and Dohman. "You can't mean that... that they...?"

I cried as if the ferocity of it might bring our Mother and Father back; as if, by sheer force, the news could be undone, the words could be unsaid.

"They couldn't be dead." I tried to scream, but the words were unable to come out, no matter how much I forced them to. I often found myself shouting at the words, telling them to leave my lips, but they were stubborn and refused to listen.

Dohman looked to Oskar, prompting him to help, but Oskar couldn't hear under the tobacco fumes.

"No, they wouldn't do that. They loved us..." Tomas' voice was cracking. So, too, were his eyes. They were like the sky. His voice changed mid-sentence.

"Why did they have to die?"

You can't blame them for dying, Tomas.

My cries were then replaced with silence, and my silence was a lie.

"Don't cry." Dohman seemed to collect his words in his hand, flatten, and throw them across the room at Oskar.

Everything was silent for many more difficult breaths. Not the kind of silence where nothing happened, but the kind where everything happened. All at once. A collection of colours, sounds, and smells.

Then Oskar entered the script.

"You understand him, *ja?*" Oskar finally said, placing a hand on my brother's head.

"Yes," Tomas promptly agreed. Quick answers were appreciated here in Inland.

"And you?"

I nodded my head, salt on my tongue.

Dohman pulled a small, ceramic bowl of sweets from his drawer and held out the peace offering. "Take some."

Our sadness reached into the bowl and picked out a sweet. I chose one, Tomas picked up three. Our hands were of frailty and caution.

"Ah!" Dohman's voice was a whistle. "What do we say?"

"*Danke,*" Tomas delicately spoke. I could hear his pain. He could feel it in his throat. And occasionally, it would work its way up in the prickly form of a sharp cough.

But I didn't speak.

I couldn't. I looked at Dohman with my mouth slightly opened.

"Excuse me. What do you say?" He loomed over his desk and whispered it to me.

Still nothing.

"You sure they didn't send us a retard?"

Oskar sighed, leaning forward on his chair.

The bowl was pulled from my reach, and I was forced to drop the sweet.

"You will get one when you learn some manners."

I knew my manners, but I didn't show them to adults that didn't know theirs.

Oskar was in mid-roll of a cigarette when Dohman called upon him again.

"Frederick!" I jumped. "Take these two outside and show them what we do to boys with no manners."

Before he did so, Oskar clicked his heels together, shot his right hand in the air, and said in a deep, loud voice,

"Heil Hitler."

Dohman copied him.

What do they do with boys that cry?

In Inland, the way love was shown happened to be strange. It involved being beaten, with fists and words.

But this didn't happen to us. Not yet.

"Don't worry – I won't hurt you," Oskar said, with kind eyes and a cigarette in his mouth.

"But if you don't stop crying," he poked Tomas' *Stupsnase*, Tomas' button-nose, "*he* will."

The beatings made us forget our names, and almost ourselves, too. We wrote line after line when the other kids were playing.

"My name is Josef Schneider."

"My name is Josef Schnieder."

"My name is Josef Sch…Schh."

People are hard to understand. The men surrounding me are far away from my comprehension. They're puzzles missing a piece, and trying to make a beautiful picture from the pieces they have.

11

THE BACKGROUND PEOPLE

*BEAVER*BITTERSWEET SHIMMER*

THE LANGUAGE OF INLAND CAUGHT ON RATHER QUICKLY. I
don't mean that they spoke in tongues, or used secret codes, or
anything exciting like that. I mean the profanities spoken – so
impassioned and vehement.

Every other person was referred to as '*eine Fotze*' or '*ein
Arschloch*.' Sometimes, Oskar got creative and yelled out, "*Deine
Mutter geht in der Stadt huren*" to other youth leaders and older
students.

If you're unfamiliar with these terms, and I assume most of
you are, I should explain.

Fotze, of course, refers to a woman's genitals. But, in this
case, it refers to an unpleasant or stupid person – a cunt.

Arschloch means arsehole.

And, lastly, Oskar's creative masterpiece can roughly be
translated to your "Mother is a whore."

Roughly.

A man like that needs to be quoted at least once.

Tomas didn't know what a lot of it meant, and for the first
few days, the other boys thought it would be funny to ask him

to repeat them. Even to various youth leaders. It was always met with mocking laughter.

My first overripe banana taste came from the mouth of a stern woman from the town of Inland, Frau Teichmann. She was in charge of everything. She called me a *Miststück* after I refused to get undressed for a shower the night we came. A bitch, a piece of dung.

"Why won't you get undressed, child?" she said. "You're filthy!"

Being naked in front of three people I didn't know was enough for one day, thank you very much. They forced us to shower with a strange green substance that, apparently, would make us "cleaner."

Frau Teichmann was an immensely holy woman, and she led a strictly catholic based life. Despite this, she was good at complaining. After church on a Sunday, she always made a point in seeking out other women for their weekly Sunday gossip. It truly was a gift of hers. Mothering, on the other hand, not so much.

The woman's nose stuck out like a star, but not in a good way. It was stuck out like a pinch of clay fashioned into a beak, and her eyes were strange too; she had the kind of eyes that always looked like she was glaring at you, intense and harsh – even if she was in a pleasant mood, which wasn't often, but it did happen. She was thin in appearance and always wore black and stockings that bunch at the knees. It was like someone had thrown a blanket over a broom.

Despite the complaints about her job, she grew to love some of the children of Inland – myself included. She just had a rather strange way of showing it.

As you can imagine, I showered in anxiety that night, and yes, clutching my paintbrush. Teichmann tried to take it away, but she quickly learned there would be no way in hell I'd be getting into any shower without it, or into any bed for that matter. Both of us had to bathe. My arms clutched to nothing. There was nothing but dried soap, various chattering from outside, and the deluge insults from Teichmann.

We listened as we bathed.

"Those bastards better pay me extra for this? I work my ass off all day, and then they make me do this." She complained to us. I was still silent, but I was listening.

"How do they expect me to get everything done?"

By "everything", she was referring to the meals she had to prepare for the students. She always had help from other cooks, but Teichmann was in charge and gave the orders.

"You done?" she scolded.

Tomas answered for both of us.

After the torture ended, I backed myself into a corner and waited for what was to come next – more words from Teichmann.

"You would want to sort out your attitude before going to school, young man. Quick answers here and quick answers only."

Then Oskar.

"Would you leave him alone, you bitch?" His gentlenesss slipping in front of her words.

"Let me handle him."

The tiles were shivering. Oskar came closer.

"Lick my ass. I'll speak to him whatever way I want." The ground shook slightly.

"Don't tempt me, Teichmann" Oskar winked at her.

"Shut up!"

The echo of her swearing followed Oskar up the tiny washroom, to where I was squashed, almost halved in the corner. He rolled his eyes.

I watched as Tomas folded sheets after Teichmann told him to be quick about it. Despite all the swearing, he agreed.

"Don't listen to that bitch, little man," Oskar mocked. Swear words still bouncing off the walls in the damp air.

Trust in children is like a murky pond: the true depths are out of sight, and even when the bubbles surface, you need to know where to look and what exactly to look for.

Oskar Frederick knew where to look.

He sat beside me, his back to the wall.

"This one is for you," he smiled, giving me chocolate he pulled from his coat.

"You don't have to say thank you," he added quickly when he saw me hesitating.

With a half-smile, I took it.

"Danke," I said quietly. "Thank you." Almost so quiet that I wasn't entirely sure Oskar heard it. But he heard it all right. The grin of his face confirmed it.

First bubble coming into view.

I didn't eat the chocolate. I held it. I felt the stickiness of Oskar's friendship on my hands, mixing in with the sweat present on my palms. I don't think I ever did eat it either. Its new home was my pocket, and I'm sure Teichmann would have been cursing my name when she came across the stain.

"Now that we have you talking, can I ask you something, little man?"

I nodded.

"What's with the paintbrush?"

I didn't know how to answer that. All I knew for certain was that I needed it. And:

1. It represented the last time I saw my grandmother.
2. It represented the last time I saw Father.
3. And it represented a dream.

I shrugged. "I don't know."

"Do we have an artist, maybe?"

I smiled. I've always hesitated to call myself an artist, but others did, and I accepted that with humble satisfaction.

Some notable things about Oskar Frederick, twelve-year-old Josef edition.

- He was born in laughter and with the sense of knowing that the world is mad.
- He loved cigarettes. His favourite part of them was the long drags, the rolling, and the taste of tobacco on his lips as he licked the paper. The only thing he loved more than cigarettes was his beloved Elsbeth, who will make her debut very soon. She will enter from the scene in the rain.
- He was a teacher by trade and a good one at that, which was the reason he was targeted, let's say, by the school.
- Being the oldest of six children, he had to take on the role of his father when he left years before.
- He cheated his whole life, and he would soon cheat death, too, when he was put into a war he didn't start, and all because of a boy, pink triangles, and stubbornness.

"Then, the Führer will love you!" Oskar laughed, his smile crooked.

"He himself is one."

I knew that I wanted to know more about the staring man on the wall. All artists are interesting.

Oskar Frederick was an odd-man-out. A non-existent person. He had wisdom beyond the years of any twenty-four-year-old I've ever known, and he was a good man. Somehow, though, and I'm sure you've met people like this before too, he was able to blend in. A background noise. A background person. Oskar was always just there. Not a person, but light and colours.

The background people come to live, breathe, work, and die. Floating through life unnoticed, rather like slaves. Going where they need to go and doing what they need to do because they are just energy.

Fortunately, however, lights and colours were not invisible to everyone. In a line of people, I would always choose him first. His colour was the loudest to me.

His eyes were a strange blue, too. Like that warm, wool jumper that you put on when the air gets chilled – comfortable, cosy and familiar. Mix as much white and blue paint as you wanted, but you could never duplicate it, for there could only ever be one such colour in the world. His eyes were that kind of blue. As soon as I saw those eyes, I knew he was worth an awful lot.

Oskar stood with a patch of damp on his back.

I was led into a cabin-type room with bunk beds of cheap, stripped pine that smelt like cologne, cigarettes, and hormones.

Rough, canvas mattresses were jammed end to end on both sides of the draughty room. The last bunk bed, on the second row, would be mine. I was holding sheets, pillowcases, a thin duvet, and some more hand-me-downs. I had to make my bed up.

I could still feel the Führer's gaze. That man was everywhere. He stared from the front wall where his portrait had been crookedly hung.

Without the beds, the cabin would have seemed quite cavernous. With its stone floor and corniced ceiling, it might even seem quite grand. Like this, though, it was reminiscent of the economy section of some clapped-out train carriage. Light shone dimly through the mullioned window, onto the moss green bedding and dusty floor.

Boys were playing marbles. Two of them were drinking from a brown bottle. It seemed important.

"Save some of the burning juice for me, Manfret," a boy named Penn called out. Some were smoking cigarettes. The smoke stung my eyes. The boys and the smoke all stared at me as I made my grand entrance.

The walls were alive and decorated with posters – some of war heroes like Otto Skorzeny, and legendary fighter pilots and U-boat commanders like Günther Prien. Oskar kept a poster of a popular blonde-haired actress, Winnie Markus, (who Oskar thought was gorgeous) by his bed. At night, when he thought everyone was asleep, I caught him staring at it between the sheets and hard breaths.

Outside, to the horizon, you could see only where the grey sky blended into the grey pavement. If there were a colour to sum up life in Inland, grey would be it – an anthem for life here. Wearing grey clothes, eating grey food, to the grey drone of pointless chatter.

Tomas and I were separated. Another wet departure.

I'd be sleeping in the same cabin as Oskar, the familiar, cozy jumper, and five other boys. That night, I was cannonaded by questions.

It was an interrogation of colours.

The part of Stefan Rosenberger was played by pansy purple and fatty bacon.

Penn played by burnt orange.

They all fell on my face, landing somewhere near my nose and further exaggerating the pungent smell.

Stefan: "What's your name?"

Me: "Josef."

Penn: "How old are you?"

Me: "Twelve."

Stefan: "Twelve? How could you be twelve? You're so short."

This was true and a constant disappointment for not only myself, but Mother, too. I was a boy incapable of ageing.

Penn: "So, you must only be eight then."

He was persistent.

Me: "No, I'm not! I'm twelve!"

I protested, fleeing the scene – dodging the colours.

From across the room, the warmth of the blue fell.

"Leave him alone, boys," Oskar shouted, ending their interrogation, but that didn't stop them mocking me.

"Josef's not twelve; he's only eight. He's a baby," Stefan spoke in a sing-song voice that only intensified the colours.

An older boy, whose freckled face was covered with occasional areas of skin, introduced himself. He jumped from the top bunk.

"Rouvon Bacchman. Nice to meet you, Josef."

We shook hands and exchanged a look that made me certain that we would be friends.

It took everyone else a little longer to warm to their new roommate.

The teasing continued for several weeks.

"Did you see Josef's eyes?" the line of boys announced.

Questions.

"He's defiantly one of them."

Cruel answers.

"He can't be. Don't be stupid. Jews aren't allowed here."

Jew.

Whispering. Questions. That word.

The word itself didn't mean much to me. My only link to it being my father, and he didn't have much to do with it. But when I arrived in Inland, I started wondering what it really meant. Was it a bad word? Was my father a bad person? Everywhere I went, there was that word. It stood on top of closets, crouched in the darkness. It followed me around, tapped me on the shoulder, tripped me up the stairs.

Jew.

Jew.

Jew.

But not to worry. That word would soon be replaced with another; the gay F-word and I was seemingly the only boy in Inland who didn't know its meaning.

I am laughing now. I really should stop spoiling the story for you. Not to worry, I will work on that.

I'll try.

Continuing.

12

SWEATY PYJAMAS AND SWASTIKA SOUP

*SAND DOLLAR*SAFETY ORANGE*SELECTIVE
YELLOW*

After a few days of being in Inland, a tailor from
the small town delivered our new uniforms. We had been
measured upon our arrival.

The town itself was relatively poor, despite the apparent rise
in the economy since Hitler took power. Many of the towns-
people got work from the school, including Teichmann. She
lived on buttons to support herself and her adult son, who will
make a cameo shortly. *Shit, I did it again.* Despite what I
thought back then, Teichmann did not live in that kitchen, but I
was close. She lived under it, in the basement with her son.

Our uniforms consisted of a black shirt, black corduroy
shorts, a belt, and a glowing red armband with a swastika
embroidered onto the white stripe. There was some difficulty
securing the neck scarf. Oskar helped. On my upper sleeve,
Inland was embroidered onto black triangles, with a yellow
border and lettering, acorns intertwined on branches.

I examined my new uniform. It was too clean.

The tailor, who was an older woman and had the longest
plait in her hair I've ever seen, noted approvingly,

"These two are going to be such good looking young soldiers. Some competition for you, Oskar."

I wasn't too sure whether or not I wanted to be a soldier, but the choice was not freely given.

Again, adults and their rules.

"No one could compete with this face," Oskar joked.

Oskar wore the face of a teenage boy. What made up for it was his height. He was over six feet tall.

I could see Tomas' lips stretch wider into a gaping grin, and his eyebrows arched to the sky as he looked in the mirror and gloried in his new-found status. What he coveted the most was the dagger that came with the uniforms, an eagle perched proudly on the leather with a Swastika on its chest.

Swastikas were all the rage back then.

A fashion piece.

I peed next to swastikas.

I wrote on desks with swastikas etched on them.

I ate fucking swastika soup.

You understand.

Very popular.

Engraved on the knife, "*Blut und Ehre.*"

Tomas studied and traced the letters.

"Blood and Honour."

Oskar didn't say much about it. The most he did to acknowledge my uniform was make a thumbs-up sign and pat my shoulder, which was all I needed.

Afterward, we walked back to our cabins and listened to the sound our feet made on the cobbled ground, and Oskar had a cigarette – or two – or three.

The first few months in Inland were no doubt the hardest.

A nightmare a night.

I can't quite recall all the details, but this I know for sure.

There was a van.

A rope.

A boy.

And one word.

"Run!"

The bed on the other side of the room, which belonged to Manfret Wünderlich, drove through the darkness. To a noose.

"Run." A voice in the distance.

A boy reached out his hand for someone to take hold of it.

Then slowly, more rooted in the nightmare, he sank, presumably to the floor – the bed and boy. I tried to run to him, but I was too slow. When I finally reached him, the rope was tied tight around his neck. I could see only blue eyes staring, just like Grandmother's had been.

The boy was my brother, and it usually took a long time for the screaming to stop.

I would drown in my sweat, while my brother was on the other side of the room, drifting and dying.

I couldn't help him.

Cue the screaming.

The nightmare seemed so real and was good competition for the equally terrifying reality.

The six other boys would sleep with hands over their ears. Sometimes, they swore. *"Zur Hölle mit Josef."*

"To hell with Josef."

They cried to Oskar.

What did those boys dream about? Sliding down banisters? Playing soldiers with their best friend? Pretending to be Robin Hood? In their dreams, they'd be the heroes, and there would most definitely be a happy ending. In a way, I felt bad for waking them from their beautiful, innocent, and childlike dreamland. But I was a boy incapable of dreaming.

The dreams would return, of course, and when they did, I would hold onto them and breathe them in like the air. When that little voice started to become louder in my heart, that's when the real fun would begin.

At first, Oskar looked upon me with pity. He soon realised that his gentle touch was not enough.

Nightly, he sat sleepy-eyed, waiting for the ruction to begin. He sat in a ball of sadness as a stranger at the bottom of my bed. After a few nights, he sang his mother's words. Quietly.

"Aber heidschi bumbeidschi, schlaf lange,
es is ja dein Muatter ausganga;
sie is ja ausganga und kimmt neamer hoam
und lasst das kloan Biabele ganz alloan!
Aber heidschi bumbeidschi bum bum,
aber heidschi bumbeidschi bum bum."

"Sleep long,
your mother has gone out and won't come home again.
And leaves the little boy alone."

"Heitschi" is not a word you can find in any German dictionary. I've looked, believe me. It possibly originates from Bavaria and means to rock someone to sleep. To soothe them.

The tune was the same, but Oskar sometimes changed the words a little, depending on varying degrees of drunkness. He sometimes sang;

"Your mother has gone out whoring and won't come home again."

After three weeks, he held me tightly in his unconscious arms, as I struggled mightily to defeat the nightmares. He picked me up and sat with me on the damp ground until it ended. Something about Oskar not knowing what he was doing was very reassuring to me. He accepted my screaming words and kicking like it was gifted. Snot adorned his shirt, but he didn't mind.

We would never speak of it in years to come. I'd never properly thanked him, nor did he expect a "thank you". The most said about it was a typical Oskar response in April. We were smoothing out our beds for the daily Teichmann inspection.

"You're a horrible singer," I said.

Oskar laughed with the most beautiful response.

"Du bist ein Warmduscher."

Loose translation: you are a pussy.

But this is different. In Germany, there is a myth that warm showers aren't masculine, and so the term literally means someone who takes a warm shower. Despite the rumours, the German language can be colourful.

Many of the other youth leaders would've mocked me or beat me if they'd so much as heard an unmanly whimper. It must have been fate, sheer luck, or maybe something else entirely that brought Oskar to me.

Tomas wasn't so lucky.

He didn't have an Oskar of his own.

Instead, he had Erick 'tin eye' Kröger, so called because of the monocle fixed to his left eye. No one knew how he lost the eye, but the children of Inland liked to spread rumours anyway.

Derrick Pichler told me he lost it when he fought in the First World War. Some said he challenged a pencil to a fight – the pencil won. Others commented that a boy from Inland did it. All of those answers were right to some extent, eh, except maybe the pencil thing. But I think the number one reason can be summed up in one, small yet powerful word.

Love.

The strongest thing on earth.

He was a sharp-edged man with a nefarious glare that seemed to discourage the very idea of misbehaving. Except, his idea of misbehaving was rather odd, unfair even. If Tomas even uttered a whisper that sounded like Mama or Papa, he'd be met with a wooden cane, or worse, like on this occasion, a fist.

Kröger adopted a soldier-like posture, stiff and tense, a refrigerated voice and breath that reeked of heil Hitler.

A small lesson on parenting from the *Schulleiter* – school leaders.

Things you will need.

A fist.

If your child misbehaves, you will give them a hiding.

If your child cries, give them a hiding.

If your child gets an answer wrong in class, hiding.

You get the idea.

The answer to everything was a hiding.

Boys were beaten daily in Inland.

I learned a lot about punishment there. I learned that it happened because of love. We tried to cry out for help, but we soon realised that no one would listen. No matter how loud we screamed and cried, we couldn't stop or change what was to be our fate, and no one was going to come for us. We were tortured, and they told us it was for our own good. We needed discipline. Betrayal is too simple a word to describe the over-whelming pain and loneliness we felt.

If we questioned a sigh Hitler made, we were beaten. The younger children were too small and weak to fight back, and the ones who could, had their hands tied to a post.

There wasn't a thing that was fair about it.

Echoes of screams were in the air.

The obvious thing would have been to run away. Run away and never come back. But where would we go? Who would we run to? There was no one. The children with parents would likely be captured again by the Gestapo, and who knows what would have happened to their parents.

In Nazi Germany, it was safer to go to the root of the virus and kill it before it had a chance to spread. And kill the people who helped those people, the people who assisted those other people, and a few more just to be safe.

We believed the things we were taught because we were conditioned to believing them. And if at the end of our 'training', any conscience or social status was still left, the Wehrmacht (the German armed forces) would take care of that.

13

SCREAMING DOMINOES

SILVER SAND

We played a lot of games in Inland.

One such game was called *Totgeschlagen.*

Translation: beaten to death.

A younger boy and an older boy were taken in the night.

A team was formed.

The older of the two was forced to beat up the younger ones, or they would be beaten themselves – and worse.

I was half awake and half asleep in arms of the cotton blankets. I was terrified of the dark thing inside of me. Oskar lit a candle, so I wasn't so scared, but he didn't realise that in doing so, he also cast a shadow on the wall that mimicked outstretched hands.

On the small, single bed beside me, I could feel the sheets rising and falling with Oskar's breathing. His books on the nightstand beside me were on fire. I heard the sound of a boy deep in concentration in the bunk above me and the familiar sound of a page being turned in a book. In my half awake-half sleeping state, I thought I had imagined it – a trick of the mind.

Everything around me was still for once, and just as I found myself drifting back to sleep, misery came knocking at the door in the form of two suited men. Oskar woke up.

"It's alright."

They wore masks.

They smelt like cheap rum, sweat, and urine.

Panic stood up in my throat. Oskar's voice tightened its grip. He repeated it.

"It's alright." He told the shadows to get out.

As the darkness fell, there was a shift in Oskar that night. It travelled and wandered through the lines on his forehead. It was tense and calm, but it disclosed no answers. Not yet.

His midnight face, as I called it. Of course, this face wasn't confined to midnight, but that's when I saw him make it the most. When people couldn't read it like a bad book.

The monsters dragged Penn Pichler and Stefan Rosenberger from their beds. They were screaming in a chorus of misery.

"Nein."

I can still hear them. They smelt like pain and blood. I could taste it.

I didn't know where they were taking them, but judging by how much they resisted, they knew. And judging by Oskar's midnight face, he knew too.

For a while, there was nothingness. I couldn't hear, nor did I want to.

In the door that never fully closed, there was a small gap, big enough to see through. The other boys found themselves gravitating towards it, all pushing each other for space.

Curiosity got the best of me. I had to see.

Then I saw it.

Penn punched the sobbing Stefan, his ten-year-old hands too small to protect or defend himself, before he pushed his foot down on his head, kicking him and twisting it down on the little boy's skull.

I tried to stifle a terrified scream.

Oskar was now sitting atop my bed.

He tried to coax our gaze from the door.

"It's alright. Don't be scared. It's just a silly game."

It didn't look like any game I would like to play.

"How about we have a game of dominoes?"

But we were too curious and afraid. No one dared intervene and help the boys. I wanted to help, but what could I have done being skinny and twelve?

After being slapped again, the terrified victim screamed when a lit cigarette was thrown down his shirt by one of the masked men and –

I could look no longer.

I gave in to the dominoes and Oskar, letting him pull me close to him, and I covered my ears with my hands. The screams could not be defused.

I was given seven, small tiles.

I did nothing. I said nothing.

I wished I did.

It was easier to just keep quiet, sit back and take it all in. If you did that, you'd have a reasonably good life in Inland.

Later, when it was all over, Oskar had a hard time calming down the hysterical boys. Penn sat on the edge of his bed, staring blank-faced at the wall. His brother sat with him for the majority of the night, falling asleep at the bottom of Penn's bunk. The boy could not cry.

Tomas took a beating of his own. I sat waiting for him in the cold. Only, he was taking longer than usual. I put it down to him not being able to tie the laces of his boots – something he had trouble with, and I always had to help him. Since arriving at Inland, I'd become very protective of my brother. We often came to the rescue of each other. Our dependence upon one another wasn't too unusual, because we were the only family we had left.

When Tomas came into view, for a second, I didn't recognise him. He was far away, but his gait was all wrong. He walked like a scarecrow more than a boy, and all crooked at that. As he neared, my heart fell through to my boots. He was more purple than pale. His left eye was swollen. He couldn't have seen a thing out of it, and he would not for a while. His face still bore congealed blood, and his clothes were an utter mess. When he tried to say my name, his cracked lips failed at the first syllable.

"J…"

But he didn't need to. I was already on my and feet running.

At first, I couldn't say anything to him. I just stood there; arms stretched out my side, and my legs shaking ferociously. It took a few moments to staple the words together.

"What the hell happened to you?"

"Nothing. Just leave it."

"The hell nothing. Look at you."

The look he returned seemed to suggest that he knew what he looked like, and he didn't need me to state the obvious.

"What did you do?"

"I was bad."

What had Tomas done that was so bad? He asked to see where they had buried our parents. For closure. A final goodbye. Only, the trip would never happen. It could never happen.

Tomas' grief came and went like he was jumping in and out of puddles of misery. One moment he'd be laughing, playing with me, having fun with the other boys; the next, he'd be in tears, calling out for our mother. When he cried, I couldn't bear to look at him. He had Mother in his eyes, and every time I'd stare into them, her eyes in his eyes would cry to me.

He suffered crippling separation anxiety for a few weeks, sometimes screaming at me if I got ahead of him on our morning runs, and he couldn't see me, even if it was just for an instant.

"Don't leave me."

At other times, he got angry and occasionally his words lashed out at other children, which got him another bruise. The boys were often sitting in constant states of confusion. For although anger was occasionally frowned upon, the school leaders would also encourage it and teach us to direct it towards our parents and other children.

Our childhood memories seemed so far and distant in Inland.

He would whisper the word "Mama" and see mother's face a million times in a single afternoon. When the events of our story were over, I would often find myself going back – looking at all the people I crossed paths with. How did those people breathe? How could they move? I am often in awe of what humans are capable of – especially the younger ones. Life without our mother and father was still life, and we were determined to live it.

I started seeing my father in crowds. It reminded me that he was still there. Sometimes, whenever I was completely alone in the tiny washroom, I would cry silently when I missed him, but I was still glad to be awake. Nothing compared to the night-mares. In those moments, I'd never felt so completely alone.

14

THE PAINTED MARKETS

*PAINT-PALE-RUST*PAPAYA WHIP*PASTEL GREEN

AS I'M SURE YOU'RE AWARE BY NOW, THERE WERE MANY cast members in Inland.

To be precise, one hundred and twenty four more.

Yes, there were a lot of children in Inland, but very little childhood. All of the boys had old eyes. Old souls trapped inside the bodies of children.

In my time there, only a few of them touched me, and their colours intertwined with my own, creating different hues and shades. Oskar, Kröger, and Teichmann were only a few of those colours.

Others included:

- Rouvon Bacchman – a kind boy one year older than me, with skinny legs, who slept on the top of the same bunk as me. He preferred to be called Von rather than his given name. There was an unusually light, delicate air in that boy's step. He would soon become one of my best friends, and in a sense, my partner in crime.

- Manfret Wünderlich – a squashed boy, with a nervous look in his eyes, who had a tendency to apologise. Even the air around him whispered the words, "I'm sorry".
- Stefan Rosenberger – a ten-year-old with a fragile, short life. He spoke in oddities and riddles, and almost no one questioned it. An odd boy that everyone was fond of. He didn't let it bother him, though. He took what life had given him and tossed it right back in its face.
- Penn Pichler – a boy who was constantly in fights, but also the school favourite, so he never got into trouble. He was a horrible soccer player.
- Derrick Pichler – the identical twin brother of Penn Pichler and his shadow. He had a pink river of skin painted across the joints of his arms and legs. Upon arriving in Inland, I couldn't tell the two apart.

We were Germany's future with no future.

Life in Inland went as follows.

Oskar would wake us every morning at six and not a minute before or past. Beds had to be made up perfectly, without a single thread out of place. Some of the older boys helped the younger ones when they were finished. They were inspected by Teichmann, or one of her cronies, who would often shout profanities at us and tell us, "we don't have all day". Oskar made mincemeat out of us if we made it incorrectly.

There were compulsory training uniforms: mossy green shorts with the Inland crest stitched onto our pocket; two acorns crossed and a white tank top, that was really more grey than white from all the dirt.

We were lined up for our early morning run through the countryside. Much to the shock-horror of our classmates, Tomas and I were good at this, and we got even better as time went by. We would run until the sun fell on top of us if we could. I slowed down for Von so he could catch up, and once he did, I tried to race him. I stole secret glances as I overtook everyone. He cheated and tripped me up so he could get ahead.

The countryside lay like a divine fingerprint, twisting and curving, no two parts the same. The dip and sway of the land, the patterns, the ever-changing sky, and wind. It was my favourite thing about Inland. Every day was a new snapshot in time. For even from that one place, from one of the fine oak trees on the hill, the view could never be exactly the same two days in a row. Little by little, the seasons would bring changes.

And the colours – the colours were so beautiful. They circled above my head.

My mind would wander back to the faraway city of our home. But the beauty of the countryside would draw me back. It had a way of reminding me that I wasn't apart from nature, but a part of it. When I ran, I thought of painting it – every stroke of the brush – every shade of green I would use. The wind blew them all on my face.

Tomas would reach out to touch the bark of the trees as he passed or feel the softness of the new leaves between his fingers before a group of boys would initiate a fistfight by throwing a fistful of leaves at another.

Kröger taught us about weapons. We would throw mock hand grenades and be taught how to duck and cover if one was ever thrown at us – all precautions, apparently. Compasses, maps, MG34s (machine guns) and rifles all made their appearances throughout the lessons. The rifles were too big for our tiny bodies to hold properly, but a lot of us became confident in aiming and firing at targets, with help from Oskar and the other school leaders, of course.

Others were rusty, but eager to learn. There were a few accidents that required consoling a crying child or digging out a bullet from their arms, but it deterred none of us. Great relish came from the quieter days where heads would hover and huddle together while an older boy showed us how to read a map.

Some boys frolicked around like "dastardly creatures," as Kröger put it. The annoyance lingered on his face. His forehead wrinkles shouted swear words.

Two-finger guns + two disruptive yet imaginative boys + an audience of giddy children = a highly frustrated teacher.

Boy 1: "Bang. Bang. You're dead. I killed you, you rotten French bastard."

Kröger in between and ever so small: "Will you stop playing guns and listen?"

Boy 2: "I'm not French; I'm British."

It was a time of mine that I shall never forget, along with the friends that I shared it with. It struck me as odd that the very same person who was teaching us to fire at targets, not two hours ago, forbade us to play with pretend guns. An adult mind is not very grown-up times.

We were not forced to take up arms – we did so with fierce joy.

You give a little boy a gun, and he's not going to turn it down.

Except for Tomas.

He refused to shoot at anything during our first training day.

"Mama wouldn't want me to," he said.

"Your Mama's not here," one leader told him. "Come on. Just like this."

Tomas agreed to hold the gun, but nothing more.

Little did we know that in just a few short months, he'd become the best in class.

A few days of the month were spent helping out at a farm

that bordered the village, and we practiced military discipline, we bonded and shored up our beliefs of the Nazi cause.

The town was filled with stalls. On Mondays and Fridays, we could go there accompanied by the school leaders and buy or trade tobacco rations, liquor, even sweets, and toys. Some older kids helped with odd jobs to earn money if their parents were too poor to send them anything.

I stayed back and walked with Oskar. We listened to the crunching of the leaves as we walked. Erich Kröger walked ahead with some other boys.

He walked with purpose and a slight limp in his step. Kröger knew what he needed, usually tobacco and alcohol. "In and out," is what he always said. Kröger didn't like staying in the same place for too long.

The town was home to many strange yet unforgettable characters. Pieter-pick-a-Pfennig, nicknamed so by the children, was one such person. A crooked man who collected loose change on the streets. As the war advanced, it became harder to spot even a single Pfennig.

I overheard a conversation between Von Bacchman and Penn Pichler. The twins came from a good family, amongst the wealthiest. They thrived during the war. Often times, their mother and father would send them a few Pfennigs each.

"How much money do you have?" Von Bacchman hopefully asked.

"More than you, dickhead."

It was almost dusk, and they were just a few stalls away from the red-haired sweet-shop owner. No one knew his real name, and if they did, no one ever used it. He was simply known to the children as "the sweet man".

"You know," Von started, "we could buy some sweets to share, over there, from the sweet man."

"Get your own," Penn said, jangling the money in his shorts

pocket.

Von shrugged. "It was worth a try."

His nonchalant whispering made me grin.

He gazed back at me alluringly and rolled his eyes.

No other words were needed.

I looked down at my boots.

The stalls in the village were mostly run by people who lived there, but others had come from neighbouring towns to earn much-needed money for them and their families. In world war two Germany, everyone needed every Reichsmark they could get.

One quickly caught my eye. It was run by an older lady and her daughter. The pair of them created artwork and other hand-made crafts. I found myself walking towards it without saying anything to Oskar. He followed me.

Standing there, staring at the long shelves crammed with works of art, I felt myself relax, and suddenly I was at peace.

I traced my fingertips along the paint pots – there wasn't colour that I didn't like. The older woman spoke to me, but I didn't hear.

I was tempted to steal a few from the table, but I fought against it. I would have been caught, and quite frankly, one of Kröger's corridor beatings put me off altogether. Kröger was trying to bargain with a stall owner who would not budge on the price of his tobacco. I instead focused my attention on Oskar.

"Can I ask a favour?"

At first, he said nothing. He was in the middle of rolling a cigarette, licking the paper and sticking it all together, which took immense concentration.

"Oskar?"

"Ja?" He finally replied.

"I just wanted to know if I could get some paints."

Oskar laughed. A small grin directed at the ground.

"Sure. Ask that bastard over there." He was pointing at the man whose face was lit from stem to stern.

He looked like a sagging plastic bag. I could not hear Oskar's joking tone, and I couldn't see his signals for me to return. I proceeded to walk towards Kröger after I clenched my fists hard together.

Go on, Josef.

You can do it.

I spurred myself on.

A shoulder tap.

"Herr Kröger?"

Manfret Wünderlich, Kröger, and the cider fumes turned around.

"Yes, what?"

A pause.

I swallowed.

"Can I get some paints?"

I pointed to the stall.

"Please."

By now, Tomas had made eye contact with me and gave me a look that suggested that I should just fuck off.

I didn't.

"Paint?" A sly smile. He turned to pay the shop owner, who looked at me and smiled. I smiled back.

"Yes, paints."

"Why do you want paint for?"

"To paint a picture."

Kröger's eye was like a pale blue cut-out on his face, and his monocled eye looked in different directions. You could never tell if he was looking at you or just past you. My eyes diverted to the monocled eye.

"A picture of what?" He asked.

"I – I don't really know yet. Maybe flowers."

He laughed. Kröger's laugh was a dangerous thing. "The flowers?"

I would have been less concerned if he had punched me square in the face.

Grown-ups laughing in the face of a curious child hardly inspired confidence. My face began to turn every shade of red there was.

Manfret's soft grey eyes stepped in, curly hair moving with him. "My sister paints." He almost tripped over the words as he said them.

Nodding. "See!"

"Ja. It's alright for his sister. For a girl!" Another sip of the cider and a mouth covered burp.

"Young men are supposed to be playing with toy guns and riding bicycles. Not painting."

"So."

"So!" Kröger mocked. "So, people might get the wrong idea."

"What idea?"

"You know damn well what idea."

"I don't. Honest." I reached a point of arguing with Erick Kröger that no boy should ever reach.

Kröger shoved my words out of the way.

"You're not getting the paint, Josef."

I didn't really mind. I didn't moan or stamp my feet or cry. I simply swallowed my disappointment, and the next thing to come out of my mouth would be a risk. Not a risk I calculated in my mind at all, but a risk.

"You really are a bastard!" I said it louder than I intended.

He heard me.

And he slapped me hard across the face.

I returned to Oskar with a hand-shaped ring of fire, and he mocked me for several weeks.

15

THE GOOD JEW

GOOD-BLUE

WE DID MANY ACTIVITIES DURING THE DAY, LIKE CAMPING. We piled into the mountains and slept underneath a blanket of stars. Singing songs, naming the stars, telling stories, and playing games.

I will admit it was fun.

I didn't have many nightmares when we camped out in the countryside, probably because Tomas was always there. Sometimes, when all the other boys had gone to sleep, Tomas and I would stay awake and pretend to play soldiers, and sometimes we simply sat together and didn't say a word. I loved that.

On one such night, as we lay under the full sky after a long day's work, Von started talking quite suddenly and out of the blue.

"Everything would be fine, but this thing with the Jews is hard for me to swallow." His thirteen-year-old eyes were melting in the moonlight.

Oskar paused for a moment, cautiously, looking around and making sure the other youth leaders weren't listening. The fireflies danced around him. "Hitler knows what he is doing, and for the sake of the greater good, we have to accept certain difficult things."

But I could tell Von was not satisfied with that answer. Others took his side.

"Even if they are incomprehensible?" I asked. Surprisingly, it was the children who had the questions, which seemed backward. I thought it more common for an adult to ask the questions, and the children's job was to stay inside their mental boxes because adults said so. Everything was inside-out.

"Surely, not all Jews are bad," Manfret said. "I knew one when I was little." He crossed one leg over another. "My Papa worked with one."

"*Meinst du, dass ich dumm wie Bohnenstroh bin?* Do you think I'm as thick as two short planks? Of course, they are!" Derrick replied. "Papa said it's got something to do with business."

Suddenly the attitudes in our varying home backgrounds were reflected in the conversation. Then, when a few hours had passed, and all the boys were asleep in the tent and the arguments fell away, Tomas' smallness piped up.

Penn, Tomas, and I were the only ones awake, but they both thought I was asleep.

Tomas: "I knew one, too. A Jew."

Penn: "Not that again."

Tomas, shrugging from his lying position in the tent: "He was nice."

Penn waited for more.

Tomas: "But he was always late for work."

In his mind, he remembered our father with lips like cardboard.

Penn: "See! Those stupid Jews." His ignorance was like a mild burn.

There was a pillar of silent light.

Penn argued for a good ten minutes before he finally won the argument, and Tomas was silenced. I could tell that he had more thoughts left to share.

I said nothing, but I wish that I had.

A recollected memory of the paintings in the clouds

The day was probably a Monday, but it could have been a Friday. All I know for sure was that it had a powdered ebony taste.

They were many nights where father and I spent under the stars. We lived in the city with the neon gods, so the stars weren't so grand. Mother would call out from the window, not knowing that I was there.

"Aren't you lonely down there, Ben?"

"Nein, Lis. I'm painting in the clouds."

I know it sounds mad, but I really did see them. Father's paintings in the clouds. Especially when I closed my eyes tight and used my imagination extra hard.

I caught myself laughing and stopped before anyone heard.

We spent a restless hour in that tent, but afterward, we were just too tired, fell asleep, and the next day was inexpressibly splendid and filled with even more new experiences.

After training, we would go to class, but only for four hours a day. Physical training was a priority. Hitler thought it was more important than memorising dead facts. Just about every task, no matter how big or small, was turned into an individual, team, or unit competition. This included boy's and girls' sports, the quality of singing during propaganda marches, and Winter Aid collections, all of it.

RINSE. DRY. REPEAT

*RED (CRAYOLA) RED-ORANGE*REDWOOD*RED
DEVIL

SCHOOL WAS A TERRIFIC FAILURE. ON MY FIRST DAY OF class, I thought I'd better make a good first impression and went outside and picked flowers for our teacher, Frau Simons. She threw the flowers aside and stared at me with cold eyes.

Frau Simons was a middle-aged teacher who lived and breathed for the Führer. She always had a hawkish air about her. Even her nose was curved and beaked. She had eyes of the palest blue that fixed you in ice should you dare disagree or talk out of turn. If a child so much as answered a question wrong, she took it as a personal slight. She was willow-wand thin, so stick-like that it was hard to imagine her eating much at all, at least not without wiping her narrow lips after every bite. Her hair wasn't so much blonde as a washed-out brown, like it just couldn't be bothered to be any colour at all.

One of the first things I did in class was to make sure my Heil Hitler was working correctly.

It wasn't.

"Don't you know the proper German greeting?" Frau Simons nose-dived.

She made me walk out of the classroom and enter again, this time using the proper greeting, which I didn't know, so I just tried to mimic what I saw others doing. I walked into the classroom, blushing to the roots of my hair, held out my left arm, and shouted in a pretend grown-up voice,

"Heil Hitler."

"Nein!" She roared as she tried to calm down the hysterical children.

She walked over to me, staring at me with piercing eyes and lifted my right arm.

"Your right arm, you stupid child!" She said, marching me out to stand in the corridor for twelve minutes – one minute for every year.

I never lived that one down.

In later years, the left-handed heil Hitler would be a form of defiance, and one I would be rather proud of, too. But for now, it was a source of constant embarrassment.

After a few moments, when I returned, she instructed me to come up to the front, to the chalkboard, and tell the rest of the class my name. The boys were staring and snickering at their new classmate. I looked at Von Bacchman because he was the only one not snickering.

He was worth a stare. He was trouble.

"Your name," Frau Simons was getting impatient.

My face went red again.

"J.O.S.E.F ... S.C.H.N..." I realised that I didn't remember how to spell my so-called last name.

"I can't," I said quietly.

The snickering got louder.

"What? Speak up, boy!"

"I can't spell it!" I yelled it this time.

Simons was not impressed.

Tomas' first day was just as much of a disaster.

New school, new teacher, new students, new clothes, but same old Tomas wanting to be anywhere but there.

As he lined up with the other children to go into class, a smile hung limply on his face, but it would soon come crumbling down. Everyone was looking at him, their eyes judging him. "That's the other Jew boy."

Suddenly, he could feel the muscles in his chin trembling, and he looked towards the window in the hallway, as if the light would soothe him, but it didn't bring him any comfort. It was too late.

He walked quickly away from the other boys, tears in his eyes, turning the rainy day into a whirlwind of greys and yellows.

"*Wo gehtst du?*" Tomas' teacher yelled out. "Where are you going?"

But Tomas did not care to answer, and he had no idea where he was going.

He ran right into the surprising arms of Kröger.

"*Was ist los?*" He asked him, half bent in front of him. "What's the matter?" When Tomas would not respond, he tried again. "Why the waterworks?"

Tomas sobbed into his chest unceasingly, hands clutching at his jacket. He held him in silence, rocking him slowly as his tears soaked his jacket.

"Has it got too much for you?" he asked, crouching.

"Look, I have not met a single boy who came here and didn't have a hard time at first." He said it in the gentlest way Kröger could muster.

A tiny lapse let Tomas him pull away, and he gathered his breath enough to speak.

"I can't tell you." Tomas was sniffing his words.

The pain must have come in waves, minutes of sobbing

broken apart by short pauses for recovering breaths, before hurling him back into the outstretched arms of his grief.

Kröger just held him.

That was our life in Inland.

Rinse. Dry. Repeat.

17

THE STREET WALKERS

SCHULTZ SAND

Saturdays after school were spent walking the streets of Inland with a youth leader or an older student, collecting materials for the war effort. Such materials were scrap metals, charitable donations from some of the wealthier people of Inland, and warm clothes for the soldiers on the eastern front. We'd choose a partner to walk with. Obviously, I chose Tomas, much to the dismay of Von Bacchman, who was gesturing to me as soon as Oskar mentioned the idea pairing up.

Some boys rode bikes.

Others walked.

Regardless, we were all to meet back at our cabins at six o'clock.

Viktor Link, a bossy fifteen-year-old boy, was assigned to walk with us. He didn't say much to us, and we almost always walked in silence, occasionally exchanging small smirks and smiles.

Viktor would greet every person at the door with a docile smile, but as soon as the door was shut and we walked far enough down the road, he would curse those poor people, with all their laziness. Some were deserving of the roll call of scorn, slamming the door in our faces. But most people were just people. I liked it.

See, to me, people are like colours on an easel. No two colours created can be the same as the last. You can have variations of the same shades, and some colours complement each other better than others, but never exactly the same shade. I think that's the most beautiful part of life.

"They think they're too good for us," Viktor would continue, despite our partial dependence on them. Especially later.

Tomas and I enjoyed taking it in turns to knock on each door.

"And this one," Viktor pointed up to a larger house that looked important. "This one belongs to Herr and Frau Schultz." They were two of the wealthiest people of Inland and, in turn, the most envied. Rumours with coats talked in their honour.

It stood on its own. Their house was the only house in the town that did. "He's a rich cunt," Viktor pointed. "Made all his money from his father and spent it all on hookers and alcohol."

Tomas and I looked at each other and rolled our eyes in complete vexation. He continued. "Last time we came here, his wife told us to fuck off. She's crazy." He punctuated his words. "Absolutely. Fucking. Crazy."

Tomas was horrified.

The Schultz's owned a constantly moulting teddy-bear like dog, one small enough to fit in the arms of a child. We all patted his head. It usually took a long time to get the dog hair off our clothes and the smell from our hands.

Although it was his turn to knock on the door, Tomas pushed me in front of him and stood back with Viktor and the dog. "You knock." A giant brown door with a brass knocker stood atop a small flight of steps.

"What?"

"You knock this one," he repeated, practically pushing me with his words.

I sauntered towards the door. "Move it!" Viktor yelled. "We don't have all day." I moved it. I walked the path, climbed the steps, hesitated, knocked the door, and waited for the scorn that was about to come my way.

No Scorn. Just a set of rollers answering the door.

Frau Schultz wasn't overly old, but her body had aged past her years. She wore the wizened features of an old crone. The occasional strand of her once golden hair could still be seen through the lifeless grey mane that limply framed her ageing face.

"Do you have any materials for the war effort?" I asked, so quietly and quickly that she didn't hear any of it. I had to repeat myself, as was usual.

She looked over my shoulder and saw Viktor at the bottom of the steps. That's when she danced over to a wooden table beside the door and handed me a few Pfennigs. She didn't seem all that bad. I ran my fingertips along the indentations of the coins. Frau Schultz was going to speak before a loudspeaker voice came from the other room.

"What are you doing?" I could see visions of mustard-amber squares flying down the hallway towards me like knives.

"*Danke schön,*" I said to Frau Schultz.

There was no answer – only the wooden door in my face.

Not nearly as bad as I expected.

"See! The rich bitch. Doesn't even care about our cause at all." Viktor showed little appreciation despite her just handing me something for our cause. He took the money from me and placed it in a small bag, writing her name on the notebook he carried.

In the evening, the boys compared what we were given in

the various houses we visited – the competitive nature of children.

"I think I did the best," Penn said with his signature cocky smile.

"I collected heaps of scrap metals, and I got one Pfennig." Heads nodded and agreed, half afraid of disagreeing with him, half fed-up with arguing with him.

I didn't say anything about the Pfennigs.

Oskar sat carefully, composing a letter to his family back in Mittenwald. It was his fifth one, and he sat amongst the white river of failed attempts on his bed.

"Dear Elsbeth,

Weather is nice."

Too boring.

"Dear Mama,

I got shitfaced last night and…"

Too much information.

"Dear Elsbeth,

I want to fuck the shit out of you."

Too crude.

You see the problem.

To him, his words were always too cold and flat. Too meaningless. Not what his beloved and Mama deserved. So, when he did write home, he stuck to the basics. "Things are well in Inland," and all that sort. Why can't people ever say what they mean? Why are words so hard sometimes?

In the corner of the cabin, the freckled boy sat cross-legged on the floor, reading a book with a red cover. I tried reading the front. He sat with it on his lap. Occasionally, he'd look up and catch me staring at him in the fading candlelight.

After keeping to ourselves for a while, we thought it would be a good idea to go out to play with the other kids. Well, correction,

Tomas thought it would be a good idea. I thought it was a horrible idea, but I wasn't going to let Tomas go alone, so I dragged my feet behind him. Before Tomas had to ask if we could play, a younger boy, who shared the same cabin as Tomas called out to him.

"Tommy, come play with us." No one ever called him that before.

There was something about Tomas that drew people to him. I guess it didn't hurt that he was a friendly-looking boy, but it was more than that. He was quiet, but not painfully shy. It was a kind of reservedness, let's say, like a conscious choice to observe the lie of the land before he got involved. Yet, he wasn't stand-offish either. He stood friendly-faced and welcoming. It wasn't like he sat down one day and planned to be like that. It's just the way he was. It was just Tomas.

I never saw him go out and deliberately make a friend; they just came to him. Of course, these boys were unaware of the incident that happened a few years back. An incident rarely spoken of, but highly regarded as the Robin Hood Incident.

"Can my brother play too?" Tomas asked the boy, and before discussing it over with the team, they agreed.

In Inland, friendships were important. Like any group of boys, we conducted our favourite pastime – trappers and Indians. And not just any old game. It was Olympic-level trappers and Indians.

It wasn't winning any gold medals anytime soon.

There were two teams.

We formed platoons, pinned red and blue flags onto our shirts, and we were to hunt down the enemy and rip off the other coloured armbands. This, as you can imagine, often resulted in physical fights between platoons. Younger, and weaker boys were pummelled, while platoon captains stood and encouraged the fighting.

Sometimes, even the adults joined in.

Everyone enjoyed the games.

The blue and red flags were ready, and by the standard way of division, the children would pick teams – a real confidence crusher. There were two captains, and in this case, it was Von Bacchman and Penn Pichler.

A small question and its answer

Guess who got picked last?

Yes, that's right – me.

Now, understand one thing. I know why I was chosen last. I would have chosen myself last too, were I the captain (which I never was.) I was too skinny and weedy to play such a physical game effectively, and of course, I was the new kid, so who would take a chance on choosing me? But still, just because I intellectually understood why, it didn't make in any less painful.

I didn't even remember the outcome of the game before the Pichler incident. I just remember that I was picked last.

I was standing there in the street that looked like an unfinished painting. So much of the canvas was still perfectly white, waiting for the artist's hand to return, watching as the team captains called another boy, one by one. The same boy, who called out to Tomas before, whispered something in Von's ear and soon after, he called Tomas' name.

He ran to join the straggling line of shivering children, until, finally, only Manfret Wünderlich and myself were left in the childhood battle-zone, the unlucky team captain already turning away, scowling and complaining to the others.

"Fine, I'll take Manfret," Von sighed.

It was Manfret's lucky day.

Wünderlich looked over-shoulder for support, and we exchanged looks as if to say, "I know how you feel, you poor bastard." I slinked over to my team, who all hated me by now, the other team glad I wasn't on theirs. Being the new kids,

Tomas and I were immediately jammed in between two bigger boys, for protection.

All went quite nicely for a while until the moment when Penn Pichler realised that he wasn't winning, and brought Von Bacchman down onto the mud and snow in a foul of rage. There was some struggling as Pichler tried to get Von's flag, but Von was determined not to let him have it.

Von took Penn's flag in the end.

"What?!" Pichler shouted. His faced twitched in desperation. "That's not fair!" His eyebrows were covering half of his face.

Everyone in Von's team cheered in triumph until it was only Von Bacchman and me. I somehow managed to stay out of the way, flag intact.

He crouched down on a grubby mound of snow, confident of the usual outcome. Von hadn't failed to get anyone else's flag during the game, and most of his team were still standing. It was just me remaining, and the pressure sat heavy on my legs. Von shuffled in, found his target, and I somehow dived out of his way, smashing my elbow up on the pavement.

My celebration was short-lived. For when Von got me down again, he took the flag and waved it around in front of his teammates.

By now, everyone was trying to force me out of the next game.

"Jesus Christ, Josef. You're terrible." And they made their decision. "Get out!"

"*Nein!* Let me play! I'll be better next time. I promise." I pleaded with Pichler, the obvious alpha. "I want to practise."

"*Verpiss dich,*" he replied. "Piss off!" Penn was wiping at the stray beads of sweat on his forehead.

His brother stood beside him, scratching pathetically at his pink river rash on his arm, giving him his support in the best way he could. "We don't want you to play with us, you little *Mischling.*"

You can't play with us: a childhood punch in the gut.

Also, I should probably explain what *Mischling* means.

Mischling – a foul name for someone who comes from mixed blood.

Rumours had their way of travelling quickly around Inland, despite the school's attempts to conceal our past.

"Come on, let him stay. It was our first time." Tomas pleaded.

Von nodded in approval. "It's not polite. Let him stay."

The other boys said nothing. No one dared to argue with Penn Pichler.

"I want to practice. Let me practice. Please," I said as I tried to force my way through the taller boys in front of me.

"It's five against two. He's going, Bacchman."

Despite my protestations, I was booted off the team.

Literally.

"Fuck your stupid game," I said as I kicked a stone down the painted, cobbled road.

I was sniffing into my sleeve.

A few stomps of self-pity later, I felt a palm reach for my shoulder. I thought it was Pichler, back for more. Thankfully, it was not. It was Tomas. There wasn't anyone behind me even a second ago. He must've run, and fast at that. He gave me a grin as I turned towards him and the wind. "Where are you going?"

"Don't know."

"You were so bad," he laughed, rubbing his eye.

"You didn't have to come. You should have played."

"Nein." He said, still gathering his breath. "It would have been uneven teams anyway."

"I guess." My eyes looking towards the snow.

By now, the snow stopped falling on the grimy pavement,

muddy footprints of boots embedded into the white. The next thing I remember was a flash of rosewood red and Von Bacchman tackling me to the ground.

"How do you like that?" he shouted.

"You dickhead," I whispered.

Only Tomas could hear it. He made a sound from the deepest part of this throat that best sounded like a laugh.

"What happened to the game?" Tomas asked. "I thought you were still playing."

Von Bacchman didn't answer; instead, he spoke in my direction.

"Sorry we kicked you off, Josef, but, you were shit."

When he looked my way, it was with a grin that tells me he's going to be a fun kid to know. That sort of half-smile that ticks up on one side.

He looked away again, pale blue eyes to the ground, but not in shyness, more like that withdrawn gaze that tells you you've been dismissed. He didn't care if we were his new friends or not, or perhaps that's what he wants us to think.

"That's alright," I grinned cheekily. "Next time, I'll beat you."

I sounded confident, even though I knew it was a lie.

Oskar had secretly made Von promise to look out for us, and to his credit, Von was happy enough to comply. Probably bribed with sweets from the sweet man. He was not a hostile type of boy at all. In fact, he liked me a lot and wanted to be my friend. (Hence the snow tackle.) But he would not make it so easy for me to see – not right away anyway. He would keep me guessing.

Von Bacchman was the kid that always looked punchable. Every childhood group had at least one kid like that in it, and he was ours. He had cheeks that always seemed flushed and curls that did a lively dance when he ran. I knew the moment I met him that I liked him, and he smiled because he knew.

He was the type of boy who was unafraid to make a decision. In this case, Von Bacchman had already made his mind up about me. He liked me, and he didn't care how strange the other boys said I was.

I liked that a lot.

The snow around the corner on the main stretch of the courtyard was reduced to slush. It was rarely thick enough to play in. More of a nuisance than anything, getting into our boots and making our socks soggy. Boys still threw snowballs, but the contents were mostly dirt, stones, and ice. You didn't want to be hit with one. A lop-sided snowman stood with a cork for a nose and a coal-black smile.

Soon after, the other boys caught up, and Von was showing Tomas and I some of Inland's best landmarks. At least, he managed to fit it all in between telling Stefan Rosenberger to shut his mouth and him telling Von to shut his.

"Go away, pup!" Those children bloodied and battered each other. They shared each other's secrets and broke each other's hearts, but somehow it could always be repaired, sewn together with silver threads. Some friendships never break.

"Pup?" I asked.

Rouvon nodded. "We call him that because his foster papa works in a kennel."

As was always the case, a herd of troops in training came marching past, to our right. They were freshly graduated from Inland, and students all the boys knew. They were met with cheers. But despite it all, the uniforms still kept straight-faced and marched upright, their black boots further polluting the snow. At the back, a straggler broke the act and waved to us younger boys. We were thrilled, and coal-black smiles were dotted on our faces.

The first thing Von pointed to was the fence with pointy

spikes that ran around Inland playground. "Don't ever try to climb that," he warned. "Electric."

Von pushed his way through the growing crowd of boys, forcing his way to me and trying not to stare for too long. We walked the rest of the road side by side.

A lot of the boys became faceless through the years, and most of their names space my memory. I do, however, remember Von Bacchman's face. Every simple, facial expression, and smile. His smell, his taste, his colours. Everything existing forever in my memory.

"And don't worry about Pichler. He's a dickhead to everyone. Don't take it personally." He realised that we didn't know which twin was who yet. "The ugly one!"

"Oh!"

Penn had thick, bushy eyebrows that dominated most of his face. His brother, Derrick's, was a little less wild. They still looked like two brown, dead caterpillars stuck to his forehead, but they weren't like Penn's. Those were his trademark, and how most people in Inland told the two apart.

"Before he came here, he cut his papa's face out of the family photo because he spoke against the Führer."

Tomas rolled his eyes.

"Bulls… nonsense," he said, correcting himself mid-sentence, for even though Mother and Father were gone, he still obeyed by their rules – to be polite. "You're just trying to scare us."

"*Nein!* I swear! I cross my heart." Von said, which put an end to that debate. A kid wouldn't just cross his heart and hope to die if he were lying.

THE DAY THE PICHLER TWINS CUT TIES

It certainly was the truth, as hard as it is to believe. If it makes you uneasy, I would suggest getting used to that feeling. You will be feeling it a lot. Get comfortable with feeling uncomfortable.

It was five on a spring morning – a Monday. Cloudy pink. The air felt grey and chilled.

Two brothers, stern-faced and determined, made their decision, and everything in the room was conspiring to make it happen.

The night before, there was a party. Derrick overheard his father tell a group of his friends that the Führer was a "crazed maniac". Of course, he relayed this information back to Penn, who wouldn't speak to his father for the rest of the night. To Penn, what his father said was contradictory to what he had been learning in the Hitler Youth. They were nice to him there. Made him feel important, didn't treat him like a child, and at the forefront of all of that was the moustache man and his orchestra of colours.

Their father was a Nazi, but not out of choice.

He had mouths to feed and a status to uphold. If that meant being a Hitler supporter, so be it.

Herr Pichler would stand behind Germany's leaders and watch as the less fortunate stood in line for bread.

Nazi Germany was an auspicious place if you didn't mind the spies.

It was dark, and the light in the twins' hearts grew more potent and powerful with each step, not fully realising that if they spoke out against their father, he would be marched to Sachsenhausen.

Derrick eyed the Frankfurt sky from the large window while his older brother carried out the deed. It had been Penn's idea. Derrick tagged along, for support if nothing more.

The clouds were dark and dense. A storm was undoubtedly on its way, despite being spring. German weather was often a tricky thing to pin down.

Penn used his Hitler youth knife to cut his father's smiling face from the family portrait, and I imagine that it bled. Ink all over the living room, and Herr Pichler's cutout smile on the floor.

It was the final straw for the Pichlers, and the decision was made to send to pair off to Inland. Better to send the problem away than to fix it.

The twins were asked about the school, and although there were some unexpected tears and uncertainty from Derrick, there was still a rather enthusiastic acceptance of the idea. They realised that they would no longer be trapped in their circumstances. It would be their chance to see something different – to experience something new.

On their eleventh birthday, the twins were sent away on a train – alone, with two suitcases. They were able to bring one personal belonging each, and the thought of the twins clutching a pot of raspberry jam and their copy of *Birds Of Prey* is still enough to bring tears to my eyes. Derrick embraced both his parents before they left. Pictures were taken with sideways caps. Penn wouldn't even look his parents in the eye, and their dead-eyed mother announced,

"I've lost him. I've utterly lost him."

The twins' father's camera followed his sons down the street until they were out of sight.

18

THE PUPPET-STRING MAN

* PLUM * PLUM-LIGHT * PALE-PLUM * PERSIAN-PLUM

BELLS RANG; A THOUSAND CRIES, MORE OR LESS DISTINCT, mingled with the bursts of boys running out of buildings like they were set alight. Coming from every crack in the wall, and running in the direction of the canteen, like a stampede, not caring who they would trample in the process.

"Well, come on!" Von said, as he hurried and joined the charge.

It was dinnertime.

We were boys.

That's all you need to know.

A whistle blew, and the flock of uniforms formed a neat line, give or take a few stragglers, who stood to the side, talking to their buddies.

There was an epidemic of anxiety that followed me.

Feeling oddly as though my stomach was turning inside out, I stood behind Tomas, and flexuous strands of hair kinked out of his head in random places.

I tried my best to flatten them, and told him to stand up

straight, just like Mother taught me, as we walked towards the wooden doors of the canteen.

The building itself was cold and completely colourless, aside from a Swastika mural that hung in the centre of the wall – it set the room on fire. Most of the flags were painted by the children and were giant eyesores. The canteen seemed to shiver a little more severely than the other buildings in Inland.

When we came to the doors, older students greeted us with a *"Heil"* and produced a tray. The contents were our cutlery, a bowl, and a small plate. I tried to steady it all.

Sitting with Tomas, Von, and the other boys from my cabin, I could hear hundreds of conversations that I wasn't a part of. I didn't join any of them either. I was too afraid, preferring to sit in a puddle of silence and listen. Tomas engaged in a few of the juvenile conversations. I had trouble looking them in the eye. Some boys sat alone and read the latest issue of *Der Stürmer*.

Some were happily laughing with their friends. Oskar was sitting with another youth leader shovelling fistfuls of food into his mouth. He caught sight of me, winked, and I waved back.

I had no problem looking Oskar in the eye.

Manfret's confidence stood up and began to speak to me, others listening in.

"How are you settling in?"

Food was served with dirty fingers.

"Good…" Before I could finish, his words cut through mine.

He apologised in his Manfret way. "I was saved by the Führer when I was eight. Mama said I would become brave." Bravery that the boy had not yet obtained, but he was determined.

Being saved by the Führer was a bizarre way to put it.

MANFRET WÜNDERLICH: A HISTORY

He had a strangely shaped face, which wasn't to say unattractive. His features just took some time to make sense: his huge, murky, river-blue eyes, spotted cheeks, and strong jawline.

He was the type of boy that the other children seemed to like because of how unique he was. How so not 1940s he was. Perhaps, for those same reasons, other people disliked him. People fear different. It's a disease to them. So they sent Manfret off to a clean-cut school, with boring uniforms, boring rules, dull buildings, and hoped that by the end of it, every bit of his uniqueness would be burned away.

He was sent to Inland at twelve. Herr and Frau Wünderlich sent him for his own good. Manfret's monster stood in the door frame and waited for the pantomime that was to follow. A scene ensued: a teary-eyed mother, a determined father, and a long line of strangers that would have more control over Manfret's actions than he would.

"Papa, please let me stay here," he pleaded. "I don't want to go to boarding school." He never felt so betrayed. He kicked and screamed before resigning in shock.

His father would have none of it.

His sixteen-year-old brother looked as scared as Manfret felt; he didn't know about the arrangement either.

"You must do as I say, Manfret. It will be a great experience for you. Toughen you up. I won't have any son of mine be called a sissy."

Manfret had two older siblings. A boy and a girl. In later years, one would make the bullets; the other would be killed by them.

He arrived the same way – by car.

Manfret felt abandoned.

He felt trapped.

But as most children do, he adapted. He learned which leaders would make him tea at various hours of the night, and which ones would yell at him if he left the light on past curfew.

Learned that snack food was a currency, and the wealthier you were, the more people would leave you alone.

Learned to fit in everywhere but belong nowhere.

"Well, I was..." Stefan played with his carrots."I was saved when I was ten."

"*I* was talking to him," Manfret whispered.

Stefan was tiny, but I'm sure it's something he remembered for the rest of his life. I suppose we remember the moments in our lives that force us to act not so little. He was two years old when Hitler took power, and he lived with party members his whole life.

"You don't have to be rude!" Stefan said back, sticking his tongue out at Manfret, which made me laugh.

Tomas sat to my left. Von was sitting opposite. During dinner, he loosened the scarf around his neck and took it off completely, throwing it down on the table with great defiance.

"I hate this thing," he said. "Don't you?"

"I like the uniform," I said quietly.

Tomas nodded. "And the knife. Kröger is helping me use it." Tomas was never the type of boy who liked knives and fighting, but fitting in was important, crucial even. I never understood the importance of such things. Different doesn't need fixing.

Tomas had started to warm to Kröger after the beating initiation.

"Well, I feel like a dickhead," Von said, stuffing the tie into his shorts pocket.

"I think you look great." I realised what I said only when the words came pouring out.

"Thank you," he laughed.

I looked at the enormous platter of food on the trays before me. Bread, eggs, ham. Bitter greens with tomatoes. Salads with lots of, what looked like mini trees to me. I have never seen so much food in my life. Mother's special was usually *Eintopf* – potatoes and vegetables. I knew she would give anything to have such excellent food at home.

Von turned his nose up at it all.

An adult victory is a childhood defeat.

It all looked appetising, but it was terrible. Teichmann is no cook.

Tomas' bread and jam were half-eaten on the table and curled into teeth marks. When he tried to eat another bite, that's when the whistle blew.

We stood. Von sighed, rolled his eyes, and reluctantly dropped his fork.

Dohman's puppet master shifted into position. He was ready to deliver his carefully composed, daily dinner speech, and calmed the seething mess of boys.

All was silent, but there were a few boys who continued to whisper and giggle, excitement unintentionally slipping from their lips.

"*Schweigen!*" Dohman said. "Silence." There was no silence. "I would just like to say a few words before we part for tonight." I could see his strings being pulled – clouds of delicate silver ropes on the ceiling.

There was some talk about accomplishments by other students before he got into the meat of the speech. Von leaned over the table and secretly fed himself some bread.

"Whoever marches in the Hitler youth is not a number amongst millions, but each of you is Germany's future. And with our great Führer, we will help make Germany great again." For just a moment, the strings severed, and Dohman spoke like an actual human being. "And I know we have some new students. Do your best to make them feel at home."

Von looked at me and smiled. Penn nudged Derrick on the shoulder. "I bet Von is going to have a good time with Josef," and there was some giggling from around the table before they were silenced.

Dohman remained at his table, looking out at the hunched-over mannequins. The strings returned.

"Learn to sacrifice for your Fatherland. We shall go onwards. Germany must live. In your race is your strength. You must be true, you must be daring and courageous, and with each other form a great and wonderful comradeship."

The enthralled assembly roared inside the room amid frequent shouts of *"Heil."* Von Bacchman began drumming on the table, causing all of the boys to join in.

Tomas laughed.

"Now," Dohman roared. "Let's sing!"

Excitement started to bubble at the bottom of the other boy's stomachs, and a chorus of them sang – the room filled with the colour of music.

"Adolf Hitler is our saviour, our hero. He is the noblest being in the whole wide world. For Hitler, we live. For Hitler, we die. Hitler is our Lord. Who rules a brave new world."

Tomas and I looked to each other, not knowing the words, and I laughed at Tomas trying to mime them. At the end of it, all the boys raised their right hand in the air and chanted three times.

"Heil Hitler. Heil Hitler. Heil Hitler."

I'm not entirely sure how we got anything done around Inland, with all the heiling.

Most days after that, Von made a particular point in seeking me out during the breaks, and he didn't care what noises the other children made at him for doing so. He was with me at the beginning, and he'd be with me at the end.

But evening times; those belonged to Tomas and me, and only us.

We escaped to the back of the school and climbed the hill, running alongside, elbowing each other out of the way. We sat on the grass for hours on end regardless of the weather conditions. It was a place that almost nobody wanted to go, but we did.

Everything was dark-skied, and small chips of rain started to fall.

From a distance, we could hear children playing. Occasionally, I would look behind me for further clarification that no one would disturb us, and I would watch them.

The muggy air made them look more like ghosts. Not people, but shapes moving under the grey clouds. Their charcoal pencil lines smudged with a thumb. I tasted grit in my mouth and swallowed it.

Most of the time, we sat in silence, communicating only in expressions. Sometimes, words were exchanged.

"What do you think of Teichmann's food?"

Tomas looked at me, blue eyes gangly and glowing in the dusk.

"The worst."

The sunset held him.

I don't quite know how long we stayed that way, but we would watch the sun go down together, the burnt-orange sphere sinking towards the river and painting the hills until only shadow and darkness remained.

I lay back on the grass. Tomas followed. We felt the last drops of sunlight on our legs. There wasn't always a lot to say, and that was alright. My brother enjoyed my silent words. He listened to them. He was a boy who always knew what to say in the right moment, and left unsaid the wrong thing in the tempting moment.

Most people didn't listen with the intent to understand, but to reply. To show me how bigger and better their words were. When did it become this way? Why can't we just listen to people talk about something they love, see the passion in their eyes, and simply smile? No one-uppers, no under-cutters, just bliss.

We talk about our joys, and no one listens, but if we talk about our sadness, everyone does.

I think a lot of people forgot how to listen.

19

TOMAS AND THE PAINTED JS

*TYRIAN-PURPLE*TITANIUM-WHITE*TERRA-COTTA

BEFORE WE BEGIN IN FULL, THERE ARE A FEW THINGS YOU should know about Tomas.

He was my very best friend and secret keeper.

He loved to read, but he wouldn't do so in the company of others.

And he tried his best to make sure everyone's happiness was true, even at the sacrifice of his own.

I wasn't there for the infamous incident, and it was never really spoken highly of by the Berliners. When I look back, however, I realised that I felt as though I was there – telling it through Tomas' stories. I was in the crowd, cheering him on. It became just as much a part of my story as it was his.

The date was June, 1937.

Grandmother gifted Tomas a book as an early present for his eighth birthday, the *Merry Adventures of Robin Hood* by Howard Pyle. He couldn't understand a word of it, but one of the towns-people did, and Tomas would spend countless hours sitting by their fire, listening intently to the words, inhaling them through his nose and breathing them out as colours.

Robin and his band of Merry Men offered Tomas more than enough adventures and thrills to keep him turning the pages.

What eight-year-old could resist the arrows, flying, danger lurking, and medieval intrigue? The book itself was an act of defiance all of its own – an anti-hero doing bad things for good reasons.

Three years prior, on the night of May 10, 1934, students and brown-shirted soldiers tossed hundreds of books into the flames, burning an evil spirit from the past, while giving the Hitler-armed salute and singing Nazi anthems. Such books were "un-German," and getting rid of them was for the greater good of the people. Robin Hood was a black sheep. All copies were forbidden, and the people watched as the words were set alight, burning childhood forever, but imagination was not so quickly smoked out. I don't think any of this was Howard's intentions for his beloved book.

Howard Pyle pitch–

Howard: "It's about a legendary outlaw."

Nazis: "Yes."

Howard: "Robin protects local justice by banding together a group of outlaws to prey on the rich and give to the poor."

Nazis: "Burn it!"

My father's mother kept it hidden in a shoebox, wrapped up in a blanket until a certain curious little boy claimed it as his own.

We played many pretend battles in our back yard that summer. Tomas told me about the story, but I never actually read it.

Naturally, he was Robin Hood, while I was his right-hand man, his partner in crime, Little John. There was some arguing about the fact. Boys tend to move through life quickly, and it's hard to see the love that passes through, but if you look hard enough for it, you can find it. You just have to dig around a little.

Every Saturday morning, Mother and Tomas would go into town to shop. I was asked to go but thought better of it. I'd rather be getting lost in a painting than being trampled on by a swarm of people who didn't even know me. I hated shopping. I hated crowds, the queues, and the aching feet.

But Tomas loved it. What added to the adoration was the weekly gift mother and father would let him pick out if he was good. He would usually spend it on sweets or toys, and when I went, I would usually spend mine on well, you guessed it – paint.

Tomas would breathe in the colours, the aromas from the food stalls and the atmosphere like an elixir. He thrived on interacting with the stallholders, each one almost a caricature of bubbly friendliness. Mother often went there back then, so the owners knew Tomas by name and often kept something back for him, like lollipops or chocolate.

Everyone liked Tomas; they just dealt with me, but always seemed genuinely fond of Tomas, partly because I never really looked at them, even if I was addressed, much to the dismay of my mother, who would tell me that I was rude.

Nevertheless, Tomas was the favourite.

This particular day, he edged through the dense flow of people, with mother's bags getting fuller by the minute. The air was perfumed with produce. The ground was porous stone, and there was a perfect summer chill: no irritating music, just a busker with a violin. Beside him was an old dog that never moved.

Tomas was mesmerised by the music and the statue dog, of course. The crescendo coming out of the violin reminded him of waking up after a sweet dream. When he heard the *pizzicato*, he remembered playing hide and seek with me in our back yard.

The vibration of the magical shoulder instrument reached inside him and struck a chord that he didn't know existed.

The man was standing on the steps of a church that were damp from the morning rain, just across from the busy markets. Mother was having a seemingly important conversation with the stall owner about identity cards: something about a J, the name Sarah and poisoned blood.

Staring at the man's face for as long as he dared to, Tomas made his move. Mother had only let go of his hand seconds before. Edging closer, he continued to study the man's face. It was skeletal. Not human-like at all.

Tomas thought for a moment about his beloved book – Robin Hood. He gives to the needy, he thought. He rattled through his satchel, digging through the marbles and tissues, and grinned maniacally. Mother was still talking and didn't yet notice the boy's absence.

"Hallo, sir. Are you needy?" Tomas asked.

At first, the man wouldn't speak, just frowning down at the small boy and away just as quickly. Tomas was not deterred. A shrivelled, toothless man, he was feeble and walked with a cane, using the railing to keep balance. His hand trembled to play each perfect note – lungs starved for air.

"Halloo," Tomas said again, but louder this time.

"Excuse me?" The older man was impressed with my brother's persistence.

Tomas sighed and repeated. He verged on eye-rolling exasperation.

"Are you needy?"

"Excuse me."

"I'm Robin Hood," Tomas replied, like it was the most obvious thing in the world.

"Are you now?" He smiled down at him this time. "Where's your mother? You shouldn't be here."

"She's talking to someone over there." Tomas reached in for the Pfennig note. "I wanted to give you this." His eyes glowed.

"I can't take that, child. Go back to your mother."

"But I'm trying to play Robin Hood. He helps poor people—"

"What makes you think I'm poor?"

The man's eyes never met my brothers. He thought Tomas didn't notice, but he did.

"You must be. You're filthy and out here playing violin for money."

The man leaned against the railing – slowly. He blinked briny tears from bloodshot eyes, his thick lashes stuck together in clumps as if he'd been swimming. "I'm a doctor, actually."

"Oh." Tomas had never met a violin-playing doctor before. His eyes were stumped and caught hold of the frozen dog. "Can I pat him?"

"Yes."

Something about the way his hands hung limply over his knees caused a black mist to settle upon Tomas' shoulders, and no matter how bright the day was, he felt no sun. Secretly, when the man was bent over on the steps, Tomas placed his Pfennig into the violin case. Maybe now he can go back to being a doctor, he thought.

"*Was zum Teufel machst du da?*" A strangely familiar voice called out to Tomas. She stood there like the bogyman. "What the hell is going on here?"

Something became knotted up in his chest when he saw a woman standing in front of him with a box of half-rotten apples in her arms.

The old man, too, was frozen. The voice belonged to Frau Walther, the woman Mother had been talking with.

"Everyone has been looking for you."

Tomas exhaled. "I was being Robin Hood," he answered

happily, as though it was the most natural thing in the world for a boy to be doing. There was even something implicit in his tone that suggested something along the lines of "What the hell does it look like I'm doing?"

"He's a Jew, you stupid boy," Frau Walther said. "A filthy Jew – look at him!" She stuck Tomas' head in the Jew's face the same way a dog owner holds their pet's head in its filth.

Tomas looked back at the man and tried to find what made him "Jew-like." He saw nothing. Tomas had no eyes.

Mrs Walther was an amiable woman, providing that her rules were followed, and everything was normal. Giving money to needy people was not considered normal. She obviously hadn't read Howard Pyles' book.

"We told you before; you can't play music here. Go! Shoo!" she said like she was scolding a stray animal.

The man was beginning to speak before agreeing and moving on. He waved to Tomas.

She smacked Tomas over the head with her clammy hands, wrapped her whole hand around Tomas' forearm, and dragged him through the crowd of people, who were staring at the pair of clowns and the hectic scene on the street.

"You want to stay in the party, teach your son!" she said, as she delivered Tomas back to Mother.

Mother didn't really want to be in any party. She did so as a front, thinking that it would be better for her family. It was for a while before Hitler wrapped the entirety of Germany around his little finger. The only thing that kept my father with the family was their marriage.

"We don't teach the children about politics."

"Why?"

"Why? Well, because they're children. They shouldn't be learning about politics and war."

Walther's face turned every shade of disgust there was. "I can see the problem now." She sniffed.

Mother didn't say very much. She simply watched as the shades became like shadows over her face. Her thoughts, also, were murky. She took Tomas by the hand, but Frau Walther wasn't finished with her yet.

"Your blood has been poisoned, Lissette."

Then Mother turned. The small boy's knitted cardigan turned with her.

"Haven't you ever sat down and thought for yourself?" Mother didn't regret what she said, but she did fear the listeners – the people who are somehow always present. People like the suit men and the monsters. "You might learn a great deal."

"You're not welcome here anymore, Lissette. Your father would be ashamed of you."

"Good. Your fruit is off anyway."

On the way home, Mother gave Tomas a good talking-to.

"You can't do things like that, Tomas."

Tomas was interested and confused. The sun was undone, and free to move and drip down on his face, making his face shadowed, like his thoughts.

"Why not, Mama?"

"Because they'll take you away."

"Why?"

"Because you shouldn't be giving money to people who are... not like us."

"Why?"

"Because... people around here don't like Jews very much, Tomas."

"But Papa is Jewish."

"Yes, but see, Tomas," – she searched for the sense in her words – "Papa is good. A good man."

"Oh. And that man was a bad Jew? Why? He was a doctor and a violin player." Thinking. "Why are Jews so bad?"

Antisemitism, Tomas: an age-old phenomenon.

Contrary to popular belief, Hitler did not invent the hatred of the Jews. The true inventor can be traced back to the Middle Ages. Many Christians, for instance, saw the Jewish faith as something of an oddity that had to be terminated. Hitler just came along and fed into the fears of the people. Fed the madness.

"I don't know, Tomas." Mother was carrying the shopping with one hand and steering Tomas with her other hand.

She was having trouble steering the conversation in her favour.

"It's because Hitler said that some Jews aren't so good for Germany."

Then why did you marry one? "Ohhh. Is Robin Hood a Jew? A bad one?"

"What? I don't know!"

She was losing patience now.

The bottom of the cheap bags fell out. The fruit went everywhere.

"Jesus Christ," Mama sighed.

"Sorry, Mama."

Tomas ran after some of the loose fruit and returned a few seconds later.

They walked in silence for a while, until Tomas broke it.

"He was a bit strange though, the man. And a liar." Tomas talked to the ground as he walked. "He told me that he was a doctor. But he couldn't be, because he was playing a violin for money." He tried connecting more dots. "Is Papa a liar, too?"

This time, Mother placed her hands on Tomas' head and explained.

"Tomas, listen to me. Your Papa and this family are Germans through and through."

She looked briefly at her purse.

"They can decorate our cards with as many J's as they want to. They can give your Papa a ridiculous fake name." She held tight to my brother's hand and her pride. It came dripping from her lips with a smile.

"But we are Germans. Never forget that. You hear me?"

"Ja, Mama."

She kissed Tomas' hand.

But Tomas heard nothing. He understood nothing.

Two years later, the violin would be pried from shaking hands, reduced to broken wood, and the man would be thrown into the back of a van of his own. Only, the man wasn't taken to Inland or any school for that matter.

Also, I can tell you now because I know. When the old man discovered the money my brother had left, he cursed the boy and later thanked him. It was because of Tomas that he was able to get his granddaughter a book for her birthday.

Of course, like many things in childhood, phases often go as quickly as they come. The Robin Hood book sat under my brother's bed for years after that day, gathering dust and cobwebs. The Robin Hood story was one that my father liked to bring up at dinner parties with his friends, much to the apprehension of my mother. My brother smiled with awkward slouching that was usually unique to me. I suppose we were more alike than I remembered. Tomas' benevolent nature never changed, though.

That night, Tomas and I sat outside on the steps of our house, and he related the whole saga to me, even the smallest of details.

The clouds were being wrung out like the washing, and a few stray bits of rain fell on our faces.

"… And she even hit me." Tomas said.

"She hit you?" I laughed.

"Right across the snout." He nodded.

There was some laughter about the whole incident for a few minutes, but I could not shift some thoughts from my head for days after.

First: the Js. Try as I might, I was unable to see their importance or purpose. I tried asking questions, but as always, I was met with silence.

Second: a nice thought.

My little brother, the money giver.

I painted the thought.

My brother on the stitched clouds throwing down Pfennigs from the sky and surrounding him, the Js floating. My ten-year-old hand controlled by the brush.

It made me smile.

He was the boy who gave money to Jews, and I was the boy without words – two outcasts together. It was the perfect grounds for a great friendship.

20

OSKAR'S TOBACCO HEART

*OFFICE-GREEN*OLD-ROSE*

SCHOOL CONTINUED AND REMAINED A DISASTER. WHEN WE were homeschooled, the curriculum was home to many fantastic subjects, like art, German literature, and science. In Inland, we were taught only the basics that any flourishing Nazi boy in training needed to know, with a heavy emphasis on physical activity and history. Most of the boys in Inland lacked the most basic maths, science and social skills. Their minds were too full of the Führer.

When Miss Simons waddled into the class, the students would stand and raise their right arms. "For the Führer, a triple victory," answered by a chorus of "*Heil*."

Mornings woke with a song, with the almighty man keeping watch from the wall. The uplifting melodies, brilliantly written and composed, transported us into a state of enthusiastic glee. Rouvon would quieten for parts of the songs, before roaring the rest. Hues of pinks bounced off his dimpled cheeks, blurring the boundaries between sight and sound. I caught Simons smiling a few times, and even laughing in a way that looked like she was coughing, like the idea of humour was a foreign idea.

Simons drilled a daily dose of Nazi instruction into our heads, which we swallowed as naturally as our mother's milk. We were defenceless receptacles for whatever they crammed into our young minds.

Mein Kampf was used as a study guide, and staff and students in Inland were expected to memorise it. Tomas began to read it during our evening trips. It wasn't the kind of reading material I enjoyed. Hitler, whom we suspect of being an envious, traumatised loser, presents himself as, well, an embittered, envious, traumatised loser. So much pent-up rage was stored away for his father, and even though my own had committed the ultimate betrayal and died, I still held no resentment towards him or my mother. It was more demoralising than inspiring. I doodled in the margins of the book and wished with my hands that it would end. Simons hit me with her weapon of mass destruction – a ruler.

Humans were divided into categories based on physical appearance, establishing higher and lower orders. At the top, according to Hitler, is the Germanic man with his pearl skin, blond hair, and blue eyes. He asserts that the Aryan is the supreme form of human, or master race.

And so it follows in Hitler's thinking, if there is a supreme form of a human, then there must be others less so, the *Untermenschen*, or racially inferior. Hitler assigns this position to Jews and the Slavic peoples, notably the Czechs, Poles, and Russians.

Jews are devious and cunning overachievers, especially in their aim of polluting our pure Aryan race – whatever that meant. Aryans were brave, blond, tall, and slim, with eyes of the bluest ocean.

I often studied my own brown eyes and short stature in the mirror in the washroom and wondered how I could be Aryan. I unintentionally touched my nose and wished that I was different.

Every other boy listened with such pride. I was never really sure what to make of it, but it transpired so magically that it would be difficult for any twelve-year-old boy not to find it fascinating. Most notable to me was the Führer's failed painting career and his opaque father, who forbade the idea altogether. My twelve-year-old self felt a sense of pity for the man.

Still, I had questions: I often wondered what the difference was between them and us. Who woke one day and decided that they were inferior, and we were superior? I didn't understand it. My curiosity would make me a victim of Simons' frustration, but it was worth it. The truth was always worth a good *Watsche.*

It's not like anyone in Germany woke up one day and decided that they hated Jews. In fact, before the Nazis took power, Mother used to take Tomas and me to a sweet shop that was run by a kind Jewish man and his wife. The wife would always slip us an extra helping of sweets without Mother knowing. Father took us to a Jewish barber to have our hair cut, which I hated, but the man was sympathetic and calmed me into obedience, sharing stories of his childhood in Poland. Most prominent, however, was that I didn't know they were Jews; I just knew they were kind people.

One day, we arrived at a wounded building, windows all over the ground, and I, too, felt bruised. I tasted its pain. The kind Jewish man and his wife had their shop taken over by Germans, and I don't even know what happened to the calming man. I suspected he went back to Poland.

I thought there was something wrong with me for not understanding what was so apparent to others.

I suppose you could say that Germany went mad together.

Sometimes, I wished I was pale enough, so I would blend into the grey walls of the classroom and disappear altogether.

Simons wrote a phrase on the board which had to be copied and memorised.

Manfret raised a hand, dipped in apologies, but Simons could not see it. He bravely spoke anyway.

"Do we have to write that?" Manfret was full of stupid questions.

"Nein, Dummkopf! She's just writing it up there for shits and giggles." Derrick's voice, too, dripped in sarcasm.

The chalk on the board sounded like a morse code. If I knew morse code, I would send a simple message:

.-- .... .- - / - .... . / ..-. ..- -.-. -.- / .. ... / ..... .- .--. .--. . -. .. -. - -. .. --..

Translation: what the fuck is happening?

"Our Führer is named Adolf Hitler. He was born on the 20th of April 1889 in Braunau, Austria."

I was shocked to learn that our Führer wasn't from Germany. I studied the words for a second.

"Our Führer is a great soldier and tireless worker. He delivered Germans from misery. Now everyone has work, bread, and joy. Our Führer loves children and animals."

Of course, when the memorising part came, the words fooled me, and I could never get past the first sentence without having to look at my copybook. It often resulted in me getting a *Watsche* in the corridor, or even sometimes in front of the whole class, which was, as you can imagine, humiliating.

Homework was usually simple: I had to draw the swastika flag, and as I was a recruit, I copied out an oath of loyalty to the Führer that I had to memorise and recite back to the class in a few weeks.

"Adolf Hitler, you are our great Führer.

Thy name makes the enemy tremble.

Thy name alone is law upon the earth.

Let us hear daily thy voice; order us by thy leadership.

For we will obey to the end and even with our lives.

We promise thee! Heil Hitler!

Führer, my Führer, given me by God.
Protect and preserve my life for long.
You saved Germany in times of need.
I thank you for my daily bread.
Be with me for a long time; do not leave me, Führer.
My Führer, my faith, my light, Hail to my Führer."

It took me a long time to be able to say it without looking at the sheet. It felt like I was running backwards, unable to turn around, and run the way I know how. The words held me back.

I wanted nothing more than to pick up my paintbrush and let the brush speak for me.

Back in the cabins at night, Oskar would do his best to give me guidance. But even then, it didn't help much. Oskar was a good teacher, but I was a slow learner.

Some evenings, I learned myself to complete exhaustion, and even then, I understood nothing. I figured some people are just born to do one thing, and for me, that was not memorising words, but painting them.

Looking back, however, I realised this thought process is fundamentally wrong. A person who cannot do a thing could learn to if he believes enough in the art of persistence. My brother was able to master this beautifully.

I really did try to do well, though.

As Oskar gazed down at the bastardised form of the Lord's prayer, he could surely feel my eyes upon him. They reached over and gripped him, waiting for something, anything to slip from his lips. I was worried he would have given me a hiding because of all the drawings in the notebook.

"Here." He said as he shifted the book back.

"How much of this to do you know?"

I gripped my pencil and lied.

"Most of it," I said.

"Alright. Write it down." Oskar covered the prayer with a sheet of paper.

"Well," I faked confidence, and Oskar smiled because he knew.

"Adolf Hitler, you are our great Führer."

I stopped and looked up at Oskar for validation.

He nodded. "Hmm. Good."

I continued to deliver three more lines of the oath, and finally, my pencil stopped with a sigh. The lead broke from me leaning on it too hard. Oskar sharpened it.

"Very good, little man." He gave me one of his signature, smiles.

"What else do you know?"

"He… he…"

I couldn't write much more.

"Come on. You should know this, little man."

I shrugged. For two years, Mother and Father had managed to stop us from going to the Hitler Youth. Being mixed-blood, they didn't require us to join. It wasn't until later when the suited men spotted our talent and somewhat Aryan looks, did they start applying pressure.

This might be harder than I thought. I caught Oskar thinking it – just for a moment.

He lifted himself forward, rose to his feet, and walked out.

This time, when he came back, he said, "I have an idea." In his hand, there were a few coloured chalks.

"Let's start from scratch."

I saw no reason to argue.

On the hard wooden floor, he began to draw a distorted stick figure with a squiggly line moustache.

"Bitler." He grinned.

From across the room came a voice attached to Stefan.

"You mean Hitler."

"Yes, him."

I couldn't help laughing.

"Well, I'm not an artist like you, you know." Oskar said.

"We can't all be great, Oskar."

Others were now gravitating to my bed; they all watched and smiled.

"Now, write." He handed me the chalk. I wrote in big letters.

"Thy name makes the enemy tremble."

I didn't write very well, but it was definitely readable.

"And when you get stuck on something, write it down here, *ja*?"

"Yes, Oskar." My eyes grew large.

Others watched me as I filled the floor with blue and white chalk.

As I completed my homework, telling Tomas about the event was heavy on my mind. I wanted to run to the cabin a few doors down and show him.

The only anxiety Oskar Frederick ever gave me was the fact that he was always going out – for a cigarette – especially during the night. Oskar often had a hard time sleeping, because sleep required peace.

After a few months, the nightmares had quietened down, and Tomas and I had settled into our new lives as nicely as you would expect. Of course, we still missed our mother and father every day, but there were comforts now too.

Oskar.

Von Bacchman.

The morning runs through the countryside.

And escaping it all in the evening with my brother.

All of this resulted in some form of contentment, and would soon be built upon to approach the concept of being happy.

Of course, there were still nights where I'd see my brother's dead eyes staring at me in the darkness, and I'd wake up screaming.

Oskar would always be waiting at the bottom of my bed, pulling at the sweaty fabrics of my pyjamas.

When he had calmed down the seething mess of my night terrors, he'd go outside, and the frost would keep him company while he puffed on a cigarette or two – or three.

Sometimes there would be stars.

On those occasions, he would wait a little longer before a voice from the cabin called him back, or the stars would disappear and dissolve back into the vast German clouds.

"What a fine night this is, world," he said.

I'd look at the moonlight shine through the crack of the wooden door that Oskar hadn't closed properly, lie on my back, and wait for him to return before going back to sleep.

On a particular life-defining night, I had a distinctly unpleasant dream, and I followed him into the moonlight. I couldn't explain it, but knowing he was close made me feel at peace.

I couldn't understand how I couldn't explain it.

I stood and stared as he gazed down at a photo of a pretty dark-haired woman he pulled out of his shirt pocket. He didn't yet notice that I was there. Oskar looked at that photo often, especially at night, when no one was looking. I thought about asking him who the lady was that night, but I didn't.

The sky was usually like a spillage – cold and heavy, slippery and grey – but once in a while, more colours would have the nerve to appear. Dark blue, like a piece of velvet, had been lined over the sky and sprinkled upon by shining gems.

"Hallo, little man," Oskar said, when he saw my small stature standing at the door. "It's okay. Go back to bed."

I remained upright and didn't speak.

"Or you can come sit by me," he smiled.

I smiled back at him.

"But we'll have to be quiet, okay?" he whispered. "Don't want to wake the others up."

Kissed by the rain and glistening, the wet ground was cold underfoot. One sock on and another barely hanging on, I stepped off the path and into the shaggy grass. I felt the squelch of the mud beneath. The water rose and ran between my toes.

"Do you know how to roll a cigarette?" Oskar turned as I sat.

"*Nein.*"

By the end of the twenty minutes it took Oskar to smoke a few cigarettes, I could roll moderately well.

"Why do you smoke so much?" I asked.

"Trying to kill myself quickly, Josef," he answered, puffing on the end. "It calms me down."

"Like painting calms me down?"

"*Ja*, I guess so."

I felt the kind of sadness that seeps into your bones. Oskar's face studied mine, scratchy hand on whiskers, and then the light.

"Want to try?"

"No. I'm not allowed to."

"Says who? Your teacher?"

I stared at the cigarette between his fingers and took it. At first, I didn't even inhale. I didn't know I was supposed to. I just sucked in, held the smoke in my mouth for a few seconds, and blew out.

Oskar rolled his eyes and told me to stop wasting it.

"Just get it in your lungs already!"

A sickening image: a twelve-year-old boy with a cigarette hanging out of his mouth.

As I sucked in the smoke, the hardest part to get over was the psychological sense of breathing in something that wasn't air

– like breathing underwater. It tasted horrible. It was very dry and stung my throat. It was pointless to stifle a coughing fit.

Oskar laughed.

"Shut up," I coughed.

But then, through the coughing and the burning, I wasn't thinking of my Mother and Father anymore. I wasn't thinking about how they abandoned us or how much I missed painting. My headache went away. I didn't even know I had one.

It was relaxing – clarifying.

That was the beginning of the midnight smoking lessons.

Beginning with supposed happiness and ending with devastatingly cruel sadness and a beat-up man.

Cheery, I know.

In Inland, 99.5% of boys were indoctrinated to the Nazi ideology.

That left the 0.5% that still had questions. But they were only half questions – half thoughts. Our childish inquisitiveness was peaking, and we became very fond of specific, curious phrases. Considering most of them were answered with a hiding, most boys kept their mouths shut. It took me longer to catch on.

Tomas was an intelligent boy, well beyond his years, so he could comprehend rather quickly.

The price to pay for not comprehending was the bruising. But nothing was as bad as the *Watschen* he got in his first few days in Inland. Kröger not only learned to stand the boy, but he actually grew to like him. My brother remained quiet and listened.

Together, we'd fill up the entire floor with facts about the Führer. The progress I was making was respectable – or so I thought.

No paintings lived in Inland, and there was little to no talk about art at all. Everyone was so opaque. They forbade me to nourish even the slightest of hopes that I'd someday be able to study art. The best I could do was pretend to paint in the cabin at night with my grandmother's paintbrush when all the other children had gone to sleep. I spoke the colours under my breath before I was told, in no uncertain terms, to shut up by the other children who woke up from all that mumbling. The colours spoke back. I recited the pages in my grandmother's book in a way I couldn't with other words. I remember the painted handprint birds, the beautiful colours of yellows, blacks, and reds.

Handprint birds.

What you'll need:

- Poster paint in a few colours.
- Fine paintbrush
- Medium paintbrush
- An old magazine or newspaper
- A lot of creativity

After the day's lesson had finished, at two, Tomas and I would come back to my cabin, and he would help me with homework. We sat with the words and watched as the sunlight shone through the windows, setting the ground alight. Many times, Von would enter and try to join us before we told him to get out. We screamed at him. A lot of the time, he was trying to egg us on.

On a Thursday, at 6:15 pm, we were preparing for our usual evening on the hill, but Von had other plans.

"Tommy is playing soccer with us today. We need more players."

He looked at me and grinned. "Not you, Josef. You're horrible at soccer."

"Sorry, Von, I'm going with Josef."

Von had his hands in his pocket and didn't even bother looking up from the ground. "What? Come on."

"We're going to play dominoes," I said. I handed Tomas a steadfast smile.

Now we had his attention.

"Can I come?" A cutout smile.

Tomas was thinking, almost considering it.

"No, you can't come." I butted in. "You're horrible at dominoes" This wasn't true at all. Von was rather good. I just wanted my words to sting.

Children can be so cruel.

Soon, we were on the main courtyard, passing brown shirts and upright walkers. Just as we were about to turn the corner, I looked back to find Von still watching. When we locked eyes, he shouted out, "I hate you, Josef," putting his hands to his mouth to amplify the sound. Some older boys stared, but Von didn't care.

"Dickhead," I laughed under my breath.

Von's eyes followed us until we were out of sight.

No one hated me more than that boy.

21

HANDPRINT BIRDS

*HOLLYWOOD CERISE*HELIOTROPE*HEGARTY

IN A CLASSROOM WITH SUN OVERFLOWING ON THE WALLS, names were rattled around in the shaker-box that was Frau Simons' head. She stood at the back like a human smoke detector, just waiting for someone to slip up so she could begin her cries.

"Pichler, Wünderlich…"

Each boy in turn stood up, walked to the front of the class, and rhymed off the oath to our Führer. The words rolled off their tongue. They made it look effortless.

"Bacchman."

Von stood confidently, with his hands behind his back and answered. He was surprisingly good.

"Brilliant, Rouvon." Frau Simons looked down at her book. She wasn't finished with Von just yet. "And I don't suppose you could tell me what are some characteristics of the Jew?"

He didn't even flinch.

"Hooked nose, like the shape of a number six," he said, tracing out the shape of six. It was velvet purple. "Ugly, puffy lips, a deceitful look, and fleshy eyelids."

He was showing off now, one eyebrow raised.

"Fein gemacht, Rouvon," she answered. "Very good, Rouvon. Sit down."

He looked and smiled at me, but I would not return the smile. I looked at the desk and went over the words. The wrong ones kept blocking them, and the colours. "Draw different colours onto each finger-tip."

No, Josef!

The oath.

Throughout the test, I sat with a mixture of trembling anticipation and hot fear. I desperately wanted to measure myself. To find out, once and for all, how my learning was advancing. Was I ready? Could I even come close to Von and the others?

Each time I sensed the teacher looking at me, a string of nerves tightened in my ribs. It started in my stomach but had worked its way up my chest, and soon, it would be around my neck.

"Very good class." Frau Simons picked up her ruler and spoke once more. "Now, let's move on to…"

I raised my sweat-soaked hand to explain. "No, Frau, I have been practicing," but she took no notice.

Von Bacchman intervened.

"Josef has his hand up."

He didn't shout out of maliciousness or to embarrass me, but because he was proud of me, and he wanted me to prove myself to everyone – but most importantly, to myself. "He can do it. I've heard him."

Frau Simons wasn't impressed.

"How dare you call out without permission in my classroom." Two strikes on the hand were a severe enough punishment for speaking out. But he didn't care. He rubbed the *Watschenabdruck* – the slap mark – and continued.

"It's not fair. Give Josef a try, Frau Simons."

"No, no, Rouvon. Josef can't …" I was a lost cause in her eyes.

A *Mischling.*

A stupid child.

No.

I am no lost cause.

Determination caused me to raise my hand. I cleared my throat and spoke with quiet defiance; it shocked me.

"I can do it now, Frau Simons."

I left behind a drawing of Frau Simons on the page. The majority of the other kids watched in silence. A few of them snickered quietly.

She had enough of me. "No, you cannot, Josef. What are you doing?"

By then, I was already on my feet and walking to the front. Looking down at my boots, I turned. A swirl of light and faces. I couldn't bring myself to look directly at Simons.

"I want to do it."

"Okay, Schneider. Do it then."

I could do it.

I smiled and looked down at my boots again – just for a second.

When I looked up again, the room was pulled apart, then squashed back together. The children were growing wider and then mashed again. In a moment of brilliance, I imagined myself reciting the oath in a faultless, fluency-filled triumph of which the Führer himself would be proud.

Yes, that's what I imagined.

"Come on, Josef!"

Von broke the silence, clapping me, not caring what the consequences might be.

I started well.

"Adolf Hitler, you are our great Führer."

I coughed.

"Thy name makes the enemy tremble."

I looked down at the undone laces. I swayed gently. It soothed me enough to continue.

"Go on." Von mouthed it this time. "Go on, Josef."

My blood loudened. My words blurred.

"Bitler...thy... oh.. Hitler..."

Suddenly, in my head, the words appeared in another tongue. The colours were blurring, and it didn't help that tears were now forming in my eyes.

And that sun. The sun was awful. It burst through the window; glass was everywhere – a light shone directly into my useless body. It shouted in my face.

"Hurry, up, Josef. We don't have all day." Simons said. Her body smugly stood in the back.

Children were now taking part in the beautiful art of childhood snickering.

I didn't know what to do.

I just stood there frozen.

Mental pictures were blurring in my head, and my mouth tasted like alphabet soup. The urge to cry was strong, but I was determined. I would stand in front of that classroom forever until I got it right.

What should I do?

I looked around for inspiration.

Inspiration also slapped Frau Simons in her face. A *Watsche* from her hand.

"Now children, this right here is an example of some un-Aryan characteristics." She used a pointer, talking at the classroom, not to it. I looked down at my hands, hoping more words would reveal themselves, but none did. My mind twirled, but my body could not make any sense of what I saw.

Simons continued in typical movie Nazi smugness. "His

eyes, for one." A blue river of sadness leaped in front, drowning the classroom. Von mirrored it. He spoke again. "Frau Simons. No..." She would not let him finish. A ruler came down on the table.

"His eyes are brown mud piles."

More children added. "Ugly."

Do something, stupid. I said to myself.

Something.

"When they are finished with the rest of them, they will come for him."

Anything.

A quoted song."When the Jewish blood splashes on the knives, things will go twice as well."

Tears started to blind me now.

"Is he crying?" Came a voice.

"He's crying." Another.

"Shut up. That's not nice." The voices seemed to be originating in the walls, not the children.

The snickering was getting louder now. I couldn't hear over them.

In my hand, I held a paper bird, and written on it were two words.

"Be brave."

Then it came to me – a solution. Not a good solution by any means, but while I was up there, standing in hand sweating misery, any solution would do.

I wiped my blurred eyes.

Breath. I breathed. In and out.

I began rhyming off every page from my grandmother's book. Every page, jigsawed together in my mind. None of it made sense.

"Cut a wave out of a piece of cardboard to make the template."

"Make sure the template is a bit bigger than the paper."

"Paint the lines onto the pap..."

"Josef, stop it!" Frau Simons' voice called from the back of the classroom, but I wouldn't. I looked her in the eye.

"Dip the marble into the paint."

"Josef!"

I heard grandmother's voice in my head, reading to me.

"Repeat with different colours." My U cracked.

I listed them off – every useless fact. Every. Single. Useless. Fact.

"Josef Schneider!"

It ended.

Von Bacchman and several others joined in on pity applause.

"Outside now!" Simons demanded as she pinched my ear in her bony hands.

Maybe if I'd kept my mouth shut, the punishment might not have been so severe. But in true Josef fashion, I opened my stupid mouth and let the stupid words spill out. And I had to suffer the consequences.

"Fuck this stupid oath!" I said it in my loudest words yet. "I don't want to be a soldier. I want to paint." She dragged me on, not hearing a single word.

As I was given twelve *Watschen,* I could hear them all laughing inside the classroom between Simons' striking hand. I saw them. All those mashed children, grinning and laughing, bathing in the sunshine – all of them laughing but Von.

I thought it was over at twelve – a strike of the clock – but Simons had another idea. I didn't know what would be next, and I wished it would have stayed that way. When she returned, Erich Kröger marched alongside her, and as soon as I saw him, I quickly shielded my head with my hands – a reflex action.

But it was useless.

"Come here!" Kröger's eyes were narrowed and set hard

on me.

By now, my knees were shaking. Kröger shook me so violently that the room fell on top of me.

"You little bastard." He took off his belt. I didn't even notice. No time. For before I did, the metal buckle came down on me. His hammer-hands too delivered punishment. Red marks looked like footprints, and they burned. I didn't stand a chance. From the ground, I pleaded to his feet.

"I'm sorry. I didn't mean t..."

"Shut up!"

There was a silver rope and pitch-black lines – all together. I blinked.

"Say the oath."

"What?" I asked – eyes, nose, mouth. Everything wet.

"What you fucking learned, you retard." Kröger's words too stung.

His belt snapped my back once again.

"I don't know it. I don't know it." I screamed it.

Handprint birds. Handprint birds.

With each slap, I could hear the buckle scraping my bone. I could taste metallic. The pain seared through my body more fiercely than a branding iron. My mind was conceding to the torment, unable to bring a thought to completion.

I realised I wasn't even making words anymore. I was repeating the same stinging syllable.

Without meaning to, my body curled.

The other children carried on with their classwork. A screaming child was nothing more than a playground sound – Inland's soundtrack.

I couldn't make sounds anymore.

"Stand up."

One feeling stood out amongst the colours. Anger.

I stood with every bit of energy I had left, raised my left arm, clicked my heels together, and in a pathetic voice coming from a pathetic body, I said it.

"Heil Hitler."

What came to me next was the dustiness of the floor, and the sudden realisation that I'd be here forever and I would never see my mother or father again. The reality of it gave me a mind-*Watsche*. It stung me, and it did not stop for many minutes.

Above me, Kröger was smudged, but he soon clarified, and his cardboard face loomed closer. Dejected, he stood in his soldier-like posture, holding his belt to his side like a club.

I'd been in Inland long enough to know that Kröger hadn't hurt me because he was a horrible person. He was a man. Like so many boys here, he'd never known anything but brutality. He had rules to follow. I broke the rules.

I had to be punished.

I knew that.

The welts grew larger on my skin as I lay there in the dust, dirt, and dim light. My breathing calmed, and a stray tear trickled across my face, around my nose. I could feel myself against the floor.

It was cold, especially on my cheek, but I was unable to move.

I would never see Mother and Father again.

I lay there for a good twenty minutes. Only when I saw Tomas' face did I start to recover. His face was broken but still perfect. His bottom lip trembled, and he hurried to my side. His eyes wandered from one injury to another. I could see the conflict in his eyes already.

"It's alright," I said. "You can cry."

I thought that was all the permission he would have needed, but Tomas didn't cry. Crying would be going against orders. He simply buried his head between his hands, and he wouldn't look at me for several minutes.

"Did you have to do that to him?" That was Oskar's gentle voice, entering from above.

"It's the only way they learn," Kröger replied before walking on. He coughed many times.

Later, from a kneeling Tomas, "Josef, you're alright. You're just in shock." Tomas said to me. He sounded more like our Father than my brother.

"It's alright, little man," Oskar said. Voices were everywhere. The calmness of his voice reached down to me, it picked me up. He stayed with me in the cabin for many minutes. Later, he rubbed my foot in the hopes that I would laugh. I did not.

When I thought back to that day in the years to come, I held no animosity towards my parents at all, or towards Erich Kröger, for that matter. To me, it's clear that external events were the reason for their predicament. Had circumstances been different, this would have ended differently.

The only thought that continually recurred was the lack of colours. There must've been colours, I thought, but I failed to remember them. It had been dark, I said. No matter how many times I tried to imagine that scene with the colours, that I knew had been there, I had to struggle to visualise them. I was beaten in the dark, and I had remained there on a cold, dark hallway floor.

It was the first time in my life I couldn't see the colours – only darkness. And, as crazy as it sounds, that's what hurt more than the beating. I didn't want to see the world through an ordinary lens.

They only returned to me when I saw Tomas.

For about an hour that evening, I remained in my cabin, spread out on my bed, until I saw Tomas stood in the doorway, dominoes under his arm, and only then did I sit upright and smile.

Tomas and I played for several hours. My mind had drifted

back to the colours many times, and I was unable to concentrate on my moves. Tomas won every game we played.

"Do you miss Mama and Papa?" I asked him.

"I don't really miss them. It's more like just being sad all the time." As Tomas said the words, he could surely feel the weight on his shoulders lifting. A weight that he did not know was there until he spoke.

"It kind of feels like... being empty all the time. Especially when I sometimes forget they are gone, and I remember all of a sudden."

We shared a sideways glance.

The shadow of our friendship grew bigger with the setting of the sun, and Von Bacchman's shadow loomed at the door, coming back unusually early from his regular game of Trappers and Indians.

At first, he bounced around on his bed and tried to occupy his time by talking to the other boys, but I could feel his eyes on me, even if I wasn't looking at him.

He left again and returned a few minutes later. In his hand, he had ice that he had stolen from Teichmann. He wrapped it in a towel. "For your face," he said. That boy must have been brave to steal from Teichmann.

He held it on my face, and I kept my gaze on him as long as I could. I took the ice. "*Danke*, Von."

If only he could see the colour of my thoughts when they circled around him.

Nightmares reinforced themselves that night as I began to realise that this is how things were, and how things would always be.

I was ready now.

I was ready to serve the Führer.

Heil fucking Hitler.

22

OSKAR'S GIFT

*OCHRE*OGRE*ORCHID

EARLY IN SEPTEMBER 1940, HITLER BOMBED LONDON.

Regarded, today, as the Blitz.

I woke to the news. Pages were flying; children were cheering, people were laughing – their hearts beating as one. All were chasing visions of their imaginary futures.

All while a city was ripped apart by bombs.

The London sky burst into fragments: orange pentagons, circles, and squares – the silent hysteria of searchlights. The blinded buses rushing somewhere with their lights extinguished. The patter died away, along with the humans left behind who lay frozen on the asphalt. They didn't make it to the shelter. Doors slammed, and lights were put out. And the city lay deserted, swept clean by a sudden plague. London knelt and cried, kneading the blue and white in its arms.

The word Blitz came from the German word *Blitzkrieg* or "lightning war".

The first of the fifty seven consecutive nights of bombing, and it would continue until May 1941. Hitler took France, and it was only a matter of time before he set his voracious eyes on England.

Germany sought to wear down the Royal Air Force in antici-pation of a land invasion but failed to cripple Britain's air power. The attack was ruled out as unrealistic; Hitler chose sheer terror as his next weapon.

For a brief second, the colour of ash flashed. It took me to a place I couldn't pronounce – Shoreditch. The air was beginning to erode and smelt like death and false hope. Four children: two boys, two girls. They sat in the wasteland of rubble that once was their home. The eldest of the children sat upright, cradling the youngest of them in his arms. When she stopped breathing, he still held on, and I have a feeling that he stayed like that for some time.

Tomas looked like an odd boy out as he sang with the others. Their colours were bright and vibrant with pride. But some of them had tints of despair mixed in for effect. "We bombed London. We bombed London."

They didn't fully understand the seriousness of the situation. How could they have? The ones who were supposed to shape us were behaving like maniacs, so we followed suit.

All that was known was that Germany was winning the war and we, the youth, would be the future. They say what you don't know can't hurt you, that ignorance is bliss. But ignorance is also a grenade, with a pin waiting to be pulled.

Young youth leaders entered like a parade of colours. A mixture of red and black, blue and yellow. All together. They gave Oskar a newspaper he didn't read. Instead, he stuffed it into his coat. The words were stapled to his chest like a tattoo.

We were all made out of darkness, foolishly thinking that we could save the world by breaking it, and making lives better by ending them.

"Did you hear the news?" I asked Oskar.

He spoke from across the room.

"*Ja.* Germany bombed London." His voice was not even remotely patriotic.

"That's good, right? We're winning the war?"

"Oh, yes. Fantastic."

There was that face again – his midnight face.

I turned thirteen that day. The age where I turned into a backstage adult, waiting on my tiptoes for my chance. The age father described as "when the fun would begin".

Yes, the fun certainly did begin.

Inland birthdays were not a day to boast about. Celebrations included dunking in a nice cold bath. Children would often hide birthday cards and gifts from their parents to stop the older boys from learning the date. Everyone in Inland remained ageless, and I was often mistaken for a much younger boy.

The only thing I desired was an impossible gift – Mother and Father, for them to share in my birthday as they had before. To hug us, to kiss us – even if it was only a second.

That couldn't happen, of course. I knew that.

But Oskar had the next best thing.

He waited till the other boys left the cabin that day, and then he spoke.

"I have a surprise for you, little man."

From behind his back, he pulled a tin artisan box and sat it on my knees. When I traced my fingers over it, the tin made the sound the wind does in the trees. It was red. Different kinds of hues and shades, some light and some dark; some in between light and dark. A little boy was painting a ship on the front. Oskar said the boy reminded him of me, and that's why he got it. He even wore the same uniform as I did – Swastika and all.

Written in gold at the top of the box was

"Watercolour paintbox."

I had owned a selection of watercolour paints at home, and

they were my favourites. I loved the way the paint glided onto the paper, blending and mingling with the other colours; creating new, unusual colours. It was magical. At least, I thought so.

When I opened the box, the red of the tin mingled with the sunlight and glowed. A large sketchpad, some paintbrushes, and an unlimited collection of colours. Bleached blue, dusty grey, fast orange, and yellows.

With wonder, I smiled. My toes curled up in my boots with excitement. I couldn't believe that such a wonderful thing was happening amongst the chaos.

"I know it's probably not what you're used to, but it's the best I could do."

"No, it's perfect."

I hugged him. Neither of us expected it.

He drowned in it.

"Thank you, Oskar." The words spilled over my mouth.

He wrapped an arm around my shoulders and pulled me closer, gently rubbing my arm. He sunk into my warmth, appreciative of the simple gesture. His touch made the room warmer, somehow. The walls seemed a little less bleak.

"But now, I expect a gift back, you know?"

I grinned. "With what money?"

"You can paint me something. Call it the Oskar." The words halted and got stuck at his teeth as he was trying to light a cigarette. "That way, when you get your big break, I can tell everyone that one of your first paintings was named after me."

I nodded with great sincerity.

It was a happy day.

A beautifully evil day.

23

TUMBLING COLOURS

*TENNÉ*THISTLE*TESZOPIGGYT

I STOOD WITH A QUIET VOICE AND A LOUD MIND IN THE line of boys. A picture was taken, and plausibly would have made it into history books in years to come. Perhaps you even saw me. I wasn't hard to spot. An awkward boy in the back, with a forced, painted smile. Can you see Tomas, too? A black and white angel in the back. Yes, we teased him relentlessly for that. Somehow, Tomas was even paler than the rest of us. In pictures, it made him look colourless and waxlike. He was someone you noticed.

In the end, boys were already starting to fix their appearance. Untucking shirts. Pulling down neck scarves. You needed just the right amount of scruffiness. I was in mid-tease of Rouvon when Kröger plucked me from the line.

"You."

"Yes, Mein Herr?"

"You like to paint?"

"Very much so."

"Then make yourself useful."

And just like that, red, black, and white paint cans were

shoved into my arms. It was my new job to paint the flags. At first, I did just that, but as my predisposition for trouble making grew, the banners I painted changed, too. Disinterested in the dull red, black, and white, I made pink. Light pink. Dark pink. I mixed and mixed until the shade was just right. I quivered with excitement. Rosy cheek pink was much nicer, don't you agree?

The world loved the Swastika until Hitler stole it. It's a symbol for German people, but not in the way you're thinking. For years, it was a symbol of well-being and good fortune in many parts of the world, used by Buddhists, Hindus, and Jains. Yet, in the twisted telephone line game that is history, it became something that invoked fear and dominance. Add a little black and red, and it's suddenly chilling. I wonder if it will ever dust off its evil associations and walk freely.

My painting style changed throughout the years. I was no longer concerned with tiny details. I used broad, energetic brush strokes. I painted with anger. Instead of holding it in and letting it slowly destroy me, until the old me didn't exist anymore, I took it out on my paintings, in the flags.

Those who came to observe didn't scold me – a silly child with a vivid imagination they presumed. The flag dominated the walls. Every colour was bold and innocent. They seemed to be stable but tumble at the same time. Like myself, I think. Seemingly stable, but always free-falling on the inside. Soft, but lampooning anyone who sparks my insecurities without meaning to, often feeling painted onto the background, like there isn't really anything of substance inside. I hope there is. I hope there is more meaning in my bones than tumbling colours and chaotic lines.

Years earlier, painting in the basement was one of my favourite things to do. Mother's face was lit with vexation. I hadn't completed my maths homework because I couldn't. I tried to explain. "The numbers get mixed up…"

"I can't hear you." Mother cut through. Anger continued to travel across her face.

"You would if you listened."

Mother always complained that she never got to spend time with me, but when I tried to speak of my paintings, she never listened. Like this part of spending time together didn't matter at all.

The colours were alive in my eleven-year-old heart.

"Josef, you must grow up." A pencil-sharpening hand moved from the table. I turned from the easel and listened to the speech. "The world has artists, my dear. It also needs bus drivers and shop keepers." I let my feelings boil over inside. I kept painting. "You have such big goals inside that little head of yours, but sooner or later, you're going to have to settle for less because sometimes it's all you have."

The starlight sucked up the room.

"You don't need maths to be a bus driver or a shop keeper, Mama." I thought of saying that much later – a *Treppenwitz*.

Literally, a staircase joke. A witty comment that dawns on you after the fact.

I sat at the table.

I suffered from day-dreamer's disease, and there was no cure.

24

THE FIGHT

FIREBRICK*FRESH AVACADO*FALOOBANG

Over the next few weeks and well into the winter, the friendship between Von, Tomas, and I continued.

Von's father was sent to Paris to recover from the horrors of the eastern front. Germany took over the world. Nazi banners littered the French flags. Foreign signs were replaced with German ones so that the German troops could feel at home – that was nice of them. They practically recreated Germany in the higher, elite places of France. German language book stores opened and cinemas were permitted to play only German films, however many French productions still carried on. Von's father wrote it in his letters, and the information was passed to Tomas and me.

They didn't care that I was endlessly teased.

"Look, it's Beckmann himself." Penn laughed, a stupid, thirteen-year-old grin of smugness. His *Backpfeifengesicht*. Derrick was like a shadow behind him, partaking, but never actually delivering the blows himself.

Backpfeifengesicht: the meaning of this word is far more familiar than you might think. Do you know those kinds of people whose face is enough to make you want to slap them? Well, from today, I kindly invite you to use the German word, instead of "punch-bag face."

"Come on, Beckmann." Penn was carving my skin with his juvenile words.

Max Beckmann: a famous German expressionist painter.

At first, I didn't speak. I couldn't, for I would certainly scream or cry.

Tomas was beside me. "Don't listen to them." He held my shoulder, just to be safe.

"Easy to say," I replied with a quiet laugh. "They're not making fun of you."

"Come on!" Penn walked backward in front.

Grins were stuck to the emotionless faces of the children around me. They seemed to mock me without saying a word.

"Shut it, Pichler." Von's words stood between us.

"I'm not talking to you. I'm talking to your boyfriend."

That shut Von up. Unusually quickly.

I tried to walk away. I did, but I could feel their thoughts, like poisoned darts.

Their words turned poisonous, too.

"If your Mama had kept her legs closed, we wouldn't have to deal with filthy little *Mischling* like you."

Stay calm, Josef.

It was nearing the end of the break now. The comments stood by the door, blocking my way.

I snapped. It was Pichler, back for more.

"Come on, you filthy little *Mischling*. Show me what you got."

My heart accelerated.

"Shut up."

Tomas was playing a dangerous game of holding me back, but he was losing.

"Get off!"

I don't know what happened next, but I heard Pichler's fist colliding with my jaw.

My tongue soaked in the taste of my blood.

It tasted good.

He began to laugh.

"Come on," he said, showing off now. "Or are you too chicken?"

My breathing calmed. With a gentle finger, he reoriented my face so that I held the gaze I didn't want to give him, stealing the passion from my eyes in a way that only magnified the spark. Now, there was no smile on his lips, only the white-hot intensity of his gaze that we both knew was the start of what was to come.

"Show me what you got," he yelled.

I showed him alright.

I stood up, and as he smiled over his shoulder at some other children, I threw my first punch and kicked him as hard as I could in the vicinity of the groin.

My passion arrived unannounced and ended explosively.

Well, as you can imagine, Penn Pichler was certainly startled, and on his way down, I punched him in the ear. When he landed, I pinned him down with my knees. I slapped, scraped, and screamed his face off. I was so utterly consumed with rage.

His skin was so warm and soft. My knuckles were so frighteningly fearless and loyal, despite their brevity. "You bastard." My voice, too, was able to punch him. "Show me how tough you are now. Go on."

The clouds gathered to watch; big and grey.

The fight stood and made an announcement, "Come and witness the suffering for yourself," throwing its light at the children and attracting them to the scene. Youth leaders didn't break up the fight. They were cheering me on. They were watching me give Penn Pichler the hiding he deserved. Blood, teeth, and guts were strewn around the playground. If hatred were visible, the air would have been scarlet.

For Tomas, the playground shook.

"I'm going to kill you," I said.

Stefan Rosenberg's absurd gigglings were heard in the stones. Manfret's unique "Oh, fuck."

Relax, Relax. I did not kill him.

But I came close.

Probably the only thing that stopped me was the pathetic scratchings of Derrick Pichler. Still crowned in adrenaline, I caught sight of him clawing at his skin with such audacity that I dragged him down and began beating him up too.

"What the hell are you doing?" He wailed, and only then, only after I smashed his head and I was pulled off by Rouvon, did I stop.

On my knees, I sucked in the air and listened to the whispering. I watched the sound cloud of voices, left and right, and I made an announcement. The colours hurt so bad.

"I will be a painter."

I could feel something sharp in my throat.

No one argued this time.

No one laughed.

You're weak if you think violence can sway me from my passion.

There was just the sound of still silence – an unusual sound for a playground.

A whistle blew. The cry was attached to the skinny, stocking wearing legs of Simons. The skirt halved her.

Shit.

Its sound rattled through the crowd, making the clones part like, well, like children who were going to get into some serious trouble.

I was in the air, being dragged away once again – this time by Simons.

I was sure Kröger would come back with his belt. If he did, I would be ready. He didn't. He congratulated me with a packet of sweets. Chocolate.

Cut to the end of the school day. Tomas and I walked back to our cabins together, arm in arm, which was nothing out of the ordinary. My throat was still stuck.

"I don't know what's wrong with me, Tomas." He didn't speak. Simply listened. "I have such a stupid passion that I would do anything to anyone who speaks against it."

This time, Tomas laughed and looked up at the pale plum purple rain. I tapped to the beat of the colours. "You're like Mama."

Far away, in the forgotten sunshine, there lived my highest ambitions. I may not ever be able to find the sun again, but I can listen to it when it calls to me and applaud the powdered gold flakes on the grass. It might lead me somewhere remarkable someday.

Curiously, I responded. "What's wrong with that?"

"Nothing."

Nearing the cabins in a brisk walk of thoughts, colours of misery swept over me. It locked me in – the forgotten sun, the demolition of my family, my nightmares, the humiliation of the day – and I stood, half-bent on the courtyard and wept. Uniforms passed like they were back-pedalling, but no one stopped. Perhaps a few stares, but nothing more.

Tomas stood by my side.

It began to rain nice and hard. Hailing actually. Each falling block of ice punched and punctured my skin.

The sky was eerily silent.

Silent and safe.

Oskar called out to us from the doorframe, but neither of us dared to move. I stood painfully now, among the falling chunks of hail, and my little brother stood right beside me – waiting with a book over his head for cover.

He loved me just as much in pieces as he did whole.

"No one will be messing with you anymore." Tomas searched for the humour, his small hand gathering it all together and patting it on my shoulder. But still, I did nothing. I said nothing.

When I had finally finished and stood straight, he gave me an awkward hand-pat hug, and we walked on. There were no words said, no teasing, nothing like that.

Some steps later.

"I will make sure never to call you Max Beckmann," he said.

There's that light again.

It radiated outwards through my body and came out in high waves of hilarity.

I dried my nose.

When the hail ceased, and the clouds had sewn themselves back up, we continued under the guarded sky.

A few words from your older self:

My dear Josef,

People's words will hurt. So much so that you might feel like you'll bleed from the smallest ones. And I am not the type to try and save you from you. I think, perhaps, it's words you need to hear. But, you have two choices:

To believe them.

To show them they are wrong.

There is nothing more soul boosting than proving the cynics wrong even if it's not today.

25

THE PINK SWASTIKA

*PAPAYA WHIP*PERSIMMON*PERINTO

WHEN I THINK OF LIFE'S MOST DEFINING MOMENTS, I'M always taken back to childhood. For some, it's a Robin Hood incident. For some, it's a moment of midnight vomiting hysteria.

It was mid-December and in the height of Winter. The snow was late that year.

Earlier, there had been a parade. A minor calamity occurred in the morning before school. It involved a radio.

To ensure that even the poorer homes of Munich could afford a radio to listen to Hitler's infamous speeches, Goebbels arranged for the production of two cheap types of radios priced at 35 and 72 Marks. They were known as the *Volksempfänger*, or people's radios.

We had one such radio in the cabin. Hitler was due to make a speech, so we gathered as Stefan tried to find the channel.

And eureka!

The man from the radio: "Winston Churchill has announced…"

The die hasn't been cast (yet).

Derrick knelt at his brother's knees, and Penn cut his hair –
the classic Hitler youth undercut. Penn's eyebrows spoke. "That's
not the Führer."

"Munich has been a betrayal of principle in the face of
threats...."

Manfret cut in. "That's not even German."

Oskar was running to Stefan now. "What the hell are you
doing, Pup?"

"I don't know. It went to this."

"Let me see!"

Stefan protested, but Oskar had a seriousness to his tone.
"I'm not going to jail because of you!"

I looked up from my sketchpad to Von. "What's wrong?"

"Radio of the enemy. No good."

Eventually, we found the Führer hiding between stations two
and three, and we listened as we dressed. From his voice, I imagined a man with eyes of utter rage. Instead of imagining myself
there, I imagined a giant radio in the middle of a booming
crowd, gathering the information and reporting back to us. I
sketched that thought.

"I would like to develop a couple of ideas for you on the
question of homosexuality. There are those homosexuals who
take the view: what I do is my business, a purely private
matter..."

I stared at the eagle and the swastika. The boys' voices
babbled happily like a mountain river.

"If we continue to have this burden on Germany..."

I buttoned my shirt and got ready for the school day.

THE PARADE

We had half the day off to prepare for it, and everyone did
their share. There would be music, singing memorised songs,
dancing, and a fire.

Boys on bicycles had publicity signs. "Are you a German

boy?" said the sign in childish penmanship. "Come and join our *Jungvolk.*" I wanted to have the chance to do that, mostly to ride the bicycle, but I never did. I was not diligent enough.

"Bist du ein deutscher Junge? Komm zu unserem Jungvolk."

Like always, we walked the streets, looking for war materials. Only this time, it wasn't for the soldiers on the main front, but for the fire itself. We collected posters, old books, and any found propaganda of the enemy to burn in the Führer's glory. I walked with Manfret, and on the way past, I pointed up at the Schultz house. "Fuck that," Manfret said. "That man scares me. And that big old house."

Such events in Inland were anticipated. Not only for the half-day, but because some parents would travel from all over Germany to see their sons marching in the sky like the clouds.

Manfret Wünderlich was especially excited. His mother, father, and sister would be coming from Frankfurt.

He had a puddle of excitement in his stomach.

That day, I watched as he was extra careful to tie his laces just right for his mother.

Stefan Rosenberger had the honour of pinning the swastika banner on the window of our cabin. He stood, hidden behind it, waiting for his moment.

"Can I do it yet?" he asked for what seemed like the hundredth time that day.

Oskar sighed at the small boy. "Yes, Pup. You can do it now." He smiled over his shoulder. "Now, will you shut up for two seconds?"

"Schwein!" The voice from the flag replied. "Pig!"

I examined the pair, examining my handiwork. I broke the silence. "Do you like it?"

Oskar's posture tensed. Stefan's brow furrowed. "It's pink," Pup replied.

"Do you like it?"

"No, I do not like it, Josef," Oskar said with a shaking head delivery. "You changed the colours."

"I like those colours."

It would have to do, he thought. Oskar helped Stefan throw it over the ledge of the window, like washing being dried. It was different and raised eyebrows, but still, it was there.

I took the time to polish the glass on the Führer's portrait vigorously. Mostly with spit and the bottom my jumper. Tomas and some boys from his cabin decorated new photos of the Führer with some flowers they found in the grass. The Führer with school children. The Führer petting a fawn. The Führer kissing an unsuspecting child. You couldn't make it up. Unbeknownst to the children, however, they were adorning their beloved Führer with weeds.

Some boys from Inland were selected to participate in the later parade. Tomas, Von, and I were not amongst those boys. We didn't mind. It was nice to watch.

I took the opportunity to paint on my gifted sketch pad. It was one of my happier sketches, showing the Führer on his podium, and the children jostling around to get just one good look at him. My brushstrokes were more controlled and petite as I dipped my brush into the poppy-pink and painted the tiny walking uniforms. The rest of the painting was a mess of colours.

The brown-shirted extremist members of the NSDAP (otherwise known as the Nazi party) marched down the main road of Inland. Their banners worn proudly, their faces held high. Voices were full of song, culminating in a roaring rendition of *"Deutschland über Alles.* Germany above everything."

My hands burned from applause.

I stood at the side of the road with Tomas, Von, and Oskar – three of us had faces like lanterns. Oskar stood with the curtains pulled.

When the boys from Inland passed us, identified by their

mossy green armbands, they were spurred on as they walked to who knows where. Von called out to Penn, and he replied with a middle finger.

People on the road stood and watched, some with straight-armed salutes, some with smaller ones on shoulders. Some kept faces that were contorted by pride in the rally, like the red-haired shop owner. And then there were the scatterings of shadow men, like Oskar Frederick, who stood like a human block of wood, clapping slow and dutiful. And beautiful.

A man with a beard for a face stood beside me. "Look at them all. Proud as anything." I looked up. That was Penn and Derrick's father. Unmistakably. Their mother was taped to his side, heating her gloved hands. She made several attempts to wave to her sons, but only Derrick would wave back. Penn's eyebrows remained straight and marched in the wind, not daring to improvise the script slightly.

Oskar's hat looked down; its shadow looking up. Herr Pichler's words seemed to sting him.

"They look like dickheads! My father followed Hitler into war, and that ended with him being blown up." His voice was stretching out his sentences more than usual, his movements were clumsy, and he had a whisky breath.

"Don't be so negative," Herr Pichler said. His wife nodding in agreement. It was evident where the twins got their smugness.

"You call yourself a member of the party, with thoughts like that? You should be proud of your father. You owe him that."

"I don't owe that man anything. My mother raised me and did a damn good job of it. And Hitler is doing all of this for attention. For followers."

"Attention?" He looked at other faces that took his side.

"That is the most fantastic story I have ever heard. Shame on you. He is doing all this to make this country better. For those children and your own – and what is he reading?"

That was directed at Von Bacchman and his book, kneeling on the ground.

"He should be reading *Mein Kampf.*"

Von stood and closed the book.

"I did, Sir. Three times already." I had never seen a red book move so quickly. And above it was the moss green shade of Herr Pichler. His breath more diluted.

Frau Pichler was appalled at Oskar just enough to speak.

"How can you say you love your county if...?"

"I love my country. It's the war I hate."

Oskar was not a member of the Nazi party, despite working in a Nazi school, which he only agreed to due to bribery. Appearances can be deceptive.

If I squint hard enough, I can just make out the two figures sitting in *Die Kneipe*, bonding over cheap whisky, and an offer was made. Oskar kept a close eye on his brother, Alfred, who was drinking lemonade at the bar. The man in the hat offered Oskar a cigarette, which he declined.

"You would be a great asset to our school, Oskar."

"I'd rather hang from the rafters than work with those snobby parents and bratty children."

The man knew about Oskar's husband-less mother and young brothers. Knew that money was a hard thing to come by, and going to Inland earned the families a small government salary.

The hat rolled a cigarette and talked to the entire bar. "Then maybe your brother. I'm sure if I called the lad over and explained, he would love to join. Support his mother."

Now he had his attention. "You don't want him. He's fifteen. Just a little kid."

"No, we want you, Oskar, but we will take what we can get."

Hat-man leaned back on his chair, laughing, thinking he had trapped Oskar Frederick. Oskar drank the last drop from his glass and smiled a whisky smile. "If I agree, you won't take any of my brothers?"

"No."

"I'd like that in writing. And signed. *Bitte.*" He leaned back on his chair and laughed. "Please."

Increasingly impressed with Oskar, the man knew he had met his match. "You want a cigarette, Oskar?"

"Yes."

The parade continued. Behind the Inland children, boys and girls from other divisions walked proudly. The girls skipped with braided hair.

The sweaty boys walked behind the girls like smiling fools and dared each other to talk to them after the parade.

Pat. Pat. Point. Pat.

"Look, it's a real-life girl."

"Shut up. I can see that."

Some mumbling was exchanged.

"I'm afraid to talk to them. They look bigger."

"Even if we are afraid, we should go talk to them."

The boys did not know, but the girls heard it all and giggled in front.

We didn't see many girls in Inland, and a lot of the boys were at the age where they were starting to find them interesting enough to examine them further. I had no time for such things. There was a parade to be watched – people to heil.

Derrick Pichler managed to trick one such girl who lived in the village of Inland. The colours in that girl's eyes changed when she saw Derrick in town. They met that evening behind an old oak tree, and I imagine their evening consisted of awkward banter and formulating a cover story. The girl's father called her home. Derrick returned with a fake-victorious smile. I caught him ruffling his hair and roughing up his uniform on the way back.

"Did you do it?"

"Ja." He lied. "Until that humpy old bastard called her back."

Manfret Wünderlich kept an eye out for the people who would never show up. He cried later, telling Oskar how much his parents must hate him. Wünderlich often cried for his parents, especially in the morning. The hardest part of Inland for him was waking up. "I'm sorry." He said, swimming in self-pity. "I miss my Mama."

Oskar gently soothed him with his words. "Yes, I miss mine, too. But we must be brave, and we will see them soon." Oskar was an excellent teacher because he was genuinely fond of children.

On that particular evening, after dinner, it was one of those rare occasions when Teichmann baked. She was a better baker than cook, but just barely. Tomas had three of Teichmann's *Wibele* biscuits, as did I. Von managed to scoff down a total of six different desserts in the space of ten minutes. Tomas warned him that he'd pay for that later, but Von wouldn't listen.

He would pay later. That night at midnight, to be exact.

More of that soon.

26

FROM DESTRUCTION TO ABSTRACTIONISM

DARK MODERATE MAGENTA*DANDELION*DAMON

In the night, I dreamed again. At first, I only saw brown-suited marching and swastikas glowing. Then, the figure of a boy outlined in stars appeared above my bed, only for a few seconds. I couldn't be sure, but the figure appeared to be Bacchman-like. It tasted sweet. Eventually, they all led me to my brother, and I saw him lying face down in the snow.

When I woke in a panic, Oskar was there, on the edge of the bed. I attempted many times to speak, but the words wouldn't allow themselves to leave. Oskar knew what to say. He always did. He sat up straight. "Smoke?" He smiled, his blue eyes lighting the dark.

I smiled back at him and agreed. "Smoke."

During our smoking lesson that night, everything was going as usual. I was looking at the stars floating above me, blowing smoke into the sky and watching it disappear, and I did so until Oskar spoke or until I smoked the cigarette down to the end.

I sat in the darkness, tracing out what would be my second painting that I created in Inland – a boy sitting on the moon, cradling a fallen star in the palm of his hands. It burned, but he didn't care. Below him, colours were dancing in the German waters, creating waves that reached the sky.

Recently, I had run into trouble with the number of emotions I was leaving behind – the amount I was revealing. Words were sometimes hard for me, but it was more than that. I had not yet figured out how to describe my paintings without the viewer feeling uncomfortable. If I could explain my art in words, I thought, what would be the point of the painting? Simply saying, "oh, I like those colours," or "that house reminds me of my home," forces us to miss the point of art completely. Art is a process, thoughts underlying the execution. The way another views the world can be charming, and at the very least, cause the viewer to see things they would have otherwise overlooked.

Many artists of the '40s focused on abstract art, from destruction to abstraction. I understood the reasoning, even as a boy. In a time of war, who wants real life? However, I loved painting about life. Humans themselves are mysteries and adventures, and happiness. I tried to portray them all. The smaller stories of life that everyone forgets.

All told, I would create a total of ten paintings during my five years in Inland, but I saw my story as being made up predominately by four of them. The marching brown shirts and glowing swastikas, one painted with stolen paint, one painted for a trusted hand and the painting I didn't finish.

I wondered that night, about the stars. I often wondered things in my head, but I was almost always too afraid to speak them. I wondered if the stars were just crumbling bits of moon that refused to fall, and instead became stars, became something better, something more than they should have been – rebelled against their fate. I decided that the stars are where the good people live.

As usual, Oskar held a photo like it was broken glass.

I bit down on my lip, but I couldn't resist this time. Curiosity got the best of me.

"Who is that?"

Oskar broke his gaze and looked down at the ground, then back to me. "This?" He shifted the photo to my hands. "That's my sweetheart, little man – Elsbeth."

Elsbeth Frederick (Elsi, for short) was a thing of beauty.

Of course, that was not the thing I shifted my mind towards, despite my teenage-boyness, but her colours. The colours that made up her character.

There was something unreal and eerie about Elsi. Her face, somewhat luminous, had a pale tone to it. Eyes were a sharp shade of grey. She had black, woollen hair that framed her enchanting face and fell to her hips. Overall, she was unearthly.

Oskar and Elsi's love story was a thing people write novels about. A love story to some and a tragedy to others. You can decide for yourself which one it is.

I liked to think of it as a bit of both.

Oskar met Elsi at a bar called *Die Kneipe.*

Translation: the bar.

A wonderfully creative name, I know.

It was there where Oskar spent most of his free time before arriving in Inland, and where one of the suit men would learn of him. He loved to sit with his whisky and his thoughts and let his mind wander. Oskar drank nothing but water and alcohol. He was either hydrated or drunk. Sometimes, he'd look at the trees. I've never been there, but from what I have heard, Mittengwald has the most beautiful trees in Germany, especially in the autumn: greens, yellows, reds, oranges, every shade in between. Their dazzling colours glowing with the sun.

The other half was helping his mother and six younger brothers at the farm they inherited from his father. His brothers battered, annoyed, and loved him. Teaching his thirteen-year-old brother, Albert, how to fight was a training ground for his future. Albert got a little too good, and soon he was the topic of discussion at a table in *Die Kneipe*.

I realise I keep getting off-topic a little. This is *your* story; you might be saying. Why are you telling me about Oskar's life?

From somewhere in the back row, there is probably a voice calling out, "What's the point of all this?" Others might agree or disagree, but most will sit with hanging heads and Catholic stares. A Catholic tut made its way through the crowd.

What's the point of this? What's the point of life? Well, that's precisely why we are here. To understand why.

To sum up what I think going forward, the best I can do is to say this: the purpose of life is to find a way to forget about the question, "What is the purpose of life?"

But you see, Oskar's stories are essential, and very much a part of my own. My life story is the product of the stories of everyone I have ever met. A mixture. A blending of colours that connect like dots.

They all had their part to play.

Yes, Oskar's story is very important, indeed.

WHO WAS OSKAR FREDERICK?

His life is not easy to explain. Before coming to Inland, it had not been the rip-roaring adventure he'd imagined for himself in his younger days. But it wasn't totally absent of colour either. Oskar himself would tell you that he was a simple man with pure thoughts. His face would someday fade to yellow behind a glass pane, and his name will be forgotten. But the simple things in life are often always the most important. It just takes a smart man to notice.

Oskar was a son, a brother to six younger siblings, and a life-long friend. Above all of these things, Oskar loved Elsbeth with every ounce of his being.

He inherited a lot from his Father: as mentioned before, a farm was one such thing. His tireless eyes, for another. He also picked up his fondness for puzzles, figuring out how things worked, and – albeit to a lesser extent – fascination with machines. Like his father, Oskar was a quiet man who worked hard for small rewards and would have done anything for his family.

But there was one quality that he inherited from his mother. A quality that he had wished for many years that he did not possess.

He always stayed.

Despite the persistent itch on his skin to leave Mittenwald behind and begin a grander life elsewhere, he would not scratch it. He was afraid that scratching would relieve the itch, but also cause one as well.

Oskar didn't have leaving in his heart.

But oh, how I wish he did.

Yes, I wish he did indeed.

His father was to blame.

Herr Frederick always craved something more in his life. The beginnings of that adventure came in 1933, in the form of a small, charismatic man with a square moustache stapled to his lip.

In the 1930s, the mood in Germany was grim. The great depression had hit hard, and many people were out of work. It was especially tough for the small shop and farm owners like Oskar's family.

Hitler was a powerful and spellbinding leader, who attracted the attention of a despairing Walter Frederick, who was desperate for change, and he abandoned his wife and sons to follow in the puny footsteps of his beloved Führer.

I wish I could tell you that it all ended well for Herr Frederick, I really do. But this isn't such a story.

Oskar was seventeen years old when his father died.

He left his family behind with a single bullet through the head.

As long as Hitler was alive, people were dying in his name. Long before the death camps and public executions.

Somewhere between all of his pain and sadness, Oskar made a vow. He would never leave the people he loved as his father left them.

I imagine it.

The light on the window was grey and the colour of summer.

A woman with a battered heart on the floor, cursing the kitchen tiles.

The six father-less sons squashed together as they breathed and cried.

And a seventeen-year-old boy surrendering to his emotions.

I can almost see them leaving Oskar that day: the pain, the shock, the denial, the abandonment – leaving him like ghosts of the past, and in its place, some words.

"A man who leaves his own family can hardly call himself a real man." He spoke the words, and no one heard them.

But he did.

They were lies.

Oskar's face wasn't filled with resentment, either. It was more a face of acceptance. This would be his life now.

He was worried about abandoning his family. Worried about disappointing them. Worried that if he was to trust his gut and follow his heart that he would disown the very people he owed his life to.

He would be no better than his father.

The boy was afraid. Afraid of not following his dream. The

only remedy was to move forward – get on with it. Oskar was not the type of man who would have died overthinking.

Personally, that was one of the things I loved the most about Oskar Frederick.

Yes, I liked that a lot.

And then he met her.

She opened a beer with her teeth, and Oskar gave her his necklace.

They got married one year later in borrowed clothes.

And that was it.

"A hell of a woman, this one." Oskar grinned.

He kissed the back of the photo and put it in his pocket.

Oskar got to the bottom of his cigarette, and he leaned over and stubbed it out on the pavement. "Enough for tonight."

"Can we just have one more, Oskar." I smiled at him. I was enjoying the stars that night and the stories.

Oskar had fallen into my trap. "Oh, alright," he laughed. "One more and then bed for you." His laughter intensified. "I've created a monster." He rolled two more cigarettes.

"Thank you, Oskar."

He patted my hair.

Occasionally, I'd be smoking and painting at the back of Inland with Tomas. Oskar halved his tobacco with me.

Tomas was arched on the ground, legs crossed, and nose buried into a book he was assigned to read about the importance of physical fitness.

Colours in my head, smoke in my lungs, and paint on the paper. My words, too, were in the paint.

Inhale. Exhale.

Tomas would cough hard from all that smoke. He hated the smell and taste.

"You stink," he'd jokingly tell me. "Like cigarettes."

That was usually my cue to take a bath.

Sitting in the bathwater, I imagined the colour of the smell of it lingering on my clothes. The scent reminded me of my happiest moments, which would otherwise be forgotten: my father, my grandfather, and Oskar. See, sometimes we capture a moment in our hearts, but sometimes things change, things fall apart, and memories are forgotten. Smells are not so easily forgotten, and it lingered in my mind.

I would sit in the cooling water and watch the grey tones dance on the water.

I smiled.

At a quarter past twelve and mid-smoke of a cigarette, we heard the most horrid sound coming from the cabin. It caused my senses to blur. Suddenly, I was tasting the colour green. It tasted bitter and sweet at the same time. It was a mouthful of taste. Oskar immediately put out his cigarette on the wall and ran back inside. I followed apprehensively behind him, throwing my cigarette on the grass.

We scanned the room for the perpetrator, but all that could be seen was a room of curled up sheets. All boys still surprisingly asleep. But somewhere in the semi-darkness, sat Vons crouched over form, stars outlining his figure, his muscles contracting, expelling his guts over his bed and onto the floor.

The bulk of the vomit was already cold on the sheets – too many cakes for dessert that night, just as Tomas warned.

Von sank further into the bed, resisting the urge to touch his face with his fouled hands. As he leaned forward, the last of it dribbled from his lips.

At first, he tried convincing himself that nothing had happened, but when Oskar came closer and held him, he cried and admitted the fact into his ear. His tears were a mixture of pain and humiliation. But I didn't care. I ran to fetch him some water.

Teichmann shouted sleepy words at my head. I ducked and dodged them.

As I turned off the tap and looked back at the door, there was a masterpiece of imagination.

Father stood like a ghost, except not. More like a shadow of the past.

"Josef..." he said.

I dropped the glass and it shattered on the floor, and as soon as he was there, he was gone.

The feeling was one that could not be related to the other five senses.

"I'm going mad," I thought.

Teichmann woke up fully and made me clean it up with a brush and mop.

Oskar lifted Von gently from his bed and carried him down to the washroom, where he cleaned him up and returned to the cabin a few minutes later.

"Josef," Oskar whispered to me upon returning. "Can you take off the sheets for me? I'll go get a washbasin."

When Oskar left the cabin, as Von helped me with the sheet, something that had been wedged between the mattress and bedframe loosened. A red book with yellow and white lettering came running towards me and landed on the floor between my feet, with one sock hanging off.

I looked down at it.

On the front cover of the book, there was a photo of a koala with a blonde little girl.

I looked up at Von, who shrugged his shoulders.

Fear dripped down his face.

I tried to read the title of the book with high concentration and a lot of stammering:

"*Easy to learn...*"

"*Easy to learn English,*" Von interrupted.

A patch of silence stood among us – Von, the book, me, and the colours. I picked the book up and spoke as soft as cotton.

A conversation between two boys at 1 am.

"Is this yours?"

After a short silence.

"*Ja*, Josef."

I looked at the book and then to Von with ample confusion.

"It's to learn English."

"Why do you want to do that for?"

"Mama gave it to me."

I laid the book beside him, climbed on to the bed, and sat opposite. His pale blue eyes stared into mine for a brief moment.

Silence.

I could feel the pointy, jagged fibres of grandmother's paintbrush digging into my hips as if it was trying to spur me on. I took it from my pyjamas, stared at it, and smiled.

I offered it to Von. "It belonged to my Oma."

He smiled and studied it.

Surprisingly, he didn't tease me.

Then he spoke again.

"She was a teacher." Stammering. "Mama. Before I came here, she was teaching me and my sisters English. She said it'd be important to know for the future."

"But German is the most important language."

"It's not if you want to travel the world."

"You want to travel the world?"

Nodding. "I think so."

Gentle words fell from the bed, landing on the floor like powder.

"And I know French, too." He continued. "You can't tell anyone I have this, okay? They'll take it away from me."

"Why?"

"I don't know why. It's just not allowed."

His eyes looked as though an ocean had been encased inside small glass marbles.

"Please don't tell."

I thought he was going to cry, so I sputtered, "I won't tell anyone. I swear."

He slid closer to me. Hand gliding down my arm, folding over my hand. His fingers laced with mine, palms kissing. I could feel the fast thud of his heart through that single touch.

"Promise?"

I was shocked, but only mildly.

A feeling so strange; it stretched through my whole body. It was overwhelming, yet made me feel full. It had no bound nor length nor depth; it was just absolute. It felt like I was in a dangerous fire but completely safe at the same time. I felt sick.

I couldn't explain it.

I had only one thought: curse blue-eyed, hand-holding boys.

"Promise." I nodded.

A few minutes later, Oskar returned, wearing a face of stone.

"What is this?"

"Nothing."

His face softened.

"She almost killed me."

She, of course, was Teichmann, and she very nearly did kill him. The word *Arschloch* made its appearance regularly in the administration of his punishment. She slapped him with her rolling pin and made mincemeat out of him.

I roared with laughter as he told us.

"Ssshhhhh. We have to be quiet, little man."

There was a slight flash of a smile on Von's face.

"Good night, *Arschloch*."

A quiet one-syllable laugh.

"Good night, Oskar."

27

THE WORD WHISPERER

WISTERIA

VON SHOULD'VE SPENT THE NEXT FEW DAYS IN BED, AS instructed by the doctor, but he refused and came to school anyway. He even joined us on our early morning jog, and as usual, I raced him. On Saturday, I walked with Von around the doors of Inland with our new shared secret.

We knocked the doors, ran away before anyone answered, hid in the bushes, and laughed as the towel-wrapped heads and walking-stick men complained. Von further stirred the older villagers by throwing his ball into their gardens.

"God damn kids!" a voice from the window cut in. "If that ball comes into my garden one more time, I'll pop it, ya little cunts."

Imagine calling a thirteen-year-old boy a cunt.

The man had tiny swastikas on his tie.

A bizarre addition, but I remember it.

As I got *Watschen* in the cabin from Oskar, Von smiled at me, and I tried not to laugh.

Tomas walked with Stefan Rosenberger.

He "fried his brain," as Tomas put it.

No one would walk with him, and since Von had called dibs on me, he didn't see a reason not to.

There was a reason not to.

The boy carried a small notebook, marking off the houses they had already visited and noted what the people of Inland had given them and said to them. People in town knew that they had to be careful what they said around Stefan. He would have no problem reporting them if they stepped out of line.

The gate of the Shultzes remained guarded by the teddy-bear dog and, walking past it, Tomas would greet him. "Hallo, puppy."

Tomas later told me that Stefan would also comment on the homes that didn't hang up their flags. "I will tell the Führer about you," he would say, his blood pumping around his tiny veins. All for the Führer.

Tomas would keep his head down and try to restrain a smile.

The boy was dead devoted.

Tomas liked it.

Little boys like Stefan Rosenberger were Hitler's purest creations, beholden only to him, unaware of a non-Nazi past and unable to see the propaganda being throwing at them from various channels.

Hell, none of us did.

Perhaps the only reason I questioned it was because of my Papa and the stuff we were force-fed about the Jews.

When the materials were collected, the pair made their way to the River *Seehund* which flanked the town of Inland, and ate sandwiches and some precious *Fliegerschokolade* they had managed to liberate from the kitchen. The bitter-sweet chocolate came in round tins with a bright red and white label on the lid, screaming SCHO-KA-KOLA. It was normally reserved for troops at the front, but the elite status of Inland had obviously enabled Kröger to pull some strings.

The river ran in the direction of the camp, which we only learned about from scary stories, and later, we would get a front seat look at the suffering.

Yes, calm down. We will get to that soon.

But for now, we will talk about Stefan.

I think he deserves to be remembered.

Don't you?

THE SHORT LIFE OF STEFAN ROSENBERGER

Stefan didn't have a happy beginning, and you could argue whether he had a happy ending.

He and his brothers were taken from his young mother when he was four years old and placed in a children's home, waiting for his new family.

Apparently, his mother was crazy. It turns out she was just young. Very young.

He delivered the information to Tomas that day on the river.

He came home from school on a rainy Friday afternoon, and his brothers were no longer there.

And he never saw them again.

"Do you remember them?" Tomas asked, wiping the flakes of sweat off his forehead.

"I remember them." He started playing with the badge on his belt. "But they are with new Mamas and Papas now."

Tomas looked out across the river, his heart aching from Stefan's memories of his lost childhood.

Tomas tried to explain to me why he was sad, but nothing came out when he tried to speak, and he realised that he didn't know why either.

But I did.

Compassion.

Tomas always wore it like a cloak.

He tried to change the subject.

"Are you excited about Christmas, Stefan?"

This was a little more appropriate for a ten-year-old to be thinking about.

"Fuck Christmas!" Stefan shouted. "And fuck St Nicholas, too."

Tomas didn't expect it. He almost choked on saliva.

"Oskar said he doesn't come here." The boy was cut, his knees to his chest and head on his palms.

Tomas looked out. The river was everywhere.

Stefan remembered it clearly, the day he arrived in Inland.

Aged nine and a half, he was taken, hand in hand, by his foster mother up a tree-lined driveway, smartly dressed in a suit with sleeves too long. His blond hair neatly brushed and styled. In front of them was a country house. Stefan thought he was going to the doctor's. He was sick. His foster mother spoke to a lady he didn't know, and then, with only a trunk, three shirts, and a pair of pants, he found himself alone.

A scared, lonely boy. That's how careers in Inland usually began.

He was taught to be self-reliant, stone-cold, and hold himself high and poised. They taught him how to conquer the world in the name of the Führer, and suddenly, for the first time, he had meaning, and he belonged. He had a family – a home.

He was taught to cry on the inside, behind closed doors, in the dim of the candlelight. If no one sees your pain, does it mean you're in pain at all? Much like when your Führer bombs a country, killing thousands of innocent people because of his stubbornness. Just because you can't hear their screams, you could almost believe that it didn't happen at all, right?

Stefan Rosenberger was not alone.

The majority of Germany had the same mentality.

You might call us cowards.

Call us fools.

I called us humans.

Scared humans.

That didn't make us good guys. We were still assholes. We had a good reason for being assholes.

Stefan was a broken soul in the body of a happy boy.

I could smell it in his laughter.

Such a sad existence.

To never feel true happiness.

To not know how real love looked.

Tomas played trappers and Indians that evening. He was the team captain and chose Stefan first.

Later, when we met each other again, Tomas hugged me.

We even invited Von along.

"Are you coming or not?"

"You're letting me come?"

"What did you want? My permission?"

We walked to the back of Inland as we usually did. Von tried to be a gentleman and carry my paint set for me, but I knocked him out of the way. Von walked to my left, Tomas to my right. They both usually engaged in a conversation about the latest game of trappers and Indians, Von's parents, or anything else that came mind. Occasionally, I would give some input, but not very often, and not unless Von or Tomas called upon me. I didn't always find it easy to make words, especially when others were telling their stories so well. I questioned my voice and wondered if speaking out would cause more trouble than needed. I tried to break through their words, but more words came and stood in my way, keeping guard. So I simply sat in an ocean of unspoken thoughts and waited. I'm not sure for what or whom I was waiting.

Inland was darkening. The cold rising from the hills.

We got to our destination, and I sat on the grass, taking out my paint set.

"What's wrong? Is this it?"

"No, he's just stopping for fun." Tomas teased, adequately out of character I might add. Not only was the language catching on fast, but so were the personalities. Yes, the building itself had its own unique personality, and it was rubbing off on us all.

Von settled into the long arms of the grass, laying back on it. For a while, he watched me paint, watching as I did the basic outline of the figures on the paper in a lighter coloured pencil and then began adding detail.

When I was first gifted the paint, I wanted to ask Teichmann for some water. Nearing her cabin, I heard the roll call of scorn coming from the kitchen, and I ran. She was probably talking about something pleasant, but it sounded threatening. I would not accept my fear as an answer, though, so I made the brave choice to put out the anxiety altogether and steal the water when she wasn't there.

My painting was surreal, using shades of blues, blacks, and reds. They worked together in perfect harmony to bring out the visual illusions and abstract figures. That, or clash together in a violent frenzy. Either way, I knew it would be beautiful. Just three colours perched on the page, working together.

"That is beautiful, Josef."

That's what Von thought when he watched me paint, but teenage boys don't know such a vocabulary.

For now, Von Bacchman's fourteen-year-old mind could only manage three words.

"That's shit, Josef."

Naturally, I punched him in the shoulder, and we all laughed. "It's the best I can do, Von. I paint how I paint."

"Show us the book then."

Ah, yes. The book.

Von's secret.

Admittedly, it would have been engulfed in the flames of the 1933 book burnings, and the Führer would stare in awe at the beautiful chaos. When people think of Nazi Germany, the image that floats to the surface is generally fire. Go on, try it for yourself.

We didn't start that many fires.

Thousands of people stood clear of the volcanic scene. The smell was grotesque.

Some watched in unwavering, patriotic excitement, the Nazi songs tattooed on their hearts. Others watched from afar, hands in pocket and heads bowed, their guilt anchoring their heads.

Nazi flags flew, rising upwards with the warm German heat. Speeches made by suit-wearing, roaring humans, all beginning with the same words.

"*Heil Hitler.*"

All starting with the same right-armed salutes.

A fire was lit.

And an evil spirit of the past was burned.

Smoked out.

But see, Hitler didn't just burn the books that day, he burned everything. History, culture, life, death, and peace. All up in smoke.

What was left was the ashes, and German citizens would breathe it all in as they cried. The weak-kneed people would try to cram in as much information as their brains would allow – eating the pages. The brave ones would hide books.

Von's Mother was one such human.

She hid every book she could find in every nook and cranny in the shoe-box like house; above it, under it. It didn't matter. All that mattered was they were unable to be found.

As mentioned before, Von's mother was teaching her children English and French before her middle child and only son was taken to Inland. Or rather, Von volunteered to go.

Von Bacchman: the boy who never stood still.

Never stood still and let the people he loved suffer, never stood still when he was holding an assembly, listening to Dohman mumbling on, and never allowing his thoughts to stand still. I imagined them dancing in his mind. At first apprehensively, then growing comfortable with the familiar ideas.

His family was poor, and Von knew that going to Inland would give them a small allowance. The choice was an easy one for him to make.

Von's Mother, Maria, would write to him. Children in Inland often got letters from their parents. The letters were carefully read by youth leaders first, and any messages that contained anything suspicious, un-*German*, let's say, were discarded, and a fake letter sent in its place.

At first, Maria's letters appeared normal, appropriate for a flourishing Nazi to be reading. But secretly, just like the books, a small message was written in English.

"Keep learning."

Von told us the meaning. "*Lerne weiter.*"

He ran his hand along the indents on the paper like it was the most fragile thing in the world.

Also enclosed on the hill were the secret picture books, which fascinated me. Since English books for children were difficult to come by, Maria decided to make her own. It was expensive and took some time, but occasionally she would, and sent it to a man who owned a small farm near Inland, who would exchange it when the time was right.

Von stumbled over the words. He sat lost in that book. The only thing alive. I made occasional sideways glances until I realised in a toe-curling panic that he noticed.

He smiled.

I stopped.

I listened.

Everything I heard sounded like an indecipherable code with bizarre, mysterious intonations. It sounded like an imperious series of declarations and resonated like a landscape of rolling hills. So many little words have big jobs. So many little words have long rules. Although, some of the words were very similar to their German counterparts: father – *Vater*; water – *Wasser*; I have – *ich habe*.

You get the idea.

Almost identical.

The two languages were like distant cousins. They had changed, intermingled, and drifted apart due to many invasions of Europe, but they were still family. Their core was the same.

Well, compared to when Von would speak French, and every R he said sounded like he was choking on a large piece of *fromage*.

"However" was a problematic word. It was too soft and round: nothing my mouth touched when I said it. I had to pretend that I had a ball in my mouth to remind myself that I couldn't close my teeth.

Hawovever.

"Is that how you say it?"

Von laughed into himself. "No, but keep saying it."

Years later, I would be saved by the words and an apple, but they saved me in my youth, too. Or rather, Von Bacchman saved me. From what, however, I'm not entirely sure, but it was certainly something. Perhaps from my loneliness and the what-would-be thoughts of fear, had he not entered my life at the opportune moment. Von Bacchman saved me from *me*. He rewrote my story by being my friend.

"Fuck," Von said.

"What's wrong?"

"I keep forgetting this one word."

"I have an idea," I said, as I turned to the back of my sketch-pad, ripped a sheet out and started writing. I drew a little stick man, with very skinny legs, in the centre of the page.

"What are you drawing?" Tomas asked over my shoulder. Von, too was interested.

"It's you, Von."

My eyes returned to the page.

"A for what?" I said.

Von smiled.

Now he was catching on.

"A for ..." He thought. "Apple."

I smiled back at him and wrote the German word for apple in big letters.

Apfel.

I drew a line opposite it and shifted the page onto Von's lap, and he wrote the English word.

Appel.

Well, he tried to at least. He spelled it wrong. I didn't know it was wrong, so I nodded. Tomas etched closer, took the pencil and drew a misshapen apple under the word.

We all laughed. Tomas was no artist.

"I'm blinded by how shit that is, Tomas."

"Shut up! Now for B," I said.

As we progressed through the alphabet, Von's grin grew larger. He had done this before with his mother, but it's always better with your friends. I knew he liked to watch my hand write the words, and he loved watching Tomas construct the primitive sketches.

I couldn't explain why his happiness made me happy. Tomas and I didn't know what any of the words meant, but that didn't matter, for we could surely feel them. And more than anything else, we had fun.

I have never been so attracted to something I couldn't understand.

"Oh, come on, Von!" I said later when he was having trouble.

"Something that starts with P! I'm very disappointed with you."

I wasn't, of course. I didn't know English at all, so I couldn't have been angry at Von. But when Tomas and I would forget silly things when we did our homework at home, Mama would say, "You know this one! I can't believe you don't know it. I'm very disappointed in you," which always made us remember the thing we couldn't remember. I thought the same thing would work in this instance.

He couldn't think.

"Come on, Von," Tomas joined in. "Something that starts with P." His words played with Von.

That was when a word stuck on his face. A reflex grin crept up. "Pussy," he shouted before roaring with laughter, then quieted when he realised we didn't know what that meant.

He explained, we joined in on his chorus.

Scandalous.

Tomas' cheeks grew red as he realised he didn't know what to draw for that one, and the laughing commenced again, but louder. We drew nothing.

Von sat in the middle of Tomas and me; he placed his arms on our shoulders and looked with warm, pale blue eyes.

We'd fallen into Von Bacchman's trap.

Later, and alarmingly past curfew.

"Now for T," I said.

When we went through the alphabet, and Von studied it a thousand times, we decided that would be enough for today.

"Just one more!" Von pleaded.

"No. We'll be in so much trouble," Tomas said.

"Please, Josef."

It was hard not to give in, but we were persistent.

"No, Von."

I let Von keep the paper. He folded it up a million times and put it into his pocket. It was almost eight o'clock by the time we got back, and we were all ready to accept the *Watschen* to come. On the walk home, Tomas spoke.

"Your paintings are getting good, Josef." I looked down, realising he was right. I shrugged.

"I paint in a way that makes it feel real."

"Such as? What's that one about?"

"…Ahh, well. I don't just paint the moon. I show people how it glistens through the window."

Don't become silent. Art is about emotions, experience, and thoughts. Be ready to feel. The same applies to life.

I smiled, and he returned it, nodding shyly. He had no idea what I was talking about, but that didn't matter. What mattered was it made me happy. I hope that someday you have the chance to smile and nod at something you don't understand to make someone you love happy.

"Pussy!" he added, with a quiet one-syllable laugh, running away from me before I could react.

All three of us chuckled.

We said our goodbyes to Tomas and entered our cabins.

The fun didn't last long after that.

"Welcome back, fags." Penn Pichler sat upon his bed, the harsh, hate-filled cruelness of childhood alight with the hellish, rotten stench that is unique only to the armpits of teenage boys.

At the time, and other times after, I never let the word bother me much, but it did inspire a feeling I never felt before inside of my stomach, and it was a different feeling to the feeling I felt when I first heard the word "Jew". I knew what that meant, and I knew the reason for my anger towards it.

I had no idea what this meant.

Was it fear? Disgust? Who knows. Von had no answers, nor did I.

I brushed it off and sometimes laughed, but I did internalise it.

Watching Pichler and Derrick get a *Watsche* of their own was, if not a true comfort, a relief. But the feeling in my stomach made me unable to find it as satisfying as I probably should have.

That word. You are probably afraid to say it yourself out of fear that you might offend someone. Don't be afraid. It's a word, like many others. 6 letters. 2 syllables. It starts with fa and rhymes with maggot. Say it with me.

Faggot.

F-A-G-G-O-T

Faggot.

The word wasn't spoken a lot. Hell, I don't think the boys could even comprehend what exactly it meant, and it never seemed to bother anyone too much. But it lingered in my memory, popping up in the late of the night amongst the starry yellows, dancing with the colours, lurking from the distance. Something was always watching. The puddle that was forming in my stomach was getting deeper, and before I knew it, my thoughts would be drowning.

That night, in the dark cabin, I continued with Von's figure. I could tell Von had the words on his mind. I had the colours on mine.

28

FORGOTTEN LETTERS TO THE FÜHRER

FANDANGO*FELDSPA*FLAVESCENT

NEARING CHRISTMAS, WE WROTE LETTERS TO THE FÜHRER. It took me two hours and three drafts to perfect it – cigarettes scattered around me with the words and light.

A lot of boys declined to send letters, believing that it was only for the smaller kids. In hindsight, I knew that the whole exercise had been rather pointless. Had Hitler cared enough to speak to the boys he was creating, then he would have already done so.

The harsh scent of drink could be smelt on Oskar's person. Stefan was on his lap. "My pals said that he is not real, but I have to believe anyway."

The two were reading his letter. "Of course he's real, Stefan. We'll mail it to him directly."

We all use our imagination, but when we are children, we are often unable to tell the difference between fact and fiction. I believed the things adults in Inland told me because it was the adults who told me. Add a little childhood imagination, and you have the makings of the biggest lie in history.

Hitler and his radio waves kept me company as I tried to

collect the words and stamp them on the page. I ran away with my thoughts.

"Dear Hitler," it started.

The ways the grown-ups of Inland tried to shield the truth from the children multiplied and evolved yearly. The biggest threat, of course, was other children. They love to point out lies.

The impressive thing about myths is that they can live in the truth.

Hitler was, sadly, a real man, as well as an imaginary one. But the version of him the boys of Inland created in our minds did not exist.

Youth leaders were piled on top of each other, sitting on stools and smoking. The air was grey with smoke. The walls were yellow.

"Listen, men. And I'm just throwing this out there to see if it sticks, and don't twist my words."

"Just say it," Viktor Link said.

"I've heard that Hitler is orchestrating all of this." Whispering. "The hangings on the main street, the camps... Now it's just a whisper I heard. Don't go around repeating it."

"Supposing it's true, what else is he hiding?"

Orchestrating. I knew the word orchestrate had two meanings, but I still thought of the music anyway. The soft, Hitler-orchestrated songs were blowing on my neck. I scratched it with my shoulder several times before the images floated away and got stuck in the whirlpool that was my mind.

The German word for orchestrate is, similarly, *orchestrieren*.

Now, I think of the German men, and how their doubt was preyed upon. We all know what Hitler did, but the men in the cabin that day did not have the eighty years you did to internalise it. There was a tiny fraction of them that believed they could be wrong. People like him prey on doubt. It's that same doubt that makes us humans. The doubt that stops us from becoming Hitler ourselves.

Ignoring the sense of foreboding, I told the Führer about Inland, that we were learning all about him, and how I wished he could see my paintings someday. The words in my letter looked backward and upside down, but Tomas convinced me that it was suitable.

We placed our letters in envelopes, and the leaders would mail them for us. I was anxiously waiting for my reply the moment it was sent. An answer never did come.

Penn was waiting for a reply of his own, not from the Führer, but Von Bacchman. He gathered the nerve to ask Von for a lend of his yoyo.

"Von, come over here for a second."

"Not a chance."

"Why not?"

"You'll take my yoyo."

Penn Pichler had a mantra: "What's yours is mine, and what's mine is not yours."

29

STOLEN TOBACCO

*SADDLE BROWN*SALMON PINK*SEA
BLUE*SHOCKING PINK

WEIHNACHTEN, 1940.

Christmas.

Oskar had permission to go back to Mittengwald to spend some time with his family. Some pupils went home, but many stayed in Inland, only receiving letters from their parents.

Tomas made his way to my cabin as soon as he woke up. He and Kröger were getting dangerously close.

A conversation.

"Herr Kröger, I shot from the corner."

Kröger had a cigarette smoke grin. "From the corner? Right on target?"

"Ja!"

"Good boy!"

They were not a likely duo, but they were friends. Tomas passed Schultz's terrier daily when he went to shine shoes with Kröger. He gave a bag over the shoulder, bent-over "Hallo, puppy."

"Christmas just doesn't seem the same without toys," said Penn Pichler as he played with the wrapping paper. He was awake before most of the others. "But, I suppose we're too big for toys now." He had opened his parent's present without Derrick. Hair clippers. He wouldn't hear the end of it for the rest of the day.

"*Ja*, toys are for babies." Manfret hid his Hitler miniature in his pocket. An odd snapshot in time. Of course, such toys were quite normal back then. You cannot deny history.

To Stefan Rosenberger's surprise, sitting under our makeshift Christmas tree, there was something wrapped in newspaper and addressed to him.

"From Sankt Nikolaus," Tomas said.

The rest of us were not fooled.

Stefan practically tore the paper apart, unveiling a small, wooden car with a missing wheel. It didn't bother Stefan, though.

He hugged Tomas around his shoulders, snow still sticking to his delicate blond hair, and for a few moments, Stefan could not hear anything but the pounding pulse of his excitement.

My smile could not be restrained.

Afterwards, Stefan would carry that toy car under his arm wherever he went. Whether he was eating or sleeping, the car was always there. Later, Von and the other boys huddled in a circle and watched as he played, all while the youth leaders drank cider and talked about something we didn't understand in full – politics.

I listened and drew. They spoke of "blackies" and people who weren't like us. Not handsome, or tall, or slim, or German. I intervened with words directed at Herr Link. "But Link, Hitler is not German." Their heads cocked and they looked at me with patronising eyes. "Goebbels is very short, and Göring is a fat shit."

I did not receive the beating I thought would follow. Instead, they laughed at the ceiling and gave me a cigarette. "Yes, quite right, Josef." The explanation I was seeking was not given.

It wasn't until later that another thought occurred to me while I was watching Tomas take two bites out of Teichmann's grey-coloured sausages. I didn't even think they were cooked properly. I don't know how that woman managed to keep her job.

"Where did you get the money?"

My brother's eyes lit up.

"For the toy?"

Tomas grinned into his fork. "It's from Sankt Nikolaus, Josef."

The hall and Tomas waited for my counter-attack. "Tomas! I'm serious."

"I traded some tobacco for it… from the old lady down in the market?"

"Tobac…" It was then that I realised a large portion of my tobacco was missing. I was too impressed to be angry. I laughed with a mouthful of burnt pastry.

"And this one is for you." Tomas passed a small paint pot.

A two-toned blue. A riot of colours.

I could feel the colour.

"And how did you get this?"

"I stole it."

"Jesus."

30

THE RIVER OF SOULS

ON THE ARRIVAL OF THE HOT DAYS, OTHER DISTRACTIONS were learning how to swim in the River Seehund. As usual, it was a competition. Kröger, Oskar, and a tobacco-pipe-man made bets on who they thought would win. It was safe to say that I wasn't a favourite. I wasn't a powerful swimmer.

To get there, we had to swim through a river of shit, as Von called it. It was not shit, but it was up to our knees and deeper in parts. We had to step carefully. Tomas explained that I should follow his steps. He was a true eleven-year-old leader.

"Okay," I assured.

It was not okay, for when Tomas turned again, I was waist-deep in the mud. A single purple-splashed word came from my mouth. "Help." Laughing, Tomas pulled me out by my arm. I used a rock for leverage.

The river itself was grim. As children, we weren't aware of the souls who entered the water with the intent of ending their own lives, believing that they would find the answers they sought at the bottom, in the reeds. I hope they did. They jumped from the bridge. Inland was such a sad little postcard town, haunted by tragedy.

We swam amongst shame and fear, sucking in their misery and regrets.

Tomas had trouble swimming, and Kröger took it upon himself to teach him. By 'teach him', I mean throwing him into the deepest part with his shorts still on and hoping he wouldn't drown. "Just kick your legs."

Thankfully, Tomas was able to swim to the side and took instruction from Kröger for the rest of the day. By the end of it, he was able to float on his back.

I sat bare-kneed on the mud, wrapped around a *Sehnsucht* thought. I drew the boys in the river. Von interrupted. "This is my place" – a bare hand on a bare shoulder. I come here to think and read. I found it."

Sehnsucht: a painful yearning of the heart. Germans love to romanticise.

For most of the day, I managed to sit on the safe riverbank, dipping my toes into the water. "It's freezing."

A few times, Von tried to pull me in by my foot, but I quickly kicked him away.

"Come on, Schneider." Von tried coaxing me in. "It's not so bad once you get the dangly bits in." He did a handstand underwater and stood up in victory. Just as I was cornered, Kröger came from behind and launched me into the water. I dog-paddled for dear life, despite almost choking on the swollen intake of water.

"You *Arschloch*," I scolded him when I found my way to the side. I spoke to his feet. He repeated his regurgitated phrase. "Kick your legs." Adding to it. "Move your arms."

Tomas was hunkered under a tree and trying to wipe away his smile.

"Are you alright, Josef?" Von made sure to keep away from

me. He saw what I had done to Penn and Derrick Pichler with his own eyes.

"But you're in now, aren't you?"

He grinned it, rather than spoke it.

How dare he?

Dummkopf.

I reached for him, grabbing only water. "I'm going to kill you!"

I suppose that was love for two teenage boys.

When the fun was over, we bathed in the river. We didn't yet possess the embarrassment an adult would. Nudity was quite normal in Inland.

I changed in silence, between over the shoulder glances, until Penn broke it with a bar of soap to the face.

"What's that for?" Penn was hiding behind the cigarette. I tried to throw it back at him, but I missed, hitting a tree instead.

"Ew, don't touch me. I might catch your gayness."

Von interjected and breathed, "You mean like this?" He held the boy down and spat on him.

31

COLOURS

By March 1941, Inland had managed to escape the bombings of the invaders, but we would not be so lucky for long. The adults had some suspicions, for school work turned to preparation: how the death siren sounded, how to keep under cover, and get civilians to safety.

Tomas spoke highly of it when we played together. He loved to be a helper. There are many Tomases out there, too. You might even be one. Shy and quiet, sitting under trees, chuckling, and living for others so cheerfully that no one sees their sacrifices until the sunshiney presence vanishes, leaving behind only silence and shadow.

I was determined that the world would not make me grow up so fast.

Kröger took that day's class. Simons had been sick. Roll call was taken, and I became fixated on his glittering eye.

"Bacchman."

"Here." The volume of my voice turned down.

"Becker."

"Here."

"Pichler 1."

(Louder than the rest.) "Here, Herr Kröger."

"Pichler 2."

"Yes."

"Dietrich."

"That's my name."

More names and reckless responses stirred around the classroom, and I examined the bruises on my legs.

"Schneider." It was repeated. "Schneider."

"Here."

Silence.

"Schneider?"

Louder. "Here."

"Wünderlich?" No answer. "Where's Wünderlich?" Nervous laughter and scattered questions.

Just on cue, Manfret Wünderlich flew through the door. He stood nervously, drenched in rain, as though a storm cloud had mugged him, and the light caught on the ends of his curls. "Sir," he panted. "Jakob left his shorts in his cabin, so he is just getting them now."

Kröger's one good eye twitched desperately. A sigh escaped through his clenched teeth. "Get down there and tell him to get his arse in here before he dies!"

Manfret practically tore through his clothes, tripping on his legs.

Kröger sucked in the air, holding it in for a few moments before exhaling with exertion. "Someone throw brains from the heavens. Or stones. As long as they don't miss."

Tomas won a Reichsmark for his morning run. Pure excitement – a solitary, corroded coin.

"Look at THIS." Tomas held it out to Von and me. The eagle stood out remarkably nobly on the coin.

By then, Pieter-Pick-a-Pfenning had also spotted it. I saw his coat before I saw him. He was circling, just waiting for Tomas to slip up and drop it, but he kept hold.

Von swooped in before I even had a chance to react. He could spot money like a starving, stray dog can sniff out a half-chewed piece of steak. "Not today, you humpy old bastard," he said, throwing Peiter a middle finger. He walked away, wordless, holding my brother's prize.

Pieter stood with sad, empty hands. "Sorry." Tomas and I said it together, but our meanings were different.

The excitement almost stung as we rushed to the market, sprinted up to the tin-sweet shop, and stood before the red-haired shopkeeper, who regarded us with contempt. After some searching beneath the counter, he spoke.

"I'm waiting." His orange hair was swept to the side, and his black shirt practically choked his body. I stood, wondering what he was waiting for, and it came to me.

We were German citizens during world war two.

The framed photo of the Führer waved to us.

"*Heil Hitler*," Von led.

"*Heil Hitler*," Tomas followed.

I stared at the shopkeeper's orange hair. I had never seen hair quite like his before.

"*Heil Hitler*," he responded, straightening taller behind the counter. "And you?" He glared at me, and I promptly gave him my defiant left-handed "*Heil Hitler*". Von laughed, but the shop owner and Tomas were not impressed.

Tomas gave me a look that could only come from a judgmental sibling. Without words, he was able to convey his growing frustration. "Why can't he be normal?" I swallowed the bitter taste of sadness, but it lingered.

When the heil Hitlering finished, it didn't take Von long to dig the coin out from his pocket and slide it along the counter under the ash-coloured eyes of the shop keeper. "A hundred one-

Pfennig frogs, please." The look on his face said something like "See, you bastard. I have money now."

The shopkeeper smiled. His teeth elbowed each other for room in his mouth, and his unexpected kindness made us smile as well.

He bent down, did some searching, and finally found the box of Pfennig frogs. They were Von's favourite. We watched in awe as the cardboard man scooped the candy frogs with his shovel-like hands. He counted the first ten but afterward made no real attempt to count them at all. I was sure we had well over a hundred. He threw the sweets on the counter. "Here."

Von took them, grinning. "*Danke.*" He said it cheekily, ran out, dragging me with him, and we carried on our way. "Thank you."

Von walked slower than usual behind us; then, something flashed beneath the surface of his glowing expression. It was just a small change – a slight grin. But still, I hurried to investigate the sudden shift. Quiet Von meant trouble.

"*Was ist los mit dir?*"

"What's wrong with you?"

Von could hardly control his excitement as he pulled the coin out of his shorts pocket, waving it around like a flag. He was showing off again.

It took a few seconds for me to realise.

"Where the hell did you get that?" Tomas asked.

He hadn't caught on yet.

"He's a little thief," I explained, snatching the coin from Von and giving it to its rightful owner..

"The idiot didn't ask for the money," Von argued.

We laughed like it was the best thing to ever happen to us. If only this kind of humour could have spilled over into adulthood. But sadly, like many things, you have to leave it behind. For the better, apparently. The red-haired shop owner caught on later, and when Tomas came the next day to get more sweets, the man asked for payment. Tomas laughed a grin of compliance and handed the Reichsmark over.

The April air cut through our skin like razors as we sat on the kerb, just outside of our cabin. We shared the sweets with Manfret Wünderlich, who got kicked out of the daily game of trappers and Indians for being too slow. We decided to share them out equally. It was Tomas' idea, and Von Bacchman had what was left. Talk turned to Kröger. A stern man with a tragic past that no one knew about. He was sent to Inland as a bit of cruel punishment.

"Tragic. It was tragic," Von Bacchman said.

"What happened?"

He shrugged. "He doesn't want it getting out."

Ahead of us, a youth leader was giving Stefan and other younger boys cider and cigarettes. They performed rather well in training. To their left, a little boy sat with a bandaged-up arm and a bruised face. He was sobbing. I gave him a sweet.

I could only just see the setting sun, hiding behind the dips and dives of the hills, colouring the sky various shades of orange, each one more beautiful than the next. I tried to recreate that colour in my paintings, but my attempts were fruitless. I didn't have enough colours.

One day, I swore, I would paint the perfect sunset, but could never find the words. It didn't feel right. I realised I wasn't painting with the right emotion. I should have been painting with resentment, not adoration. Sunsets are an illusion, making us believe, foolishly, that we want the day to end quickly so we can have another.

"Tomas." I nudged him gently. His blond hair turned first, his eyes second, the warmth of the sunset still trapped behind his eyes.

And then I saw them.

Mother and Father.

Memories were fading and made anew. Our last name was gone.

Mother and father were gone.

And soon our childhood would be gone, too.

The last memory.

We were sitting by the fireplace in our tiny living room. Mother knitting mittens on her chair and Father reading his favourite book, hiding behind the pages and his fringe.

I would love for it to be more than just imaginary; I'd have loved to be back in the comfort of our small home and the lovely hearth. The warmth of that fireplace gave me even more comfort than the sunsets I learned to resent.

Oh, how I missed them.

Tomas was waiting.

"Do you see th—"

"The colours?" My brother's words collided with mine. "Yes, I see them, Josef."

It's not very often that you meet another boy who not only sees the colours but speaks them.

32

YOUTH AND PUNISHMENT

*YALE BLUE*YELLOW-GREEN*YELLOW ORANGE

I was in Inland for five summers. One pleasure was the smell of hearing the older boys wheeling down the projector on a trolley. Its sound meant that we would be watching a film. We slid down banisters and hoped to make it down alive.

We watched these films three times a week.

Somehow all of the buildings in Inland felt cold, even if you were previously warm. I could feel the room ever so slightly shaking from the children shouting. It smelt like the sort of smell that got bigger the more you smelt it and then burst open like a balloon. A boy behind kicked my chair, but I said nothing.

We sat slouched in our seats, some legs dangling, unable to touch the ground, as music was projected onto a large wall. Younger boys sat on the floor. A ten-minute sequence showed Hitler's emotional appearance before the enthralled assembly inside a sports stadium amid frequent shouts of "Heil!" In his speech, he told us, "Regardless of whatever we create and do, we shall pass away, but in you, Germany will live on." Hitler burned like the sun on that wall.

Our eyes were held open with sticks, and our mouths gaped

with grins. Some boys wiped away tears with their shirt sleeves. Derrick Pichler realised he could play with the shadows, making various animals with his hands, sound and all. He continued for a while until he was told to shut up, which he did and started paying attention.

Some things to note about Adolf Hitler (thirteen-year-old Josef addition): the strange man behind the monster.

He loved animals – except cats. He had a phobia of them. Believed to be a vegetarian, during the war years, Hitler was addicted to cocaine.

In a strikingly bizarre turn of events, Hitler became the first European leader to ban human zoos.

They made a shorter film about the Jews in the camps, and everything was shiny. People were playing soccer on the street, laughing, dancing, and drawing. We were told it was better this way. That they were happy. And every one of us fell for it.

We were Germany's highly impressionable.

And history would judge us severely.

I cannot recall much more about the strange students that sat around me or the musty, crowded room. But I do recall something vividly — the picture projected onto the wall and the room seemingly tightening around me.

A boy. A Jew in the camp. It felt like I was looking in a mirror, and the glass was breaking from the hammering of the cerulean stars.

Manfret tapped my shoulder. The same coloured stars. I jumped.

"Look, Josef! It's you." The children nearby had quiet laughs. "Sorry if I scared you."

A harsh hush came from somewhere at the back.

I closed my eyes and breathed in the colours and air until the slides changed, and the stars disappeared. I was squashed like laundry in a basket.

The concentration camps, as we know of them today, were just scary stories parents told their children to frighten them when they were naughty. We knew nothing of the atrocities and unfolding destruction that took place.

Flash forward to 1946.

An eighteen-year-old boy sat in an unlit room. Paint and guilt on his hands, the walls and Herr Müller. On the page, the colours tried to stretch out and give him the comfort he needed, but he did not want their pity. He was undeserving of it, he thought.

The ones who were deserving of the pity were the ones forced into bunkers one and two. Trucks carried the ones too infirm to walk. Everyone else marched, unaware that they were fated to die. Told instead they were going to a work camp. The hope-filled, hopeless humans got undressed and went for a shower. They never came back out.

There was no punishment harsh enough for us. The boy wanted them to torture him. Wanted them to pull him out of the house and throw him into the fire, colours and all. When retribution was to come, the innocent ones would suffer too, he realised. But we were all guilty. Directly or indirectly. Many things felt wrong, smelt wrong, tasted wrong, and still, we said nothing. We did nothing.

But then, what could we have done?

Between fighting the tears with his words, heavy breathing, and battling a hug, he managed to break through the tiny amount of air that remained. Enough to speak. A whisper through a crack.

"I should have done more."

Hitler deceived many.

I'm not interested in being a Nazi apologist – we all know Nazis are bad, but I'm not going to stand here and lie either. At one point, I thought we were the good guys. I realised later how naïve that was. You might be able to see the scattered tears I left behind on the page if you look really close.

Hitler found my weak spot through the arts. In 1909, he was just a starving artist walking the streets of Vienna for a second time. He sold paintings he had copied from postcards, and he was filled with burning denial when they told him he was unfit to be a painter.

Although I now recognise the resentment-filled words burning on every page, as a child, I felt for him. A feeling boy would. I could taste his pain on my tongue, and I swallowed it whole, letting it seep into my bones. They thought he was stupid like they thought I was stupid.

I'm not stupid.

This alone was reason enough for a thirteen-year-old boy to subordinate himself to him.

We all want to be more than what we are.

And we truly believed that we could change the world in that classroom. Many others, after us, thought the same thing. What they somehow always failed to see was that war was not the answer. War was the cause of the pain, not the cure for it. How do we keep getting this so wrong?

A collective identification of humanity is war.

1950-53 Korean War.

1961 Cuba.

1961-1973 Vietnam War.

1965 Dominican Republic.

1982 Lebanon.

1983 Grenada.

1989 Panama.

Somalia.

Haiti.

Let's not forget the 1994-95 Bosnian war. Kosovo.

And Iraq. Afghanistan. Libya. Sierra Leone. Chechnya. Ukraine. Syria.

All in a lifetime. All since the square-moustached man and his army of fanatical Germans. It all happened again, and you didn't have to be German.

When the films were over, and the tears dried up, we were glowing in Nazi pride, and it triggered a wave of excitement in our stomachs. We ate Teichmann's terrible food, and we joined in doing drills around the main building of Inland.

Even Penn and Derrick were friendly. They weren't so bad. I started separating the two in my mind. Unique personalities.

Younger boys jumped onto the backs of the older ones.

Pure joy filled their souls. They breathed innocence into their lungs. Naïve hearts, perhaps, but I liked the fire we were playing with.

If only this could be a picture painted more often in Inland.

We climbed the highest tree in Inland so I could have a better view of the playing children. I sketched them. Von and Tomas told jokes that no one would understand, and I watched the sun wrap around their faces.

If you're beginning to think that it's all a bit too happy. Too safe. Well, don't worry.

Life will throw us a curveball soon enough.

This story is not for the faint of heart.

I will give you a glimpse of what's to come in part two if you will be joining us.

I realise, of course, that I keep spoiling the story. How rude of me. But if you are reading this, I'm sure you have ideas about how it's all going to end. What's important is the how and why, the story, and the humans, not just what happens. So, don't try to rush through. Just enjoy the colours.

Come with me on a tour.

This tour is unlike any other.

A tour of pitiful humans.

We all love a good tragedy. Not to be a participant, of course, but to be a spectator.

Pop corn-filled hands at the ready. Here we go.

Right now, I'd like to take a minute to familiarise you with some safety precautions. First, I ask that you remain seated until we reach our destination. No flash photography is permitted. If you must be sick, do so in the paper bags provided. Or out of the window. Either one. But please, not over the leather. It's new.

Strap in.

To your left, there is a man hunched over in pain. A sadness in his bones that only gets worse with each grief-fuelled movement. His little boy lies beside him, a single bullet in his head. Killed by communists. What did the boy do? He was in the legally compulsory Hitler Youth.

To your right, there's a Jew with a golf ball head, his ribs protruding, and the lines on his face rendering him a scarecrow.

Please, sir, no flash photography.

And please, remember that there are better places to learn how to walk on a balance beam – not the site which symbolises the deportation of hundreds of thousands.

Sorry. It's probably not a shock to learn that offensive things offend me. Moving on.

Above, the men with pink triangles. Witness as they are forced to kiss each other and dance for the enjoyment of the prison guards. Nothing is funnier than faggots dancing.

Look straight ahead – down the tunnel of colours – melon-pinks, earthy-greens, soothing-yellows. It tastes like disappointment.

Disappointment for the human race.

Now that you're prepared for the road, our little story will resume; I will take you back to where we left off.

The tree.

I have no idea how we got back down. The only thing I recall was Von Bacchman's taunt directed at Tomas. "Jump, you fucking pussy."

That evening, the three of us, Von, Tomas and I, sat atop the grass overlooking the hills. Moving on from the sketch, I painted the sky green and the grass blue. I was inspired by the film. There's nothing like a bit of madness to inspire madness. I spat into the watercolours. No water. I splashed scarlet red on the page that was propped up on rocks, some of it missing the paper, landing on the grass and my hand. I almost always had brightly-coloured paint stains on my skin.

Red clouds went quite nicely with a green sky. Then the word again: faggot. You're a faggot, Josef. I painted over it.

Tomas lay on his stomach, legs kicked up on the grass, looking through a book. The grass was wet, but we still sat on it.

Each boy was given a performance booklet, detailing his progress in athletics and Nazi indoctrination throughout his years in Inland. Tomas sat with shame on his shoulders as he read his, and Von tried to point out what he should work on to make improvements. Rouvon taught my brother how to do pushups, helping his body lower to kiss the grass, before showing off by doing 'clapping-pushups', as he called them. It was truly impressive, omitting the small detail that he rushed through the twentieth push-up and face-planted the soil.

"Do some training to get a bit stronger, and you will do fine," he told Tomas. I could feel Von's corner-of-the-eye gaze. "Better than Josef, at least." I was unable to hear him over the sound of the colours. Certainly, I wish I could have listened to every unheard thought that came out of that boy's mouth, but the Josef of my childhood did not understand the complex emotions of an adult. The mid-life emotions that catch up with us when we least expect it. He shouldn't have to understand it. I go back to that moment on the hill many times, as well as others like it. I pause, I rewind, I laugh, and I cry.

After a few hours, Tomas still had his head stuck in the book, but now Von was beside me, staring at my painting with varying questions marked on his face – in each of his freckles.

"That makes no sense, Schneider."

"The world doesn't make any sense. Why should my paintings?"

A rush of contemplation. "Maybe you could paint the pictures and make them make sense." He wiped at his light-coloured, growing hair. It was a question, as well as a statement.

"Maybe by painting them, I am."

After many, now vexing statements from Von, it was decided as a team that we would steal something from Teichmann. We didn't know what, but something better than water. Something more theft-worthy.

Something like chocolate. Yes, it was to be the coveted *Fliegerschokolade* chocolate again.

Now understand this, I know it would have been easier to simply ask. We may have caught her in one of her bizarre moments of being nice. But where's the fun in that? Something about the stealing was thrilling. It fuelled something inside me. Perhaps it was just a case of childhood stupidity, but damn it, we made the plan and acted it out like our very lives depended on it. We were like the three musketeers that evening. We meant business.

When childhood dies, we come back as the corpses we call adults. I think that's why most of us hate children, even if we love them. They show us the state of our decay.

When in the hell did I become so boring? Afraid to take chances or break the rules? And afraid to live?

I think the exact moment I died was at age twenty-three when I received a letter penned from a trusted hand.

I died three times in total.

It was past curfew, and Tomas kept watch. He was terrible.

Von and I entered the cabin, not even considering that Teichmann might be there. Her green-eyed glare hunted us down in the dark. The rocking woman sat on her chair with a cat for company – a stray.

"*Scheisse.*"

She dragged us both by the ear to Oskar, who whipped us back into shape. We did drills around Inland, to which we grew accustomed. One-hundred push-ups and fifty sit-ups. I must say I enjoyed it.

We were punished with chores, too. Well, it indeed began as a punishment, but for me, it became something of a gift. I would help Teichmann in the kitchen after school every day.

God help me.

"Come." Oskar dragged me and the words roughly, with calloused hands. "Since you like to cause so much trouble, you can help out in the kitchen. No more fun."

"But…"

"Don't 'but' me, Josef. If Kröger got his hands on you…"

"I know." I stopped him because I knew how the lecture would end. "Yes, Oskar." I heiled my best heil yet.

"Yes Oskar," he jokingly repeated. Oskar was great imitator. A passionate one. "And don't do that. I want to talk to a human being, not a… a robot."

"Sorry, Oskar."

A few steps later. "I'm sorry. I didn't mean to raise my voice at you." He was concerned that I would report him to the Gestapo. You had to watch out for friends betraying you back then.

"Yes, Herr Frederick." Saying those words were a good way of staying out of trouble in Inland, as was doing as you were told, and from then on, after class, I would make my way down the Inland courtyard. At first, Teichmann gave me a solitary job, washing dishes outside, out of sight. She complained a lot about everything. "Make sure you use the soap and give them a good scrub." Her sentences practically glared at me. "Those bastards will come for me if they see so much as a speck of dirt on that plate."

"Okay."

"You hear me?"

"Yes. I heard you the first time."

"Don't give me lip."

I got a *Watsche* for that one.

She could complain about the entire school in that kitchen: the men, the women, the little pricks and the bigger ones, too. To the pots and pans, knives and forks. Even the walls covered their ears.

Von and Tomas also got a punishment, but theirs was different. Tomas was forced to tag along with Kröger in the village of Inland and help him shine shoes and listen to him complain about his back pain. Kröger took him under his wing. Again, what started as a punishment would soon become a surprise reward for Tomas. He told Kröger he had nothing to do with our plan that night. He always had trouble with the truth. I hated my little brother for it. The truth certainly hurts, but I deduced that it was the lies that hurt more.

Von became a youth leader at the age of fourteen. "*Danke, Mein Herr.*" It was the first time Von was given the title – I knew he liked it a lot. Undoubtedly, the only reason Von accepted the new role was down to vanity. In the age of the Reich, we were all a little vain.

Mirror. Mirror.

I like to think about it – beauty – in terms of its cultural connotations: who it includes, who it excludes, the prejudices involved, who is favoured, and who isn't?

Who is: blond-haired, blue-eyed, slim, small-nosed, robotic Aryans.

I was beginning to take extra care with my appearance. I was proud of who I was and how I looked. Despite this, I was plagued by the whole idea of attractiveness, and deep, deep down, I wanted to look like my peers. You likely understand self-obsession – you are human. However, it made me feel greasy. A selfish thought. A not-very-Josef colour.

All of the new responsibilities meant that our time together would have to be postponed and used wisely. It turned to the mornings, just before I had my shift with Teichmann. And although we were only being punished, I was not yet done with breaking the rules.

One of those rules was broken just days after the administration of our punishments.

I was washing the utensils from the evening meal, being hurried, and told to speak up as usual. "You'll never get on unless you speak up." Her hands moved fast with the knitting needles. "Like the Führer."

"I'm speaking as loud as I can!" My blood was loud that evening. "Fuck the Führer!"

I was waiting for the saucepan fist to chase me through the kitchen. It never did.

"The cheek of this one. You should never talk about the famous Hitler that way." The strange voice sounded like an eye roll.

"Sorry." I looked at my boots.

"My husband is in the SA; my eldest son is in the army, and my daughter is part of the NS women's organisation."

I knew Teichmann didn't have a daughter or a husband, but I played along. "Do you ever see each other?"

"Oh, yes. We meet up every year for the Nuremberg rally."

I laughed. She reached out and ruffled my hair.

Teichmann sat like a ghost in the rocking chair next to the sink. She was knitting. The sound of those threads stitching themselves together appealed to me greatly, and I hurried to finish washing the fork, for I had a question. At first, I was afraid, but after the question made itself at home in my mind, It was delivered as I stood.

"Can you teach me how to do that?"

I was met with tremendous resistance. "Knitting?" I could tell that word sat behind her ear and peeked over from time to time.

Faggot. Boys don't knit.

"I can't. You're left-handed."

"What does that have to do with anything?"

Faggot. Faggot.

The blackness in Teichmann's eyes melted and grabbed hold of my shirt. "Come, sit down. I will show you only once."

I shied towards the coat rack woman and watched with such concentration; I thought my eyes might bleed. The needles pressed and created an itch.

"Like this?" I said fifteen minutes later, when she gave me control.

"No. No. Like this."

We continued for two hours, and I realised that I had missed our daily hill meeting. I asked Teichmann if I could make a scarf for Tomas, Rouvon, and Oskar. She agreed.

I brought the needles back to the cabin and continued working on the scarfs. I was folded on the ground. The boys were also partaking in the weirdness that is boyhood. I liked a little spice in my humans. I hate ordinary people.

I was staring and laughing with my brown eyes, throwing in comments here and there, that almost always went ignored. I felt so much love, and I didn't even know it. If only I could be that naïve again.

Rouvon unexpectedly gifted me a compliment. "You have nice eyes, Josef." Von always stopped to listen to me, and being in my moment had enabled him actually to hear what I was saying. Others were more concerned with loud, great words, and since listening to me required patience and silence, they chose not to listen at all.

Embarrassment rendered me speechless, but it didn't take long to find the words. "I want blue eyes, like yours."

Von shook his head at the floor. "You shouldn't."

A shout across the room that echoed for miles. "Stefan, what's your favourite eye colour?

"Purple."

The whole room turned to stare at him.

It continued like this for months.

Until everything went wrong.

And right.

When I had finished the scarfs, I stitched a V, an O, and a T.

33

THE FIRST BLACK MOON

FRESH AIR

MOST AIR RAIDS TOOK PLACE AT NIGHT, AND THEY GAVE US boys jobs. We were called upon to go door-to-door and examine houses to see whether they would be suitable for housing air raid shelters. Anyone that protested would have a visit from the Gestapo, but I would never report them. I'd write their house down as unsuitable: *ungeeignet.*

The Schultz family happily offered up their basement, and soon there was a scattering of air raid shelters in Inland. More were needed. You could never have enough. We were stationed outside them, waiting for the bombs to arrive, but they never did. Our one order was this: do not surrender.

The bombs *would* come. They were being carried over Germany by the red, white and blue stripes and roundels, and soon they would be dropped on Inland. Stars would be every-where, dripping down on everyone's caved-in faces.

We were given helmets that didn't fit our heads. I remember when we first received them, Stefan would jump from the top of his bunk to the floor, hoping that some non-existent wind would carry him and his makeshift bedsheet parachute away. This only ended in bruises and disappointment.

"I told you that wouldn't work," Derrick said, composing his best attempt at a love letter to the girl in the village.

"Maybe if I try again."

Children make no sense.

Memories like these are the ones that torment me the most. They harass my memory. Boys as young as Stefan should never have to worry about air raids, and they certainly shouldn't be forced to witness them from the front seat and be told that surrendering would make them weak. Children turn to the adults to guide them in life, but in times of war, adults act like maniacs. So, what chances do the children have?

Oskar and I watched the first bombing of Inland from our usual smoking position; a night like the rest. The air felt different, though. I could taste it. Oskar's face screamed as he exhaled the smoke. I wish I could tell you what was happening inside his brain, but we are not given such powers. A sense of relief washed over him as his eyes found my sketchbook. I sketched a moon, deciding that this moon should be black. I rubbed black and white paint between my fingers until the shade was just right. It made the pencil lines' charcoal just right. I smiled. My art wasn't great, it was good. I was no child prodigy. What I did possess, however, was the ability to try. I figured that if you do what you know, then you shall learn the truth you need to know.

Oskar leaned over. "Is that painting mine?"

I didn't want to lie. "No. I'm sorry. Yours is coming."

"So are the '50s, Josef!"

I transferred blue paint to the paper. "I've been busy."

"Oh yes, being a boy is very time consuming indeed." When he wasn't looking, I gently touched his arm with the brush and watched as it dripped down and onto the grass.

I was sucked into his grin.

The word flash: "Faggot."

Oskar: "What's wrong?"

Me: "Nothing."

Then the first bomb, a hideous red glare, transforming the spring night and its full moon. "*Um gottes Willen, was zum Teufel war das?*" Oskar said. "For God's sake, what the hell was that?" I had never seen a face so pale The trees were scattered in the dark.

"Oskar?"

"Fuck." He said. The sirens arrived a few seconds later. They were late. Oskar's hair stood up, and his blue eyes grew grey.

Heavy breathing. "Oskar?"

His thoughts were chaotic as he bent over to catch his breath. "How could Inland be a target?"

The simple answer: we were not.

In the sky, men spoke with voices we wouldn't understand. To the horizon, I could see a trail of light and smoke, presumably where one of their own went down. I pointed and tried to get the attention of Oskar, but he was not there. His mind was with the men in the plane. He tried not to show the severity of his fear.

When I looked up, I saw them. The British men.

The sky was the colour of madness.

The need to weep filled them and the plane shook ever so slightly.

But there was no time for such things.

Black, reds and yellows were coming. We were coming. They had to get away.

The men had a decision to make.

Humans always arrive too early or too late, particularly when in distress. They miscalculate or over calculate. Who could blame them? Wives and children were awaiting their safe return. They had Tomases and Oskars of their own to hug.

They dumped their bomb loads on what they presumed were empty fields, enabling them to gain height and speed to make good their escape from the Luftwaffe *Nachtgeschwader* pilots hunting them in the moonlight.

They could not see my friends asleep in their beds or the midnight smoking lessons.

Inland was merely a town caught in the crossfire. We were victims of a nightly air raid gone wrong.

The men in the sky collectively exhaled when their plane was successfully in the clear, but their relief was short-lived. The guilt would chase them for decades.

We heard the muffled bombs announcing their arrival in the background. "What do we do?" I asked, knowing full well what we had to do, but fear was speaking. Stefan Rosenberger clutched to Oskar's side and tried not to cry. In the end, I noticed that we had all been clinging to Oskar, and embracing each other just for a moment. Our duty to the Reich tapped us on the shoulder. It forced us to our feet. We glued our helmets to our heads, and we ran to the wreckage, the people, and the colours.

The flawless sky was a gigantic sheet of fire and a flash came before my eyes. The bombs were delivered to the village, and I should note that they were never directed at the school. But it would take us twelve minutes to run to the civilians, so that left twelve minutes that the victims at the scene had been gasping, gagging, and dying.

Groans and screams came from perhaps ten boys in front, and when I got closer, I could see the origin. A cow lay dead at the side of the road. I knew Tomas would stare and cry for several minutes. I looked for him, but he could not be seen. The war was gaining on Inland, and I was being dragged along for the ride. I brought along hope in my coat – a pocketful. My grandmother's paintbrush among them.

By ten that night, most people had already made it to the shelters, but a few stragglers limped through the streets, and we directed them. One woman had two young boys – one in her arms and one by the hand. "Young man, what about our homes? I cannot afford to be homeless for the summer with these two." I did not turn to her. Instead, I talked to the rubble and my grip on her hand tightened. "You won't be."

My reassurance charmed and shocked her.

"How would you know that?"

"If we have to rebuild your house brick by brick, then we shall do it."

As we parted and I delivered her to the shelter, she kissed my hand and whispered, "*Bleibe sicher.*" The cherry tobacco flicked my ear. "Stay safe."

A roll call was taken before making our way back to the cabins, and when I reunited with my brother and Von, no words were needed because our faces spoke. We were afraid. Later, Tomas managed to speak. "Josef, Manfret thought he was shot." I laughed about it, thinking it was fiction, but a few days later, I learned it was the truth.

The boys were stumbling, crying, and guiding. Steadying giant buckets on their heads and hoping a bomb wouldn't come. One tried befriending them a few minutes later. It was still too far away to cause them harm, but it disturbed the brickwork on the ground and one came for Manfret. A thump on the helmet. "I've been shot!" The boy fell to the floor. Tomas grabbed him by his armpits and dragged him to safety. "You're not shot."

"I'm sorry," Manfret spoke through his fringe of brown, curly hair. We wiped snot from his nose. "I'm useless."

"You're not useless."

Panic was pushed aside in some boy's minds. When they knew they were out of peril, they teased Manfret. I would have chosen some choice words and torn a new one for them, but

Tomas was not such a boy. Possibly an easily led boy, but not a rude one. The words were ignored, but Manfret held his knife, blood and honour overflowing in his veins and busting open.

Arms were linked, and we went home.

Yes, home. For Inland became our home. With the friends that became family. We were a strange-looking family.

That night, I reimagined my painting as I listened to the silence of the cabin. It was eerie. My friend's conversations usually served as great background music for painting. When I painted the red sky, I thought about poking them or shaking them to make them speak. I didn't. Von Bacchman peeked his head down to my bunk but didn't say a word.

I searched for him. "Von?"

"*Ja?*"

It felt like I had melted in the bed and sunk into myself. The starry outline of colours. This time, more vibrant.

"Nothing."

34

THE DANGEROUS KISS

*DARK LAVA*DARK SEA GREEN*DARK RASPBERRY

A LOT OF THINGS WERE DANGEROUS IN 1943 GERMANY.
Being in love with a boy was one such thing.

Keyword: boy.

Many changes occurred that year, and for me, they can be summed up like this.

Flak gun crews were manned solely by the boys, and when Kröger called upon him, Tomas had no trouble volunteering.

Kröger, I thought. He did this. It wasn't him at all. He just pointed at the sky, and Tomas wanted to fly.

I was fifteen. My painting ability had improved greatly, but I had a long way to go before I could be great.

My voice was deeper. And I realised the best things in life make you sweaty and breathe loud. Socks went missing on a regular basis.

Tomas sightings were getting more and more scarce as he preferred to spend his time with Kröger, training. There was an altercation that involved Tomas, two boulder-like boys, and a bridge.

Tomas said it went something like this.

The art of the fight.

"Where's your fag brother?"

"My brother is not a faggot."

A push into a fence. Tomas almost broke it. His face also began to break.

Do not cue your favourite fight song, for this stopped there.

Tomas was filled with thoughts of burning his fag brother, his weakness and kindness. The thing that scared him the most was the relief that he felt in his stomach. How could he feel this way? How could he? He didn't want to, but he was helpless to it. He had escape to collect his thoughts. In other words, the boy ran away.

Ran, as usual, to Kröger. He was breathing heavily. A quick explanation and Kröger was not pleased. "You don't ever run away from a fight, Tomas. You make me want to throw up. I will make a man out of you if I have to break you in two."

Kröger woke his body. Tomas screamed at him. He pulled his knife out.

"What the hell are you going to do with that?"

Tomas said nothing. He didn't know either. The weapon was dropped. "Don't take it out on me because you fucked up your own life." Kröger readily accepted the words.

He made a man out of him, alright. Little boys do what little boys do. They try to fit in, then lose themselves by the age of fifteen and have to start all over again. Crossing out what isn't them and keeping what was. The problem, however, is that the two overlap. They meet in the middle. Most people, I decided, are in the middle. It takes an act of true madness to push people to the truth of themselves. Like saying, "I want to be a painter." Or "I want to be Robin Hood." I want to be more than what small minds will allow.

Rouvon accompanied me most nights to the painting hill. Just the two of us.

The sky had pink stripes, but there was an absence of clouds. For once, it was calm and so too was my mind. Gentle colours gathered but didn't protest. For once, my mere existence was not difficult.

Von wanted to be my muse, and I let him. I liked watching his brows furrow, his lips tense up. "Relax your face," I told him. "So serious," he replied. I laughed. I was caught in an emotional experience. I have always been captivated by the white magic that is art.

Von was intrigued. "I think art is fascinating."

"I thought you didn't like it." I held out my thumb to get his proportions correct.

"I find it fascinating when you talk about it."

"Shut up." His choice of words was strong and meant something. "I don't even know what to say to you sometimes."

A laugh."With eyes that smile like that, you don't need to speak."

Again, with my famous counterattack. "Shut up, Bacchman."

Dinner time was in progress. Food was getting more scarce by the minute, so Teichmann did her best. Hitler promised us many things that he could not deliver.

We had a gulp of air for breakfast. A feast had to be prepared for us growing boys. Tonight it was potatoes. It was my job to deliver the food to the tables, and as Teichmann handed the plated tray to me, her body deflated for a single moment and sank into the tiles. "It's pathetic, I realise. But it's the best I can do."

I took the trays and her *Weltschmerz* smile." It's not pathetic." The smile was returned, and I shot a capricious joke at her lips. "Maybe we can ask some rich kids' Papas for money."

Weltschmerz – literally, world pain. Melancholy.

Teichmann laughed. "They won't admit it, Josef, but they are struggling, too." Everyone in '43 was struggling, even the ones who weren't. "And you have paint on her hands again. Wash them."

That evening, boys shoved the potatoes into their mashed mouths as they had various discussions in boyish breaths.

"Frau Teichmann is a ride." Conversations always turned sexplicit in those days.

Swear words fell on the table.

Derrick called out to me from across the canteen and tried to launch a spoonful of potatoes.

"Josef, have you done it yet?"

Again with the "IT". Apparently, Derrick Pichler had, in fact, done IT with the neighbouring Inland girl. However, I still hadn't decided quite what IT was.

Allegedly, hormones made Teichmann look somewhat desirable. I couldn't see it. I made a sound that was too quiet for them to hear and rolled my eyes.

The usual five from my cabin sat together. The hall was warm with teenage bodies, but Manfret still sat with his jumper on, nervously looking out.

"Don't you ever sweat?" Penn asked.

"No." Wünderlich painfully scratched as his acne-covered face. His Hitler Youth knife was impaled in the table, sitting upright and yelling in his face.

It was true that he didn't sweat. He was in the larva stage. The pained shedding of the child's body. This is what boarding school was for. To store children away during years like this, so they didn't have to suffer the embarrassment of their parents watching.

Tomas sat with older boys who were tutoring him on fist-fighting and swearing. I watched as my little brother poured his unique, individual light into a mould. His muscle rivalled that of Oskar, but you wouldn't know it under his baggy clothing. It didn't happen overnight, of course. His love for the Reich and his willingness to learn pushed him forward. The boy achieved things that others only dreamed of. He could shake the stars that boy – he could do anything if he only dared. A smile tapped him on the shoulder when I'd walk past, and he'd roll his eyes because he knew it was me.

Too many conversations were happening at once, and there was a constant flow of flavours dripping onto my tongue, one taste after another, varying in flavour and intensity and overlapping in my mouth.

The sun rose through the window, bathing the trees in vibrant hues. Finding Oskar outlined in the blue was the best part of dinner for me. This day, it looked like he too was in transition. His happiness was like a cloudless spring day and he didn't notice the weather or colours at all. He was showing the other youth leaders a letter, and they patted him on the back. After some staring, he caught me and waved.

The unmistakable colour of burnt orange came into view in front of me, like a circle of light. I knew that it was the voice of Penn Pichler.

"He's a right nancy boy, that Josef."

The others protested. It was mostly Stefan, just reaching over the rest of them. His purple colour and taste of fatty bacon fell on my tongue.

"He can't be, Penn. He kicked your ass. He's very brave."

I understood that in their minds, I could not be gay and brave. For them, the two were incompatible.

What's it like being a faggot? The words that were getting louder chased me.

They cut a nerve in Von Bacchman that night. He rubbed his eyes. Recently, it was like his smile was not fully complete until he received a letter from home, or when he read on the hill. I watched him play with his potatoes, cutting them with his frozen eyes. He tried to numb it, but after some more cutting, he could listen no longer.

He was on his feet. I saw more legs than boy.

"Where are you going?" I called out to him, rather loud, in fact. Brown uniforms turned to make sure that the voice was coming from me.

By then, I was also on my feet, walking towards the brown oak door.

Tomas pulled at my coat when I walked past his table. "Dohman will be giving his speech soon, Josef."

"I'll be back soon."

That was a lie.

I found Von Bacchman sitting in our usual spot, and I could just hear the beginning of the speech. Von's legs were dangling over the crest of the hill.

"*Sieg Heil!*"

When he turned, it was with such a great relief that he asked me to come sit with him.

We sat in silence and listened to the speech. The longer Dohman spoke, the more the crowd was whipped into a frenzy of enthusiasm. They interrupted his words with impassioned shouts of "Heil!" I imagined Dohman clenching his fists hard.

"Are you alright?"

He nodded and offered me a cigarette.

"I don't have a light."

A match-box rattle.

Von shielded the cigarette from the wind, and it lit. It was wonderful. Life's most mundane things become beautiful when they are done by a loving hand.

"… more disciplined, fit, and trim."

Von laughed.

"…do not want to see class and social differences anymore… must not allow it to happen."

"What's wrong? Why are you laughing?"

"Nothing."

Von's skin smelt like the light – it tasted like the stars.

"We want our people to love and honour... you must declare... in your youngest years."

"Have you ever felt love before, Schneider?" Von asked.

"*Nein*. Never really thought about it."

That was a lie. I thought about it often.

"Have you?"

A cloud of smoke sat between us.

"...demand for you, boys and girls."

"I think so." He laughed at the grass.

"What's it like?"

"I don't know. Hard to say."

"Alright. What does it feel like then?"

Dohman silenced to gather his notes.

"...Everyone's heart runs over with joy when they see you."

"Hard to say. Many things are difficult to explain, Josef." When he smiled this time, the freckles and dimples danced upon his face.

"Alright."

"I know it cannot be any other way."

"I can try to show you... if you want."

I took a nervous drag of the cigarette. Again, I tasted the damn cherry tobacco. "Alright."

I'm not sure how to tell you this, but I want you to imagine Von's freckles moving towards me, his sleepy eyes closing, his lips puckering, and all the other sounds of the world going silent – the rustling of our clothes, the chaos from inside, the birds' song – all silent. I'm not sure if the speech ended or if I stopped listening. I gripped the damp grass as Von's highly educated fifteen-year-old lips met mine.

A balance of soft wetness and firm strength. Everything felt intense and bright.

Somewhere, in the middle of it all, it occurred to me that he'd been leaning towards me throughout the speech, so when his moment came, he'd be in the perfect proximity to make his move.

What a dickhead. I wanted to punch his shoulder.

And then, somewhere below it all, my heart reacting. An unexpected touch. I broke the kiss. I sat stiffly on the grass with my arms across my knees.

"Did I hurt you?" Von sounded genuinely concerned.

"No." I stared at the painted landscape. "That wasn't bad."

But *we* were bad.

I knew it. Faggot.

Rouvon stood as though he didn't feel it, offering his hand to me.

"Do we have to go right now?" I crossed my legs.

"You're a sweet boy, Josef." Grinning again, at the grass, he sat down, and I thumped his shoulder hard.

I lay in bed awake that night. It was just past two o'clock. I played with the colours in the darkness, and I couldn't shift one recurring thought from my head: that word. Faggot.

I gulped the air.

I counted with the colours.

1 – poppy red.

2 – cigarette ash grey.

3 – green, like the rolling hills.

4 – the powdery, perfectly harmless, blue-grey.

When I got to five, I turned to Oskar.

"Oskar?"

He didn't hear me. He was asleep and clutching the photo of his beloved with the letter, but I didn't have the selflessness to allow him to sleep. I was a boy with questions. Questions that needed answers.

Louder.

"Oskar? Are you awake?"

A slight twitch.

"Josef." Oskar rubbed at his swollen eyes in their tiredness and made a noise from his throat. "*Ja*, what do you want?"

"I'm sorry, Oskar," I sat up in my bed and leaned toward him. There was a long breath and a scratchy voice. "What's..." Quieter. "What's a faggot?"

Oskar stared at the ceiling. "Why do you want to know that?"

In my head, I circled the moments in my life. I heard that word but declined to tell Oskar. "Don't know. Just want to know."

Oskar's face turned towards the incoming daylight, and as he did so, I could see the light shining onto his blond whiskers – he needed a shave. He couldn't seem to get the sleep off his eyes.

He gave a slight laugh. "It's just two fag..."

Oskar stopped there when he looked at me and saw the concern on my face. "It's just a word that people call homosexuals. A stupid word."

"But what does it mean?"

"It doesn't matter what it means. People's words... people's words are exactly just that, Josef. Words." His whispering continued.

"Am I a faggot?"

He sat up now. The colours were foreboding. Dark or light. It didn't matter. The room spoke to Oskar.

I was dragged outside.

Oskar lit two cigarettes before he spoke again. It was the last of his tobacco. He looked at it like he may never see another cigarette again. "Don't ever let anybody call you something that you don't want to be called. People don't get to decide who you are. Only you can do that."

We sat with backs against the door. There was a five-minute silence, and I realised Oskar had decided to close his eyes, to get the left over sleep he so desperately needed. He didn't get it.

"Everyone always says words here like they are bad, but I don't think…" I couldn't find the right words to finish.

Oskar considered it. He dodged the sentence, leaning forward.

"I have some advice for you, little man."

I waited.

"Talk less, smile more. Don't let them know what you're thinking." He winked at me Oskar-like, and I threw a confused smile at him.

"Does the Führer decide?" I finally asked. A fifteen-year-old boy is many things but stupid.

"Fuck the Führer." I could see the regret spiralling yellow as he spoke.

I nodded. "I think a lot of boys would if they could."

A deep sigh mixed with a laugh.

"You're killing me, Josef." I had warmed Oskar's heart like the sun.

The wind changed direction on Oskar's face that night. I studied the stars, and as usual, Oskar was perched on them. But I could not comprehend the lines on his face. Oskar and his many night faces. More questions. "What's wrong?"

He was waiting for me to ask that question all night. He explained by reading the letter. The letter was already taken from his pocket.

"My dear Oskar,
This is a joyous letter to write. I hope as joyous for you to read,
despite the intuitive shock I know you will feel."

He skipped a few parts because he knew I didn't have the maturity to weigh the words. I stared at the moon as he read, my head on his shoulder.

"I didn't want to tell you until I was sure, and now I am. You are going to be a father."

"So, this is why I can't afford tobacco." Oskar's excitement peeked around the corner. I was happy. There may have been tears, but I can't recall.

Oskar found my eyes. "I know now is not the best time... but..." The sky poured over him, and so too did my heart. Oskar Frederick, as a father, was something that simply made sense to me. I was pulling at him to keep reading, which he did.

"You may have guessed from the way I was floating in mid-air for these past few weeks. I am happy. You have made me very happy."

Oskar felt my head get heavy on his shoulder. It finally struck him that I had fallen asleep when he heard my breathing deepen. Nothing can ever be perfect, but things can be just right. This moment was the just right kind, and I know that half of my fifteen-year-old heart belonged to only one man. The other belonged to a boy.

Oskar was a good man.

I had not yet made up my mind about the popular dichotomy of good and bad. But here is what I knew back then.

Good: Oskar; Tomas; and, I think, the Führer.

Bad: me; the Jews.

You cannot be gay and good.

35

THE PRINCE AND THE THIEF

*PALATINATE BLUE*PALE CARMINE*PALE SPRING BUD

THE CLOUDS WERE ONLY JUST COMING BACK TO LIFE AFTER the air-raids. They happened nightly. The people of Inland were still trying to comprehend how a simple little town could be a target, even by accident, but we were preparing for the worst anyway. Signs were removed from the road, provoking many passer-by conversations.

"They can't come for us if they can't find us."

Newspapers filled the sky. Berlin was the talk of Munich.

The front page read like this: "Hundreds of German women saved their Jewish husbands from death camps."

Frustrated by the lack of information, they stood in the freezing temperatures. They chanted, "Give us our husbands back."

When lethal force was threatened, some of them were afraid, but most of the frost-bitten women stayed and faced them. "They can't kill all of us."

Goebbels ordered the release of the men and children at Rosenstrasse two days later.

They were loud, and they listened. I can only think of the words stapled in the sky.

The sky was fake and painted like it had been put there to fool us. Many vans passed by the farm when we worked. More than usual. I pitchforked hay into the *Schubkarre*, and I do not know the English word. Perhaps you can find out. Learning a little German is not such a bad thing.

The van could be spotted from the bottom of the hill, and I followed it until it was out of sight.

It was just after seven and three friends sat on the grass, still in our training uniforms. Earlier in the day, we ran. The sunset chased us. Tomas beat us all, much to the dismay of Penn Pichler, who sat with arched eyebrows for the rest of the day.

Tomas knew he was improving, and he knew he was one of the best in Inland. He would always let himself feel the pride while making sure to remain humble and help others rather than patronising them.

We ran along those winding, country roads and air filled our lungs. On the cliffs, it felt like we are standing on the shoulders of a giant.

Stefan fell back from the pack. Herr Kröger ran alongside him, but not for encouragement. "I'm surprised at you, Pup. The rest of them only have two legs, but you have four." The boy was not amused and kicked him as hard as he could in *die Unaussprechlichen*. One's unmentionables.

Stefan certainly made a statement, but Kröger didn't appreciate the boy's fearlessness, and the screams sounded like they were part of nature. Stefan reappeared later with a black cutout for an eye. Kröger stood like a pillar behind him. "If you're not careful, you'll get the other one to match."

Von was given another book, and we all sat laced together, my head on Von's lap, Tomas leaning on his shoulder. He cleared this throat and began. He was an English language genius.

"Once there was a prince who lived far from here. He was handsome and sincere." His words moved in a way that made us laugh – such funny, little words.

"Soon, his pp…arents wanted him to find a wife, but in his heart, he could find no freedom."

I was drawing a memory. If only there was a way to tell that you were living the good old days while you were still living them.

"Until one day, a person entered. A stable boy with hair of embers." I did not understand the story, but I did understand Von's smile. Soon, he was wiping at a tear that had the nerve to fall from his eye – an uninvited guest.

A stray memory tear. It was yellow. I recognised that tear. It was recognition, realisation; surprise, also, but that was small and sprinkled on top like crumbs. It was a 'pieces coming together' tear. His mother knew about her son.

"Von?"

"I'm alright."

"*Lies weiter,*" came from Tomas. "Keep reading."

In my hand, it felt like I held a blue, paper bird and written on it were the words I wanted to tell him.

In the evening, we played with Oskar. He had other work, of course, but Oskar thought it was acceptable to occasionally drop everything and play with little kids, for they don't keep. They spoil in the sun if they are left too long.

We grew up slower in Inland as well as faster.

Tonight, it was football by the farm in Inland. He had a ball. We reluctantly shared our road with the cars. I didn't usually play, but that evening I did.

"Can I play?"

The boys looked to the ball, to Manfret, to Penn, to Derrick, to Oskar, and back to the ball again. The musky air stood in patches above me. The unconscious air blew.

Penn answered in the negative.

Oskar laughed, balancing the ball on his foot. "Be nice, Penn."

"It's not your ball," I explained to Penn, but he would take no part in it. His eyebrows twitched violently. Derrick scratched at his rash. Von gripped his shirt sleeves. "Oh, no. Here we go again. *Der Teufel wird los sein.*" He had to duck to avoid Penn's fist, and before he could catch him. "The shit is going to hit the fan."

"I wasn't talking to you, Rouvon." A mumble. "Someday, I'm going to kill you." We laughed, but Penn was the type of boy who kept to his word, and it would not be long before this promise was met.

I know huffing isn't a good thing. At least, that's what Mother always told Tomas and me, but there are just times in a boy's life where huffing is absolutely necessary.

Within a few minutes, Oskar's clemency entered the scene. "All good?"

"*Ja*, Oskar. All good."

And then the van. The rumours appeared on the hills, spilling over the side. I wiped my mouth. "Oskar, what's in those trucks? There's an awful lot of them." Oskar kept opening and closing his tobacco box, and each time it got emptier. I felt sorry for him. He would love nothing more than a smoke. "Oskar? The people say all kinds of things."

"Don't let them scare you, Josef."

Nothing would give me more pleasure.

"Nothing there but pigs and sheep."

36

WHITE FEATHERS AND RADIO WAVES

*WILD BLUE YONDER*WILLPOWER ORANGE*WHITE SMOKE

IN THE MORNING, THERE WAS A FIGHT. IT WAS WHAT homophobia tasted like.

Good violent fun.

I was at the farm when I heard the cheering children.

What I saw: Von Bacchman on the ground + Penn Pichler on top + a knife.

Stop it! I tried to push through the bodies, but they held me back.

"No," said Derrick. "He'll kill you."

Von could not move, and he could not breathe. Penn held his arms with his knees.

The knife was pulled.

"No!"

The knife found Von's crotch. Penn didn't have the guts to go further and risk expulsion.

"Oh, you do have a penis in there after all. Act like it!"

When it ended, Penn let him go, and they both stood. Von staggered towards me.

The sheer force of the grief caused him to collapse around me.

The rest watched. Penn crumbled.

"I'm sorry, Von. I didn't mean to."

Two crumbling bits of boys on the pavement.

I was not sure what Von had done to stir him like that, but I didn't matter.

When it had ended, apologies were made, and I sat with Von under a blanket of the setting evening.

"Are you okay?" Stars were in my eyes.

"I am now."

"Don't be stupid."

"I'm not."

There was nothing like a good shower conversation between boys when the adults were gone. It was a play. We spoke like men in those showers: politics, girls, and nakedness.

There was a stage, an audience, and applause. Colours and questions were making our minds just murky enough, and boys who were previously silent were beginning to speak.

Here's a snippet of ours.

Me: "What about the Jews?"

Derrick: "They're in the camps. It seems mean, but they are happy there."

Penn: "You have seen the films."

Me: "You don't believe that, do you?"

Derrick: "Sure, I do. It's what we're taught. You don't suppose the adults have been lying to us, do you?"

Manfret: "I've heard rumours."

Penn: "Grow up! You know enough not to listen to rumours."

Manfret: "The adults could be wrong."

Penn: "They could be wrong, and that mountain could fall down tonight and kill us all. You're supposing."

Rouvon: "My mama says it too, Penn. She is a teacher. You can't argue with a teacher."

Penn: "I think it's possible that some teachers are just plain stupid."

Rouvon: "Take that back, you dickhead."

Penn: "Josef is trying to confuse everyone. Get us all mixed up."

Me: "I'm not. It was just a quick thought. I won't speak again if that's how yo—"

Ensemble: "No, don't be silly, Josef."

The Q&A turned to the next day's work. Neither boy wanted to go to the Schultz's house, and for some peace and quiet, I decided that I would go.

"I'll go to the Schultz's." It silenced the arguments from my peers for a few seconds.

I made my way there alone that day. I was afraid, so I walked afraid. My grandmother's paintbrush followed along like a good friend. It spurred me on to knock the door. I knocked – an answer.

"Come in," a grey face said from the door. Tomas' friend was sniffing at my boots. Frau Schultz was searching for her purse.

"Where did I put the damn thing?"

In the hallway, I was shocked by the quantity and quality of the paintings. Gerda Wegener, Ernst Ludwig Kirchner, Otto Dix. The collection of colours continued for miles. I had always looked at such works with a respectful kind of envy. I eyed the portrait of Herr Schultz.

"Does my husband scare you, too?" came a crouched-over voice.

"No. Not one person can scare me."

I spotted the Führer.

Frau Schultz smiled.

"Don't let him scare you. He's a bully, and you know what they say about bullies? They are weakest in the group."

"He doesn't scare me either." I pushed away the fear in my mind. "Did you know that the Führer gives to the poor?"

She thought. "Does he?"

I nodded. I tried to fill the room with conversation – colour all of the gaps.

"My brother likes your dog."

"Does he?" She searched her catalog of faces and colours. "Tomas?"

I nodded. "Yes."

"Sweet boy." She looked down. "His name is Ralph. You can tell him for me."

Frau Schultz was like me. "Quiet" could be a word to sum her up: quiet voice, quiet posture, quiet hair, quiet mind.

The room had a quietness of air around it until the loud-speaker man entered. In the flesh. He stepped out of the painting and into the room, leaving behind some colours on the wall. His face was still not dried and dripped mustard amber. He looked at my uniform. "What's he doing here?" The wire-like moustache spoke with him.

Frau Schultz stepped between us. "He is our guest, and we must treat him as such."

"He is one of them."

"He's is just a boy."

This back and forth continued for some time. I was some-what afraid. You do not want to be in the middle of a husband and wife quarrel.

In the end, the money was delivered. My hand was shaking slightly, and I dropped it. We watched it float down to the carpet, and I bent just before Ralph got it. In doing so, I didn't notice my paintbrush had fallen. Frau Schultz picked it up. She inspected it, but her eyes could not be drawn away from the F.

"Is this yours?" Her eyes had a blue F reflection.

"It was my Oma's. She died, so she gave it to me."

"I see." The green carpet eyed us.

Herr and Frau Shultz were helpers. The paintbrush whispered the fact into my ear. Did they also have secret meetings with their merry men? The loudspeaker voice suddenly made sense. I said nothing. We all knew, but we would be silent.

The walls had ears, and he who argues disappears.

Heil Germany indeed.

The realisation fell back into Frau Schultz's face. "Are you an artist?"

"Kind of." I was being humble again. "At school, I get in trouble for drawing in the margins."

"I see. Could you paint me something?"

I stepped back with shock. "Nothing like those. I'm not – " I pointed at the wall. "I'm not Gerda Wegener.

"Thank God. We already have her."

An awkward giggle. "And I don't have the materials."

"What do you need?"

"Ahh… more paint and brushes."

"Then take the money and get it."

I considered it. "I couldn't." I held the money. "They'd find out, and I'd be dead."

"What money?" She winked. "If they ask, I will tell them I gave you no money. Hitler has ruined our economy."

More awkwardness invited itself into the room. Who asked you?

She walked me to the door, and at first, I didn't say anything. I couldn't. Then came a voice. Realising how rude I was being, I wasted no time. I hurriedly turned. Clumsy words. "Have a good thank you." I was too embarrassed to correct myself.

"Yes," She tried to tuck the smile back into her lips. "You too."

I ran home to explain to Von, but there would be no Von waiting for me. Instead, I got a boy holding a box of feathers, and he was sobbing. Not Von at all.

It was unknown where the feathers came from, but it was suspected to be from the farmer. They symbolised cowardice. A big, giant box of white goose feathers delivered outside of the cabin and addressed to Von. It took a long time for Oskar to calm him down.

"You're not a coward, Von." Stefan said. "You're the bravest one of us all."

Everyone agreed.

Von only saw me. He got lost somewhere in the mud puddles of my eyes, and I stole glances for as long as I dared.

One question: *"Kannst du mich umarmen, Josef?"* He was a lonely boy with a desperate heart. "Can you hug me, Josef?"

"Of course." A few moments later, I whispered, "Haoowever." That brought a little Von Bacchman colour back to his face.

Making someone laugh after they have just been crying is one of the most beautifully painful things to ever exist.

Von Bacchman didn't fear his attraction to the same sex at all, and the other boys just accepted it for what it was. Of course, he didn't say it aloud or make it obvious to the adults in Inland. I didn't want to think of what might have happened to him if he was discovered. The children couldn't care less.

Adults are always complicating things. There are so many unneeded rules about living.

"Well, the Bible says right here..."

Yes, we know. We get it.

I think it best to decide on what is right by what's right and not what is written. What was so wrong with our friendship? Are you going to sit there and tell me that this beautiful and limitless thing that we all love has rules? And a proper way to do it?

We should not be forced to live by the rules other people put in place for us.

In the night, I speculated about Von Bacchman and the way he touched me, wondering how many other people he touched like that. I was lying with my hormones and colours, hoping that Tomas was alright. But my thoughts suddenly turned to the boys in the showers. Von, if I was honest with myself.

And then, he was in my bed.

Verdammter Mist! Damn it!

An outstretched hand with a radio underarm. The colours around. "Come."

He took me to an unused cabin. He had stolen candles and a sweet smile.

At first, it was the Führer. "Fuck."

He turned it down. Too loud.

As hostilities broke between Germany and the Allies, listening to enemy radio stations was punishable by a sentence served in a concentration camp. All radios came with a chilling warning attached to the tuning knob, "Listening to foreign broadcasts is a crime." A Führer order punishable by prison. Later, the Gestapo was ordered to execute anyone who was found doing so. But many Germans took the risk. How could music ever be wrong?

A song played. We listened. I felt, tasted, saw, and smelled.

"This is illegal, but it's fine." Von came in.

"You're going to get us shot, Bacchman."

Juvenile laughter.

I stretched out my hand, feeling the music.

"I remember memories that I had through songs," Von explained.

I had never spoken of the thing I had inside of my mind to anyone. Only because there weren't the words to describe it, but I wanted to share it with him. "I do through smells and colours."

Von was a little surprised by this but, it being a product from my mouth, he smiled. "Well, what smell do you smell right now? And what colour?"

"It smells like..." I smiled. "It smells like books, and the colour is... like a rose."

Von's smile was understandingly sweet – but much more than that, too. It was one of those rare smiles that you come across maybe once or twice in your whole life.

"Then I will remember that forever. This moment we spent together smelt like books and was coloured like a rose."

"And the song that got us shot." Our laughs sounded like chaos.

I can't even remember what we talked about. I just listened to the sound of his voice and his laugh and listened to the sound of him listening to me.

Then it came. The countdown to goodbye. It started.

"I'm going to take the test to join the SS."

"What?" I can't say that I was completely shocked. It was just a shock that I refused to prepare for in full: the worst kind of shock.

"They need people, and I think they are interested in me."

"I don't think you should bother."

"Why not?"

"Because I'd miss you."

"Josef, Mama and Papa need me to be brave. I have to be for them."

"What about you? You said you wanted to travel. It was your dream."

"My dream is to help my family. Keep them safe."

His hand found mine; fingers walking across the floor boards and twisted. He explored my painted hands with a curious heart.

"Josef, just because my dreams look a little different than yours, it doesn't make them less important."

I wore broken eyes. We had so much to say and no ways to say it. Von found a way through.

"You know, I was thinking. When we win the war, we could move out to the countryside together. You could sell some of your paintings for extra money."

"What about Tomas?"

"Tomas is a big boy!"

"And you think it would be a good idea? With how people think around here?"

"Then we will move somewhere no one knows us. As far as anyone's concerned, we are good friends." He brought his knees to his chest. "I can't wait to get out of here, Josef. Munich feels so lonely."

"You're crazy," I said.

"Forget it then!"

"No. Don't be like that. I like it, but you're crazy."

Perhaps this was Von's way of telling me, "*Ich hab' dich lieb.*"

After I hit puberty, it was like a switch inside me flipped, and instead of becoming a testosterone-driven sex monster like most of my peers, I failed to find anyone I wanted in my life in that way.

Von could have told me he loved me a billion times, and it wouldn't have meant a thing to me. I didn't want to know if he could love me. I needed to know that he could understand me.

Rouvon sat the test at a sweaty, wooden desk. The pencil was getting hotter from the kerosene lamp. When the test was finished and sent away, Von's childhood was no more. The colours were around him. All together, the sound was beautiful, harmonising with the light from the lamp.

Two days later, a reply came. The concrete was so tall around him, and the rain fell in place. It was well known to the German ground. Tones trembled down his spine. He could not open it himself. He let Kröger break the news to him.

"Did they say no?"

"A no would have been disappointing, but we would get over it. It's a maybe."

For me, a maybe was better than a yes.

Maybe meant no.

A SMALL RALLY STORY

The word homosexual made its appearance regularly.

The crowd seemed to grow thicker around me. We all looked the same but our minds were different. I wanted to leap inside one of them and see for myself.

Did those boys know who they were? Did they like it? Even if I didn't always like who I was, I always knew who I was. The boys in Inland, Tomas included, liked who they were but didn't know who they were. They only liked who they were told to be by various adults. Now, tell me which one is worse?

To know who you are, even if you don't like yourself?

Or to not know who you are and love yourself?

"*Heil Hitler.*"

Their arms shot into the sky. "*Heil Hitler.*"

After the second 'heil', it was decided. I did not want to be some background noise. When the next 'heil' came. I wanted to give them my best defiant left-handed heil Hitler. A heil Hitler to beat them all, but I had the sense not to. This was real life, and in real life, people die – even children – if they speak out publicly against the moustached man. Instead, I felt. I tore through the curtains of boys. They spoke backward.

I couldn't understand what it all meant, and the more I learned, the less I understood.

Heil Hitler.

Reltir lieH.

I closed my eyes, heard, and held my head on the steps.

37

THE LADDER TO THE STARS

*LASER LEMON*LA SALLE GREEN

OSKAR HAD NOT COME HOME THAT NIGHT. I FOUND OUT later that he had been stumbling around Inland, eventually reaching the deserted train station, where he cursed at the Bahnhof air. "They should have been safe!" he cried over and over.

His once kind, blue eyes, like the winter jumper, had gone grey, and he had plans. We heard him drunk outside, banging on the cabin doors and sweating.

"If he tries anything, I'll kill the bastard," Penn said.

Our fear grew in larger patches on the wall, but we resisted the urge for hysteria.

Bravery even tried to stand up in Derrick, but its knees quivered as he made his way to the door, to see the damage.

Penn ordered him back to bed.

"*Nein! Bett*, Derrick." His voice was calm and firm.

A few minutes later, Oskar entered the room. I could only just make out his shape at the door. Whisky and guilt filled the air. He did not speak but made his way past the door and under my covers. Everything was quiet. We were noiseless and opaque. We did not breathe.

He took me. I did not struggle. I did not scream. "What's wrong, Oskar?"

The night's blackness hung suspended over my head. I wanted to stay hidden in the shadows, but the yellow light that lit Inland's courtyard dragged me out by the collar.

Naïvety shone out of me.

It was Oskar that spoke. "Punch me."

There was a fleeting moment of pity that washed over his wrinkled face.

"No."

He tried again. "Punch me, you little faggot."

That did it. Tears and blood. I punched him, and he fell. It wasn't enough. He wanted more.

And more—

And more—

I pounded him harder, even though my hands were breaking.

"Harder! If I were your Papa, how would you hit me? Hit me!"

"I'm not angry at my Papa."

My fist bled.

I stopped.

"Then where is this anger coming from?"

With my loudest voice. "You're making me angry!"

Oskar's legs didn't work. Neither did his hands. Or his fingers.

He collapsed on my shoulder.

And then he told me.

There was an air raid at Mittenwald, but the sirens were late. By the time the farm was alerted, it was too late. They had to run. Elsbeth fell. When Oskar's brother stood her up, they made their way to the shelter, and she noticed she was bleeding.

Howling misery.

Sweat, sick, and tears were soaked into him, and I felt the kind of sadness that starts as a lump in your throat and stretches its way out of your skin. The night was as black as the whisky he was drinking.

I thought about Oskar – not his sadness, but my own. He made me hit him. He frightened me. No one so good could do that, I thought. He fell off his perch. The stars were crumbling.

We went to Teichmann's shed, where we stayed until Oskar had sobered up and could take the abuse from Kröger. "You think your wife and family would want you to act like this? Get a hold of yourself and grow up, Oskar." It was just the right amount of harshness that could only come from him.

He was right, of course. When we are grieving the loss of someone we love, we become selfish. I could tell that Oskar didn't feel comfortable with the grief – that it was unjustified. "I'm not going to be a Papa anymore, Josef."

If he'd have known, Oskar would never have left Elsi alone under those stars.

"I'm so sorry, little man." Oskar laughed and covered his mouth like he was mad at himself for forgetting his sadness. "God, I'd love a damn cigarette."

His tobacco heart was breaking.

That night I realised how fundamentally wrong the idea of good and evil was. Sometimes the people we think are good aren't as good as we would have hoped. I had to stop decorating people.

It was a quarter past two, Oskar climbed a ladder to the stars, and they fell and knelt around him.

Oskar was the man who taught me that you don't have to have fame, fortune, or status to be remembered. You can be good. As a child, kindness was the only thing I required from anyone, but it was hard to come by. I will always remember Oskar and his kind blue eyes, like melting wax.

"I could give myself a fair bit of advice if I was your age, Josef?"

"What would you say?"

"I'd say smoke less and fuck more. A whole lot more."

38

BLOOD AND HONOUR

HONOUR

In the last few years of the war, class was a disaster. I felt sorry for Simons. Von was kicked back on his chair, talking to another student when the ruler came down on his desk. "Fuck!" It startled the boy.

The rain outside sounded like a mandolin.

"Language, Rouvon!" Simons spoke from behind the ruler.

"Oh, I'm fucking sorry, Frau." The boy didn't realise he had said it. The class broke loose with laughter.

He wasn't off the hook yet. She instructed Von to the board to draw a graph. He set the chalk between his fingers, rubbed the powder on his shorts, and began. The line was coiled from the boy's jocular hand.

Derrick's neatness called out from his seat.

"Wow, Von. That line is as straight as Manfret."

"Shut your whore face," Von replied from the board.

"The language of it!"

Poor Frau Simons.

I was halfway finished with the Schultz painting. It was one of my best works yet. Every colour of the painting conspired to bring your attention to the dog who stood between the grey pillars. His expression was strangely human-like and bore the expression of one comfortable with being superior.

Snow danced in the light, my face shone timidity.

The river was ice.

Von was bored. He wanted to play soccer, and in trying to convince me, his face came dangerously close.

"How do you know when it's done?" He looked at my painting.

"At some point, I stop."

A playful smile crept on his face. He picked up my painting and did a pretend swing.

"Play or the painting gets it."

My heart jumped out of my chest. "No! That's mine. Give it back. It belongs to me." My eyes were swollen.

"I'm sorry." The painting was gently returned as quickly as he stole it.

"I didn't want you to cry. I'm sorry, Josef."

I was held. I asked Von to sit with me, close on the ground, in the snow. This was the closest thing I would ever get to asking him to stay. I explained everything to him.

A difficult conversation.

Me: "I don't know. I have always been quite content with my paintings." I shrugged skeptically. "For the most part."

Von listened, hand on mine. My thoughts bohemian.

Me: "Everyone always talks about how grand is to be expected to lose but to try anyway." The sky was the only thing holding me up. Even as my hands pressed against Von's, they trembled.

"Everything is raw. They tell you that you must do it for all the other hopeless hearts out there, and to prove the cynics wrong, but it is soul-crushing, Rouvon. I feel invisible – unimportant."

Von: "But do you love to paint?"

The world was a blur of colours that melted to greys. Just the sound of my heart in my head.

Me: "Yes."

Von: "There you go." A slight nod. "You are very clever. I think you are a good artist."

Me: "I want to be great, not good." I continued. "Good gets you a slap on the back. I want to be great and be brilliant forever."

Von, his freckles looking down: "And you will be, Josef, but on your own merits. You will not be great like the greats, but you can be great on your own terms. Your kind of great *is* brilliant."

My eyes welled up as he spoke. These tears were words.

At one point, I laughed. I learned to thank my tears and accept them as a gift rather than a watery reflection of weakness. It might sound like an oddity to you, but if tears are the only thing that can stop me from becoming a puppet string man, someone afraid to feel all of life's feelings, then crying is the smartest thing a boy can do.

BLOOD

A call came from the grass. "Manfret cut his arm off!" Boys were running.

Naturally, I had to investigate. Crowds do what crowds do and gathered to the scene of the suffering.

Manfret did not cut his arm off, but he came close. He'd been cutting deeper and deeper over the years. We had no idea. He was in ten shades of agony on the grass. The colours inside hated him. The scars were discovered when he was made to remove his shirt.

He locked everyone out of the cabin that evening, but I found an opening in the window and snuck in. The boy was spread out on the mattress.

"It's snowing outside," I said. "You should come out. Everyone is playing." For me, the very fact of snow has always been amazement.

Manfret looked up. The soft lines of his childhood becoming chiseled. "I'm a mess, and now I can never go home. They hate me, and I'm ugly."

He said it with the ugliest cry I have ever seen. It was the cry that was ugly, not him.

Second World War Germany was a very superficial place, and it seeped into the bones of the children.

"No, you're not." I told him.

"You don't know what it's like."

"I do." I crouched beside his bed and gave him a glimpse into my mind. "Josef needs to speak up. Josef is too quiet... Josef is too... Fuck that."

He smiled.

"I can't be anything other than what I am."

"You'll go mad trying to please everyone, Manfret."

Hands on soft cotton sheets, an image came to view. I wondered what the world would be like if every strange, little child got to be what was in their hearts.

The prodigy son the Wünderlich's wanted never arrived. Missed his train. One got shot in Russia. The other was a disgrace.

Herr and Frau Wünderlich didn't receive a single thing but money. Rich people got richer. During my time in Inland, I learned that people feel safe and important with money. They would do anything for it, even give up their children.

"I wrote to them, and I told them I was unhappy." He had a cigarette in one hand, a toy car in the other.

"They sent me this toy and told me they were sorry." His anger and resentment lit up the cabin walls.

"They weren't sorry. If anyone told me I was privileged, I would laugh."

Manfret spent his entire life trying to forget those childhood moments.

The door spoke in various tongues.

"Manfret, are you in there?"

A choir from outside. Snowy, gloved hands.

"Let us in. I can't feel my toes."

Even the light laughed at them.

"Do we even need toes?"

I offered my hand. "We should let them in."

When we did, Manfret was piled upon, and we played games for the rest of the night. The simple things of life became love.

We always think we aren't good enough.

We are always hiding.

Always hoping that no one would see, for fear of everyone knowing.

What if everyone knew?

What if they all came to witness?

Would they like what they saw?

Or would they hate it, too?

Too many people hate themselves. What if for once we said something good about ourselves. Not about everyone else, but ourselves.

Go on, try it. Say something nice about yourself.

I'm waiting.

Repeat after me.

I am _____

39

THE MUSIC MAN

MISERABLE-TOBACCO MADNESS

IN THE DAYS THAT FOLLOWED THE AIR RAIDS, PEOPLE WERE still being dug out five days later – wedged between the fallen beams. The youth leaders would tell us to look away when another body was brought out. I did, but a lot didn't. The British knew that Nazis took residence in Munich, so our unlucky town was caught in the in-between – collateral damage.

I watched as Tomas was given a hand-written advertisement for a street sale. People sold belongings that weren't destroyed in order to keep afloat.

I sat in the rubble, observing a thin lamppost through a shimmering twilight puddle. I thought it was so beautiful that I had to show Von how it looked, and I made the most beautiful, tender, little drawing of it. I was the only boy I knew who would bring a sketchpad and a pencil to a bomb site, but I did it so cheerfully, you couldn't help but be charmed.

Tomas was not. He and Kröger sat eating sandwiches on a pillar. It was wet from the rain and soaked their trousers.

"Do you think there's anything wrong with my brother?" I felt Tomas' eyes on me. I heard it all, but I didn't look up.

Flecks of bread came out with Kröger's words. "What do you want? A numbered list?"

In the peaceful Europe we live in today, it is hard for those who did not experience the war to understand it and the bitter emotions to which it gave rise.

That night, our sky belonged to the bombs. It froze the stars. Inland was a small town, and bombing for the third time held no strategic benefits. I realise that they didn't mean to bomb Inland, that it was a big mistake. But it made no difference. More bombs.

Oskar searched for his calming tobacco, but there was none left. My compassion looked up at him. He tapped my hat.

Some Germans were left traumatised by the war. Children's first memories are hiding behind screaming mothers. They remember the muggy bomb shelters and the burning smell of human remains. Through all the helping, guiding, and digging, I would see the littered scraps of humans. An old searchlight man stood still in a crowd, tears in his eyes and he couldn't breathe. I knew the person he was searching for was one of the humans that would never come back. He moved with the others until he was out of view.

The stars sang from behind the smoke, managing to let a little light slip in front. The people, too, sang German lullabies, and the sounds were so delicate that it gently brushed the hair on my skin. Manfret Wünderlich was singing along.

I imagined Hitler above the town, like a musician on the hill, orchestrating the musicians, the instruments moving to his will. Below, notes formed on the pavement, and bombs dropped from the sky.

Herr Hitler happened to be in Munich that air-raid night, and before the alarm had been sounded, he was already safely tucked away in a private shelter complete with rugs on the floors, baths, and, reportedly, even a movie projection-room.

While hundreds and hundreds of people were buried under rubble, struggling horribly to breathe, he might well have been watching a movie.

In the wake of it all, he announced that everything would be built better than before. We heard him in the radio wave colours when we were cleaning up the next day.

The whistle came. It meant safety and the end. German civilians would come out in turns – some running back home expeditiously to inspect the damage to their homes. The purple ones came slower, linking arms. It was those people that would thank us, with a hand-patting smile. "You did a great job, young man."

Lines were formed.

Another roll call.

Screamed orders.

Von found and stood with me. Children were fidgeting and playing with the rubble.

"We're missing a few." Pages of names and upside-down words were flipped. "Schneider for one."

Von's arm tightened on mine. "Josef, we have to stay here."

"Tomas!"

I rounded the corner, and I saw it.

A boy was lying amongst the rubble, patting a dog. The moulting dog could care less, but he did let Tomas pick him up.

That fucking dog.

Some quick words were needed.

"I'm sorry. I couldn't leave him, Josef."

"I don't want to lose you to a damn dog! He doesn't even care."

He does care, Josef. He cares very much."

But I knew. As I hugged him, I realised. Tomas could not have left that dog there, the same way the purples in the bomb shelter couldn't help but sing.

The words "galavanting" and "don't" were used a lot by Kröger in the delivery of my brother's thirteen *Watschen*.

Von and I carried the radio to the unused cabin that night. Well, it was actually morning. The orange peeked its head through the window we sat under. The starlight and air was sucked into the room.

I asked Rouvon to teach me some English words.

I almost broke my tongue off. I mispronounced words, lost words, and pronounced letters the English don't use. I said the B at the end of lamb. The word "girl" was the funniest to me. In German, the word is *Das Mädchen*, which sounds cute and innocent, like a girl. But this English word was harsh.

"Guurrll."

Von and I laughed.

The word laugh made me want to cry.

The song that morning was delightful. An English one. It let me run away with my thoughts and bathe my senses in the water of prismatic lines. Rainbow stars.

"You know how to dance, Schneider?"

I grunted a reply. "Not well."

"Who cares? Dance with me."

"No."

As absurd as it sounds, we danced that night. Really slowly. Two boys in the dark. No-one around to watch, but the colours; The purples and blues, and the taste of young love. Von's eyes danced too, and his freckles. His adolescent face was changing, as was his body.

The rhythmless rhythm of my thoughts and body. The chaotic flapping of my arms. Clumsy movements with the red and white pentagon music. I scratched my neck. I looked ridiculous dancing. I looked ridiculous not dancing, so I figured it was best to dance with Von that night.

I wish you could have seen it. I wish you could have been there.

"What. The. Hell. Is. *That?*"

"Dancing."

"It looks like you're having a stroke."

I couldn't stop laughing. "Can you turn the music up?"

"Yes. If you want me to be shot."

"You won't be shot."

We danced on the edge of the page.

But someone was watching, and it took me some time to learn who it was. He thought we were insane, but the boy could not hear the music.

Years later, he would say, "Thank you for telling me."

"Of course I told you, Tomas."

40

KALEIDOSCOPE WAVES

*KOMBU GREEN*KEPPEL

DECEMBER 25.

Christmas Day, 1943.

Von's letter was still lost in the post. No one had heard anything in months.

Tomas trained until his legs fell off. He was tired, but he did not stop. He put his body through so much agony that he suddenly forgot about the dreams of his youth. Somewhere along the way of growing, loving, and fighting, he lost his self-worth.

"Do you want a smoke, Tomas?"

Clouds were big and fluffy.

I painted a cobalt line so delicately that I thought it would crumble to dust had I touched it. The kicking words inside my head screamed. I emptied on that page.

Tomas coughed from breathing in too much air. "That's bad for you, Josef."

"But it feels good."

"Try fucking."

"Tomas!" Disorganised shock.

"Alright, Josef. Don't lose your blob."

The phrase stopped my sentence in its tracks. A raised-eyebrow smile. "Blob?"

He scrunched his nose and gave me his best smile.

He laughed, as did I.

"You've lost your blob, Tomas."

I painted, and Tomas did drills with Rouvon. He ran a vertical desire; a horizontal dream. His sweat lit up his face just right, his paperback-skin colour melting, the blending freckles.

A kaleidoscope beam from Von. I waved back.

The days leading up to Christmas 1943 fell thick and heavy with snow. I made what felt like hundreds of sketches of concepts for paintings, but did very little actual painting. When I did put brush to paper, I could only think of one thing: Von. On Christmas Eve, I made a decision about Von. A final decision.

At sixteen, Von had reached a level of maturity I had not, and he and this new-found maturity had plans for me. I'm sure you're aware of the thoughts that circle the minds of teenagers on a daily basis, but fifteen-year-old Josef didn't fit into that category.

Von had now grown out of his uniform, and the tailor had measured him for another a few days prior. He stood in the cabin, trying it on. Under the door, there was a small circle of light, and the sunset was undressing itself. I watched. Earlier, just before dusk, he had told me that he had a present for me for Christmas.

"Where is it?"

A tired grin. "Just forget it then."

But I knew. I had seen him like this before. Risky eyes and sticky fingers. The breath of love was all around, and I could smell it.

"You don't really have a present, do you?"

"*Nein.*"

I guessed. "What is it then?"

Von laughed, head to the ground, cheeks turning pink. He continued. "Do you think I have any money, Schneider?" The snow was still falling. A few more layers, and we'd be shin-deep.

Von and I walked around the cabins; he still wouldn't discuss this secret present. I had only felt like his one other time.

The dangerous kiss.

Puberty corrupted what was left of my innocence.

I walked faster to keep up with the long strides of Von, and he was telling me to hurry up.

The other boys and youth leaders were in the hall, stuffing their faces with pudding, not even noticing our absence.

We reached our destination – an empty cabin.

The windows and walls of the cabin wore a thick layer of grime and mud. They hadn't been cleaned since the day and hour that I arrived.

The cabin was empty, as were many of them in '43. Germany was losing the war, and we were desperate. Desperate humans don't always make the best choices, and Hitler's choice was anything but. They sent boys to the battlefront, knowing full well that it was a suicide mission. Some of those Inland cabins would remain empty forever.

Von entered. His first instinct was to hit the light switch, but the electricity had been cut off.

"Are there candles?" He whispered while holding the door open for me. "Are you coming or not?"

Nervousness made me feel nauseous, almost like I had two hearts frantically beating inside my chest instead of one. I still don't know why, but I could not enter that cabin.

"*Nein.* I'll wait outside." I did not want to know his reasoning for being there.

Von looked down in a single, sorrow-filled motion and

rubbed his nose."But Josef." He tried again. "Josef." I shook my head. He would have to think of another gift for me."Wait for me then."

"If you're not long, I'll wait for you forever."

I watched the door shut with both relief and disappointment. I waited with the *Weihnachten* air. On the edge of the grass, there was ice like broken glass.

The light was disappearing fast. All of Inland was beginning to close up for Christmas, and then, after a nervous silence, Von reappeared and held out the light of a candle for me to see. The light was like a pillar, shining onto his refined uniform. It lit up his battered shoes and dirty shirt beneath his jumper.

"Merry Christmas, Josef." He said. His eyes were red. In his dirty hands, he held three Pfennig frogs. I could tell it was a cover-gift, but I did not dare speak.

I continued my examination. I moved around him and shrugged.

"That's it?" I grinned.

"That's it? You know what I had to do for that bastard to give me these?"

"You probably talked shit to him. Got him charmed. The one thing that lets you down is your face."

Von placed the candle on the snow and came towards me in mock anger. That same nervousness as before gripped me. When I watched him fall and slip on the ice, it was with a sense of both relief and disappointment.

On the ground, Von laughed.

Then he closed his eyes, clenching them hard.

I rushed over, almost slipped myself. I crouched over him. I was laughing now, too. I helped him to his feet.

I helped him tie the red scarf I knitted for him. Once, twice, and on the third time, I tied it properly, overlapping it twice to be certain it would stay. Our faces were close. I could taste the sweetness of his breath when he laughed that big-bellowing laugh of his, the sound of it making me laugh, perhaps awkwardly, but laughing nonetheless. It was the kind of evening that should never have been possible for me, but this evening it was: Von, the scarf, the laugh – all of it.

"Are you alight, Von? Rouvon?"

"I'm going to the SS," He said sideways. "They sent me my acceptance letter three days ago."

At first, I couldn't say anything. If I spoke, I knew I would cry. Or worse, I'd ask him to stay.

"*Frohe Weihnachten, Arschloch.*" I replied. I straightened his scarf and smiled. "Merry Christmas, arsehole."

Cleaning the paintbrush was the most satisfying thing I did that day. The warm running water against my palms as I moved it back and forth until all the paint rinsed from the brush.

A conversation about Herr Amling.

"See that man Amling and his friend are up to no good."

"How can you be sure?"

"Do you see the way he walks? He couldn't be anything more."

I knelt over the sink and wept. The potato skins and paint-brushes were looking up at me. Teichmann noticed a few seconds later.

The kitchen hands were dismissed. They lit up a cigarette, leaving behind its fumes like an old friend. The woman in black placed her hand on my shoulder, and her wrinkles looked at me. "What's wrong, Josef?"

"I can't tell you." The door was closed tight.

This time, Teichmann made sure my eyes were on hers. "Josef, I have been the mother of a teenager long enough. You can tell me."

I rubbed snot on my jumper, breath getting stuck in my throat. "It – it's Von." I was unable to finish, but I didn't have to.

"Oh." Teichmann had her suspicions before, but now she knew for certain. "Oh, dear. Dear. Dear. Dear." Her hand still on my back. Pat. Pat. Pat. Her gentle pats soothed me more than she knew.

"Sometimes, life sneaks up on you, doesn't it? You don't realise how you feel until the goodbye is staring you in the face."

"I'm a mess. I don't know what's wrong with me."

"We're all a mess, Josef."

For the first time ever, Teichmann's face was grave. She lay dormant with the kitchen. Highly unusual. If it continued any longer, it would have begun to frighten me, but to my relief, it lasted only a few seconds. "My boy is going, too."

She planted her hands on the sink, and it overflowed with colours. Her apron was sinking around her waist.

"Being a parent is hard. You do your best to raise them. Then they turn eighteen, and you think they will be alright. But they still need help."

Then the moment came.

Von Bacchman had his ticket, his suitcase, his leaving smile. I pulled at his hand. I would not let go.

"I'm not going to sit here and tell you that I'm happy you're leaving, because I'm not. Not even close. But I want you to be happy, and I hope that you will be. I hope I will be." I said it all without breathing.

He was the greatest story I ever painted.

"You make me happy," Von wiped at his nose.

"Do I?"

"Yes."

The sun burned my eyes. We stood on the main courtyard, balancing on a razor blade. I would not look at him. Could he feel it, too? The silence of my loud, oh so loud heart?

"Look at me," Von said. "Why are you crying?"

"Because you're leaving and I'm going to miss you." My breath tightened on the last few words.

"You don't have to cry about it," he grimaced, no movement on the cheeks." Come here, you hopeless, boy."

He kissed my forehead. I can still taste it.

And he left. I never saw Von Bacchman again.

I thought that I would always have the memories, but as I got older, I realised that time would take those from me too. Time was always taking things that didn't belong to it.

41

SYNESTHESIA

*STARRY PURPLE *SMOKEY TOPAZ*SPANISH VIRIDIAN

A TYPICAL TEICHMANN CONVERSATION.

"You know your man?"

"Who?"

"Your man that comes here."

"What man?"

Later: "I knew you had to have a little fag in you to paint like that."

"That has nothing to do with it. You know the greats weren't gay, Teichmann."

"That's what they say."

Teichmann's stories gave me inspiration. I would breathe them all in and exhale them in the form of paint on the paper.

A man with three twigs for hair delivered the milk. He was deaf and mute, but Teichmann wasn't falling for it. This day, eggs were also needed.

"*Eier auch.*" The man's scalp was moulting. "Eggs too." I knew this man had stories to tell. Tuscan sun hexagons danced on his lips like a curious child, but his listless eyes simply stared.

I jumped in. "Teichmann, he's deaf. He can't hear you."

"I'll give him deaf."

In the end, Teichmann had to jump around, mimicking a chicken to get her eggs. I covered my mouth and held in the blurred-green laugh.

The kitchen was big, but somehow Teichmann's voice was large enough to dominate it. She owned that kitchen. There was nothing but the sound of chopping food and pots. I often thought of Von Bacchman and hoped that he'd be safe. He started writing me letters that would die out by '45, but the first one was a treasure.

"Dear Josef,
    They tried to make me get a tattoo, but I refused. It looked ridiculous, and I simply wouldn't."

In the end, Von's refusal would be the only thing to save his life.

He had just the right amount of recklessness. Sometimes I rolled my eyes out loud.

Colours were in my head – too many.

"What's wrong?"

She walked like a broom.

"Well, sometimes, I see colours."

She looked down her nose. "Everyone sees colours, Josef." The statement sounded like a question.

I gave a short, nervous laugh.

"But not everyone sees the colours. I see them everywhere, and even in my memories."

A candle was lit. I could almost see it. "You might have synesthesia."

In hindsight, it was pretty presumptuous of her to think that a little boy growing up in the '40s would know what synesthesia was. "What's that?"

"I don't know exactly. But you have it."

Potatoes were thrown at me. They were everywhere. "Take them out to the hall."

I was given instructions.

"And use two hands."

"God help you if I find you've dropped them."

In the evening, I watched the bunk above me, seeing the colours of Von Bacchman flying overhead just for a second and disappearing into the dark. I often had the urge to go to Tomas' cabin to play dominoes. A distraction, if nothing more. But not even my brother could protect my teenage heart from missing Von Bacchman. I held his letters to my chest, the words leaving a permanent scar. He was the only boy whose absence made the world feel ordinary.

I never stopped missing that boy.

Derrick Pichler had a date, and he was preparing.

A collision of colours, tastes and smells.

Oskar: "You're not going to go with those whiskers, are you?"

Derrick touched his face and realised he had grown some hair. He hadn't noticed, nor had he shaved before.

"I don't have a razor."

Oskar produced a small box, and inside it held a blade. He gave him instructions on his bed.

Stefan: "Derrick, make sure to tell me all about the night when you come back. But don't go falling in love and leaving us like Von."

Manfret: "Shut up. Josef is here."

Me: "I'm alright"

Penn: "Derrick, if you get a stiffy, just tuck 'er into those shorts."

The room laughed.

Oskar: "When did you get so wise, Penn?"

Penn: "I've always been wise, Oskar. You were just too busy seeing what was wrong with me."

A few minutes later, Oskar noticed Derrick wasn't making any progress with shaving.

Oskar: "Derrick, you're not trying to tickle those hairs."

Derrick: "I don't want to cut myself."

Oskar: "You won't. It's a blade. Here, let me do it!"

The bed screamed, and I'm sure the windows had cracked open.

Derrick: "Oskar cut my face off!"

Oskar: "I did not cut your face off."

Stefan Rosenberger gave his best, side-splitting laugh.

Hysteria in the cabin.

Herr and Frau Schultz hung my painting in their hallway. Beside the loudspeaker man and the red flower wallpaper. I stood in that hallway forever, just trying to get one more look at it, memorising the colours and the words.

"You notice things in art that other's don't. Those eyes are special."

I couldn't disagree.

The sun dripped on my face.

"People want beauty, Josef. People need it. They don't realise how needed art is. Please keep painting, my boy." I couldn't disagree for I knew that she was right. Both times.

It was my last visit to the Schultzes. Two days later, they'd be hanging in Munich city centre, paper stuck to their lips. I heard it in the newspaper sky. You do not have secret meetings with your merry men.

I should have cried, but I didn't. Instead, in a moment of hopelessness, I would later regret, I sold some of my paint for two cigarettes.

Watching Oskar take a drag out of a much-needed cigarette moderately numbed the pain, but only just.

"Josef, what did you do?" the top bunk called out. It had the breath of bacon, the crispy taste caressing my tongue. "You didn't sell your paint, did you? It's your only talent."

"I don't care much for things I can't take with me when I die. I want purpose and moments." My friend's eyes were big and alive."Things I can remember." Besides, I didn't have it before the Schultzes gifted it to me." My dignity was stood upon.

At night, I sat on the cabin steps. The rain was staining the grass, and I let some tears loose on my face.

In the distance, a boy walked ten feet off the ground. I tried to cover my face as he approached, but it could not be hidden.

"Josef, what's wrong? Have your nightmares come back?" It was Derrick. That laugh could come only from him.

I was feeling mightily sorry for and laughing at myself.

"*Nein*. It's my paint. I'm pathetic, I know. You can laugh. It's funny."

"We will get you more. I promise." He lowered himself to the grass and looked at the stars.

I was angry at myself for the selfishness.

I am a greedy person; I want many things in life. I want to be selfish and unselfish, have many friends as well as solitude. The simple pleasures in life have never completely satisfied me. The same green hills could never content me forever. No matter how much my body craved the pleasure of a little life, my mind was unwilling to let me. No, I am not like my friends, but I do envy their laughter.

42

THE MEN WITH THE PINK TRIANGLES

MAJORELLE BLUE

FROM BEHIND THE CLOUDS, I COULD TASTE AND SMELL THE van nearing.

"Look over yonder." Penn pointed. "They are taking them to the camps."

"Who?" I hammered in a nail.

"The fags. Or the Jews. I don't know."

I disagreed. "Nothing in there but pigs and sheep."

He scoffed. "There are pigs in there, alright."

Derrick slapped his brother. "Don't say that."

"Alright. Jesus. I'm sorry."

I had no idea where the convoy had travelled from, but the drivers were past students on Inland. It was perhaps four miles from the school, and many more to the Dachau concentration camp.

Shovels landed loudly on the concrete, and many of the boys were laughing and telling jokes, but not a word was heard from the van.

I could smell sadness from whatever or whoever was in it.

Recollections tell me that many voices were going through Penn and Derrick's minds, too.

Why them and not me?

Thank God it isn't me.

I thought about Von and the pink armband men.

If there were people in there, and the rumours were true, Von couldn't be in there, could he?

Did they find out?

I could not quarrel with the curiosity any longer. Fear was not able to hold me down. We had stopped for refreshments when the noise arrived in full. The farmer's wife and daughter had brought us water.

"The Jews." She announced. "The poor souls."

Everyone turned towards the sound of stumbling feet and the muddled colour of my voice. I ran to meet the van. Straight up the hill would get me there quicker.

"Josef, where are you going?"

Voices just missed me. I was travelling too fast. But their sentences followed me up the grass and onto the road. I waited as the vehicle approached.

There was an added emphasis in the shouting from the soldiers driving. If there were people, I thought they were most likely Jews, homosexuals, and other criminals. Perhaps some of them were mothers who wouldn't let them take their children. Some might have the name Schultz.

I imagined the men. Not people, but swastikas with faces and voices. Colours dribbled from their lips.

I didn't want to, but I watched.

When the men saw me standing like a shadow on the road, they stopped. They weren't going to run a boy over.

They moved their arms.

I would not move.

"What's wrong, boy. Get out of the road," one called from out the window.

I said nothing.

I watched as the working boys made their way up the grass and onto the road like a catalogue of colours. Among them was Oskar. I could spot his face in the back. It was the deepest shade of grim that I had ever seen. When they arrived in full, the noise of their feet throbbed on top of the road. Their eyes were enormous. And the dirt. The dirt was moulded to them. They had all come to watch my act. A one night only performance they all had tickets to.

Questions and Answers.

Sometimes they took hold.

Arguments broke out.

Applause. Applause.

Oskar watched above the heads of the crowding audience. He tried to push through, close the curtain, but there were too many boys. I'm sure his eyes were blue and strained. I looked through the gaps.

Tomas arrived. I could smell the taste of his boots on the road. He bathed in the sunlight.

The men evacuated the van. These men were not farmers, but uniforms with badges. "You, what are you doing?" He pointed at me. I ignored his calls. My focus was on the back. I had to see for myself. I had a depleted face – not full of fear. I was beyond that. Now, I just wanted questions.

I found a window – a peering hole into the suffering. In a moment of sheer desperation and foolishness, I walked towards it. "What's in there?" I could smell them – the pigs and the sheep – of course.

A hand grabbed firmly onto mine, and I went struggling by. I could feel my hand getting slippy and sticky.

It was Oskar.

Familiar and warm.

But I wouldn't go with him.

At my side, the soldiers also made their way to the crowd, ordering the entertained children to move on. The men were just boys. The had the Führer in their eyes.

Louder now.

"I want to see."

The uniforms spoke. "What's wrong with him? Is he slow?"

We struggled on the road together, and now Oskar was part of the show. An act all on our own.

"No. I can handle him." He remembered the faces. The men were graduates. No, they were not men. They were boys. Viktor Link was one of them.

The boys made their way back to the van, confident in Oskar's answer, but foolishly, I left his grip and ran again.

"Josef, what the fuck are you doing?" Oskar's voice tasted like fear.

And then I looked.

At first, I saw only my reflection until my eyes adjusted. Yellow stars were everywhere. I rubbed my eyes with black hands, and the stars turned to stripes – rosa.

And then I saw them.

Men and boys with raw and charcoal coloured eyes. They were raw in their skin. They felt paper-thin. The men were not Jews, but Germans. Criminals – gays. They had pink triangles.

I felt cold in my skin. I withered and tried to peel at the wood on the side. How could I help them? I fell off the wheel, but I had to get one more look. Surely, they couldn't have people in there. No, those vans were for animals. Bodies slammed against the inside of the truck. They were animals, not people. Animals. Tears formed. But Oskar said. Hitler said. The film said. They all said.

Boys at the scene laughed at me, unaware of what was to

come. Some stood serious and overlooked. Some tried to help Oskar reach me.

I did not look again. There was no time. For when my nerve got up again, the soldier had me. "I said, get off." I was thrown to Oskar.

Wading through, another soldier arrived at the scene of the crime. He studied his accomplice, me and Oskar, and he looked at the crowd. "Don't. Please." That was the grappling voice of Oskar. He clung to my clothes and my tears. "I'll take him now. We will leave."

It did no good.

After another few moments on the road, he took his fist and began.

I was the first victim. He shoved Oskar aside and made his way through. One held me; the other beat me.

A sudden flash came before my eyes.

Oskar was on his knees. Everyone was loud. So loud. I covered my ears.

His fist sliced my cheek open. It reached across and grabbed hold of my ear.

"Josef!"

I knew that voice.

As the soldier swung his arm, I heard the voice of a distressed Tomas in the gaps of the crowd. He called out again. I could not see his tortured face. "Josef, get out of there!"

I could not get out, for I was held. Or were my legs incapable of moving? I cannot recall.

I closed my eyes and caught the burning sting of his fist, and my body hovered above the warmth of the road. It heated my legs. The man managed to hold me just above.

I understood then. The poor voiceless humans were not taken to shiny camps where they played and sung songs. The Jews, homosexuals, gypsies, and every one different was taken to die. I should have been in there, I thought. And the one who orchestrated it all was him.

Hitler.

Hitler, the lover of children and animals. Hitler, the charity giver. The man who banned human zoos. Hitler, the artist. Hitler, the good. More tears. More blood. He did all of this. It was him we had been heiling. I let the realisation run down my face and sting my cheeks.

More words arrived – this time from Link.

"Stand up!"

The sentence was not directed to me, but the kneeling Oskar. It was elaborated upon. "Get up, you dirty asshole. His voice broke. "Get up. Get up!"

Oskar hoisted himself up.

His feet moved.

"You know me!" His voice dragged and travelled on. "We ate together!"

I was let go of and fell to my knees. The onlooking wall of children crumbled around me. So many voices. So many shapes. I believe that it was Tomas who had begun to cradle me. Blood soaked his shirt. My knees heated on the road. Smoke rose.

Then it was Oskar's turn.

"Please. I'm a teacher at the school. You know me."

Nothing cared.

I swallowed as Oskar was beaten on the road. I expected cracks to appear on his face. He was struck four times until he, too, hit the ground. Oskar was helped up and held.

The men continued. No surrendering. That's what we learned in Inland. I knew the colours in their minds tried to break through, telling them to stop this madness at once, clipping them on the ears, but they did not stop. This minor inconvenience would not deter them.

Homosexuals needed to be taken to Dachau.

I was not finished.

Pause.

What happened next was my fault. I was to blame.

Please don't hate me.

Resume.

I heard the men in the truck – the broken, bruised, and insane.

I followed it.

I imagined Tomas and the other boys helping Oskar to his feet. Every breath I took was a different shade of green.

Some watched in shock. Some were crying themselves.

All Oskar could think of was one thought: "Where is Josef?"

I recognised his voice. "Jesus Christ."

I watched the van stagger further down the road, my selfish mind unable to think of Oskar.

Cars drove past, some stopping at the side of the road to see the show. Some drove by, staring out of windows.

And I ran. Quickly. My personal best for 10,000 metres was 48 minutes. I could catch the van.

The men must've seen me, for they slowed and eventually stopped. Now I had done it.

We were stopped at the bridge.

I looked again at the men. Through the window. Once in a while, a man – no, they were not men, they were homosexuals – would find my face among the crowd and their blue eyes would stare into mine. Dangerous eyes. I could only hope that they could read the depth of sorrow on my face, to recognise that it was true and not fleeting.

I am like you.

But I knew that it was utterly worthless to these people. They could not be saved, and in a few moments, their true hopelessness would reveal itself to me.

In a small gap, there was an older man – much older than the others.

He wore desperation so well on his face.

"I will save you."

Herr Link.

Herr Link.

I was addressed personally. "Josef!"

My classmates arrived, but the second soldier would not allow them to come any farther.

"You want to see so desperately?" Link pointed.

I knew what would come next. "No, I don't...." I wept bitterly. "Leave them alone! You can't."

I was punched. "You see these medals, little boy? I can do any damn thing I please. I'm in charge! Me!"

He opened the back and pulled out a man. He forgot how to walk. Forgot what the sun tasted like.

Oskar secretly made his way through, as did Tomas, but for now, he would only watch from the grass. Soon, I was wiping at tears again. Oskar stood with me.

I could not hear over the crashing water below our feet, but my friends' screams were getting louder. The soldiers practically became a human wall to hold them back.

I escaped Oskar again and made my way to the man. I grabbed his shoulders.

"Don't touch him!" Link tried to pry my hands away, and soon, Oskar was pulling at my waist. We wrestled on the road.

The man used all of his remaining strength to stand. His gaunt face was stressed with torture. He avoided the eyes of the people at the side of the road. His eyes pleaded with mine. "Let go of me, boy."

He fell at Oskar's knees. His legs could take no more.

The homosexual looked at Oskar's coat and expected brutality. Oskar would not give it to him. "I'm sorry, young man. I'm sorry." The man watched with everyone else as Oskar Frederick helped the man to his feet. "It's alright. I'm sorry."

You do not say sorry to fags, Oskar.

The man slid down, and he buried his face in Oskar's shins. "Thank you."

I watched with tears in my eyes.

I looked into the van. "Run," I whispered, but they were stuck there – all of them watching this small futile miracle.

When the man looked to me for the last time, he looked with sadness at the child who was now kneeling on the ground. At least, he would die like a human. Knowing that he was one.

And that was when he ran for the bridge. "Freiheit." The voice amazed me. It made the sky white from shock. The man was going to jump.

I stepped towards him, but a weight pulled me down. "Tomas, get off me!" He wouldn't. Never had a single moment been so long. My heart had never felt so tired.

Struggling, my voice trailed fell away completely. I had to re-find the courage to speak again.

"Don't."

I called to the man.

Louder.

"Don't jump."

I struggled.

He heard me. And he leaped over the bridge. I heard him hit the water. I would have leaped in, too, if Tomas had let me go. We were like a human twister on the grass.

My brother's face fell on mine. It reached down and spoke gently. "I'm here, Josef," He repeated it. "I'm here now."

There was an intense sadness in his eyes. They swelled.

From within the stream of people, I caught sight of the van door closing. They were leaving. I could not save the man, but maybe I could free the others.

My face was burning, and there was such a committed ache in my arms and legs that it was numb, painful, and exhausting. I stood for the last time. I shrugged away and began to run.

"Josef, what the hell are you doing?"

I escaped the grip of Tomas' words and the eyes of the gathered people. Most of them were mute. Hair was in my eyes.

Everything began to fade. I cried out.

"They lied to us."

"Please forgive me."

"I'm sorry."

It felt like a joke that the whole world was in on but me. Like every time I laughed, they would cry; and every time I cried, they would laugh.

Tomas ran after me. It made perfect sense that it was him.

I didn't get far before Tomas tackled me once more. Hands were clamped upon me from behind, and he was able to bring me down. My brother collected my tears, words, kicks, and punches. I begged for him to let me go, but he was able to hold me down so beautifully. When I tried to lift my head, it was again met by the roughness of the road. It tore at my skin. Blood was everywhere.

When the outcast people were gone, Tomas and I stood. I did not speak. There were no answers to Tomas' questions.

I saw Oskar weeping on the road. Cars slammed on brakes and beeped horns.

Anger overtook me. "You said it was pigs and sheep, Oskar." My tears punched through him. Others stood and watched. "Pigs and sheep!"

"I didn't know, little man. I didn't know. I swear it." He tried to grab me by my elbows. "Come here." He wanted me to give him the same comfort he gave me all those years ago, but he did not get it.

I did not go back to the cabin, either.

I went to Teichmann. Of all people.

My shift was due to begin.

Everyone found me.

The usual gang gathered outside and listened, but they were sent away.

When she found out what had happened, she hit the table with her fists.

In Teichmann's kitchen: five pm.

Picture it.

Oskar leaned forward. His arms outstretched on the wall. He was tripped up by sheer shame.

"What have we done? What have I done?"

I did nothing. I said nothing.

If I could relive one moment from my past, it would be this one. I would have taken Oskar Frederick in my arms. If only my fifteen-year-old heart was old enough to know.

Tomas said nothing. He did nothing. He assembled the puzzle and left.

"Tomas?"

But he was gone. A slam of the door confirmed it.

43

THE COLOURS ON FIRE

*CHROME YELLOW*CLASSIC ROSE*

A HARROWING BUT OBVIOUS LECTURE

TOMAS DIDN'T DISTURB ME FOR THREE DAYS, BUT ON THE fourth day, he came.

"Come on," he said. His smile was faint.

His voice did not sound like him. "Bring your sketchpad, too."

I went, sketchpad under my arm.

When we got to the tree, I realised that we wouldn't be going much further.

We sat on the grass, and for a good fifteen minutes, Tomas searched for the words. When they arrived, he stood to deliver them. He rubbed his eyes and sniffed hard. First, it was a question. "Do you love Von Bacchman?"

The noise of the shock poked me. "What?"

The question was repeated, and he elaborated. "I saw you and him. That night with the radio."

I breathed. "Yes."

Tomas exhaled and smiled. "Okay."

"You're not angry?"

"You're my brother."

"But, I'm a homosexual."

Silly Josef, is what Tomas was thinking.

"You're still my brother."

I smiled, but it would soon be erased. Tomas was not finished.

He spoke about our past – about our mother and father and their band of merry men. About the executions in Munich city centre, black coated men in funny hats, and the men with the pink triangles. I listened to it all without looking up. I was drawing nothing on my sketchpad – invisible circles.

Then came more words – the crucial, life-and-death, no laughing matter words.

"Josef." He stood proud while I sat. He walked back and forth between the tree and me, the sun magnifying his shadow. It turned him into a giant.

The painted words were scattered about, perched on our shoulders, and dangling from our arms.

He remembered what happened three days before.

"Josef, if you do anything like that again, we will all be in serious trouble."

I had no words. I cradled my head.

"Act like a man. People are dying out there." He had my attention now.

"I know. Everyone treats me like a child, and a stupid one at that."

"You act like one."

He walked a fine line between making me want to punch him and soothing me enough to keep me calm. He fed me sentences and watched with his pale eyes: desperation and placidity.

"You will be taken away."

"It's not fair." I shook my head.

"Life isn't fair, Josef."

Tomas was worried that he was on the verge of upsetting me too much. But he took the risk. Better to swerve into the lane of too much sadness rather than not enough. My compliance had to be absolute.

He took hold of my sketchpad, flicking through the stories of our pasts. The boy who sat on the moon, the man who climbed a ladder to the stars, the marching coats, and the freckled-faced Von Bacchman. Tomas stood with no emotion on his face. I realise, now, how much bravery that took. How could such a thing come from such a tiny human? That boy was meant to change the world.

I retorted, "I want us to win, but to do that through fear?" I felt nauseous.

"No." More head shaking.

"That's a coward's way out." I was sure Tomas could see the colours flying, landing on each strand of the grass until the whole field was covered.

"A last choice plan." I was tearing apart at the seams. I must say it was beautiful.

"Cowa…" Towards the end, Tomas looked at me and made certain that I was focused. "Josef, listen to me."

He gave me a list of consequences.

"If you keep doing things like that…"

The defiant left-handed Heil Hitler.

Listening to music from the enemy.

Loving freckled-faced hand-holding boys.

And running into the road after men with pink triangles.

It didn't matter what it was.

What mattered was that they were all punishable.

"For starters," he said. "I will take each of your paintings –

and I will burn them." He was acting like a tyrant, but it was necessary. "Got it?"

My frown hardened.

He wouldn't, I thought.

Tomas must've heard me because the next thing was a match being struck and the colours on fire.

"No. What the hell are you doing? Stop it!" My eyes could not sustain my tears any longer. Tomas' words restrained my attempts to reach for my sketchpad.

"Tomas!"

The flames caught rather well.

He stopped it before it lit entirely, and he put it out on the grass, stomping hard. I don't know who was more shocked: Tomas, myself, or the sketchpad. I picked it up and hugged it.

In anger, I turned to my brother. "Tomas, I was always there for you." Heavy breathing. "Always standing by your side when you called." I had to speak in short sentences to avoid the inevitable breakdown of emotions. "But I can't live my life only for your cause."

He tried his best not to show it, but I was sure that it broke his heart. Quietly. "It's not for me. It's for Germany. You act like you don't even like your country."

The shock made a hole in me, very neat and precise.

"Do you understand me, Josef?"

"*Ja*. But it's not fair." Tears welled. "What about *my* dreams?" I bit my tongue. "They forced us here and made us wear all these different coats." A painful pause. "What if we didn't want to?"

"Don't cry, Josef. Please."

"What about my hopes and dreams? What about me?" I was crying now, in earnest. "I am so sick of all of these conflicts forced upon me by adults."

Tomas decided again on the contemptuous.

Two big, stupid words.

GROW UP.

He had to remain hard, and he needed to strain for it. "They are going to take you away. Do you want that? I can't lose you, too."

"*Nein.*"

"Good." His grip on nothing tightened. "They will drag you away, like those men in the van. And you won't ever come back again."

And that did it.

I was now sobbing uncontrollably, wiping at my eyes with my forearm. I knew that Tomas was dying to pull me into him and hug me. He didn't.

Instead, he squatted down and took the eye contact I wouldn't give him. He unleashed his quietest words so far. "*Verstehst du mich?*" Do you understand me?"

His face hardened.

"Stop crying."

I nodded; I cried, now defeated and broken.

I loved to paint.

I loved Father.

And I loved Rouvon Bacchman.

But I loved my brother more.

Tomas sat beside me and produced a small bag. He tried to stop his hands from trembling before he offered it to me. "Want a Pfennig frog?"

"*Nein.*"

My feelings were on fire, and all I could do was sit on the grass and cry. I was still that twelve-year-old boy who clung to the door in the Inland snow. I hadn't changed at all.

Two brothers sat side by side on the Inland grass and watched the sun fall into the River Seehund.

"Are you alright?"

No answer.

But he didn't need the answer.

Life is one big contradiction. My sense of wonder was a little tired, but I knew it was beautiful. Life is amazingly awful, and then it's awfully amazing. But we have the in-between emotions, too, and those are the ones people take for granted the most – the in-between colours. We have to let in the in-between.

"I"m sorry."

"I'm sorry, too."

Days later, the air in Inland was different. Oskar did not smoke, Tomas did not speak, and I did not defy. When I was called upon, I went; when questioned, I answered; and I did not cry.

Sadness came to visit me every night, and all I could do was push it away and say, "I'll see you again". I never spent time with it; I never got up and showed it to the door. It sat on my bed. I pushed it away and refused to befriend it because I was afraid of the darkness it would have unveiled in me.

Compassion is difficult. You feel for undeserving people, and you can't speak of it for others would not understand your heart.

I was always only one step away from becoming like Hitler myself.

Almost.

One thing always stopped me.

Humanity.

Some facts about Adolf: fifteen-year-old Josef addition.

If I were born in your shoes, I couldn't promise that I wouldn't turn out like you.

How were we supposed to know? You don't speak unless spoken to. That's how it was for me growing up, at least.

It's hard growing up. You try on shoes that they expect you to fill and you realise that they don't fit. They were never made to fit. So, you tailor your own shoes, but they are not good enough. They have holes and let in water, but you patch them up so beautifully. They all think you're mad because you are.

Every generation has one. Every generation has someone like you in it.

You were a boy who had paint in his blood, but others ridiculed you. They burned your paintings to the ground, and you were reborn from it.

I am that boy, too.

Everyone is.

We all have some darkness trapped inside us. What makes us who we are is the road we choose to travel.

I wish I could have known you back then. When you had that paintbrush in your hand, and you told the world how you would paint it many different strokes of brilliant. Maybe we could have been friends.

Now – now I just pity you. I pity you because you will never know how it feels to be remembered for being good. And I realised that being good is far more important than being remembered.

It frightens me, what humans are capable of. A modern, advanced, cultured society can rapidly sink into barbarity and genocide.

44

THE ROAD TO GOODBYE

*ROYAL BLUE*RUSSET*RUSSIAN GREEN*

IN THE LAST COUPLE YEARS OF THE WAR, THE CHILDREN were mobilised in the *Volkssturm*, the German version of the Home Guard, and fought on both eastern and western fronts. A lot of them were sacrificed in Berlin, some as young as twelve or thirteen.

In '44, some of us got letters, too – half of our class.

Our moment had finally come.

I was doodling when I saw the men in black delivering the letters.

Penn Pichler came bursting through the door. "They're here. They're here." He nearly fell over Simons' feet.

"Who? What's all this commotion for?"

"Our conscriptions."

I was already at the letterbox. What had remained empty for so long had a letter. A giant letter that was heavy on my hands. So heavy.

Simons delayed finishing the class that day. She prayed with us, and when we left, she wept. "We are robbing these children of adulthood," she said. I placed a daisy on her table, and she did not throw it away this time.

For most Germans, the guilt began after the war had ended, and our crimes surfaced. The majority of us would suffer in the east and the west; some in their minds, others would be punished with starvation and poverty. But two souls whose colours were ready for their punishments were Oskar and me.

I could not save the men in the pink triangles.

He could not save me.

Both were punishable.

It gave Teichmann a good reason to swear – she was not a good woman for a crisis. We were sitting around a table in the hall. She raised her voice at Oskar before lowering it again. What she said was the truth.

"We can't send those boys off to war. It is a suicide mission, Oskar. An absolute suicide mission. Josef will be killed in an instant. No, you must... write to them, and tell them that we will not send our boys... we will not send our boys."

Teichmann was not talking about us then. Oskar's hand found hers.

"It's my fault, Oskar. I shouldn't have gone to the van. I shouldn't have."

Oskar placed his hand on my shoulder. "You needed to, little man."

Teichmann's voice was not wavering, but it was smiling.

Tomas burst through the door when he learned of the news. This was what he was afraid of. He did not receive a letter.

He began. "No, he can't go. He is too young, isn't he?"

"He got a letter. They want him." Teichmann said.

"Why does he get to go, and I don't? I trained for it. He didn't."

No use, Tomas.

It didn't matter.

"Tomas…"

"It's not fair." Tomas went to the wall, standing with his back to the table and looked at the smiling Führer. His fists turned to stone.

Returning, he took my upturned hand and cried into it.

The goodbye was the most difficult.

"*Bis zum nächsten Mal.*" I hugged him for many, many seconds. "Until next time." When we separated, he said nothing. Just raised his middle finger. It suggested something along the lines of "Fuck off, Josef," but it wasn't in acrimony. He was a cavern, like his face. In fact, I thought it was absurd, and I laughed.

Goodbyes don't have to be painful. They can be, under some circumstances, and with the right person, tear-trippingly hilarious.

A love from brother to brother.

No. We were not brothers that day. We were just two teenage boys saying goodbye. There was no need to forgive or forget. He knew my mistakes, and I knew his.

One last time.

I was given the beautiful gift of desperation.

"Josef, maybe you don't have to go. If they come for you, we can run away. You and I would be brilliant forever and never die," Tomas cried.

"A bit late for that, Tomas," I said.

I held my brother's face in my hands.

"Stay safe, Tomas. Alright?" I brushed his darkening blond hair. "Promise?"

"Yes, Josef."

One's heart is always heavy when goodbyes are near. It is like we are not only carrying our own breaking hearts but the hearts of our loved ones too. Standing in that train station, I was sure that I carried the fragmented pieces of Tomas' heart in my palms. I took them on the train. It was so heavy. A boy of fifteen should never have to say as many goodbyes as I did.

I refused to tell Tomas goodbye. Even if everyone left everyone, I would not leave him. The sadness fell through his boots. He felt it fall to the floor of the train station like it was gravity. Sadness is this way. Just follow the footprints.

"Do you have your papers? Sketchpad?"

"Yes."

He was trying not to run out of last-minute miracles to put off my going away.

I opened my mouth and felt the words stuck like glue in my throat. That's when I knew I was making an awful mistake.

Oskar made a promise. "I will take care of him."

Tomas threw it away, onto the railway tracks. "That's my job."

One more hug and I was gone. I watched as Tomas' figure became smaller, and I held nothing but the remaining colours of Tomas.

On the train, Oskar prayed, hands clasped on the table and whispering shapes into the void, praying someone was listening.

He prayed for his family, his Elsbeth, his boys. He hoped they would at least make it to the day that they turned twenty eight years old. He only spoke of religion that day.

He was so devoid of colour that he didn't even remember what it meant. He smoked his dreams away. Tobacco tears streaked.

"Only fools and children would choose fire every time. But I wanted it, Josef. I wanted it so much. I wanted to be more. I wanted to be important – remembered." His passion was nice.

"You had to come here, Oskar. They were going to take your brother." You cannot separate yourself from what you create.

I understood in the end. "I'm a bad person."

"No, you're not. You could not have known," Oskar said.

"I don't believe you, Oskar."

45

THE FORGOTTEN WAR FRIEND

*FACES OF LIGHT*FULVOUS

WE WERE GIVEN HALF A DAY'S TRAINING AND SENT NORTH
to resist the Allied attacks along the Rhine.

When I arrived, I wondered what those men had done do
deserve such a fate. They didn't look like men at all – they
were grim reapers in uniforms. They had blackened faces.
What had they seen? What had they heard? What had they
done? Many of them must have been asking the same of me
for they were pointing. Oskar was already making friends with
the cigarettes.

The army reminded me of how easy it can be to get humans
to act the same – much like Inland. Humans really do want to
belong to a herd, but no one will admit the fact. I did not. You
should never, under any circumstances have to sacrifice your
dignity for your destiny.

Questions arrived.

The first: "*Welcher Tag ist heute?*"

"*Montag.*"

"Jesus Christ. These fuckers thought it was Saturday."

The second question arrived from a man made from broken

glass and was succeeded by a statement from another wearing a bruised leg.

He tapped my shortness, and I felt the cold bitting his hands. "Jesus, look at this. They're conscripting children now." It was met with short spurts of laughter. "Just remember that we're not Hitler lovers here." He told me to watch my back. "They won't show mercy because you're a child. Bullets don't discriminate."

Before I could ask the obvious question or give them the story about the homosexuals in the van, I was restrained by another voice from above me. His face has been erased from my memory, but his influence never had – even today.

"*Hallo*, my name is ____."

He dragged me with his words. "In here." The building was damp, and the smell was horrid – the second question.

"How old are you?"

"Sixteen."

My words fell on him. He took a short breath. "You had better walk out, come in again, and tell me different." The nameless man was said to have heard the horrors of the boy soldiers, and although he didn't want to face it, he was prepared with a stash of lollipops. It was better than liquor and cigarettes, he thought. I was given a red one when I arrived.

I did as ordered. I told him I was nineteen. Despite him already knowing, my real age revealed itself to him when I broke down in tears under shellfire and was hauled before an unsympathetic officer.

Old men today – the survivors tell stories and tales about their youths in the army. One story that face-plants my mind the most is the story of a young boy who could barely see over the trenches. I was that boy.

Horrors of war soon got caught in my boots. Always dust and smoke. To me, they looked like paint clouds. A paintbrush dream, but it helped me cope, and I found it so contagious. All that was left was our voices, and we had no choice but to raise them. Screaming. So much screaming. A grown man called for his mother and believed, really believed that they were there. His blood-soaked hand grabbed my coat. "Johan, take care of Mama, little one, take care of her." He believed me to be his little brother. I let him coat my hair in blood-paint and held his hand. Only when I stood did I realise. "Medic!" But it was too late.

Walking away, the medic explained. "His little brother was killed three months ago."

Over the next few months, I would learn that the days were bearable, but the nights were excruciatingly painful. I read and composed letters to Tomas. Every word I read felt so lonely.

"*Dear Josef,*
   Everything is good here. Come home soon.
   Your brother."

The night sky drowned the stars, and I buried my face in the letter. There was a fresh sketch of a dog beside me.

The faceless man stared at it. "You look so serious, my friend. What's wrong?"

A forced laugh. "Nothing."

"Tell that to your face."

"It's just that."A sigh."During the day, when there are things to do, I'm so focused on my training." My fingers were blue – my toes in a worse state. The real enemy of the war was general winter. Hitler thought the war would be won by winter, so we were still wearing our summer uniforms." But I think about death at night. It doesn't scare me at all. Right now, I think death sounds so fucking peaceful." I stretched my arm. The damn gear practically tore off my shoulder blade.

In your visions of how this all might end, you probably see a young boy fulfilling his dream and his paintings going on to mean a lot to thousands – remaining a symbol of hope forever. A holiday might even be held in his honour. There was nothing like that.

Reality doesn't work like that.

Some people are destined to go down in history.

Some people are destined to be forgotten.

Everything was chaotic, messy, and matched my mind.

"You won't die here. We'll get you home. War doesn't suit you."

A drunken man staggered in, offering me a cigarette. God, did I want one? He was led away by another. "Don't give the boy cigarettes. What's wrong with you?"

"No, I see you as – what's the word – a creative type. One of those lucky bastards."

I had a dirty laugh. "I'm an artist, actually."

"See!" He practically slurped the air. "Why do you want to be an artist?"

"I don't think I *want* to be an artist. In my mind, I'm already there." I picked up the colours trapped on the page. "I just have to prove it to the rest of the world."

Fear rolled down and dripped off my shoulders. Dreaming is hard.

Back in Inland, the skies were on fire and the grass was a sea of black. Dispatch riders were coming on their bicycles; my brother was manning the searchlight. Blue shadows hit him under chin. The *Flak* guns were shivering, and the boys could hold on no longer. A platoon took a direct hit, and all fourteen members were killed instantly. Their bodies were dragged like colourful rags along the shallows.

"Keep safe, Tomas." I repeated it nightly and let the words carry me to sleep.

I taught myself not to think during the day. The weight of

the kit tripped me up. God, I fell so many times I lost count. The rifle gripped my arms in support. So many runners, so I followed them, stars in my eyes. They came out and ran beside me on the grass. I ran straight into a boy. An English boy.

"Get up!" An order came from the boy. He looked around thirteen.

"*Nicht schiessen!*" We held our guns together. They kissed, and I thought of Von. He would know what to say. "Don't shoot!"

We let each other go. Unnamed war friend was not impressed. He picked me up by the collar. "Don't you know how to shoot?"

I was crying. "I forgot Herr Kapitän. I'm sorry."

"What? The amount of training they gave you in that school..."

I controlled myself. "But this is real life war, Herr Kapitän. This is scary, and I am not good enough for it. I'm scared." Wiping my tears did no good. The dust and dirt drenched them. "You are very brave. I need you to teach me to be a man. Please, Sir."

"No." His face fell back. "I am afraid every day, Josef." He gave me a lollipop. "It's alright. Don't lose the boy just yet."

I realised I had pissed myself when I felt the hot sting in my socks.

A gift was sent to camp later. A 155mm shell inscribed "Unhappy New Year, Nazi pigs." It was retrieved from the rubble. As I made my way, German men spoke. "The fuck do they know? We're not even Nazis."

A younger man with whiskers like Oskar's replied. "Why don't they just go home?"

"England is a shitpile. Suppose they don't want to."

When I did make it, I could not contain my anger within

the box it sat in any longer. It spilled out. A bit at a time and then all at once. "They think we're terrible."

Oskar replied. "We are."

"Tomas isn't." My forehead creased. "If he were on their side, he'd be called a martyr."

The only reply I got was from the bombs in the distance.

"Fuck me, your arm, kid!"

"My what?" It was then that I realised my arm bore a large gash. Blood was everywhere. I must've trailed it all over Holland. Panic made me vomit.

My unnamed friend stood, looked up at the sky and breathed. "Medic!" Someone snapped a photo. Who the fuck are you? The sky was falling all around. It was no time to be afraid. The medic arrived, cloaked in adrenaline. I do not know what happened in the room he came from. There was a lot of scream-ing. "Stitches," he said and prepared. I was laid on the grass.

"No anaesthetic?"

"Not for this, sir."

"Fuck."

"Josef, listen to me." He was hovering. "This is going to hurt a lot, but I will stay with you…" He saw my eyes trail off to my arm. "Josef. Josef."

"What's he going to do?"

"I'm scared." Hands were clamped down upon my arms, and my chest was knelt on with such force, I thought my lungs would collapse. "Don't look at it. Don't." It was needed, for when he began, I screamed. A primal mind crying out for the love I was taught to expect. When it ended, my arm throbbed with the cold and pain. I was offered another lollipop, but I wanted nothing to do with it. I cried into the chest of my forgotten friend, and he held me in the trenches for ten minutes.

A flash. Again with the camera.

The one nice memory I recall was listening to Oskar's stories. Men were shaving each other, revisiting old memories out loud. Some simply wanted to go to a bar for a beer. Laughter was creeping on our faces. In the distance, death was rubbing his hands together.

Oskar spoke: "I bought us a house. It was cheap – very cheap, and I knew she would kill me, but I took the chance." He was already laughing. "We were walking around this house, and I was talking about the view from outside, and just at that moment – you couldn't make it up – the back door fell off." Others joined in. "I said, 'A view out,' and she very nearly did kill me."

I knew that the story shocked Oskar. How did this particular story come into memory above all others? We are all filled with stories we don't know about until we tell them.

Unnamed war friend was killed two days later, shot in the chest by the same English boy that let me go. It was a tricky situation. Being cornered by two Germans was a predicament. The ground was all around him. He raised his gun, and he stitched two bullets into my friend's chest. I returned the favour, unwilling to acknowledge it was me that caused the corpse to lay face down.

"Is he dead?"

"No."

It's funny how we lie to be kind.

My friend slowly flattened on the grass – so much blood.

I saw a medic in the white. I only spotted the cross.

Englishmen.

"*Hilf mir. Bitte.*" They did not help. I was the enemy. I was responsible for their fallen men. "*Bitte.*"

My hands were caked in blood.

He tried to say the word. "Go," but what came out was a watery grunt. Coughing exploded more blood on my face.

The sky was swollen. The boy did his job. I can't blame him.

In his mind, he killed the enemy. But in my mind, he killed my friend.

In my thought catalogue, there are many men whose faces I can recall, and some that I cannot. Their words have stuck to my lips like glue, but my eyes don't remember the lines and cracks on their faces. How do you forget the unforgettable? I don't think it's people we do remember. We remember moments. That's why I paint them.

We can't decide who lives and who dies.

Who is important enough to be remembered and who isn't.

But we do have our stories, and maybe some hopeless little boy will pick yours up someday, and he'll walk around with it in his heart forever.

You cannot plan for such things.

There cannot be songs for every soldier.

There cannot be solace every time we cry.

Stories keep the world revolving. Make sure you're around to tell yours. Don't miss out.

46

BROTHERHOOD

*BUD GREEN*BUBBLE GUM*BURNT ORANGE

HOMECOMING, 1945.

Our transport arrived on the Inland grounds. We sat with bruised hearts and broken bodies. Above all else, I was happy to be alive.

A flash of blond, just for a second. Diamonds and purples. I ran to the back of the truck. In the time it took the street lights to illuminate him, the back of Tomas' head was spotted. I knew it was him because the blond kicked out just right. "Tomas!"

I stood. My eyesight was flimsy.

"Sit down, will you?" A man said.

Oskar laughed. "He won't listen."

The reunion was gaining on me. I jumped from the back, and I ran.

"Tomas. Tomas." It must have been repeated several times.

Stefan and Manfret held drinks for the returning men.

I took him. "Look how you've grown, Tomas. You're so big. Look at you."

His head stood beneath my chin. His arms held me tighter.

When I held him, it made it easier to breathe.

Stefan practically threw his happiness and the water into the wind, and watery footsteps and fatty bacon arrived. We were tackled to the ground and more piled on top.

"*Willkommen zurück.*" The light was fuzzy. "Welcome home." The bodies had grown, minds expanded, and the street crumbled some more, but the chalk, I deduced, is always stolen. Their chalky hands pressed through my skin.

Excited questions for Oskar. "Do you like my new uniform?" The man with woollen-jumper eyes went from medal to medal just for a second. "I don't care. Come and hug me." The boy did.

My worries lost their keen sting, and the optimism raised its head from the ground. Perhaps, the hope had been there all along, but without some love, it was trapped, like crystals in a stone. But like all happiness, it didn't last forever.

The inky darkness set in, and a boy stood before me. Tamed eyebrows, bandaged head, and crutches for legs. His grief leaned over it. It did not look like the Derrick I had left.

I didn't have to speak.

"Where's Penn?"

Loss takes many shapes. Sometimes, the form of someone we knew well. He remembered his brother's wild eyebrows, his knack for trouble, the way he always sang slightly off-key, and the corny jokes they couldn't help but tell.

I was in shock but composed myself.

"Penn is dead," said Derrick, and he delivered the blows so beautiful that I staggered; everything blurred, I was unable to speak.

Derrick's face was decorated in frozen streams of steam.

Then I saw it. Derricks' arms were heavy. He shivered. He was scared. Death isn't fast. It's excruciatingly slow. There were bits of hope in between, and Derrick would whisper, "Stand up and tell it to go away, Penn." Derrick held his brother's hand until the moaning and breathing stopped.

The boy that should have lived.

When Derrick's parents delivered him back to Inland, he held onto his mother's jacket, and he cried.

"Shh. No. More crying, darling. We made a promise."

"Oh, look, you're making your silly mother cry." Her eyes screamed.

This is not supposed to happen. First, your parents die, then you die, and then your child dies. You should never have to pick out a coffin for your boy. The puzzle doesn't fit. There's nowhere that piece of the puzzle fits.

"No more crying."

She left him in the capable arms of Manfret Wünderlich. He was soothing him into calmness.

When we ate that night, the chairs sat empty.

Derrick had a face caved and drawn amongst the gashes, eyelids of paper.

"You were ever so brave in the war, but we are glad you are home," Stefan said. He ate with his mouth open. "Working in a field like us isn't going to save this country."

His face was drawn to the man-sized uniforms that dominated our frames. "You're uniform is nice."

The table was quiet. "Penn looked excellent in his uniform, too." Derrick gave a small laugh.

"Don't Derr…"

"What?" His lips quivered.

The walls were singing Hallelujah.

Derrick's breath grew shallow. "Penn was hit in the back. It blew most of his guts and intestines out the front. It wrecked his uniform." His words got caught between the in-and-out struggle of his breath. "Get out of my sight."

Breathing is hard when you're weeping. I held his hand on

the table. Derrick Pichler looked like he lived too much life, and he was afraid. He was scared that his brother would disappear.

That he'd be the dead kid no one remembers.

I don't want Penn Pichler to be forgotten.

No one deserves to disappear.

People keep saying things like, "He shouldn't have left us now," or "It was too soon for him to go," but is there ever really an opportune moment to say goodbye to someone we love? There isn't. Nothing can soften the blow or dust away the feeling of sorrow we feel when they leave us.

To lose someone when they are old and grey is certainly bittersweet, but to lose a boy so young is a tragedy.

A remembered conversation.

I didn't see its importance at first, but now I realise that no feeling felt is ever random – something accidental.

I was mopping the floor when the twins entered, showered by the empty hopes.

"You have to go, Penn."

"Why should I?"

"Mama asked us." Derrick had see-through skin.

"She hates me."

"She doesn't hate you. She's just trying her best."

47

VICTORY

*VIVID AUBURN*VIRIDIAN*VIVID BURGUNDY

WE STOOD BANDAGED AND BRUISED, SOME WITH WALKING sticks, some in wheelchairs. My hands and toes still hadn't got their colour back.

A recurring thought: what the hell are we doing?

The ceremony took place in honour of the boys who fought for their country. Derrick refused to go. "I don't want a damn medal. I want my brother back."

Hitler couldn't even be bothered to show up. Another Nazi took his place and came to decorate children with medals for something. The event was captured on film, but I don't need a camera to remember. It chronicled the collapse of Hitler's thousand-year Reich, as the tottering, senile-looking Nazi is seen congratulating little boys who were staring at him with worshipful admiration.

Watching Tomas on the stage, my hands were clenched in rage.

The flags climbed high into the light. There were no birds. No angel could be born in hell.

I wondered how everything looked from the clouds. From

above them to be precise. Would I see beauty? Or would I see chaos? Or would I see both?

I painted on the hill for the last time.

The sky was powdered gold and caught between clouds of silver rope. The grass murmured.

"Do you live in that book, Josef?" Tomas' voice came from the tree.

My emotions ordered every line I drew, every stroke I painted. "Yes."

The sky had an eerie silence.

"What are you painting?"

"It's an owl. A story." I showed him.

"A little owl who didn't have any wings. The sky forgot his name. But then he grew up and grew wings much bigger than everyone else's…"

Being an artist is like being an author. You pick the colours that work and exclude the ones that don't. My hands had blisters from leaning so hard. I worked for three hours that night, using a bucket as a chair.

"Josef…"

"I'm proud of you; you know that Tomas?"

"Of course."

I had to stop treating moments like they would last forever.

It was Tomas that spoke this time.

"I'm so tired."

I thought about it, and I realised I was also tired, and I had been for some time now. It wasn't my eyes, though. No, it was my heart. A sixteen-year-old heart shouldn't hurt this much.

"I always thought that when my life flashed before my eyes, I would see you, Mama, Papa." He drew on the dirt with a stick.

"How I learned to run and fight with Kröger, and maybe there would be girls." His words were alive in the paint. "But, I saw nothing."

The world will always want to change you from time to time for the worst of reasons. Fight it. Even if it breaks your body, it'll never break your soul. Not unless you let it. It is who you are inside that matters, and the rest of the world will never change that. Not to me.

A Final Exchange Between Brothers

Tomas: "We should go get some Pfennig frogs."

Me: "We should."

Tomas: "To the red-haired-shop owner."

Me: "Red-haired-shop owner."

Tomas: "Let's go."

Me: "Let's go, Tomas."

48

THE LAST COLOURS

THE COLOURS ARE FADING NOW. BOTH FOR MYSELF AND the young boy you have come to know. My life was good. It was fleeting, beautiful, and over in an instant. And the people, the people were so good. They changed my life. They saved me, made me believe that I was worthy of such love, and permitted me to give it to another. Goodbye is the emptiest and the fullest thing I can think of.

My throat ached and my heart slammed.

The sirens must have gone off. They must have. They should have. Regardless, I heard nothing.

THE SOUND OF SILENCE

The cabin was dead, muted punctuation catapulting through the walls. We were asleep and innocent. Stefan's little toes stuck out from the bed; Derrick Pichler slept with his mouth open. Oskar slept, waiting. It came.

The only words I could understand were Oskar's words. They

were tame and polished; warm wool was melting everywhere. "They are here. Run."

Defeat was imminent, and the Führer was shaking. His bride of two days slumped beside him on the sofa, dead of cyanide poisoning; her blue dress was wet. The bunker, too, was shaking. I hope it hurt. I hope his complexion was ashen and sunken in tone to something so lifeless it would scare me to look at him. There were over forty assassination attempts on Hitler's life, and in the end, he took his own. Five shots stitched across his back.

I got a great sense of loneliness from that moustache man, and I was glad. The speakers announced it. First, quiet, sombre music and then a shaking voice. "Hitler is dead."

The news rattled me, shook me awake. Women sobbed with Hitler salutes. One such woman was sitting in the rubble that used to be her home, rollers in her hair, and sucking on a cigarette. Not to worry, Germans. There will be another Hitler. The world is spoiled for tyrants. My friends were already digging the bodies out. There was something vague and incoherent about me that day. The edges were blurred, and I was formless, simply doing what needed to be done, helping whoever needed help.

For the first time in my life, I got emotional walking through those country lanes of Inland. All the bends and swoops I've come to know my whole life – the village, the stars, all of it.

Our bravery was reckless. Stefan was given a hand grenade, and he would use it. However, when his time came, and he saw the Americans' faces, he ran and cried. It was much easier to hate the other side when they were faceless.

Boys were already captured, and no time was wasted. I hid behind the life-saving wall. They held each other. Even when they were told to keep their arms above their heads, they did not. Those teenagers got two bullets – one in the head and one in the Inland crest. Teichmann arrived, and I imagined her saucepan hands taking all those Americans, one-punching them with her words. She pleaded for the boy's lives, but there was no mercy.

They held her back, and she watched each boy die. In the end, she walked into rifle fire herself. No one can live forever, but I wish she could.

I don't want to die.

"Tomas," I thought. "I have to find Tomas."

No time. For soon, the bombs would arrive. Then, the cameras and shouting people.

It came. I felt my lungs inflated with rubble, air, words, and pain.

Once I was alive.

Death told me: "Come with me and be free."

"Not yet," I screamed in its face. I should have died. Since you can only die once, I would have chosen to die there under that blood-red sky. I was surrendering just as I was pulled out of the rubble. I was carried. "Tomas," I whispered. Adrenaline and fear took over next. I struggled so hard; the man dropped me. English words. "What's wrong?" There was a woman, too. "What's the matter, little one?" She spoke a little like me, but not entirely.

"Tomas," I said.

We've only got so much time. I'm pretty sure that it would kill me if he didn't know that pieces of him are pieces of me.

There was a light, a flash. It stung my eyes. I carried waywardly on.

The camera arrived. I covered my eyes with my hands. I tried to rub them, but it did no good. I could not see. "I'm scared."

More fluorescence. I struggled horribly to breathe. The air was death.

God, the pain. The screaming. Please make it stop.

Picture it: a sobbing boy, stumbling blindly through the

streets of Inland, grabbing at the shadows and begging for his brother. The man found me again, but I pulled away. Then they all arrived. More English speakers. Their sentences ended with so many esses. It was mostly gibberish, but some words could be understood. "What, boy, come." Another camera flash. I held my eyes and screamed.

"Wo sind meine Augen?"

No one understood. "Where are my eyes?"

"Ich will meine Augen. Bitte." I looked like a human dipped in white. Everything was dusty. "I want my eyes. Please."

"You just have dust in them." The female voice attempted to clean them with water. It did no good. "We need to get him to a hospital."

A desperate breath that told me I was alive.

When they pulled Tomas out of the ruble, he didn't do what was expected of desperate humans. He didn't wail or scream for me, nothing like that. Shock and the soldiers managed to keep him in their powdered hands. They took him to the remains of the church, fashioned into a makeshift hospital, and it wasn't until he realised I wasn't there did he begin his song of sorrow.

"Where's my brother?"

The Führer told us we could fly, so why are we here, drowning?

He was covered in the colours but tearing apart at the seams. Yellow coats answered. "Who?"

"Josef." Quick breath. "You have to find him."

It would be another five years before Tomas would find me.

The stench-filled hospital played with my senses. I saw without seeing. I heard without listening. Colours without colours. People with voices, not faces.

They told me the blast rendered me blind. I needed surgery.

I was so frightened. The German translator was not there, so the Americans had to make do. *"Mein Bruder. Ich will meinen*

Bruder. Tomas." I spoke in riddles, as did they."My brother. I want my brother. Tomas."

They brought me belongings of the dead. I could feel them.

A tobacco pipe. *"Nein."*

A ring. Or maybe a bolt. Fuck me, I can't recall. *"Nein."*

A scarf. The scarf. Scarf. Scarf. Scarf.

Tomas.

"Ja. Der Schal. Ist es Rot?"

"What?"

"The scarf. Is it red?"

"Yeah."

A hand led me. The hallway dragged me with it. I walked into walls, frustration making me cry. I kicked it. Seemingly, the Americans mistook me for a younger boy with my youthfulness, for they used big, friendly words.

The room had the kind of silence that stinks. The body they knelt me beside felt large, not Tomas-like. *"Nein."*

"What do you mean?"

"Das ist nicht Tomas."

"Darling, we can't understand you." The consciousness arrived just in time. Red, knitted scarf. The needles. Teichmann's stories. "Oskar."

I only have him in my stories, and he knows I've told them right.

Oskar didn't get to see the man he made. He wasn't there with me. Sometimes, I think I see the way he looks and speaks. I still spot him in crowds with his nothing, more than nothing colour. Why are some people forgotten? Oskar was a man I will always remember.

Stefan clung to Oskar as the Americans arrived. Even as Oskar pushed and pried his fingers away, they would not move. "I won't leave you."

English words stamped on Oskar's head.

Stefan's scream.

Both men agreed that Stefan should not see it. His college was called upon, unclenching each of the boy's fingers from Oskar's coat. Secretly, Oskar wanted to pull him back; just one more hug, but he didn't. The saliva and tears fell on his forehead, and the boy was dragged away. It happened in seconds. There was no fine goodbye – nothing like that.

Then the sound of bullets, like sand sweeping through fingers.

"Oskar, it's my turn now. My turn to chase those monsters away."

I was glad I couldn't see because I could not have looked at Oskar Frederick. His eyes could never be cold. He had warm eyes, not dead ones. I rubbed his foot and cried until I was gently taken away.

One day I will grieve for him, but first, I would have to accept he is really gone.

"Oskar, please don't leave me."

It broke my heart, but I was still glad I was there.

I asked for his coat. *"Oskar's Jacket, bitte. Können Sie mir es bringen?"* After some confused silence, they brought it to me, and I drowned in its largeness. It helped me feel safe. Ironically, it would also be the clothing item that gave me away – Nazi symbols on the cuffs.

"Him."

"Eh?"

"Arrest him?"

"He's just a child."

"He's a Nazi."

I understood the word Nazi, so I pulled the words together as I was dragged. *"Nicht Nazi."*

I was taken to a liberated Dachau. The poor people that first made the discoveries must have knelt and wept under that burning sky.

Brutality, torture, murder, starvation. I was tortured because I wore Oskar's coat. My friend's coat. Store owners that flourished due to the rise of Hitler were also subjected to this horrific abuse. It wasn't me they hated, but Hitler. We had to pay for what he did.

I don't care what country you live in; your news is propaganda. It's fear and misdirection. They tell you who to hate, who should live and die – show you how the enemy is barbarous, and the powers that control your life are heroes.

Maybe they have names you can't pronounce and no-one to speak for them. Maybe they call their God by a different name than you do. Maybe they pray differently, eat differently, have a different family structure. Do any of those things mean they should die? Be expendable in war? Does it mean they should be allowed to starve to death? Are they so good at dehumanising the 'enemy' that you will turn a blind eye or even support war? If you were to meet these 'enemies' in real life, you might become firm friends very quickly.

Love is the answer, not hate. Let's have grace over intolerance; critical thinking and genuine research over ignorance and impulsiveness. If you were back in Nazi Germany, how would you avoid being swept away with anti-semitism? How can you avoid hating people you don't know? Likely people from another culture and religion? Are any of them expendable? For a fraction of what we spend on war, we could save them all.

There was a kind man. One that did not make me stand naked making Hitler salutes, one that didn't tell me I was a criminal.

I wish I had a face for the name. I do not. His name was Stephen, and he sounded like the sun. He brought me an apple.

"It's alright. You can have it." I was looking through a cracked screen. I studied it before I realised it was safe. "Appel."

I heard his face shoot up. "Do you speak English? Eh – *Englisch?*"

More conversation

"How old are you?"

I thought for a moment before I started counting. "Ein, zwei, drei, vier... fifteen, sixteen, seventeen." Seventeen. I could see the blurry American's fingers counting along with me.

"You're seventeen?"

He said something in English. I didn't understand. Then something I did.

"Jesus Christ."

We spoke a language both of us understood.

Kindness.

I wished I could understand him fully. He spoke to me so carefully, knowing that I couldn't understand him. The only comprehensible words where. "Child. Boy. Fourteen. And one sentence. "I will get you out."

And that he did.

The sun stung my eyes.

I'm not sure how, but he found the Müllers. They took me in. Frau Müller cried when she saw me. They tried to touch me, but I wouldn't let them.

Questions.

"Is there anything we can get you?"

The first thing I said was Tomas. The second was paint.

I felt and tasted the photos of the children they had saved in the past. I threw up a meal from Frau Müller before asking again. "Can I see the paint, please?"

The houses were jammed together, like the ones from my family street, and neighbours would tell stories over the years – stories about a boy.

My voice cracked like the paint I had messily strewn on the page; most of it landed on the carpet and walls, much to the dismay of Frau Müller. Her husband managed to gently wrestle the brush from my shivering hands and held me as he listened to the nonsensical ramblings of the would-be Oskar painting.

Being a blind painter is not recommended.

"I'm sorry I didn't paint you anything, Oskar."

"It's alright."

"It's not."

These nightmares were worse than the Inland ones, for they didn't just happen at night. A glass smashing on the floor was enough to send me into a panic.

Every night, a scream would come from my room. I'd be hanging off the bed when Herr Müller arrived. My sweat was sweet.

"Do you want me to stay with you until you fall asleep?"

Nodding.

I'm sure you want to know about the others, as much as it might break your heart.

Derrick: he was captured. A forced surrender. Someone's little boy was taken from the world that night. He didn't die, but his soul did. It was so beaten at that point, and it tasted bitter. I sat in the sky and watched him breathing for the last time. I watched the stars and the stripes, the bends and sways, the heartbreak and heartache. The French took him to their camp because he was wearing a coat with the tainted symbol. He married the girl from Inland two years later and lived painfully among his memories. The strongest was that of his brother.

Manfret: if he could have burned the words from the past few years, he would have burned them. He stumbled around and helped dig out bodies after the war. He never forgave his parents. No wonder: they stole his childhood and replaced it with uniforms, routines, and structure. They didn't let him dream and forced him to be mediocre. All under the guise of wanting greatness for him. That was wrong. It still is wrong. They wanted silence and resilience. Don't they know how cruel that is?

Stefan: as much as I couldn't imagine it, Stefan Rosenberger did grow up. But first, the pain and confusion. He was delivered to another foster family at fifteen. When they removed the framed photo of Hitler from above his new bed, he wept. How do you un-indoctrinate a boy?

They loved me and left me. I remember them.

I remember the games that were our childhood: the hopscotch with the stolen chalk, the stones that were free, and the memories we would never forget. Yes, my childhood remembered me.

And don't think I forgot the most important cast member.

Tomas.

My brother, best friend and secret keeper.

49

TOMAS. S

*TULIP*TUMBLEWEED*TUSCAN

TOMAS WAS THE BEST OF US. THE KINDEST SOUL IN OUR
strange little family. The rest of us were a mess.

He remembers that night well. Everything seemed to be
falling apart because it was. Kröger's veil was lifted, and Tomas
knew he was scared.

"What's happening, Kröger?"

The eye turned. "We're done, my friend."

Tomas, sensing Erich Kröger's discomfort, wouldn't pry any
further. He hugged him around the shoulder, and he left
without looking. How could he do that? He wanted to kill him
and save him at the same time. Before leaving, Kröger told him,
"if they catch me, they won't catch me alive."

The buildings bent over and fell to their knees, while the
walls howled for blood. People were flattened on the road. The
red-haired sweet-shop owner was scissored. Tomas searched
through the colours for me, but he could not find me.

"Why did you leave me here? Why didn't you take me with
you?"

He realised, I left him so he could look after what I left behind, and make a life I would never have.

After a few years, I began to fade. I know they say that people don't fade, but I did. Maybe that's the reality of it all.

Germany changed.

The Germany of my childhood no longer existed.

We went from burning pride to not being able to wave our country's flag.

The people of Germany changed, too. Many of them fled after the war. Many learned English to help fit in with their new country. The colour was a grey fog of shame.

But there was no feeling sorry for itself.

It stood itself up, marched on, and tried to act as though nothing had ever happened.

That's how it had to be.

No.

No German.

No German here.

Keep walking.

For many children, being a German was to be a bad person.

But the thing is, you must live.

In 1952, when the war had ended, and we were far enough away from the destruction of Inland, I worked for Herr Müller in his paint shop. I wasn't of much use, but that didn't matter. What mattered was the distraction. I was in my early twenties with a twelve-year-old's thought process.

A man entered the shop. "Is there anyone here by the name of Josef?"

"Yes. Who is this?" Müller was confident, but he wanted to be sure. When the blond man's voice trembled, he knew.

I came from behind with paint on my hands and tired eyes.

"Josef."

At first, I didn't know.

"What happened to you?" He cried it rather than spoke it. "I'm so sorry."

My hands studied his face. Stupsnase. Yes, it was him. He sounded so old.

I collapsed into Tomas' arms, and we wept on the floor.

But it didn't end there.

There was more.

Sit back down.

They stole my breath and heated my skin. My defences were just paper. Paper soaked by the falling drops of rain. Beauty like a book and cherry tobacco. Mama and Papa.

My heart has been ripped out so much, so why, then, does it feel so full?

My body cried for the missed time we will never make back. My head was pulled in with a calloused finger. They ate me with their eyes as if they couldn't quite believe I wasn't part of an almost forgotten dream.

My name is Josef Shulman. Tomas took back what they stole from us.

EPILOGUE

I DIED IN 1957. I WAS THIRTY.

It was far away from the destruction of Munich, and even farther from my childhood in Berlin. I felt like an outsider in my own hometown, and there was something profoundly saddening about that. When I returned, the only thing that changed was me. We didn't learn a damn thing. Tomas and I moved to a faraway suburb in Melbourne, Australia, and that is where we remained.

I met a lot of characters who taught me the meaning of life, but none came close to Rouvon Bacchman and his freckled face.

I received a letter penned from him. The page felt so light, but the words were heavy. The contents are unimportant to you, but I memorised the words. He told me he was getting married to a nice German girl, that the tears he cried that Christmas evening in '43 were true and he was sorry. Our memories kept us in touch.

A man on the train became a life-long friend. He helped me to my feet when I fell in my blindness. His hands were chapped and raw – all calloused up, like a sailor's thumb. I didn't care that he was an Arab, nor did he care that I was German. We just knew we were friends.

How can you live a lot of life without living a lot of life? I somehow managed it at thirty, and it made me both want to do no more living and live a lot more.

It was the small, mundane things that made me hold on.

The colours, the paintings and sometimes the people. The people who showed me what it's like to live.

Tomas.

Oskar.

Mama and Papa.

Rouvon.

The unnamed war friend.

They were just a few of those souls who touched me more deeply than they realise, existing now only in my thoughts – as colours, not people.

We are our stories.

CPSIA information can be obtained
at www.ICGtesting.com
Printed in the USA
LVHW091510270520
656710LV00001B/195